A LIFE LESS CHARMING . . .

I wiped a trace of blood off my lip, took a look at my bruises in the compact. Everything about me ached and the cold seeped out of the shadows into my bones. Nights like this make me wish I never got started in this business.

Not that it was ever my choice. No one chooses to be traded by their parents to pay a magical debt, certainly not when they are sixteen. Still, if I had to be a debt slave, Grimm was about as good an employer as I could ask for. For instance, he let me stay with my parents until I was eighteen (which I think was saving him room and board) and he insisted I attend night school at the community college (a smart agent is a good agent), but it was still slavery.

Grimm is a Fairy Godfather, and he is good about making wishes come true if you have the Glitter to make it happen. My parents didn't, but they needed a wish in the worst way, and Grimm gave them one. My little sister got her miracle; Grimm got me. So I did what he told me to, mostly. One day, I told myself, I wasn't going to be answering calls in the mirror, or going monster hunting at the movies.

Free Agent

J. C. NELSON

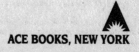

ACE BOOKS, NEW YORK

THE BERKLEY PUBLISHING GROUP
Published by the Penguin Group
Penguin Group (USA) LLC
375 Hudson Street, New York, New York 10014

USA • Canada • UK • Ireland • Australia • New Zealand • India • South Africa • China

penguin.com

A Penguin Random House Company

FREE AGENT

An Ace Book / published by arrangement with author

Ace Books are published by The Berkley Publishing Group.
ACE and the "A" design are trademarks of Penguin Group (USA) LLC.

For information, address: The Berkley Publishing Group,
a division of Penguin Group (USA) LLC,
375 Hudson Street, New York, New York 10014.

ISBN: 978-0-425-27267-1

PUBLISHING HISTORY
Ace mass-market edition / August 2014

PRINTED IN THE UNITED STATES OF AMERICA

10 9 8 7 6 5 4 3 2 1

Cover art by Tony Mauro.
Cover design by Danielle Abbiate.
Interior text design by Kelly Lipovich.

For Donna

Acknowledgments

When I began writing this story, I didn't know where it would take me, or what it would become. I also didn't know how many people would help me along the way. First off, thanks to my critique gang at critiquecircle.com, who dealt with the insanity as I discovered the story I really wanted to tell. Leslie, John, Jim, and Andy, I can't say how helpful you were.

My wife and kids put up with late-night writing and early-morning editing as I worked on a story I just couldn't let go of. They didn't roll their eyes as I went through the stages of writing, from "This is awesome" to "This is awful" and back around to "awesome" again. I couldn't have done it without their support.

My agent, Pam van Hylckama Vlieg, may be the most awesome agent in the world. I'm certain you can't prove otherwise, and I probably wouldn't believe it even if you could. Thanks, Pam.

My editor, Leis Pederson, patiently answered all my questions, guided me through the process one step at a time, and most importantly, loved this story the same way I did. The story simply wouldn't be the same without her sharp eye and invaluable feedback.

Finally, thanks to all the readers who took a chance on a modern-day fairy tale. Until next time, happy reading.

One

~⚬~

THE NEW YEAR'S Eve countdown told me I had five minutes until the ball drop. That gave me six minutes until somebody got killed. I spotted the shoplifter in line at the theater and worked my way across the street, through the teeming crowd. She had no idea what she was wearing, which made her both stupid and dangerous. Stupid was dangerous enough by itself.

"Marissa, I might remind you of the time," said a man's voice. It came right out of the store window beside me, the dry voice with its not-quite-English accent. He watched me with critical eyes.

"I got it, Grimm." I walked along the theater line, head down.

His image followed me, reflecting from the windows and even the brass banister knobs that held the velvet rope. "I'll believe that when you actually do."

Call it women's intuition, or maybe the slippers she wore tipped her off, but the shoplifter turned and looked right at me. Our eyes met, and she knew why I was there, if not who

I was. As the crowd surged forward, she ducked into the theater, disappearing into the throng.

"God Damsel-it." I spat out the faint taste of soap. "Doesn't count, not a real curse."

"Watch your language, young lady. Only proper women live happily ever after. Now, go get those slippers back." Grimm appeared in the ticket window, beckoning me on.

If I had enough Glitter to buy a happily ever after, I wouldn't have spent all day chasing a thief. There were easier ways to make a living, and definitely safer ways.

I breathed in the warm lobby air, which was laced with enough butter, fat, and salt to make me gain a couple of pounds just from walking through.

The ticket man watched me as I approached, jiggling my leg. "I've got to go. Could you save my spot in line?"

He rolled his eyes, the apex of teenage angst, and motioned me past. I'd been to my fair share of balls and knew where I'd go if I had a pair of shoes that were killing my feet. I headed straight to the bathroom. Nobody in the prep area, but I listened. There, soft sobbing, and the click of high heels on ceramic.

"The slippers won't come off like that." I hoped I wasn't talking to a Grandma, but the sobbing cut off.

Grimm coalesced into the mirrored wall, his white hair framing the bald spot on his head. He looked at me over horn-rimmed glasses that masked eyebrows like a yeti's. "Marissa, two minutes."

If I'd had something handy, I'd have thrown it at the mirror. In the name of not having a magical disaster, I decided to commit the cardinal sin of the ladies' room. I tried the stall door. As my hand touched it, the door burst open, hitting me in the face. Pain made the world flash white. I put my hand to my nose and felt the blood as she dashed out of the restroom. Grimm told me the shoes were enchanted, but the fact that she could run in three-inch heels meant serious magic. Now I knew I had the right girl. In the lobby, the fire alarms wailed as I came out of the bathroom, and I caught a glimpse of her running out. I charged after her, through the fire exit and into the alley.

I wasn't afraid of your average dark alley. I had standard Agency-issue spells in my coat and a nine millimeter in my purse for dealing with the less dangerous pests, but even I knew you have to be careful with an upset woman.

She pulled at her feet and limped down the alley. "I'm not giving them back."

No way was she going to outrun me. Tennis shoes might not be the height of fashion, but I wore them for their practicality. I slipped a bag out of my pocket. "This will let me take them off. You can't remove them because you stole them."

She stumbled, then slumped against the wall, her feet out in front of her. Passing taillights made the glass slippers glisten, moving and shifting, like something alive. That made sense, since Grimm said they were. The glass filled with red, like she'd cut her toe. The bloodstain spread up the sides of the glass and she began to gurgle and cry.

I pulled out my pocket compact. "Grimm, I might have a problem."

"Tell me you have them."

"Just about."

"Get out of there, Marissa. She's not going to turn into a pumpkin." His voice was firm and commanding. I'd never been the type to listen to firm or commanding. See, there was this thing about magic slippers. Use them with permission, and at midnight the whole deal expired. Steal them from a custom boutique on Fifth, and at midnight turning into a vegetable was the least of your worries.

She curled into a ball, kicking, growling, and making noises I'd never heard outside of the labor and delivery room. Running through the theater was out; heading back in there would introduce a whole load of teens to a different kind of monster than the movie ones. The loading bays down at the end of the alley didn't look too promising, and now Princess PMS rose to her feet. The bloodred stains covered her from head to toe. Shadows covered her face, but where the orange wash of the street lights hit her she looked maroon.

"You want to let me help you?" I asked. The growling noise she made ruled out diplomacy. "Okay, we do it my way."

She leaped at me. I'd mastered seven different forms of self-defense and I wore all four of the major protection charms, but one thing was constant: Whether my assailant was a drug addict or a bridge troll, pepper spray would leave them blind. So I ducked out of the way and gave her a dash of the scent I was sampling that day. It hit her like a brick, leaving her clawing at her eyes. I realized as she stumbled past that her nails were now at least three inches long and razor sharp.

She started sniffing the air, then like a dog, she ran straight into me, knocking me back to the Dumpster. Dumpsters hurt. I caught her arm before she could give me surprise plastic surgery and slammed her into the ground, pinning her underneath me.

That should have ended it, but she rolled over, throwing me to the side, and I barely stepped out of the way of those nails. She kicked at me and I caught her foot.

"Gotcha," I said, rubbing the shoes with the bag. Grimm said the bag was made of genuine werewolf fur, but whatever it was, the effect was immediate. She thrashed and choked and kicked and I held on tight until she went limp. The slippers came off in my hand without a fight.

They glimmered under the streetlight, and for a moment I saw an image form in them: Me, walking down the street in them. No Agency bracelet on my wrist, a bag from shopping in my hand. I could be free, if only I put them on.

"Marissa," said Grimm, speaking from the reflection in the shoes, "put them in the bag."

I did, and the fantasy blew away like dry leaves down the sidewalk. My back hurt where I'd hit the Dumpster. My arm throbbed where she'd grabbed me, and my cheek had that hot feeling that said somewhere in her thrashing, she'd managed to nail me with a foot.

"I'm going home," I said to my compact mirror. "What do you want me to do with her?"

"Leave her for the police. They'll be there shortly. Evangeline needs your assistance on the Upper East Side, and there's the matter of a troll."

"I'm going home." I knew full well he'd heard me the first time.

"I've got work for you, Marissa, and if you are ever to get your own ever after—"

"The only after I'm interested in right now is after a bottle of wine and after a long night's sleep. I'll see you when I'm ready for work."

"Marissa, you need to ask yourself what you want more: a night's sleep, or another job."

I wiped a trace of blood off my lip, took a look at my bruises in the compact. Everything about me ached and the cold seeped out of the shadows into my bones. I put my hand on the bracelet and made my decision. "Tell Evangeline I'm on my way." Nights like this made me wish I'd never gotten started in this business.

Two

NOT THAT IT was ever my choice. No one chooses to be traded by their parents to pay a magical debt, certainly not when they are sixteen. Still, if I had to be a debt slave, Grimm was about as good an employer as I could ask for. For instance, he let me stay with my parents until I was eighteen (which I think was saving him room and board) and he insisted I attend night school at the community college (a smart agent is a good agent). But it was still slavery.

Grimm was a Fairy Godfather, and he was good about making wishes come true if you had the Glitter to make it happen. My parents didn't, but they needed a wish in the worst way, and Grimm gave them one. My little sister got her miracle; Grimm got me. So I did what he told me to, mostly, and I saved up my Glitter. One day, I told myself, I wouldn't be answering calls in the mirror, or going monster hunting at the movies.

Monday came around before I felt like rolling into the office. When I got out of my morning shower, Grimm gave me a call.

"Marissa," he said.

I grabbed my towel and wrapped it around me. "Not here. Call back in a few minutes when I'm dressed."

He gave a presumptuous laugh. "I could peek on you, you know, and you'd never see me. We've never properly signed your contract."

"Not gonna happen, you disgusting, lecherous son of a—"

"That will do. Get dressed. I'll meet you in the office at eight thirty sharp, my dear. New assignment."

I was late on purpose.

We rented office space like everyone else. You'd be surprised how much cheaper it was than buying. A throng of wishers, as usual, packed the lobby. I nodded to the receptionist and slipped into a door marked "Staff." Down the hall, I meandered into the conference room, ignoring a stare from Grimm that said *You are late.*

"Bring in the princess," said Grimm, from the conference room mirror.

The receptionist buzzed the door and she came in.

"Marissa, meet Princess Arianna."

She didn't look like a princess. She looked like a college intern for a radio station. Five foot three, strawberry blonde, and a complexion that could sure as hell use work. Plus she was packing the freshman five on her hips, along with the sophomore seven on her thighs and, well, you get the idea. "Pleased to meet you, m'lady," I said, using the formal language Grimm preferred when I met new clients.

She pushed back a pair of wire-frame glasses. "Call me Ari, please."

"Grimm." I started, then took a breath. "Fairy Godfather, what is her destiny?"

Grimm swirled in the mirror the way he always did, and spoke in that monotone voice he'd practiced over the last four hundred years. "She will meet a fair prince and find love. They will live happily ever after." Sometimes, I was amazed he could say that with a straight face. I'd read the divorce statistics, and being a princess didn't help matters.

Ari sighed and sat down, apparently satisfied.

"I need to consult the stars in order to aid you," I said, and excused myself.

Grimm waited in my office, looking out from the full-length mirror. "Consult the stars?"

I picked up a copy of *People* magazine and flipped through it. "What's the deal?"

"Standard princess setup," said Grimm, now peering out at me from the goblet on my desk.

"Who's the guy?"

"Standard prince."

I knew the type. Pitcher, quarterback, CEO. Whoever he was, he could afford a little fortune worked out in his favor. Glitter was the currency of magic, but plain old money could buy almost anything. "I'm in." I headed back into the conference room.

I gave Ari a smile as real as the plastic ferns out front. "The stars are very favorable."

She looked relieved. The stars never looked anything but favorable, a fact we didn't mention in the sales pitch.

"It will take a few days to prepare the rituals," I said, "but Leona will set you up for a makeover and style rescue—I mean, enhancement—and everything will be ready right on time." I left her there and got down to the real work.

See, we could do magic. Well, Grimm could, and I almost could because I worked for him, but magic was expensive. If it were a prince seeking a princess, things would be a little harder, and we might have had to actually shell out the Glitter for a love potion. Setting up a princess was a whole different matter, thanks to one fundamental law of the universe: Men are stupid.

Oh, I'm not saying they are too dumb to tie their shoes. I'm just saying the only thing a man needs to fall in love is a little prep work from the wrong woman. Then, when the right woman appears, it's like magic. Only less expensive.

WE STARTED ARI'S setup with a meeting, that's how it always went, and that's where Grimm came in handy. He wasn't technically a "he," but "Fairy God Person" sounded weird. While he could appear any way I wanted him to, a balding, sixty-eight-year-old man served as a good reminder of his true nature.

"Where's this prince going to be?" I asked, knowing full well he'd already done auguries. When I was seventeen, on one of my training trips, Grimm actually took me into Kingdom to see how an augury was done. Basically, they took a living animal, opened it up with a knife, and let its insides be outsides. From the patterns, Grimm could tell what was going to happen.

Grimm always used rabbits, on account of a grudge he had with the Easter Bunny. I'd had a pet rabbit when I was little, and the first time I saw an augury I think I managed to throw up and faint at the same time. After that, Grimm had it done without me. Not that it mattered. After six years in this business, I'd gut Thumper himself for an ounce of Glitter.

"He's going to be taking a fine stroll along the waterfront tomorrow. He'll be quite hungry, and you're going to meet him there."

I knew the rest well enough to tune out the drone of his instructions. I'd made a career out of being the wrong woman. I flirted, I teased, I got them a little hopeful, I strung them along, and I dumped them like a rock. Ari would waltz in with a kind smile and a hot cup of coffee. You get the picture. It was a different kind of magic.

"I need to pick up a few new spells. I've still got bruises from that shoplifter and if I'd just knocked her flat to start with, I wouldn't look like an ink blot." Grimm didn't mind me carrying the basics. A few thunderbolts, a flame or two, but I wanted wild magic.

"I don't think that's necessary, Marissa. You handled yourself quite well, and our client was most appreciative. He doubled your payment."

"So I can take the day off, pretty up, get ready?" I grabbed my purse, hoping I'd make it out before he stopped me.

"I think not. I need you to drive into the suburbs and deal with an imp."

I sighed. Imps reminded me of teenagers, if teenagers were hundreds of years old, hyperactive, and homicidal.

"A certain young lady there had her first child."

I knew where this was headed. "How many guesses at the name did she waste before she called you?" I had a feeling I already knew what the answer was.

"I'll give you one guess."

"Did you get the name?"

Grimm gave me that stern look I get so often and crossed his arms. If there was anything Grimm was good at, it was divining.

"Of course you did. Bet you lunch I can guess too." He was paying for lunch either way, so I liked to play "Guess the Imp Name."

"Rumplestiltskin," I said, wasting my first guess.

Grimm rolled his eyes.

"Humperdink?"

He sighed impatiently. "Really, Marissa, I thought I trained you better."

"You did," I said with a laugh. "The name is Brittany."

Grimm pursed his lips and glared at me over his glasses. "You know it doesn't count unless you can spell it right." Some things never changed.

I went back to my office to call in backup. Some of Grimm's agents had magic in their blood. I got mine the old-fashioned way: I hired it. I drummed my fingers on the desk and punched in the number for Grimm's contract agency from memory. They were a bunch of lowlife scum who would never stab you in the back because it might ruin a kidney they could sell. I worked with them a lot.

The phone rang, and rang, and rang.

"Hello?" asked a woman on the other end.

I dropped the receiver. My hands felt like ice and my tongue wouldn't move, but this was no spell.

"Hello? Hello?"

After several seconds I recovered enough to pick up the phone "Mom—"

Only the dial tone waited on the other end of the line. I slammed the phone down on the desk hard enough to crack it.

"Marissa," said Grimm, appearing in my mirror. "What is wrong? I heard that through the walls."

"I called home again."

He nodded. "Did you speak to her?"

My tongue felt thick as I tried to answer. "No. I wanted to. I wanted to." I couldn't look at him. I knew this wasn't a spell he put on me. I froze every time that happened, because it wasn't supposed to.

"Marissa, if you're ready—"

"I'm not." I said. "Let me make a call and I'll get over there." It wasn't what he meant, but the answer was the same. I picked up the phone and dialed the contractors, watching each number with care. With each digit I damned myself for dialing a number I couldn't consciously remember.

"I need someone who can help me trap an imp," I said to the receptionist. "Standard pay. Hold him long enough for me to christen him, I'll take it from there." I hung up the phone and went down to my car. I was ready to face a half-demon imp that would just as happily devour my brain as my soul. My family, on the other hand, was a different matter.

Three

I DIDN'T GET down to the waterside until nearly eleven in the morning. Turned out our little slice of royalty miscounted the number of guesses she'd made at the imp's name. I had to use kinetic energy–based negotiation techniques, and those royal types got ticked when I ventilated their palace. I looked a bit like death, with imp blood in my hair. One glance at my watch told me I couldn't possibly make it back to my apartment to clean up. In fact, I had just enough time to rent a hotel room and take a shower.

At least Grimm had the decency to stay out of the bathroom mirror this time. "You're running late," he said while I got dressed.

"Sue me. And while we're at it, how do you want this played?" Grimm was a master manipulator. He'd have made a good matchmaker, if it weren't for the fact that his idea of "great chemistry" usually involved explosives.

"Same as always. Have him meet you over an accidental meal, stroll along the waterfront, spend the evening at the marina," said Grimm. He sounded tired, or maybe that was just me. He didn't sleep, as best I could tell.

"Kiss?" I asked, though I knew the answer.

"Absolutely not. You need to go now."

So I checked out of a hotel room I'd had for exactly fifty minutes and rushed to the restaurant. It was an Italian place at the corner of the pier, and I knew Grimm had a table with my name on it. "Table for Goldilocks," I said. I didn't have blond hair but that'd always been Grimm's nickname for me. If I was doing something, it would be done just right.

The host looked at his reservations and nodded. It was supposed to be hard to get a reservation here, but I practically had a standing appointment. He took me on through to my table on the patio. I could watch the ferries come and go, and the prince, well, he could watch me.

I handed back my menu to the waiter without looking. "I'll have the usual." I scanned the crowd, then popped the compact open. "Grimm. You might have left out something important."

"Marissa, close that at once, and go ahead and remove your bracelet."

Grimm was right. While most princes were so self-absorbed they'd miss a giant, there was the occasional exception that paid attention, and they might be able to see Grimm. Questions about the "Man in the Mirror" would be somewhat awkward at this stage of the relationship. I'd be flying solo for a bit. With his permission, the bracelet hung limp instead of clamped to my wrist.

"You might have forgotten to mention what he looks like."

Grimm huffed at me. "My dear, he's a prince."

So I took the bracelet off and put it in my purse. When I was younger I'd tried running once. I'd put the bracelet in a bag and threw the bag off into the water and ran. I'd made it six blocks away to the bus station when I realized the bracelet was hanging from my wrist. Grimm stood in the window of the terminal watching me, but he never said a word. I did my running on the track after that.

Without the bracelet, my compact was a round mirror attached to a tray full of base that gave me hives if I wore it. I didn't need it to tell me that my hair had enough curl to misbehave, and not enough to flow in waves over my shoulders. I worked hard at being the wrong woman. My mother always said I'd never turn heads. I told Grimm that once and he said all I needed to do was turn hearts.

I'd have loved to be beautiful. To have flawless skin and a nose that didn't look tiny, or eyes that didn't look like my father was part bat. Grimm said the men loved my large brown eyes. I didn't. I wanted blue eyes like Mom and Dad, but you didn't get a say in genetic roulette. If I ever got to go home, I was planning on asking Grimm to change my eyes to be like them. A push-up bra and a firm running regimen were the other components of my beauty treatment. To be the wrong woman you didn't have to look great, just available and interested.

I looked for a prince. He was the real deal, and that was why Grimm wouldn't take any chances on being spotted. So our prince would have the shine. They all did, and anyone with the slightest relation to magic could see it on them. Even the normal folks could tell in their own way, recognizing that man who walked by with the gleam and the look. The women wanted to melt into him. The men all wanted to be him or beat him. Life was hard for princes.

I saw him from halfway down the pier. Black hair cut short, wide shoulders, and arms that looked like they could pull a tree out by the roots. He wasn't all that attractive, but if you were a prince you didn't have to be. The tiny scar on his cheek could have been from battling a dragon, or a skiing accident, or any of those other acts of derring-do princes were known for. I waited at my seat, making sure my wineglass was just so and my fork just right.

Grimm didn't deal in essence or evocation, usually. That wasn't his style, though I wouldn't say he couldn't do it. He dealt with direction, and he was truly talented. The prince and I were two random people among thousands. I knew his steps, and the directions, and every little glance that would lead him right by my table. He meandered over to look at the Sunglass Hut, then, drawn by a force he couldn't possibly see, wandered toward me. I focused on my plate, on the half-eaten steak, and looked up at the right time.

Our eyes met, and he smiled at me. The sunlight served to highlight the shine on him. I let myself play along and smiled back.

"Afternoon," he said, his voice not exactly melodic but plenty deep.

"And to you." I took a sip of my wine.

On cue the waiter appeared. "Is the gentleman joining you for lunch?" he asked, unhooking the rope.

The prince looked a little surprised. They always did.

"Please?" I said, and he was hooked.

He sat down and I ordered for him in Italian. I only knew three phrases in Italian, and the other two were "pepperoni" and "mama mia." It didn't matter.

"I'm Liam," he said, and I thought that was a fine name for a prince.

"Marissa." I could use my real name. I wasn't the one they'd remember. "What do you do for a living, Liam? No, wait, Let me guess. CEO?"

He shook his head.

"Lawyer," I said and from the look on his face I knew that wasn't it. Those sorts of arms didn't come from crunching numbers, so he wasn't a stock trader. "Entrepreneur?"

He shrugged. "Got me. I own my own business."

"Coal?" I gave him a playful wink, the kind that normally had them so certain of themselves.

"In a way. Iron."

I'd met a lot of oil princes, quite a few stock market princes, but Liam was my first rust prince. We finished our meal with the barest of conversation, and I confess I was a little worried. Normally these guys couldn't wait to talk about their second favorite subject (their work) and their favorite subject (themselves). Liam was more the listening type. Given his face and his demeanor, he was definitely not a first son. First sons got all the good stuff—dashing good looks, a voice like a minstrel. Second sons got the okay stuff—they'd turn heads in the hall or on the field. By the time you got to a third son, the magic was sort of worn out.

I looked at him over my wine. "So what brings someone like you down to the waterfront on a day like this?"

He gave me a wide grin that looked kind of goofy. "I work hard. Sometimes it gets to me. So I decided to come down here, take a stroll. Then here you were," he said, getting up.

The waiter came over with the check. Liam reached for it and I "accidentally" took it from his hand, running my fingers across his palm. "My treat," I said, with a smile.

"That's not how a gentleman treats a lady."

I was at least two steps ahead of him. "Make it up to me. I'm done here, but I'm in the mood for a stroll."

He took my arm and we made our way down the waterfront. At the commercial pier, they had modern sculptures. We stood where the cold sea wind came in and listened to the chimes. I shivered in the wind and he leaned toward me.

"I'd offer you a jacket, but I don't usually wear one. I'm warm-blooded."

So I leaned back into him and enjoyed the warmth. That moment, right there, is where it hit me like a wave coming in from the harbor. I was twenty-four, turning twenty-five in a few months. Home was a stale apartment with an answering machine that never blinked, and I hadn't seen or heard from my family in six years. In a few minutes, I'd walk a path I knew by heart. I'd waltzed on piers, walked through galleries, held a dozen hands, and broken a dozen hearts. None of those hands were mine to keep holding, and there was never a second dance. I was tired, and though the word never passed my lips, lonely.

"What's wrong?" he asked.

I blinked my eyes. "Nothing." One more lie in a pile of them. As I moved away I heard my bracelet clink at the bottom of my purse, and something woke up inside me. It was sad, and empty, and I was sick of being the wrong girl for every Mr. Right.

"Let's go," I said, and took his hand. That was a complete violation of the usual setup script.

I didn't care. In a few days he'd be Ari's prince, but right now he was mine. We had pictures done in caricature, and he laughed at how my eyes were twice the size of my nose. We walked close together through the artists' booths.

"I don't know your last name," he said, as we admired paintings that weren't actually good. That's sort of a sticking point with me, and it didn't usually come up with princes. See, when my parents made the deal with Grimm, we had an agreement. The day I turned eighteen, Grimm hid my memories of them. He said it would make it easier, and in a way it did. Last names, phone numbers, addresses; I didn't remember any of them. We didn't often use last names in my business.

"Locks," I said. Goldy Locks was how I usually signed into hotels when I was on a business trip.

"Well, Marissa Locks, I have to say this is the best day off I've ever had."

I'd heard that a lot, but I didn't usually allow myself to enjoy this part. That would lead to tears. We passed the carousel, each horse hand-carved and over a hundred years old.

I let go of his hand and caught the fence. It was one of the things I did remember. Grimm couldn't hide the important memories. My dad brought me into the city for my birthday. I remembered riding it at night with him, when the world was a swirl of light.

Liam tugged at my hand. "Let's go."

I allowed him to pull me away from the fence and prepared to continue our walk toward the marina. He ran down into the line for the carousel. He looked over his shoulder at me. "Coming?"

Definitely a third-string prince at best, but I liked him. The part of me that made good decisions was screaming at me, but I'd spent eight years listening to it every minute of every day, so I think it was a little hoarse. I joined him and we rode around and around, a bunch of kindergarteners and two adults riding high. I closed my eyes and listened to the music and the pull and the whirl, and drank in the memories.

In the late afternoon there were theater groups (which I loved) and mimes (whom I abhorred). They set up in the pavilion and we sat and listened to one fumbled line of Shakespeare after another.

"How many brothers do you have?" I asked, knowing full well this wasn't part of the script.

"Six, but one died before I was born." That certainly explained where the magic went. "What do you do for a living, Marissa Locks?"

That question, at least, I had a good answer for. "I work part-time in loss recovery for clients, and sometimes as an errand runner, and sometimes I do whatever the boss says." It was nice to give an answer that wasn't a lie. "Girl's gotta make a living."

Liam laughed that soft laugh of his, the only true prince quality he had. In the evening sun the shine drifted lazily from him, and I wondered if he even saw it anymore. "I know how that goes. I once had a boss who was a real tyrant. It was his way or his way, and only his way. These days, I'm doing the things I want to, the way I want to."

So was I, if only for a day. We had dinner at the pavilion, and of course I let him pay. We almost didn't get a table.

"I'm sorry, madam," said the hostess, "but you are late for your reservation." Grimm was slipping. Then again, I'd probably upset his predictions by not following the rules.

Liam stepped up, and I was sure he'd have a hundred-dollar bill in his hand and a threat in his voice, as they always did. "I've had a wonderful day with my friend here," he said, "and nothing would make it end better than a meal here. Could you help me?"

Amateur. I bet his big brother would have put it differently, but Liam had his own way of handling things. He would have made a lousy king, but he was a gracious date.

"I have a table by the kitchen," said the hostess, and we followed her back. It wasn't dinner under the stars, but it was fine. When it was done we danced by the marina to the band. It turns out all those self-defense moves had another use—dodging your dance partner.

"Sorry," he said, over and over.

I wished I'd worn my steel-toed slippers.

My cell alarm went off at eleven forty-five, and like all things magic, it was time to end. "I had a wonderful day," I said, telling him the absolute truth.

We danced out the last measures, waiting until the final tones went silent before we stopped. "Marissa Locks, will I see you again?"

Part of me was happy—that question was the key to the whole assignment. The other part of me knew from here on out the lies and pain only got deeper. "Do you want to?" I knew the answer.

"Absolutely."

I had the card in my palm already. It was blank on one side, like my past, and contained lies on the other side, like that day. The only true part of it was the phone number, but that's all that had to be when you were working almost-magic. There was a moment, when I went to pull away and felt his hand on my shoulder, when I thought about it. About letting my lips steal a kiss Grimm would never know about. But my heart had already done worse things that day, so I left him.

At the stroke of midnight I felt the bracelet click upon my wrist, and Grimm spoke to me from the cab driver's rearview mirror. "My dear, did you get the second date?"

"Of course I did," I said, and bit back a tear.

Four

~⌘~

I AVOIDED LIAM'S calls for a week, because a good spell took time to put together. Meanwhile there was a ton of work to do, mostly with Ari. She'd been to see Leona, and it had worked wonders for her hair. The rest of her was going to take a lot of sweat and pain with her personal trainer: me.

I had Ari meet me down at the jogging track in the park. The pale January sun barely peeked through the morning clouds. Two massive black dogs the size of Shetland ponies followed me, padding along on silent feet.

Ari stared at them. "What are those?"

On the way over, I had stopped by animal control and picked up motivational assistance. "Meet Lassie and Yeller. Hellhounds." The dogs stopped when I did and glared at her. In the dawn shadows their eyes glowed red and steam drifted from their noses. "I'm going to tell them to follow. Long as you keep moving, nothing bad happens."

Ari gave up stretching and backed away. Her freckles stood out that much more with her face so pale. "What if I need to stop?"

"I have bandages in my purse." Truth was, unless your last name was Baskerville, the hounds probably weren't going to do much more than nip you, but Ari didn't need to know that. I gave the command whistle and they began to advance.

Ari took off at a sprint that predictably ended about fifty yards away. Lassie, Yeller, and I kept a nice steady pace until we caught up. The more times we went around, the more it began to hurt her. She spent more time looking over her shoulder than watching where she was going. "I thought there would be a ritual for this."

I laughed. "There is, and we're performing it. One ounce of Glitter removes one ounce of fat, but laps are free. You don't have jogging tracks in your part of Kingdom?"

She stopped running for a moment to take a sip of water, and one of the hounds nipped at her. "I don't know. I don't get to go often."

So she really was a third-string princess. In a way the match with Liam made a lot more sense. The thought of him sent pangs of jealousy through me. "You've been there, right?"

"Yeah, Mom—my *real* mom—used to bring me in for my birthday every year. Dad would throw a big party and we'd celebrate until midnight. Every year, he bought a whole nest of averlions. We'd toss them off the top-floor balcony and watch them fly down through the clouds, throwing off lightning as they went."

"Averlions are flightless. Like penguins. Or princesses." Back when I was in training, Grimm had me study the *Beast Lexicon*. I made it through volume three before I figured out he wasn't looking at my essay answers. The question that gave it away was "Name the creature you fear the most and how you would deal with it." I had been up for three days straight and for my answer I invented the Leperochaun, a little man who carried disease, hoarded gold, and, worst of all, was Irish. As long as the creature's name started with A, B, or C, I knew a lot about it.

I thought about my own birthday, fast approaching,

and took a swig from my water bottle. "When's your next birthday?"

"October."

"Invite me to the party and I'll teach you to toss those birds like a lawn dart, okay?" It was the least she could do, really, after I set her up. But of course she wouldn't.

Ari threw her bottle off to the side and set off around the track, leaving me behind. She left a trail of pissed-off behind her like a cloud, but I was patient and in better shape. Eventually I caught up.

"There's not going to be a party." Ari kept her eyes fixed on the track ahead, refusing to look at me.

"Mom can't afford the Glitter?" I asked. Then I caught her tone and realized what I'd missed. Stupid me. Stupid, stupid, stupid. "Lassie, Yeller, go eat a pit bull or something." They bounded off into the park. I caught Ari by the hand. "What happened to your mom?"

"Cancer." Magic can cure almost anything, but cancer is a bitch. She locked her eyes on the ground and started moving, grunting and huffing as she struggled along the track.

"Do you know your prince?"

She shook her head. I should have said "He's nice" or "You're lucky" or something like that, but all I could think of was how she'd meet Liam and swoon over him and latch onto him like a four-eyed barnacle. She huffed along and looked over at me. "I don't want to get married."

"Hey, princess, hold on."

"I said call me Ari."

"Your dad know about this?" The whole reluctant-bride act tended to screw this sort of thing up. Princes were used to women sucking up to them, and that look she gave me wasn't going to win one.

"He knows. He's paying for Fairy Godfather to work his magic."

"Why? Are you that desperate to get back into Kingdom?" Kingdom took the gated community concept to a new level, creating a private city for those with money and magic to burn. Exclusive didn't come close to describing it, and the home owner's associations there had a habit of fining folks one head per every rule violation.

Her eyes flashed the way princesses' eyes did when they were mad. I think it was supposed to make them look formidable, but I'd seen it so often it was just sort of cute. "I don't care about Kingdom. I care about getting away from—" She looked away. "My dad's new wife. We don't get along."

Fairy tales weren't the only place where stepmothers and daughters didn't see eye to eye. The solution these days involved a burly man with a truck, not a prince on a horse. "So move out. It's the twenty-first century, not the seventh. I was living on my own at eighteen, in the city."

"I can't. I'm the family seal bearer."

Finally the whole picture made sense. As her family's seal bearer she had magic, real magic, and that meant the normal rules wouldn't apply. She'd live at home until Stepmommy released her or she married. The seal bearer for a family does not run away from home. "You're going to be happy," I said, the best thing I could do at the time. I whistled for the hounds and they came. I set them to "torment," and took off running again, letting their bloody muzzles and glowing red eyes drive away the worry in my heart.

GRIMM AND EVANGELINE worked with Ari in the evenings. She had to learn to waltz, learn to speak, learn how to bat her eyelashes just right. I knew the charade, I'd had it drilled into me a dozen times at least, but for Ari this was all new. She'd be doing it for real, and if what I saw was any indication, she'd be doing it poorly.

"You let him talk about him," said Grimm during one of the training sessions, "He's a man: I promise it will be his favorite subject."

Ari looked like she wanted to puke, and since she'd been training for hours, they let her take a break.

"How's your part of the ritual going?" I asked as she leaned up against the kitchenette counter.

"I'm so tired. My leg hurts, and my arm hurts worse." She glared at me.

I looked at the tiny bandage on her calf. In my defense, I had warned her to keep moving. Yeller had spent five minutes licking his butt to get the taste of princess out of his mouth.

"He's not like other princes," I said.

Ari looked up at me with hope."You've met him?"

I nodded. "Getting things in order. Ready for you." It was about as true as what I'd told him, but it left a smile on her face, and at least someone was happy.

That night I returned Liam's call. I told him I'd been busy with work but that I couldn't stop thinking about him. Both things were truer than I wanted. As expected, he asked me to dinner and a movie, and of course I accepted. I went upstairs to Grimm's office to have a little chat.

Grimm's office had a big desk, like you'd expect, and a big chair, like you'd expect, but the chair only had a mirror sitting in it. Not *the* mirror, of course. Kingdom knows where the real mirror was; probably in a vault below a dungeon, guarded by accountants. This one worked as his business mirror.

"Marissa, dear, how may I help you?"

I looked at the wall of weapons in his office with envy. Magic swords, a lasso, that wall had it all. He used to even have a driver's license that let you get out of any ticket. I was nearly certain Evangeline had it in her purse. There was some fine weaponry on the wall, better than what he gave me.

"I was wondering, Fairy Godfather," I said, realizing my nerves were showing through, "how much Glitter a love potion actually costs. We go to all this effort, and honestly—"

"You were wondering if it wouldn't be cheaper to enchant? It's about time you started thinking about the bottom line. No, my dear. Potions are only to be used when time is not available. It's not about the Glitter, really. It's about building ties that will last."

"But their relationship will be built on a lie."

"No, Marissa. Your relationship is built on lies, but theirs will be built on truth, on rebuilding from hurt and learning to share. It's an arranged truth to be certain, but I've done this for centuries, and I'll take real love over a potion any day."

"Tonight is the second date. Dinner theater."

Grimm gave me that wry smile of his. "Good girl. Kiss him, hug him, but keep it appropriate for an unmarried princess."

"I won't do anything you wouldn't do."

He frowned.

"I'm kidding," I said. I almost was.

"Oh, and Marissa, you are not to employ hellhounds again in training the princess, do I make myself clear?"

At that moment I realized why Ari was complaining about her arm. "Sorry. I should've known a princess wouldn't bother with her infernal rabies shot. On the plus side, she's good for the next five years."

"Those hounds are a menace. If it were up to me, we'd eradicate them all."

That was not actually true. He knew as well as I did the hellhounds were our only hope of keeping the toy poodle infestation in check.

"Now that she's got her shots, I could take her to Inferno. Rock climbing, dodging lost souls, great workout for the upper body. The heat would be good for her complexion—"

"No."

Sometimes, he could be a real killjoy.

LIAM SHOWED UP at six o'clock sharp. We met at a tiny office Grimm keeps for us to use when we need to meet someone we can't meet at the agency and wouldn't dare meet at home. I took one look at Liam and decided someone needed to work with him on his fashion sense. One does not show up for a formal date in a T-shirt and jeans. I had spent two hours getting ready and had to ditch it in twenty minutes for a blouse and blue jeans.

"The limo driver won't want to be seen with us," I said.

He laughed at me. "I thought we'd do something different. Got good walking shoes?"

I wore my monster-hunting sneakers, so I was ready. We set out on foot, and to my surprise Liam took me down into the subway.

"It's going to take a bit to get there," he said.

I didn't mind. It had to be hard being the last son. And frankly, we weren't going to spend much more time together. So we sat in the subway station and talked. He hadn't bothered shaving, and his face was scraggly.

"You going to make a career in loss prevention?" he asked me.

"Not if my plans work out. This is just to pay the bills."

"So what is Miss Marissa Locks going to do someday?"

I froze. I'd thought a lot about the day when the bracelet came off and I took my memories back. In eight years I'd never thought about the day after that. "What do you want to do with your life?"

He looked down at the sidewalk. "I want to make things. Beautiful things. Then sell them for lots of money."

Maybe he would have made a better king than I thought. The subway arrived and we got on. You want to see a troll or an orc or a goblin, you've got to go to Kingdom. If you want to see weird, the subway is the way to go. We sat and held hands and tried not to point or stare. We got off in the wrong part of town.

There's Kingdom, which was so lavish it made my apartment seem like an outhouse. Then there was this place, which made living in a cardboard box seem attractive. I checked my bag, feeling the weight of the revolver and wishing I had picked up a few spells to go with me. Of course, I couldn't use them without him knowing I was more than a normal girl, any more than I could use the bracelet that jingled in my pocket as I walked. The nine millimeter, on the other hand, spoke a language both normal folk and magic folk understood.

He took my arm and pulled me close to him. "No need to

be nervous. You don't come to this part of town much, I can tell." I'd actually come there more times than he'd believe. I was pretty sure I ran over my first gnome a couple of blocks from there. I remember because Grimm made me pay to have the tire replaced. Even after the car wash it smelled like gnome guts and Johnson Wax for weeks. Plus I hadn't been able to get deliveries from Kingdom ever since, meaning if I wanted something, I'd have to go get it myself.

Liam turned and walked down a flight of steps. "Here." The dingy neon sign on the door said "Froni's" and buzzed like a giant housefly. Liam pushed it open and the scent of garlic and basil flooded out, along with the sounds of laughter.

Inside, red-and-white vinyl tablecloths covered the tables, and a jukebox in the corner blasted music from the nineties.

Liam grabbed a couple of beers from a crate by the door, and we sat down at an empty table. "Froni," yelled Liam, "I'll take the big bowl and a couple of brews."

I think several of the spots on the table were spaghetti sauce, and I eyed the silverware, which had a dull white film on it. "Tell me you don't eat here."

He took a swig of the beer. "I love it. One of my favorite places."

I'd always been a red wine kind of gal myself. The cook brought over a bowl of spaghetti and sauce and plopped it down on the table with a couple of plates. I held up the fork. "I'm not using this." Truth is, I had immunizations for almost every disease known to magic or medicine, but there was no cure for nasty.

Liam squinted at it, picked it up, and touched his tongue to it. "It's soap film. Rinse it off in your beer, it'll be fine. That fork's actually not bad, but you don't need it." He spooned out a glob of spaghetti, and to my horror, picked it up with his fingers, slurping it down.

When I came to work for Grimm, I spent three weeks learning proper manners and table etiquette. I spent more time learning to use my salad fork right than I did practicing at the firing range. One does not eat spaghetti, or anything else for that matter, with fingers. Only cannibals eat with their fingers, Grimm always said. Of course all three times I'd had lunch with the cannibals, they used forks and knives like everyone else.

"What are you doing? I thought we were going to a show, not flirting with food poisoning."

He smiled, showing a gap in his teeth. "We're going to loosen you up."

"With beer?" I looked at the bottle. It was cheap light beer, with the aroma and color of hobgoblin urine. On second thought, any hobgoblin who started peeing that color would have flown straight to the free clinic immediately.

"If that's what it takes. There's a box of wine on the bar if you'd prefer, and Froni did time in prison, so he makes a mean Merlot with just a can of grape juice and a piece of bread."

I closed my eyes. I'd done a lot of awful things in this job. I'd cleaned up after massacres, hunted serial killers, and dealt with the Internal Revenue Service. I figured tonight might actually displace Grimm's five-year audit on the list of the worst things I'd ever handled. One thing, however, remained true: I always did my job, and did it right. So I took a drink. If I'd rinsed the bottle in the toilet first it wouldn't have tasted worse: warm, stale beer. Hobgoblin urine couldn't have been that bad.

Liam picked up another handful and shoved it into his mouth. "Good. Now take a bite."

I shivered down inside, thinking about how Grimm would react when I told him about this tomorrow, and picked up a noodle. My arm hurt in anticipation of new immunizations as I reached into the bowl. Slimy spaghetti threatened to escape my fingers, but I eased the noodle into my mouth and swallowed. Anything to ditch the taste of the beer.

He took a long pull on his brew. "You have got to learn to relax."

So I took another noodle, and then a few at a time. Finally, while he cheered, I picked up a meatball and took a bite out of it, smearing sauce onto my chin and my face.

Liam laughed so hard he nearly choked. If he choked to death, Grimm would probably kill me, but Liam had a laugh and smile more infectious than any disease. It warmed a place in my heart I hadn't known was cold. To hell with Grimm's manners, at least while he wasn't watching. It felt good to be with someone I didn't have to act prim around, even if what I was doing here was an act too. I rolled up my sleeves and took another bite, not worrying about the stains.

"There you go," Liam said, "I like you a lot better when you aren't so 'proper.'"

"Do you do anything proper?"

He raised his beer and we toasted. "Not if I can help it. I prefer relaxed."

"I like that too, but my work requires proper."

"You should take time off. It's done me wonders."

"One of these days I will," I said, and I meant it.

When we were done with the meal, which I insisted on paying for, we left Froni's and crossed a bridge, and headed down closer toward the water. This wasn't such a dangerous place; it was just another neighborhood, on just another night.

"Here," he said, and climbed over the fence. I climbed a lot more fences in my job than you'd think possible. It came with the territory. I knew from experience that "No trespassing" signs gave you a good place to put your foot when you climbed over. On the other side was a playground, and Liam swung on the kid's swing, even though he was much too large for the seat.

"That thing will break," I said.

He laughed and swung higher. "I promise the steel is good. It's some of my work. All my good memories are of playing here."

So I sat beside him and we swung. The only thing missing was moonlight, but not even a Fairy Godfather could arrange everything. "You grew up here?"

Liam kicked his legs out and went flying back and forth. "I went to school here as a kid."

I looked at the worn brick buildings and dusty playground

with tufts of weeds. "I imagined you going someplace better." Too late I realized how it sounded.

"Me too, but life doesn't always bring you the things you want."

"So true," I said. So very true.

"I believe it does bring you what you need, Marissa," he said, flying off his seat and stumbling as he landed. He walked over and caught my swing, looking down at me. "I wanted you to know where I come from. How I live."

I knew it was time. I stood, letting his warmth radiate out into me. I kissed him. I don't mean I fulfilled my part of the assignment. I kissed him like I meant it, because I did, and wrapped my arms around him and put my head up against him. He smelled of wood smoke and deodorant. Grimm told me I was always supposed to say cologne, because princes didn't sweat, but it wasn't. I didn't care.

I stood there for longer than I can say, imagining what it would be like to do this every night. I knew I was in trouble. It's not that I hadn't had that thought before. I think it crossed my mind on every second date. The problem was, my heart wasn't asking what it would be like to have someone. It was asking what it would be like to have Liam.

Lost in the war between desire and duty, I didn't even think as we took the train back, and he walked me home.

I stood at the door to my apartment building, not ready to go in. I shivered as clouds moved in and the air began to fill with mist. Liam took off his jacket. "I remember you were cold last time," he said as he handed it to me. It smelled of him, and I wrapped it around me like a blanket.

"So this is good night?" he asked.

I thought about it. Something inside me wanted to open the door and invite him up to my apartment. Otherwise, I'd have stuck to the script and had him leave me at the office. The part of me that ate noodles and rode carousels and dreamed of someone of my own had plans for taking Ari's prince and letting Grimm punish me however he wanted. Then I thought of my sister, Hope. I wasn't actually afraid of anything Grimm might do to me. But he could take her part of the wish back. If that happened, I could never face my mother again.

I gave Liam one last kiss, long enough to make sure I'd remember, and pulled away. There wouldn't be any more kisses, and there'd only be one more date. "I'll call you. I pick the restaurant next time." I went inside. The sinking feeling in my stomach wasn't the elevator. It was the certainty that the next time I met Liam would be the last.

In my bathroom, I started the shower and washed my face, and waited.

"Marissa?" Grimm said, not appearing. At times he could be downright polite.

"It's okay," I said, and his face appeared in my mirror, looking out at me.

"I trust everything went well?" It was half question, half command.

"It went fine, Grimm. I kissed him, he showed me his neighborhood. He'll call again tonight, or tomorrow, and probably every day after that." I sighed.

"My dear, I've been doing this longer than your family has been on this continent, and I know that sigh. I've heard it many times, from many young ladies. Are you going to be able to complete this?"

I could. I had to. "Yes, Grimm. I'll get the job done, Ari can swoop in and mend his broken heart, and they can live happily ever after." We don't usually mention the HEA bit, but I was tired and my mind was wandering. "When I'm done with this, find someone else to play the wrong girl."

"I'll see what I can do. You know it won't always be like this. Even normal people sometimes manage to find love on their own, and in my view you are far from normal."

He was right. I knew it somewhere I didn't want to look right now. Finding true love was a lot easier with the help of magic, but normal people did it all the time. Just not me. "I'm tired. I'll be in to work on time."

He left me alone with my wishes.

Five

ON THE WAY in, I passed Ari, jogging on the sidewalk around the block. Behind her came a hellhound. It watched everyone who so much as looked at her like they were made of ham.

"I thought you were done with hounds," I said as she went by.

Ari stopped and petted the dog on the head until it began to scratch itself and thump wildly, leaving gouges in the concrete. "I was kind of worried running alone. I fed Yeller a poodle and he's been my best friend ever since."

It took me four months of training to be able to control hellhounds and even after that they still didn't like me. Ari reached down and put her hands on either side of its gaping maw. She spoke to it like a toddler. "Who's a great big demon dog?"

It wagged its scabrous tail and grinned at her, then followed as she jogged off.

I can't stand princesses.

I went inside and made a cup of coffee strong enough to chase the smell of princess out of my nose. As I drank it and read the *Times*, Evangeline came in. She was tall, at least six feet, and the rumors around the Agency were she had djinn blood in her on her father's side. The fact that she always wore a scarf and veil outside Kingdom played off the rumor. Her hair was braided into a single long cord that hung down to her waist. It would have taken me hours to care for that hair, but I suspected Evangeline had pixies she paid to do it. Waste of Glitter in my book.

Evangeline sat down on the corner of my desk. "Heads up. We're going to Kingdom."

"Why?" I didn't go there much, and I worked for the Fairy Godfather.

"Last mile delivery for Grimm. He's had a package held at the Kingdom Postal Service."

I loved going to Kingdom, but I detested the KPS like any rational person, for both normal and personal reasons. When I left, Ari was still jogging in circles around the building, followed by the incarnation of torment and pain who adored her. We took the subway and walked to the gates of Kingdom.

Kingdom is what you are probably thinking of when you think of fairy tales. The gates to it stand at the edge of the Avenue on the far end of the city. It's basically an additional layer on top of the city. Normal city blocks and High Kingdom overlap like ghosts. The only things keeping them separate are the gates.

Think of the gates like a freeway interchange. If you are magical, you take the overpass and wind up in High Kingdom. Normal folks go straight and turn up the Avenue. If you walked down that street, you'd pass everyday shops and everyday stores, and the businesses inside deal in stocks and bonds like normal banks. If I turned down that street with my Agency bracelet, everything changed. The buildings were still there (real estate is expensive), but the shops weren't dealing art anymore. They're all armor or swords or charms. Greenbacks weren't worth a dime in Kingdom; the whole damned place ran on Glitter.

There's a third road here too, a kind of an underpass to

a third layer, but I'd never taken it. I only knew about it because Grimm had lectured me. Glitter was magic made solid, according to him, and it's basically pure hope. If you turned that corner and passed the gates with not a single hope or dream left on you, not a single bit of love or happiness, you'd find yourself someplace very different—Low Kingdom.

Grimm warned me about it on my first trip, when he gave me the vial I wore around my neck. That vial is probably the only real magic I possess, absolutely unbreakable, a tiny trinket when I wore it and a full-sized bottle in my hand. Like my Agency bracelet, it came back to me if I got too far away, and even if you turned it over, not a single drop of Glitter would escape. I remember him giving it to me that first day, completely empty. Then a single speck materialized in the vial.

"That's your freedom," he said, "and one day it will be yours, I promise. As long as you have this vial, you will never be without hope."

So I couldn't accidentally wind up in Low Kingdom. The dark alleys, where ogres made their homes and witches weren't bound by contracts. In the city if you parked illegally they'd tow your car. In Low Kingdom they'd have four trucks tow you in different directions at once.

I stood at the gates and took a deep breath. I'm sure the people pushing their way past me couldn't figure out why I stopped. Passing the gates *hurt*, since I wasn't magic or related to a royal. While my lineage had three percent Neanderthal DNA in it, that qualified me for teaching high school physical education, not to enter High Kingdom.

Similarly, I didn't have any famous serial killers in my family tree, I didn't dine on human flesh more than once a year, and I'd never worked for the Internal Revenue Service. I just wasn't evil, so Low Kingdom was out for me. Grimm's magic made the difference. It cost him to get me in, like a toll, and he paid by the minute to keep me in the place. I took a deep breath and walked forward, keeping my eyes open.

Three steps in it hit me like an electric shock, jolting over my body, but I kept my eyes open. I never wanted to miss this part. I took one more step forward and the world changed. It was like I stood in a river of color that swept outward from my feet. The normal folks faded out like ghosts, and the streets rippled and became shining gold.

Banners hung from the buildings and in the sky above wyverns circled, hoping a stockbroker or two might jump. They went by the five-second rule—if it's going to hit the ground in five seconds it was fair game. I let my gaze follow the buildings up. Normal buildings in the city were never more than sixty stories high. In Kingdom they went up even farther, built on top of the shells of their normal counterparts.

The crowd on the streets cheered as a prince came riding by on a mustang (the car), his hair waving in the wind. He'd probably killed a monster on the field of battle, or killed a witch in her lair, or maybe made a killing on the stock market. It was hard to tell with princes.

Evangeline knelt down and picked something up. "Hey, someone dropped a quarter." She didn't care about the sights or sounds or smells of Kingdom. Did I mention the smell? The whole city always smelled like one big urinal to me. Kingdom smelled like someone ground breath mints into the concrete. I knew one day my vial would be full and I'd pay my debt. The Agency bracelet would only be a gold chain on my wrist. I'd gain my freedom and lose the ability to walk into Kingdom. It was a trade I'd make any day, on the spot.

We strolled down the main street together, past crowds laughing and toasting each other. My bracelet thrummed, asserting the magic needed to pin me here instead of in the middle of a midday traffic jam. The street vendors lined the sidewalks.

"Fresh auguries," said one crone, catching me looking at the rabbits. If I needed an augury I'd ask Grimm. When I spent my Glitter, I did so with care.

"Animal companions," said another, with a cage full of wide-eyed rabbits and squirrels. No doubt all of them talked, and would be happy to follow me around making cute jokes and conversation. I got lonely sometimes, and often thought about buying another companion. I say another because Grimm got me a cat from here when I first started working. To the best of my knowledge I didn't have it anymore.

"Weasel grease," cried an enchanter, holding up a bottle. "Slip any fetter, break any bonds."

Evangeline snorted. "Don't bother. I tried it once." She was ten years older than I, and had the scars to match it. The business was hard. In Kingdom she could take the scarf and veil off. She did so now, revealing a ruined mass of wet, red flesh that never healed. Rumors at the Agency said that she'd gotten into a fight in Lower Kingdom and lost. However it happened, from then on I always played the wrong woman.

We picked our way past the shops and the banks, which had enough Glitter to free me a million times over, and finally got to a squat marble building. "Kingdom Postal Service" said the engraving over the door.

The door-gnome spotted me from across the street and already had that look on his face.

I stopped at the curb. "I hate this place. Couldn't I go to Inferno instead?"

Evangeline grabbed my hand and dragged me across the street. "You don't hate this place. You hate the fact that every gnome in Kingdom has your face taped on their fridge with the words 'Beware of Killer' underneath it."

Inside, white marble floors reflected the light from massive chandeliers. The lobby had velvet seating and a butler, but it was still a post office, so of course it had a line. At the front of the line a man argued, and his tone said he was a prince.

No third-string prince or second stringer. He was the real deal, and the shine seemed to run off him like a river. "I don't think I made myself clear," he said. "I will personally deliver it."

The postal gnome leaned over his counter and shook

his head. "No unauthorized pickups." He pounded a tiny fist on the counter with each word.

The prince was obviously accustomed to getting what he wanted, which meant he obviously wasn't accustomed to dealing with the postal service. The KPS was the only organization I know of that actually got along with the USPS. I'd always believed that every normal postman had to have a mandatory gnomish blood transfusion to qualify for the job.

The prince glanced around the room and I got a look at his face. Chiseled nose, black eyebrows to match that gorgeous raven hair, and pale skin that said he'd never spent a day at the beach. Disgusting in my book. "I don't believe you appreciate who I am."

The postal gnome obviously shared my feelings, because he rang the bell and said "Next."

We waited in line like proper cattle. The prince swept up his papers and started one of those regal "storming out" things they do, and he glanced at us. Well, at Evangeline. Men don't look at me, they look past me. Evangeline might have been thirty-five, but her curves left men bent, and she was used to it. He approached and she gave him a coy glance over her shoulder.

It wasn't her shoulder his eyes were riveted to, and that was fine by me. His gaze made me feel like I needed a shower, like his eyes had slime-ray vision. If so much as one of those carefully manicured fingers touched me, he was going to need dental work.

He gave us a slight bow. "My ladies, I would like the pleasure of your names. I am Prince Vladimir Mihail, of the Second Royal Family." Of the seven royal families, the second was now number one on my most detested list. It's actually a lengthy list.

Evangeline played it to the hilt, waiting till the last moment to turn enough so he could see her face. He flinched and jerked his hand away, then got it under control enough to give her hand a kiss. She made no secret of wiping it off.

He kept his eyes on the ground, avoiding her face. "I

beg your pardon, but duty calls." When he was gone the air no longer reeked of roses.

I watched him walk out. "Jerk."

Evangeline gave me a half smile that's as close to the real thing as she could get.

I looked at her, looking at the cuts. Three long slices lay on each side of her cheeks, the edges tinged with rotten green. On one side, her teeth showed through the gashes. "Did you ever ask Grimm about—"

"About fixing me? These aren't just cuts, M. They're wounds from magic." Magic wounds were like magic spells—it wasn't easy to set magic against magic, like pushing two magnets together the wrong way. Magic could only counter magic with the greatest of wills and effort. Even then things didn't usually turn out right.

She put a hand up to her face, tracing the gouges. Her voice cracked as she spoke. "Most of Grimm's agents have worse before they're done. You'll get your own eventually."

"Next," said the postal gnome, and it was our turn.

Evangeline presented her Agency bracelet, and the gnome scanned it. "I'll be right back. It's in a secure vault." I have no idea what a secure vault actually entailed. KPS hallways had guards with guns and dogs and Kingdom only knew what else. The secure ones, on the other hand, I had heard only rumors about. Rumors like the doorway to the vault was actually a portal to the surface of the sun. Some of their gates had musical codes, and you had to play the right song on a flute or get devoured by a pack of rats. Those were the easy ones. The high-security ones, you had to play Mozart on an accordion, a feat that wasn't even possible with the proper number of fingers.

The gnome came back looking a little singed, carrying a book-sized brown paper package as tall as he was. With a final shove he dropped it on the counter. "Sign in septu-plicate, please."

I signed my name. And again. Over, and over, and over. "What exactly do you do with all of these?"

He looked at me as he spindled, punched, and folded my

carefully written slip. "Orange copy goes to records. Green copy goes to tracking. Chartreuse copy is for my trophy wall in the office, Maniac." He leaned over to the gnome in the next window and whispered, "I met the Maniac of Eighth Street and lived to tell about it."

"I didn't mean to kill anyone. What about the other four?"

"They don't stock toilet paper in the bathrooms. Whether you meant to or not, Bernie is dead."

"He was curled up in a pothole at night, it's not my fault I ran him over. He ruined my tire and I had to get the front end realigned. How did you even know him?"

"Bernie was my eight hundred and fifty-third and one-eighth cousin," said the gnome. He picked up a metal stamper and I yanked my hands off the counter.

"How do you get to be one eighth of a cousin?"

The gnome reached under the counter and took out a saw. "I'd like to show you." He rang his bell three times and the security guards came over to escort us out.

As we walked along I gave the box a shake, but it was well packed. "What's in the box?"

Evangeline shrugged.

"Not even a little curious?"

She shook her head. "Curiosity killed the cat, his owner, and most of the people in the apartment building, M."

"That was carbon monoxide and you know it."

"They're both odorless, tasteless, and deadly, M. Sooner or later you're going to learn to forget things on purpose."

She had a point. I considered forgetting to order Ari steel-toe slippers. That way she and Liam could bond over him helping her with crutches after he broke those toes in about a dozen places while dancing.

We worked our way down off of Kingdom's Main Street, through narrower roads, older roads. The bracelet thrummed less here, which meant we were not so tied to reality anymore. This was Middle Kingdom. While the High and Low Kingdoms overlapped the city like ghosts, Middle Kingdom didn't connect to our reality except at the edges of the High and Low Kingdoms. All the old fairy tales played out in Middle Kingdom hundreds of years ago. According to Grimm, it resisted any efforts to modernize, so the government built a new palace and renamed the road it was on "Main Street" but the old palace was still around. Kind of like an old sports stadium after it'd been replaced. One of these days I figured they'd implode it and build the world's largest yogurt-plex where it used to be.

We were in Dwarf Town, I knew by the buildings. Old buildings, heavy wooden buildings made of beams and planks, with second-story windows and crazy leaning sides. The other key hint was that I'd have to crawl on my knees to get through the doors. Evangeline knew where we were headed; she could read dwarvish. She read the scrawled writing on one door—it looked more like someone had let a rabid raven dance on the sign than it did actual writing. After a moment she gave the door a kick so hard it bent. A dwarf came barreling out.

He shook his fist. "You're late, and you owe me a new door." I think it made dwarves happy to be angry. If the dwarves ever got tired of forging swords and armor, they had a sure thing lined up as talk-radio hosts.

"There was a line at the post office," said Evangeline, and handed him the box.

The dwarf tore it open and took out an old-style bottle of what looked like mercury. With a tug he opened the lid and a smell like boiled cat bit my nose. The fact that I knew what boiled cat smelled like was a sad testament to my life.

I covered my face with my sleeve. "What is that?"

He scowled at me. "Fleshing silver, suspended in cat broth," he said and went back inside.

As we walked through the side streets and back toward Main Street, Evangeline cocked her head, listening. "This way," she said, pulling me toward an underpass.

Heavy feet tromped by overhead and stopped. Then, in the quiet of Middle Kingdom, my purse began to sing. Liam was calling on my disposable cell phone. Evangeline glared at me, as the muffled tones of "It's a Small World" echoed. I held my breath. I heard a strange creaking noise, and one by one the owners of the heavy feet jumped over the side of the bridge, landing on the path before us.

"Give us the box," said the largest one. I recognized the guttural voice of a goblin. Stupid muscle, but cheap. "Give us the box and do not scream."

Evangeline walked forward toward the group, a sway in her hips. "Oh no, I don't think people will hear me if I scream," she said, holding her hand to her mouth.

I giggled, knowing how this was going to go. The goblins advanced on her, surrounding her. Evangeline put her hands on her hips. "Oh, wait. I meant, nobody will hear you if you scream." Then she attacked. If all the women in the city fought like that, muggers would take up safer occupations, like wrestling rabid tigers.

"Graaabbaaaragggh" said the lead goblin as Evangeline kicked him in the crotch. The longest piece of literature in goblin language was only ten syllables long, so for a goblin that was practically a soliloquy. Evangeline tripped the next one and broke his arm.

I had my own problems of course. Two of the beasts decided they'd have better luck with five foot eight, hundred-and-fifty-pound me. I didn't carry a nine millimeter for nothing, and I hit the lead one in the leg three times as he approached.

"Always shoot in the feet," Grimm once told me. "They're so heavy it cripples them." Evangeline preferred to break their knees, which worked equally well. The remaining one made a lunge for me, closing his leathery hand around my wrist. It crushed my arm under its fingers and tore the gun from my hand. "Die."

I felt into my pocket with my free hand and grabbed a tiny object the size and shape of a walnut. Grimm said we should always be polite. "No, thank you." The only thing I detested more than Jehovah's Witnesses were goblins, so I sank my fist into his stomach with every bit of force I could muster.

The shell in my hand disintegrated, and lightning shot

through him, making his ears steam. If I had even a shred of magical ability I could have fired it like a bolt from a distance, but given my past history with magic I was just happy it shocked him and not me.

"Come on," said Evangeline, and we hurried back toward Main Street. "We'd have been fine if your phone hadn't given us away. Why do you even have that on?"

I took it out of my purse and pulled up voice mail. "I'm not built like you. I have to talk to them to get their attention. You just have to walk by." I listened to Liam complain about sitting through a tax meeting with his accountant and grinned at his frustration and the sound of his voice.

Evangeline looked through me, her face blank with boredom.

I snapped the phone closed. I knew Grimm would want confirmation that the delivery was done. Inside Kingdom it was hard to get a hold of him. Too much interference, I think, like too many cell phones in one area. The moment we passed the gates, he waited in an oily puddle.

"Trouble?" It wasn't a question.

Evangeline dug bits of goblin flesh from under her fingernails. "Not until after the drop-off. We left a bunch of goblins under the Eleventh Street Bridge. Might want to call animal control and let them know."

"Ah yes. Well, they may have been misled about where they would find you," said Grimm. "Are you hurt, Marissa?"

My arm had a bruise like an ink blot on it where the goblin had grabbed me. The shape reminded me of a tattoo I'd considered getting to celebrate surviving my first year at the Agency. If I was going to draw on myself with permanent markers, it wouldn't be Asian characters that meant "Free Fried Rice" or Celtic writing that said "Riverdance Sucks." It'd be the thing that best represented my life: a bruise. "I got squeezed, but I'll live. I fried the bastard for it."

Grimm frowned. "That was completely unnecessary, wasting magic. Haven't I trained you in self-defense? I want you to stop by the emergency room and get that x-rayed. Is this going to delay the prince's send off?"

A chill shot through me, making the hairs on my neck stand up. I'd managed to forget for a bit about that. "Won't be a problem." My arm throbbed, sending waves of pain through me, but I knew it wouldn't be the only thing hurting by the end of the night.

Six

THE LAST BIT of the prince setup is simple and easy, so long as you haven't deluded yourself about your chances with a prince. He's shared a kiss with you, and called you (and called, and called) and can't wait to see you again. All you have to do is seal the deal. You take him out in public and shred him like last year's credit cards.

Then Grimm knows where he's going to be sulking, and arranges it so the prince bumps into a princess. She's coy but charming, gentle, and quiet. She is a friend to talk to, and a hand to hold. Finally, it's her lips he kisses, and by that time my name isn't spoken between them. It's cold, manipulative, easy, and damn near magic. Unless you've made the mistake of getting involved.

I put on my sleek black dress, the one I always wore for this. Evangeline brought it to me the night I played this out the first time. I looked forward to our long-standing tradition of meeting for drinks when I'd done it. We'd spend the night commiserating, celebrating, and starting the process of forgetting by killing brain cells.

I met Liam at Skeins, a German place I'd used for all my

third dates. The remarkable thing about Skeins was the head chef. He was an absolute asshole. I'd never seen the same waiter there twice, which meant they never saw me coming. There's a bar on the top floor of the building where I'd tried to kill my liver more nights than I wanted to remember. Also, Skeins had a wide balcony perfect for making men want to jump.

I walked past the host, and caught myself at the edge of the dining room. Liam sat at a table alone, dressed in a suit that was obviously a hand-me-down from an age when people considered polyester fine cloth.

Minutes passed, and still I stood, hidden in the doorway, watching. When the cell phone in my purse went off I nearly threw it out the window. I didn't carry a cell phone except when I was working princes, and tonight would be the last time I'd use that one. No one else had the number.

I flipped it open and answered. "Hello?"

"M." I recognized Evangeline's voice.

I wondered how on earth she got the number. Then again, I worked for a being who valued knowledge above even magic. "What do you want? I'm kind of busy."

"Grimm says you aren't. Said you're having problems with this one. You need help?"

The way she said "help" reeked of "You want me to come bail you out again?" I spent the first two years learning from Evangeline. Now I worked every day to prove to her and everyone else that I could hold my own.

"I don't need you or anyone else. I'll get this done. Tell Grimm he'll be ready for the princess tomorrow." A lump formed in my throat as I spoke those words, a cold knot like I'd swallowed an iceberg.

"You have to do this, M, and do it right."

I knew that. We had a deal, Grimm and I. Grimm and my parents, Grimm and my sister. I thought of her. Last time I'd seen her she was two years old, pulling a wagon around and eating a Popsicle she said tasted "purple." I'd never asked Grimm what would happen to Hope if I didn't keep my end of the deal. I paid my debts.

I hung up the phone and walked into the dining room, careful to fix my face into the right expression of disgust.

"Evening," Liam stood up as I walked in, and he took my jacket.

I stepped away from the offered hug and gave him my most dismissive look as I sat down.

Liam reached across the table to take my hand. "I ordered the scallions for you. You said you always wanted to try them. Since we're eating on my dime, I thought you might want to try something special."

I carefully moved my hand away, keeping my eyes fixed on him, and flagged down the waiter. "I'm allergic to scallions," I told the waiter. "Just bring me veal." I'm not certain they actually had veal, but given my tone, the waiter wasn't going to argue.

"I'm sorry," said Liam. "I didn't know about that."

"You don't know anything about me." The food came out and we ate in silence. Liam would comment or ask questions, and I'd nod or answer in monosyllables, like every other time I'd done this. When dinner was done, and the band started to play, I knew it was time.

"I can tell something is bothering you," Liam said. His forehead was creased and he had barely touched his meal.

"Really?" I asked, my tone shrill. "You think you can tell what is going on with me?"

He recoiled. I knew he was realizing that something was going truly wrong. Really, it was the click of the trap. His lips moved as he tried to come up with a comforting response, but all that came out was, "Yes, I thought so." He leaned across the table to put his hand on my shoulder and I shrugged him off, looking at his hand the same way I would a dead rat.

"Look," I scooted my chair slightly away from him. "I'm not certain what you think is going on between us."

His eyes went wide and a confused look passed across his face. I knew I'd hit the mark. He began to rub his fingers together and if he bit his lip any harder he'd draw blood. I was going to draw blood anyway.

"I might have sent some mixed signals."

The cracks in his face opened wider. Any minute now he'd start trying to fix things. He put his hand to his temple. "I'm sorry. I thought, I mean, I thought maybe you—"

I went for the kill, letting my voice rise to where the neighboring diners began to stare. "You thought maybe I liked you? Because I let you take me on a merry-go-round? Because you took me to the nastiest Italian restaurant in the entire city? Because you dragged me to some burned-out playground in a slum? What part of that says 'romantic' to you?" Every word cut my own heart. It wasn't supposed to feel like this. It wasn't supposed to feel like anything.

"Carousels and swings are for children, Liam. I'm an adult, and I thought perhaps you were one too. Obviously I was mistaken."

His face looked hollow, his eyes didn't focus, and the edges of them shone. "I must have been mistaken too."

I swiped the check from the table and took my jacket. "Don't bother with the check, and don't bother calling." I marched out of the room, and on the way I gave him one last look. I wasn't supposed to. It wasn't in the script, because it sent the wrong message. I looked back anyway, hoping that he was on his feet and coming after me. The others never came after me, but for one split-second I harbored a hope he would. I remember him sitting at the table with a half bottle of wine. I remember the band playing and couples dancing near the stage. I remember the magic flowing off of him as he cried, or maybe that was just my tears.

I RENTED A room for Goldy Locks, barricaded myself inside, and wept before the mirror until my makeup ran in rivulets down my cheeks. I turned on the faucet and the shower and left them running. Soon the mirror was covered in fog. Then I called him.

"It's done," I said. I couldn't keep my chin from trembling, and I'm sure my voice did too.

He looked like an impressionist painting through the steam. "I'm sorry."

"Why did you do it?"

"A prince and princess belong together. It is the way of things."

Anger rushed through me, shielding me for a moment from the grief. I straightened up and glared at him. "I'm not the first girl sold for Glitter. Most of them wind up as handmaidens to a princess, or shopkeepers, or newspaper interns. Why did you make me an agent?"

"Because, my dear, anything else would have been a waste. You are talented beyond most I have met, and bright, and strong. You would not have been happy in those other lives."

My shield of anger cracked and my hands shook. "I'm not happy here either. Don't I deserve happiness?" I hoped he couldn't hear me almost sobbing over the sounds of the water.

He grayed out a little and came back into focus. "You do, my dear, you do."

My chest hurt with each breath. I stuck my hand into the scalding water, and held it there until the pain from it matched what I felt inside. "I don't want Ari to have him. I want him for me."

He didn't answer.

"But I'm not a princess," I said, knowing the cold truth of it.

"I will have Evangeline handle the rest, Marissa. You do deserve to be happy, and you aren't a princess, but that's never made you less important in my eyes."

"Tell Evangeline I'm not coming to meet her. And remember I keep my end of the bargain, Grimm. Always."

He left me there in the bathroom, at last and always alone.

My purse beeped, and I dumped it out to find the cell phone and a stack of forty-nine brand-new business cards with its number. They came in lots of fifty. I never needed more than one. I missed four calls since dinner, all from Liam.

I walked out onto the balcony and looked at the city street below. Cars zipped past, leaving trails of light in the darkness. In my hand the cell phone chirped again. Three voice mail messages. Tradition said I should throw the phone off the balcony and let gravity do the heavy lifting, but my heart and my hands said different. I couldn't call, ever. But I could keep the phone and listen to his voice, and have a tiny part of him. Ari and Grimm and the rest of the world would never know. So I went back inside and slipped the phone into my purse. Bruises on my arm where the goblin had grabbed sent tremors of pain through me every time I moved, but didn't compare to the bruises on my heart I'd put there myself. The hours rolled away while I lay on the bed, aching my way through to dawn.

Seven

~~~~~~

IT WAS TIME to go to work, but I couldn't risk meeting Ari, so I went in through the service entrance. Evangeline waited in the back room, going over papers, and she came over and gave me a hug. "Heard about last night. You'll get used to it eventually."

"I messed up. I got too close."

She poured me a cup of coffee. "Do this long enough and it won't be the last time you screw up." I didn't intend to be doing it that long. Then again, neither had she.

Rosa came in. She'd been the receptionist longer than I'd worked there. I figured she came with the building. "Evie, your client is out front."

Evangeline left to get ready for a day's work. Probably Ari. Probably about Liam. I tapped on the mirror. "Grimm, what do you got for me? Troll? Maybe a few elves in a shoe factory?"

He answered from the mirror down the back hall. "My dear, I was thinking that perhaps you might want to do inventory on the storage room. The lost-and-found pile has started moving on its own, and something ate everything in the office fridge last night, containers and all."

I sat up, cold shivers running down my back. "Including the cheese wheel?"

"Marissa, don't be ridiculous."

It figured. There was a running debate—one might say legend—among Grimm's hourly workers over how the cheese wheel actually came to be in the fridge in the first place. One rumor was that it was whole milk when it was first put in, and had solidified through the years, exposed to Grimm's magic. Another said one of Grimm's previous agents was a vampire, and that when she was breastfeeding she accidentally left milk in the fridge and it corrupted an entire wheel. Another said it was a normal block of cheddar. There was a reason the store owners always sliced cheese wheels into little pieces. Cheddar could be evil. Truth was, the wheel had shown up in the fridge the morning after my first "Welcome to the Agency" party, in a box with my name on it.

Every intern I'd seen attempt to remove it died horrible, bloody deaths within days. Six interns came and went. The cheese remained. Grimm was taking it easy on me, the bastard. "You don't have anything more interesting? No shoplifting? No blackmail gathering? Hey, isn't today wolf-day?"

"Wolves have never been your style, my dear." Three weeks ago he'd complained that I never wanted to ride shotgun on visits to the wolves.

"Yeah, they're Evangeline's, and she's cleaning up my mess." I opened my bottom drawer and took out my box of special ammo, labeled by problem creature. Genie, imp, cheerleader—there it was: wolves. "Either you let me ride shotgun, or I'm taking on the cheese. Assuming I don't leave in a body bag, it's leaving in a garbage bag. Either way, one of us is going."

Grimm squinted at me for a moment and shook his head. "Oh, all right. The van leaves in twenty minutes. If you aren't armed and on board I won't have them wait."

A visit to the wolves was exactly what I needed to cheer me up. A quick stop off at wardrobe and I'd be ready.

In the loading bay on the bottom floor they brought in the pigs. Not magic pigs. Normal porkers, and pigs stank. We'd load them into the trailer, hook the trailer to the van, and drive all the way into the country to make a deal.

Billy checked the tires on the van. He was a rotund man with a belly like he was carrying triplets and more chins than Chinatown. I knew from experience he was cold and calm under fire. Billy was the driver on wolf runs most days, and he was the negotiator all days. "Miss Locks, you'd best change before we head off."

"Not gonna happen, Billy. Think it'll get their attention?"

He shrugged. As a teamster, Billy got double time for doing work with the wolves, so it didn't matter to him how things went down. "Think it'll get you killed, Miss Locks. He know?"

"He knows everything," I said, though I knew that wasn't exactly true. "Not like negotiations don't wind up messy anyway." So we got in the van and he put it in gear. We drove out to a place only marginally better than Inferno: Jersey. Billy in his ball cap and me in a red sweatsuit with (of course) a hood.

Time was we'd have gone in guns blazing, but Grimm insisted on talk first, bullets later. That was a sign of his genius, in my opinion. It was damn hard to kill a werewolf, but it was easy to bargain with one if you had the right goods.

"Where's Evie?" Billy asked as we drove along the countryside. "She normally makes the dog run."

"Evangeline is busy," I said, not wanting to mention what she was busy with.

We rode in silence to the edge of a village. Smoke-houses dotted the landscape here, wood smoke rising up through the air, and everywhere was the smell of bacon and ham. The wolf guard met us by the road. I only saw him, but there were doubtless half a dozen others.

"Afternoon," said Billy. "Just here to barter a bit." He gave the brakes a pump, which sent the pigs squealing.

The effect on the guard was immediate. He sniffed the air and his mouth hung slack. "She ain't the usual one." He bared his teeth at me. If you were a person, or a wolf in human form, baring your teeth didn't actually serve to intimidate. In fact, I felt a curious urge to tell him my dentist could lighten his teeth by at least three shades.

"Get on in," said the guard.

The wolf town looked like old Amish meets trailer park. Shoebox white houses made of rickety wood and low cinderblock barns perfect for keeping pigs, kids, or both. The only real giveaway was that every house had a dog door big enough for a Saint Bernard to fit through. The village was run-down, stank of butcher blood, and was filled with ravenous creatures that would rip your throat out for a snack. All of that I could deal with. The thing that made it truly abysmal was that it was in New Jersey.

We pulled ahead to the village square, where Billy made turning a trailer around look easy. Evangeline told me that once (and only once) he'd left the van parked in the wrong direction, and nearly didn't get out.

The wolves came out in force, and not all of them were fully human. Hell, given where we were, it was possible some of them couldn't even turn fully human.

Billy got out like he was going to the feed store. He slapped the hood. "Stay with the van. Be ready." He walked across the square into a building that looked like a bar combined with a dress consignment shop.

Where would they be? I wondered, looking at the cinderblock barns that lined the square. Like I said, used to be we would go in shooting, but the results were messy.

See, wolves had a nasty habit of collecting kids. Stupid kids, slow kids, confused kids, kids who made bad decisions. Most weeks we could bargain for them. It was the power of bacon, which was also near magical. Some weeks the wolves were extra hungry, or had extra kids, and we did extended negotiations, the kind with bullets or buckshot. I actually hoped for those.

As the minutes passed, the wolves got closer and closer

to the trailer. The pigs might stink, but they weren't stupid—they knew what surrounded them and were about to stampede inside the trailer.

About the time I figured Billy would be coming out with the trade tickets, he came out all right, blood on his shirt, running at top speed for the van. We'd gone into sudden-death negotiations. I came prepared. In my view, "talk first" meant the sound of my voice needed to get there ahead of the first bullet.

The head wolf was about four steps behind Billy, and I dropped him with a nice clean shot, but the noise brought growls from a dozen points around the village beyond the square. I followed up by shooting anything and everything between Billy and me. The wolves that had been sniffing the trailer retreated to a respectable distance.

Billy slid into the van. "They ain't in the mood to bargain."

"Hungry?"

He took a handkerchief from his pocket and dabbed at his chest where bloodstains spread. "I'd say scared if I knew anything that scared a wolf."

Nothing scared wolves that I knew of. They'd run at you knowing they were going to get shot if it had been more than a minute since you last reminded them. The door to one low cinderblock building caught my eye. It had a wire gate, and through the gate I saw a tiny hand wave. I threw the door open and jumped out, grabbing the shotgun from behind the seat as I went.

"Now is not the time, Miss Locks."

I waved the shotgun at the wolves nearest to me. "We aren't leaving without them, deal or not."

Billy revved the engine, pulling a few feet forward. "Get back in. We'll come back next week and rescue some others. This is not how we do things, young lady."

"It is now." I ran back to the trailer.

Wolves stood in a circle all the way around us. The leader ran toward me at a trot. He still bled from where I'd blasted him. His voice came out like coarse gravel. "Are you an enchanter?"

I saw the look in his wide eyes, and his face was pale for a wolf. Something had them frightened all right. I held up the shotgun like a wand. "Yeah, I'm an enchanter. Back off or I'll turn you all into sausage."

He leaped six feet back in one smooth, graceful motion. With a single swing of his arm he smashed the wolf next to him in the head and tossed him toward me. "Enchant him. It was his idea."

I wasn't going to bring up little details, like the fact that I had no magic ability, at the moment. We stood as tense seconds rolled by, then the leader growled. "You've got to the count of twenty. Either we eat him or you." The wolves began to change. Arms grew shorter, mouths longer, and their smell—well, their smell stayed about the same. Wolves smelled like nursing homes and the entrails bucket at a slaughterhouse combined with cheap cologne.

I tried to think of things I'd heard the help say, or the little rhymes they used to transform terrorists into toads and such, but I hadn't paid that much attention. Fifth or sixth time you see someone turned into a toad it gets old. What came out would have made me the laughingstock of enchanters everywhere. In the trailer, pigs squealed and screamed in terror as wolf howls filled the air. I swept my arm back and forth and chanted.

> *"This little piggy made pork chops.*
> *This little piggy made ham.*
> *This little piggy made bacon.*
> *This little piggy made spam.*
> *This little piggy cried wee wee wee and got cut up for*
>   *dog food."*

With that, I threw the trailer gate open and let loose a blast with the shotgun. Pigs went everywhere.

The wolves were mostly animal by now and reacted on

pure instinct, chasing the pigs through the square. A wolf leaped on the first one and tore into it. The scent of blood drove them into a frenzy.

I made a run for the building where I'd seen the hands. It isn't hard to shoot off a lock, but there's hardly ever reason to. This wasn't designed to keep people from getting in. It was meant to keep them from going out. I pried open the rusty latch using the shotgun as a lever, opened the gate, and let a flock of kids gush out. Must have been eight of them in that tiny shed, the youngest maybe six, the oldest eleven.

"Run for the van," I said, and they did. I glanced inside and saw him. A child, a child who glowed in the darkness, and not with light. Magic. The tattoos on his face marked him as a fae child. The moment I saw him, I felt something snap into place between us, a feeling so powerful I dropped to one knee. I shivered as his fear washed through me. I couldn't leave him.

The screams of pigs filled the country air, and if we didn't hurry we'd be adding ours to it. I kicked the door to get his attention. "Come on."

He looked at me and then back down. There's this thing about the fae. You don't ever touch them. For one, their touch can be deadly, or so I was told. The other problem of course was they considered us diseased and filthy.

I stepped into the larder, ducking my head to fit, and approached him. I took a deep breath and put my hand on his back. It tingled like an electric fence, but my heart didn't stop, so I took his hand and led him out, one step at a time.

At the entrance I met a wolf and gave him my last shotgun shell. I knew I'd told everyone in the wolf village where I was. The fae child didn't flinch at the gunshot. He looked at the gun as if it were curious and then looked up at me with those gray and white eyes. I tossed it on the ground and ran for the van.

Billy had the good sense to open the van door, and most of the kids were in. A howl went up from one end of the village. The wolves had noticed my pantry raid. "Run," I yelled to the child, but he continued his plod toward the van like he was sleepwalking.

My gun carried the same wolf ammo we'd always used: silver, garlic, and holy water. Silver hurt them in a way that didn't instantly heal, garlic messed with their allergies, and the holy water was just to piss them off because they couldn't stand being mistaken for vampires.

I dropped one wolf with a couple of rounds from the nine millimeter, and now I had the attention of a bunch more, which was exactly the way I wanted it. The longer they kept looking at me, the better, so I pulled on my hood and began shooting as they came. I'd learned a little bit of history from Grimm, and the Riding Hood incident was still a sore spot with wolves.

According to Grimm's history books, "Red" was the name the wolves gave her after she dyed her cloak in the blood of an entire wolf clan. Depending which side of the Kingdom Channel you believed, either the wolves were innocent victims who barely even nibbled on Red's family, or horrible monsters who had it coming. The genocide that followed left the wolves scattered loners at the outside of society. Wearing a red hood was a good way to tick off every wolf in the village.

It worked better than I could ever have wanted—they ignored the kid and came for me with howls of rage, barely giving me enough time to change clips. Billy revved the van engine. The fae child stopped at the door, simply staring at the van.

"Get *in*!" I yelled. I ran toward the van, shooting wolves as I went, and lifted him under the arms, tossing him into the seat. My arms burned from the sheer amount of power he contained. I threw the van door shut, and in that instant my months and years of training saved my life. I can't say why I ducked, just that I did. A huge, hairy claw smashed the van window, causing the kids to scream. The van started to roll away and I realized Billy would leave me there in the middle of a pack of wolves.

I'd been left worse places over the years; once in the middle of a stampede, and once at a bagpipe concert where they played "The Sound of Silence." Garfunkel made me want to tear my ears off, but these wolves would tear my throat out.

I grabbed the trailer gate and swung myself inside. As we bounced down the gravel road the wolves gave chase. A lot of them had already started to eat the pigs, but didn't mind dine-and-dash, particularly when it might mean dining on us.

Billy kept the accelerator all the way down. With every passing step the wolves fell farther behind and I felt better about my impromptu raid. The biggest wolf realized we were pulling away, and instead of leaping at the sides of the trailer or the van, it leaped directly into the trailer with me.

I pointed the gun right at its head and it froze in place. "What a big head you have, Grandma. The better for me to put a bullet through." It bared its teeth and I pulled the trigger. My gun clicked. A guttural growl that sounded like laughter came from deep inside the wolf, as it pulled back its lips in what I'm sure was a grin.

When it leaped this time I dove forward, letting it go over me and hit the back of the trailer. As I stood I slipped in the muck and almost fell out. Asphalt whizzed by a few feet away, and I didn't have time to reload.

The wolf crouched and sprang at me, and right then, I released the trailer gate. With one arm I held on to the gate while I held the other over my face and throat. It slammed into me and clamped down on my arm right by the elbow. The trailer bounced and we swung out over the road together, me clinging to the gate, it clinging to me. The wolf had my arm in its jaw for a moment, shaking his head and biting deeper. His legs hit the pavement and he was torn away. I kicked my feet back into the trailer and collapsed. Drenched in pig filth, I sat and wrapped my arm, Little Red Bleeding Hood.

Eight

~❦~

WHEN WE PULLED into the loading bay back at the office I could barely sit still. I'd tried to raise Grimm from the moment Billy let me back in, but when Grimm's busy, he's busy. He'd be upstairs, and I couldn't wait to share our haul. Oh, the regular kids were great, and you could bet most of them would be returned for a reward—cash from the normal folks, Glitter from Kingdom kind—but Grimm wasn't stupid.

If the family couldn't pay up he'd still return the kid. You never know when you're going to need the services of a plumber or funeral director in the middle of the night. Also, if he kept the kid he'd have to feed, house, and clothe it. The real haul was the fae child. I had no idea what the fae would give to get one of their kids back, but it had to be good.

I slapped the front desk as I walked in. Rosa saw me, and her face went flush.

"Hit the mother lode, Rosa. You won't believe what we rescued," I said as I buzzed myself in. In the lobby a group of kobolds sat in matching bright green uniforms. They came every week and the answer was always the same—Grimm wasn't going to help them form a professional soccer team. As I walked back toward Grimm's office I heard yelling through the door, and Evangeline answering.

I barged into his office without bothering to knock. "You're gonna want to kiss me, Grimm." I took a lot of comfort in the knowledge that he couldn't.

"You!" he shouted, so loud a crack appeared along the edge of the mirror. "How in Kingdom did this happen?"

"Look, I don't care what Billy told you, I wasn't going to leave them. And I don't know really. I think the wolves snatched him like normal, but how'd they get ahold of a fae child in the first place?"

Evangeline looked at me and shook her head, trying to warn me of something while Grimm disappeared. When he returned, he looked confused. It's not a look I'd often seen on him. He set his face like stone. "Tell me how this happened."

"The wolves didn't want to bargain, and I couldn't just—" I stopped.

Grimm's jaw was set and he glared at me, while Evangeline kept her eyes on the floor. He wasn't talking about the wolves. "Grimm, what's going on?"

When he spoke his voice was cold and calm. It was the same tone he used to order a nest of poodles destroyed. "Marissa, I'm afraid you are the only one with the answers, but I promise you won't leave my office until I have them as well. Do you know who I got a call from today?"

An idea lit up my heart for a moment. Had Liam been so sad and desperate to find me that he'd managed to call the Fairy Godfather? "I didn't give Liam our number. The only number he has doesn't work anymore." It didn't as long as I kept the phone off.

Grimm's face remained unchanged, like a statue. "I got a call from the prince's family. They are old royalty, my dear, and they understand the practical matters of my Agency."

Translation—they knew damn well how we worked, and still let us get the job done. Grimm had probably gotten their permission before attempting the setup.

"He'll give up on me, I'm sure," I said, but secretly a hope had woken inside me that he hadn't. Maybe he had refused Ari, pining for me. The hair on my neck stood up as I wondered what exactly Grimm would do if that happened.

"I don't think we're going to have a problem in that department," said Grimm, his voice getting louder again. At this point they could probably hear him in the front office. Grimm shouted, "Seeing as how he's never even met you." Another crack ran sideways down the mirror, splitting him in two.

My head spun for a moment while I tried to work it out. "He what?"

"It seems he's not upset you broke his heart. He's not swept off his feet by your charms. He had a lovely stroll on the pier and bought two paintings and was back at his apartment by three in the afternoon."

I held up my hands. "That's not possible. I didn't spend the last few weeks doing nothing."

His eyes flashed brighter, and he practically screamed at me, "Do you have any idea how this makes me look? How it makes you look? If you didn't want the job, my dear, you should have said so. If you have a problem with our bargain, by all means, speak up."

Evangeline edged toward the door, doing her best to keep from getting involved.

"Something doesn't add up. I went to the pier, you know that. I met the prince, I did my end of the deal."

Grimm faded out of view, and a new picture came in. Raven black hair, sharp features with wide eyes. I knew the man. Prince Mihail, the only person I'd ever met who could make a trip to the Kingdom Post Office worse. "Marissa, are you telling me you had lunch and dinner and dancing with this man? If so, someone is lying to me. I hope for your sake it isn't you."

Nausea crept from my stomach up to my throat, and my mouth felt drier than the desert. I dropped my gaze. I went over that day in my head again and again. The crowds of people at the Pier, Liam. There was no denying it. "No. I must have got the wrong one."

The air smelled like ozone every time Grimm got furious. "How in Kingdom did you get the wrong person? I checked the auguries, Marissa. There weren't two princes on the pier that day. Only one, and he went right past your table, just as planned. But you were already, shall we say, involved?"

Now that hurt as bad as anything that had happened in the last month. My face grew hot. I knew they would be thinking it was guilt instead of embarrassment. "I went to the pier. I had lunch with a prince, Grimm. I saw the magic on him."

Grimm put his hand to his forehead and looked down. "He's a blacksmith from the south end. Oh I don't doubt you went down there and had a merry time on my dollar. You blew our best chance at our actual target. The one we are paid for. The man you had your dalliance with is not a prince. He's an artist who makes wrought-iron trinkets and that sort of thing. The only thing magic about him is that he hasn't managed to die of food poisoning. I expect better from you, Marissa."

I knew that. Grimm expected perfection. Pride made me look back at him, though I know he wanted me to keep my head low. "I have nothing in my life except this job. I have never done less than the best for you." I knew they could hear me in the lobby, and I didn't care. Let them hear me in the loading dock for all it mattered. "You said find the prince. You said look for the magic. You taught me what to look for yourself. Why don't you come out and say I'm lying?"

Instead he waited in silence for me to calm. "You made a mistake, my dear. You said you were tired of being the wrong woman, and I don't blame you. You said you wanted him for yourself. So I think you were looking for someone more in line with your ideals than the princess's. Really, have you looked at that man? He's not exactly prince material."

My face blushed even more because Evangeline was in the room. I knew exactly what she'd thought when Grimm introduced me as his new agent, and I never wanted her to see this. "I saw the magic."

Grimm's face softened for a moment, almost sad. "Marissa, I think perhaps you saw what you wanted to see."

I couldn't take it anymore. I stood up. Grimm probably thought I was going to walk out the door. Grimm was wrong. I walked over to the wall of weapons and picked up a case the size of a cigar box. Engravings covered the outside, except for a tiny brass plate. The carvings showed a rose in a ring of woven thorns, the standard of the Black Queen.

Evangeline told me about her. She'd been dead for over four hundred years, and folks in Kingdom were still nervous when her name came up. Depending on who you believed, she was either all of the fairy-tale villains in one or the queen of all of them, but whatever she was, she was powerful. Her magic lay in lies so strong they could twist reality itself, becoming almost true.

Grimm flashed into the stainless steel plating on the wall. "Put that down."

I opened it and inside the velvet interior was an odd thing. At first glance it looked like a gnarled tree root, and in fact the name engraved on the plate said "Root of Lies." That's not what it was. I knew the truth, and couldn't see it as anything else.

The story goes a righteous prince lopped the Black Queen's head off to put an end to the lies, but she continued to speak. They quartered her, and burned her, and finally scattered her ashes. Some of her wouldn't burn. The thing in the box, it was a part of her. Her hand, to be specific, and once you knew, the roots looked like fingernails, bones, and tendons, if bones came polished ebony black.

I put my hand down into the box, and the thing convulsed, gripping me across the palm. Cutting me. Did I mention it was still almost alive, in the box, after all this time? Grimm used it only to force the truth from the most uncooperative of subjects, because the options were tell the truth or die. If you were foolish enough to tell less than the truth while the Root of Lies held you, thorns grew straight from it to your heart, seeking out the lies. Most people told the truth.

Grimm narrowed his eyes and fixed me with a scowl. "Marissa, don't say a word, not a single word. Put down the Root and we can talk about what happened. There's no need for theatrics." As he spoke I felt a compulsion overcome me. I did want to put it back, but not nearly as much as I wanted to do this.

I grasped it harder, digging my nails into the blackened bone, and it returned the favor. "I went to the pier." It rustled under my hand, raking nails along my palm. "I thought he was a prince." It convulsed underneath me, slicing the top of my hand. "I saw the magic coming from him." It squeezed my hand so hard I thought it would break, tearing into my skin, then dropped back into the box, rendered lifeless by the truth.

Evangeline let out her breath. I think if he had had real skin, Grimm would have been sweating. He watched as I returned the Root to its shelf. "Well," he said, "that definitely complicates matters."

Nine

~~~

THE NEXT DAY I dealt with twelve dancing princesses with blisters on their feet (you would be surprised what wonders a gel insole can work). I put yet another frog in the aquarium until Grimm could deal with him. Before ten thirty I sent two kids who ate a gingerbread house to the hospital to have their stomachs pumped. Grimm was still angry, but at least he wasn't angry at me. Now it was more about how to actually pull off Ari's setup.

I risked a trip into the lion's den (Grimm's office—we'd had the actual lion's den removed a couple of years ago) to question him. "Grimm, we need to talk. What about the fae boy? I thought they were damn near invulnerable. So how did a fae child wind up in a wolf larder?"

From what I had heard from Evangeline, the fae were only one step down from Grimm. There was a healthy debate about how big a step it actually was. Wolves were great predators, but the fae guards would have blasted the skin from their skulls the moment they set claw on a child.

"I don't know," said Grimm.

The Fairy Godfather never admitted to not knowing.

Ever. If you asked him about something he didn't know, he'd say "I'll find out shortly," which meant that he'd already tried.

I wondered how long we'd keep the kid. "You get ahold of the, um, parents?"

He nodded. "I performed the contact ritual this morning. The family will be arriving to retrieve him. You are to be present, but silent. Am I understood?"

I didn't like letting someone else tell me when to speak and when not to, but I had a mortal fear of death, and dealing with the fae was tricky, very tricky. The wrong move might cost me my life, the wrong word, my soul. Rumor had it the fae could rip your soul right out of your skin, like peeling a banana. "How about you handle it?"

Grimm shook his head. "The fae requested your presence. In case you are wondering, that's not a request."

So I got ready to go down and party with the fae. It was safer to meet them outside in the cargo bay than risk them coming up in the elevators and meeting someone. I heard once a few came to visit Grimm unannounced. We were sponging down the walls of the elevator for weeks.

As the hour approached, everyone scurried about. In keeping for the magic kind, noon and midnight were the watch hours of the day. They'd arrive at noon sharp. As much as I wanted to actually see a fae, I detested having to dress up for them. Apparently, having pure magic as the foundation of your world kind of drives down fashion, because they still dressed like "days of yore." I'm guessing, by the way, that *yore* is an old English word for "Heavy, itchy, and hard to breath in."

I exited from Wardrobe in a funk. Their best efforts had made me look like I did on my dates: average. Ari was waiting for me in the waiting room as I left the office. She smiled at me. I scowled back.

"That's a lovely dress," she said.

It wasn't. It looked like I was dressed in a green circus tent. We could make over someone to look like a supermodel, or make the nerdiest prince look dashing and confident, but Grimm had chosen my costume himself. I think it was supposed to represent the medieval messenger pages. That, or a homeless carpet salesman. Ari grabbed my flowery sleeve as I walked by. "Can I speak with you?"

I shook her hand off, tearing a bit of the magenta lace. "I'm no longer handling your case. Haven't you talked to Fairy Godfather yet?" Obviously she hadn't, so I took her to the mirror and rapped on it like a door. "Grimm, what do you want me to do with her?"

He snapped into view and gained his regal appearance. "Bring the appointed one with you."

"Um, to the loading dock?" I asked, totally blowing the mystery aura.

"Yes, my dear, and hurry. Why must you always be late?"

Ari didn't strike me as a candidate for "America's Most Brilliant," but without a doubt Grimm was losing all the mystique he worked to maintain.

"Why are we going to the loading dock?" asked Ari.

"You've heard of the fae? We're about to get a little visit from them, a whole freaking family. Unless you want to make your innards out-ards, I'd suggest keeping your head down and your mouth shut."

She looked a little pale, which pleased me to no end. I ought to have been ashamed about that, and maybe one day I'd get around to it. I enjoyed certain forms of procrastination.

I stepped out of the loading bay at 11:56 and took my place in the reception line. The portal, hastily drawn under Grimm's personal instruction, stood at one end, and the makeshift throne we had constructed for the fae child (an office chair covered with a bedsheet) at the other. In between, Grimm had someone roll out a carpet, horrible orange shag.

The boy sat in the chair, gazing about with unfocused eyes.

Ari stood at my side, Grimm whispering from his best mirror the whole time about how she was not to speak.

The portal snapped open like a pop-up tent and vivid

colors drifted out like smoke. The Realm of Fae was powerful. The colors were sharper, so vibrant they hurt, and yet so delicious you almost couldn't look away. Where it interacted with our world it became vaporous, almost unreal. Also, things didn't tend to go well for our world.

I tried to keep my eyes on the ground, like Grimm had suggested, but I couldn't resist sneaking a peak. The fae didn't come to town every day (Kingdom be blessed). Fortunately for us, they lived a realm away. I wasn't going to miss a chance to see them. Two figures emerged from the portal and drifted along the carpet. They paid no attention to us.

The father was unearthly, regal and deadly at the same time, and his drift had absolute purpose as he moved along the line toward the child. He wore a circus tent with lace like mine, but the difference was on him it looked majestic. His feet didn't touch the carpet as he passed, but the carpet curled up, burned and shriveled, beneath him, and below it, cracks opened in the concrete. Grimm was going to lose his security deposit for sure.

For the first time since we'd rescued him, the boy looked up, and he leaped out of the chair and ran forward, seizing his father's cloaks. The father raised his hand, and the boy rose into the air, floating before him. Their laughter made the lights flicker and my nose bleed. The father raised his other hand and they drifted back, blowing like smoke toward the portal.

"It is a dangerous game you play," said a voice like bells and thunder. I realized I had lost track of the mother. She stood a few feet away, speaking to Grimm. His best mirror had been brought down and he watched from it. How he appeared to her I cannot say, since I was focusing on my toes.

"Yours is no safer," said Grimm, "for those who tread this world."

She walked on and stopped at Evangeline. "Your time comes soon, messenger," she said, and tread on.

I felt Ari tense and she caught her breath, and that's when I noticed the lightning playing on Ari's fingertips. I knew she was a seal bearer, but I'd never seen her use magic. She rubbed her fingertips together, her hands trembling. Maybe Grimm could teach her to control her abilities better under pressure.

"Princess," said the Fae Mother, and the word echoed in my head, "you must become what you are." She stood before me now, smelling like fields after a rain. Her gaze felt like the essence of the sun shining on me. "You dared touch him?"

I looked up at her. She had silver hair, the ends glowed like soft moonlight, and a sharp nose and chin. Her eyes were gray and shifted like storm clouds before rain. She was tall, taller than me by a foot. I couldn't tell if it was a frown or a smile on her face. In fact, I couldn't look away at all.

I stood trapped between Grimm's order to keep silent and her question. As the moments ticked by, I realized she would wait my life away, so I answered. "Twice. Once to lead him out, and once to put him into the van." I stood waiting, knowing if she struck me with magic I might never feel it, or the death might last an eternity. "Is he okay?"

The color dropped out of the world. I stood in a plane of nothing, gray without sound or color, and only dim shapes like ghosts in the fog.

"This is your world for one as young as my child." Now her voice sounded sweet but not deafening. When she said the word *child*, it changed, and sounded like *treasure*. "You shed blood to save him. I will reward that."

A thought leaped up in my brain. The fae were practically made of Glitter.

"No. Your freedom comes, but not by my hand."

My heart skipped a beat and I felt like I'd swallowed a block of ice. "It's the only thing I want."

"Not so. It is your heart's greatest longing. You will receive it at the cost of all you love. I give you the blessing of the fae, but it is a gift that must be accepted."

"I can't. Grimm would kill me."

She closed her eyes. "It may be your only hope against the curse." The word *curse* moved as she said it, like a spider in my ear. A curse. A real curse. "She comes for you soon. Our half sister, the Black Queen. Through your hand she will strike the victory blow."

I weighed my choices, which seemed completely zero. The Black Queen. A curse. "I accept your blessing."

She leaned in to kiss me on the forehead, and a tear rolled down her cheek. "You are twice blessed now to balance the scales. But you will drink from a river of pain." The world became blurry, and darkness wrapped itself around me in a hug that felt like a mountain on my chest. I couldn't move. I couldn't even breathe. Somewhere in the darkness I slipped into nothing.

"SHE'S WAKING UP," said a woman's voice in the distance. I struggled to speak but my voice didn't work.

"Calm down," said a second voice, another woman. "You can't talk until the tube is removed."

My eyes didn't work right; everything looked blurry.

"I'll call him," said the first voice, Evangeline.

"You're in South General," said Ari. She took my hand. "You've been here three days."

I croaked out something that was supposed to sound like "Why?"

"You stopped breathing. Fairy Godfather used magic to bring you here."

Evangeline came back, carrying an oblong mirror. "He says this one is certified to not disrupt electronics."

Grimm's eyes looked out from the tiny square, and he looked honestly concerned. "I'm going to have a nurse remove that tube, and when your throat is feeling better, we need to have a talk."

IN THE EVENING, when I woke again, only Evangeline waited. She'd covered the mirror with her scarf, and sat backwards across the chair, staring at me.

I worked the corners of my mouth, dealing with my

raging sore throat. "Hey." Given my state it meant a lot more, but my mouth wasn't cooperating.

"I went by your apartment and brought you clothes and your purse. Don't know what happened to whatever you were wearing on the way here, but at least you can cover your butt when you leave."

"Thanks."

She reached into her pocket and took out something, and my stomach turned as I recognized the cell phone. "Found this on your dresser, M."

I coughed and tried to force the words out. "It's not— Please. Don't—"

She held it up and snapped it in two, tearing the screen right off. "I know what it is. I won't tell Grimm. This can be our secret. Working the wrong man, keeping phones, that stunt with the wolves. Think about what you are doing. Ask yourself what you want. You're slipping." She left me alone, and she took what was left of the phone.

I waited until much later to call. Not just because it felt like I'd drunk a mug of broken glass, but because I didn't know what I was going to say. It was after midnight when I called him, putting one hand on the bracelet.

Grimm showed up immediately, his mouth open, his eyes squinting to see me better. "Marissa, what do you need? Can I get you something?" Grimm acting like my nurse. That was actually funny, except that it hurt to laugh.

"What happened?" Each word took more time to coax from my throat than an entire speech.

"The Fae Mother gave you a kiss, my dear. Their touch can be deadly."

I took another sip of ice water, letting it numb me. "How much of it did you hear?" I trusted Grimm. He'd earned it in most ways.

"That's not how it works." He glanced to the edges of the mirror. "What I heard and what you heard are two entirely different things. The fae speech is not unlike my own, and without this mirror to translate we'd have a lot harder time getting things done."

I coughed and swallowed another mouthful of broken glass. "I heard what she said to you. She said you play a dangerous game."

"My dear, that's the best that your mind could do with her words. Our conversation would have taken you three years to transcribe. I told you, what you heard and what I heard are not necessarily the same."

I made a mental note to ask Ari what she had heard. "The Fae Mother said something. I heard *curse*, but the word, it moved."

Grimm's face went impassive the way it did when he was going to tell someone he wouldn't grant their wish, or he wouldn't kill someone, or he wouldn't (we never said couldn't) bring back the dead. "Harakathin." The word spat from his mouth like aural vomit, and I shivered.

"That's it. My only hope against the Hara—"

"Don't say it," Grimm's voice came out a sharp hiss. "We don't call curse children back once they leave."

"So I accepted her blessing."

He closed his eyes and exhaled. He didn't say I screwed up. He didn't need to. I've worked with him long enough to know his face, and yes, possibly even his personality.

"I screwed up, didn't I?"

For a moment he looked angry, but then that look of concern took over. "Marissa, dear, I've been lax in certain areas of your training, I admit." Grimm flashed over to the bedside dressing mirror. Guess now that I was breathing on my own he didn't worry about medical devices. "If you worked for another fairy, you would have learned these things by now. If you had any talent with magic, you would have learned. I'd have seen to it, it's only proper." To hear Grimm tell it, sending me to community college had been the apex of learning. Hearing him talk like this felt weird.

"I've told you the word for curse. Do you know the fae word for blessing?"

I knew the tone, and waited.

"Harakathin." Again I felt the word shiver out, but it

passed by without the feeling of darkness. "The word is a spell when spoken in magic, my dear. Each one is a living creation, and they do not work in ways one might expect."

"So she cursed me?" I said, feeling the weight go out of my arms. I floated in a cloud of despair.

"It's about intent. She blessed you, but the blessing won't simply do what you command, and that might be deadly. Let's say, for instance, she gave you a blessing to protect you from sorrow. You begin a deep depression. Will the blessing cure your depression, or cause a house fire and kill you? Either ends your suffering. Perhaps she blessed you with good fortune, and you have cancer. Will it make you find out earlier, or hide it so that you die swiftly? Which do you think it will do?"

I propped myself up on the pillow to try and read his face for cues, but he was blank as a poster. "I don't know."

"Neither do I. You are tired, and you should sleep. I'll send a cab to the hospital when they release you."

I gathered myself for what came next. Now that I knew what the blessing was, I kept wanting to look around and spot it, see if it was standing there, watching me. "Tell me about the Black Queen." I heard the hiss of air as he caught his breath.

"You know about her, or I can get you a children's book in Kingdom about her. Perhaps one with rhymes and pop-up pages."

I'd sat in too many rooms with too many customers to be fooled by that. "Tell me about her. Tell me why the fae think she's coming. Tell me why she'd come for me."

The room shook like an earthquake and across the hospital the doors slammed all at once. Grimm's face flashed with anger, but not at me. "You have nothing to fear from her."

I waited until the tremors died down. "Then tell me."

"When you are better, Marissa. I swear on the Root of Lies itself I will tell you about her."

I flopped back into my bed. "You don't have hands to hold it with. That doesn't mean much."

Grimm held up a hand so I could see it. "The Root of

Lies could kill even a fairy, my dear. I swear on it, I will tell you, but you must wait for when I think the time is right."

I grasped the bed rail and sat up to get a better look at him. "Promise me. Everything you know."

"Never. Only what you need. You are young, and the story of her life would twist your own from hearing it."

"The Fae Mother said I was twice blessed." The meaning of that sank in.

Grimm nodded, like I'd told him I signed for a package. "Well, you've never been one to do something by halves."

Ten

~

AFTER FOUR DAYS in the hospital, I expected more re-action to my return. You would have thought I never left. Rosa didn't so much as tip her head to me when I walked in. Evangeline, feet up on the conference room's table, glanced over the paper she was reading, then went back to the sports section.

"What, no hello? No welcome back from the dead?"

She folded it up. "There are easier ways to get a few days off."

I glanced at Grimm's mirror. "Hey, Grimm, if I was legally dead, does that cancel my debt?"

"Debts are canceled at, and only at, the point of embalming," said Grimm, his normal business self this morning.

"Ready to serve, Fairy Godfather," I said, hoping my enthusiasm didn't sound as fake as it felt.

Evangeline gave me the "teacher's pet" look. No one ever got fired for kissing up to the boss.

"Evangeline, you will need to handle the final arrange-ments for prince project 2.0," said Grimm.

Evangeline and I exchanged glances. Every once in a

while, Grimm got the idea it was time to go modern. It never ended well.

"What's wrong? Is my new, hip dialogue not appropriate? I searched all the Internets last night and determined where we can arrange a new meeting." Grimm cocked his head, waiting for our reply.

"Last time you used a computer it caught fire," I said.

Evangeline added, "Then the desk it was on caught fire."

"Then the building it was in caught fire," we finished together.

The Agency had good fire sprinklers for a reason. Fairies and technology were a bad mix. "Grimm," I said, "You always tell me to stick with what you are good at."

He snorted and rolled his eyes. "Oh, all right. I've studied the auguries, and I have determined another opportunity to arrange a meeting between our princess and her prince."

"So we're going to do it over?" I knew I'd been out a couple of days but I didn't expect Grimm to move that fast.

"Hardly, my dear. Evangeline will handle arrangements with Princess Arianna; you will be going into Kingdom. I need you to visit the Isyle Witch and pick up a love potion."

Rosa buzzed, and I knew another client needed time with the Fairy Godfather. I grabbed my purse and headed toward the door. "I'm on it." No more screwups, no more mistakes, and definitely no more blessings.

KINGDOM ON MONDAY morning looked like the leftovers of a ticker-tape parade followed by a massive alcoholic bender. Morning sun didn't do the magic facades much good. Smoke hung in the air as street sweepers burned off the confetti and crushed down the discarded wineglasses and a few drunks who picked the wrong gutter to sleep in. The rest of the world got to work, including me.

I was two streets over from Main, which was still in the "good" part of Kingdom. I wondered for a moment what stood in this spot on the low side. I discarded the thought like so much stale wine and went into the store. "Isyle Witch," said the gold lettering on the door, and below it were all four pages of her binding accreditation. That's legal speak for "may not transform into toad without consent (and probably payment)."

Now the outside is your standard magical facade, clean and pastel and shimmery, but step inside and the witch's shop was like the aquarium section of the pet shop mixed with the heart of the Amazon. Tanks with fish, tanks with spiders, tanks with things that looked like a fish had a kid with a spider. The only thing missing was the cauldron, and that's because a few years back most of the witches went to using slow cookers so they could watch soap operas and work spells at the same time.

"What brings the pretty to my home?" asked the witch. She was old. Nobody talked like that anymore. With witches, age brought more and more power, but I felt the Agency bracelet and took courage. I stepped up to the counter. The witch's eyes were solid yellow, like the iris and pupil had been removed, and what remained was diseased.

She glanced around with those sightless eyes and gasped. "How dare you bring curse children with you into my home?"

For a moment I tried to figure out what she meant. It finally came to me. "I can't afford daycare. They're actually blessings, I think."

"So little difference." The witch laughed at me, a croaking, choking noise.

"I've come for a love potion."

"Of course you have. With looks like that, and your age, I don't blame you."

I glared at her. "I'm twenty-four, and you just said I was pretty."

"I got a better look."

"Make the potion." I won't go into the ingredients—they weren't rational, or reasonable. About the only thing that made any sense was the Valentine's candy hearts (for flavoring, of course). Potions tasted like cheap scotch, or so I'd heard.

The witch held out her claw. "Pay and receive."

I tapped the company card and it changed, becoming a

vial like my own, but full. Always full. I turned it over and a tiny pile of Glitter swept out, funneled into a tornado that came to rest in the witch's hand.

"You pay with hope that does not belong to you, child, buying a potion for someone else's man." She set down the flask.

I snatched it, ready to be gone. "Thanks."

She held up her hand, crooked, with liver spots and long yellow nails. On the counter she placed a tiny flask. "The leftovers from my brew. It is time you had something of your own. Consider it a gift for the Queen's handmaiden."

"The term is *agent*. And he's the Fairy Godfather these days." I'm not stupid. Gifts in Kingdom were like snakes. They coiled up around you and struck, and Kingdom only knew what would happen. Gifts from witches were worse, but turning it down would be like turning down the blessing of the fae, certain to bring their wrath. I took the second flask and pocketed it. I had enough enemies already.

Grimm looked relieved when I got back to the Agency with both the potion and my skin intact. It's not like I hadn't given him reason to be worried lately. The thing is, even though I was technically a slave, he'd never treated me like one. He was always polite, and often proper, and on occasion kind. So I mostly trusted him.

"Excellent work, Marissa."

I gave him a scowl for complimenting me on such a basic assignment. The potion I deposited in a safety box.

"I trust Kingdom is recovering from their weekend hangover?"

"You know it. The witch didn't have a single other customer. Speaking of which," I took the second flask out of my pocket, "you ever known a witch to have 'leftover' potion?" My fingers tingled, and I felt the urge to hide the flask someplace dark and safe.

Grimm took off his glasses and rubbed his eyes. "Never. It would be like wasting Glitter."

"She could see the blessings, Grimm."

He nodded as if it weren't important.

"Can you?"

"No, my dear. Now tell me, how much did the 'extra' flask cost you? I'll buy it from you for double."

That made no sense. Grimm held on to Glitter even tighter than he held on to money. "Double?" I asked, and he nodded.

"Marissa, I trust you, and your Glitter is yours to spend, but such potions are dangerous. Particularly for you."

"She said it was a gift. Double nothing is still nothing." My fingers cramped around the bottle, and it hurt to let go. My fingers felt like they were on fire as I thought of all the possibilities. A potion. One of my own, which would leave a man so taken with me he'd die before letting me go. I knew I should make a counteroffer. Triple my month's pay, or more. Grimm looked like he wanted it bad, but the thought of giving it away made my stomach turn.

He looked at my hand, and I knew he had seen me clutch it. "Then it is yours, my dear. Tell me, can you even bring yourself to put it down, or have you already begun to imagine using it?"

I focused on my fingers, peeling them back one at a time, until the vial fell out of my hands and rolled on the desk. I held one hand in the other, resisting the urge to snatch the potion.

"May I offer to keep it safe for you?"

My stomach turned as I looked at the tiny flask, but in the revulsion I also felt desire to take it back. I knew what it held was magic, dangerously close to black magic, but part of me didn't care. I was afraid of that part. "I don't want to touch it again. The big one didn't do that to me."

"It wasn't yours. Your desires make it that much stronger. I'll have Rosa put it away. She has a husband and six children, so it won't affect her the way it does you."

"I didn't want to make any more enemies." I sat down in a chair and put my head down on his desk.

He shook his head. "A gift from a witch. You're certainly not making any friends."

Eleven

~

THE NEW PLAN came together quickly. This time, however, we'd work as a team—Evangeline and I—because potions were not to be trifled with. Grimm knew where Prince Mihail would be having lunch, and Ari herself would deliver the punch.

"I'm not ready for this," said Ari, looking more than a little green.

"We'll get you dressed when we get there. There are barf bags in the seat pockets," said Evangeline. Given the way she drove, we often needed them.

"You do have the wine," said Grimm, looking out from the rearview mirror. He was personally overseeing the operation this time around.

Evangeline patted a bag in the console beside her seat as she floored the accelerator and took another corner at near takeoff speeds. "Of course I do. Port, 1938, exactly as you ordered."

"His favorite," said Grimm. "Now, young lady, do you understand what you need to do?"

Ari took her head away from the bag for a moment. "I

take the wine, walk along the sidewalk, he'll say hello. How do you know what he'll say?"

Grimm gave a sigh. "Does the sign on my office say 'Fairy Janitor'? I know. He says hello, you say hello, he says he was about to have a drink, and you, you look like someone who would like to have a drink with him. Does he like old port? He does, and he drinks it, looks at you, and you are golden, young lady."

Ari giggled. "It's magic."

Evangeline and I exchanged nauseated glances, which had nothing to do with the fact that Evangeline treated curbs as an extra lane, and considered any space larger than a loaf of bread an opening to squeeze into. I, for one, was used to her driving, which resembled a demolition derby crossed with a Formula One race.

"The potion expires at noon now that it is tuned to Princess Arianna," said Grimm. "So you only have a tiny window to make sure it gets delivered. Fortunately, he's going to look up at exactly eleven forty-two, giving you plenty of time for banter and toasts."

As we drove along Ari turned about the same shade of green as the plastic plants in our lobby. Her grip on the bag turned her knuckles white. "I feel terrible."

I reached over to feel her head, and as I touched her something like a static spark jumped between us. She pitched forward, gagging into her bag. Her skin felt so hot it hurt, and her face looked feverish. I held her hair out of her face and let her finish. "Grimm, you got magic for this?"

"Not necessary, my dear. There's a drugstore on the way. We'll get something there."

Ari sloshed against the window as we made another near ninety-degree turn and let out a low groan.

I took her hand. "Hold on. We're going to get you fixed up." That was the point where the tire blew out. Anyone else driving, and we'd have rolled for sure, but Evangeline cut the wheel perfectly to counter the skid. We slammed into a curb, blowing out both tires on the other side. She looked in her mirrors. "We hit something. Either a gnome or a two-foot-tall homeless guy."

Please, I thought, *please don't let it be a gnome*. I stepped out onto the sidewalk and went around to get Ari. She looked at me with feverish eyes, and I knew we were in trouble. "Grimm, is there a horse-drawn carriage near here? How about a pumpkin? You want me to buy a carpet? Or a cab?"

He spoke from the driver's-side mirror. "Blast it. There's nothing for two miles. You are only six blocks away. Secure transportation for the princess. We don't have time for delays."

Ari took a few steps and nearly collapsed. "Going for help," I said, and took off at a sprint. I passed three blocks before I found what I was looking for. A bag lady sat by an alleyway, her shopping cart filled with soggy clothing.

"I'll give you a thousand dollars," I said, pulling out my wallet. I'm guessing there was actually closer to twelve hundred there. Grimm always said a load of cash was a more effective tool than a loaded gun. I packed both kinds of heat everywhere. I shoved the money at her and took the cart.

I hope what she wailed was "Thanks," but honestly I didn't care. The front wheel squealed like a dying hamster as I pushed the cart, and it shook from side to side. I ignored it and ran as fast as I could, pushing over people too dumb to get out of the way.

Back at the car, Evangeline saw me coming and nearly collapsed on the hood in laughter. "Come on, princess. Your chariot awaits."

Ari was curled up in a ball on the curb. Grimm questioned her from the mirror. "Are you certain you ate no shellfish? How about egg salad? Potato salad? Did you eat any form of salad?"

Evangeline scooped up Ari like a sack of rotten potatoes and dumped her into the cart, squashing wet clothing off to the side. I grabbed Ari's dress and the bottle of wine and we took off again. We ran the whole way to the corner one block from where we'd meet her prince.

Evangeline grabbed the dress with one hand and put the other around Ari's waist. She lifted Ari out of the cart and onto the ground, and took her arm. "Come on. We'll hose your hair down in that salon and I'll find you a mint to take that lovely vomit scent off your breath."

I took the bottle of wine, and got as close as possible. Down the block, at the restaurant, Mihail sat. His table stood at the edge of the sidewalk. The shine looked like dandruff, which actually made me laugh. "It's eleven thirty-eight," I said to my reflection as the minutes ticked by. "She ought to be here."

"We've got a problem," said Grimm.

"If that dress doesn't fit, remember I told her not to eat that chocolate."

Grimm connected me to Evangeline, which wasn't something he normally did. Everything went dark as he connected us more or less mind to mind. It was like whispering into each other's ears, while having your faces smashed together under a blanket. Evangeline spoke, and I heard it in my ears and through hers at the same time. "It's like the freaking Exorcist in here. What did you eat, girl? What did you not eat?"

I hefted the wine bottle. My watch read 11:40.

"Grimm, I don't think the human stomach can hold anything else," said Evangeline, "but she's barely able to walk. Don't put anything in her hands you don't want puked on or dropped or both."

"Change of plans," said Grimm. "Marissa, take the bottle and move. Down the sidewalk, make the connection. "

"But—" Evangeline and I said at once.

"Evangeline, bring her out with you and walk along behind her. Marissa, offer him the bottle and tell him you don't drink. Ari will be happening by, and looking a little faint, and need a place to sit."

"We disappear into the woodwork?" I said.

"Of course," said Grimm.

I didn't wait, I took off, bottle under my arm. As I approached the prince's table I made sure to give the wine an "exactly why do I have this thing?" look. I smiled and caught his eye. Just for a moment, really. He looked at my face long enough to be certain it wasn't interesting, let his gaze ooze down my chest, and found something truly appealing: the wine.

"Ah," he said, recognizing me, "we meet again, my lady. Would you care to have a seat? I was about to order wine."

I ignored the bottle on the table, which said he was a liar, and offered him a lie of my own. "I don't actually drink. If I did, it would be something with flavor. I have mouthwash that tastes better."

There was Evangeline, leading Ari down the sidewalk, and she looked about as sick as I've ever seen anyone. Poor girl, whatever else was wrong with her, the fix for her marital problems was in the bottle.

The prince's eyes swept across the bottle, giving it the same look he'd given Evangeline's bust in the post office. "Is that port?"

"You drink this swill? Good riddance. Must be your lucky day." Every day's a lucky day for first-string princes. I set the bottle on the table, avoided his hand, and marched off with that determined gait that said I was a woman scorned.

I ducked into the nearest alley and heaved a sigh of relief. By now Ari would be taking a wobbly seat at his table, and in a moment he'd offer her a drink to steady her nerves.

The sound of a pistol cocking brought me right back into the present.

"Listen up, princess," said a man's voice behind me, "you want to stay calm and do exactly what I tell you."

"You have the wrong girl," I said, but I felt the jab of the barrel in my back and someone kicked me in the back of the knee, causing me to fall.

"Poor girl," said a woman's voice. "I saw you looking at him, and he offered you his table. Your nerves got the best of you. You're not the one I was expecting, but I can hardly be surprised there are several of you after him. You've already fallen under his spell, so you'll do."

"These things happen," said the man. "Quiet, very quiet, princess, and you don't die in an alley. In fact, I need you to do something, something simple."

"Something natural," said the woman, and she set down a box beside me. I swear it looked like a pie box, but she opened it and inside slithered a serpent with silver scales. The woman seized my hand, and I gave her the back of my fist, knocking her to the side.

"Just for that," said the gunman, and he choked me halfheartedly, pushing his forearm into my throat.

"Stop!" said the woman. "Don't hurt her." She grabbed my hand in a gloved fist and turned it over. "The fangs of the heart seeker are enchanted, so its bite does not bring you pain as it tastes your blood." She drove a dagger down into my palm and I screamed, a squelched noise as tears ran down my face. "So we do it like this." She picked up the snake and held it out toward me.

It flicked its forked tongue. As I strained against her grip, it latched onto my hand, sinking those metallic silver fangs clean through my palm. The bitch lied. It hurt a lot. As it drank, the silver eyes turned crimson, and the scales took on a rose shine. I felt thoughts and memories and feelings running down my arm and into it along with the blood. I don't know how long it feasted, but when it let go it was fat and warm. Then things got worse.

"Now that it has tasted of your heart, it will know the truth," said the woman, and the snake slithered forward, wrapping around my arm, sliding along my skin with those warm metal scales. It poked its head into my blouse sleeve, slithered across my back, and then up around my neck, flicking its tongue at my ear. I don't mind saying I was screaming at this point, but it didn't come out as anything more than a whine. It coiled upward, wrapping itself around my head like a crown.

"Think of him," said the woman. "You cannot resist it. Think of the prince. Think of the one who might love you."

The snake burned my skin where it touched, pulsing in time with my heartbeat, and so many images flashed before my eyes. Dad, Grimm, Evangeline, Ari. I knew I was supposed to think of him, of Prince Mihail, but the harder I tried to force his face into my mind the further away he got. Then I heard the sound of the carousel, or maybe remembered it, and I saw his face: Liam.

The snake uncoiled from my head and fell forward. I watched as it slithered off into a sewer grate.

"It is done. The curse goes for him," said my mugger. "Now sleep, princess."

I waited for a spell to hit me. Instead I got a boot to the back of my head.

Twelve

～∞～

WHEN I WOKE up, my Agency bracelet was burning. "Grimm?" I opened my compact and saw only my face, filthy from lying in garbage. Obviously my muggers laid some sort of damper hex on the area. That meant Grimm couldn't tell exactly where I was or what was wrong.

I had a knot the size of a golden goose egg on my head and double vision, and the skin on my palm was a lovely shade of purple and red. The moment I left the alley Grimm appeared, in bumpers, rearview mirrors, and finally a showroom window.

"Marissa!" he said, looking me over. "Thank goodness you are alive. Are you injured? Of course you are. Is it life threatening?"

"Unless you have a twin, I have another concussion. I got mugged, but I'll live."

He almost managed to hide the look of exasperation. I doubt he'd ever had agents getting mugged before. "Then get back to the Agency. We have a problem." He disappeared.

It took me the better part of an hour to remember how to call a cab. I had a business card with "The Agency" and our address in my purse. I gave it to the cabbie and tried to doze off. Far too soon the cabbie woke me to say we'd arrived.

I stepped off the elevator with a migraine like an imp was eating my skull and I knew there was something wrong. On a normal day, coming down our hall was like walking into the entrance of a hornet's nest. There were always a ton of people trying to get in or trying to get out, and none of them were happy. Most of those people didn't need real magic, but they all had real problems that needed real solutions.

Grimm kept dozens of people who worked for him part-time or full-time, and a few, very few, like me. We handled the important things. The dangerous things. The magical things.

Today the Agency looked like it was on fire. Actually, I had seen it on fire four separate times, and neither looked this busy. People pushed in like it was a Black Friday sale inside. The phones were ringing like a cancer telethon when they put the little bald kid on who sings "Somewhere Over the Rainbow." Most of the crowd was the magic type. That wasn't unusual; they were more likely to have spare Glitter. Most of Fairy Godfather's normal business was normal problems, from normal people.

I slipped into the back room and down a crowded hallway and into my office. It wasn't a broom closet, I'm pleased to say, but it didn't have a window. Just a computer, a desk, a bookshelf, and of course a mirror.

"Marissa," said Grimm, "we have a serious problem."

I winced. Grimm's voice sounded like he was screaming, and the pounding in my ears felt like a hangover without the pleasure of getting drunk first. "What? Did he pick the wrong girl? Did she drop the freaking bottle? She did, didn't she?"

Grimm waited for my rant to peter out. "She performed flawlessly, Marissa, flawless, down to the word and gesture. I need you in the conference room, now. There's a psychotic dwarf barricaded in the MRI room, but once we've taken care of him I'll get you in."

"Can you at least do something for my headache?" I felt

like I had a safe sitting on my forehead. An angry safe that made every noise sound ten times louder than normal.

Grimm smiled warmly. "Of course, my dear. There is aspirin in the kitchen medicine cabinet."

I tried not to swear, I did. I made it to the kitchen, dry swallowed two pills of indeterminate nature, and stumbled to the conference room. Inside, Evangeline was waiting. Then I saw who was sitting beside her: Ari.

"What is she doing here?" I sat down across from Evangeline. That's about when I realized Ari had been crying.

"That will do," said Grimm. "In fact, it's entirely enough. Now, Ari, you did fine."

"Then why didn't it work?" Ari blew her nose. "He poured a drink, and we laughed, and it was perfect."

Evangeline shook her head. "It was eleven fifty-seven. You had plenty of time."

"Young lady, we will correct this," said Grimm. "I give you my word. If your prince is capable of loving anyone, it will be you." That was a serious promise for Grimm.

"What went wrong?" I asked.

"Potion didn't affect him," said Evangeline. "Not at all. Not even a bit. He finished his meal, excused himself, gave the bottle of port to the table behind him, and stuck her with the tab."

Now that didn't make sense. No one was immune to potions. There's a reason people used them—they worked. "Bad potion. I knew something was wrong with it, that witch gives me the creeps."

Grimm shook his head. "There was nothing wrong with the potion, my dear."

Evangeline pulled out a digital camera. "There's an entire table of bishops who will have serious explaining to do if these pictures get out." She gave it a pat. "Which they will."

Everything was going wrong. "First there's the accidental prince," I said, "then little miss here gets projectile vomiting at the wrong time, and now our potion doesn't work. She's cursed."

Ari let out a little gasp.

Grimm glowered at me. "She means unlucky. We don't use that word around here."

I rubbed my head. "Someone was looking for Ari. Someone who thought I was her." Ari and I traded looks, both of us offended such a mistake could be made.

"What did they want?" asked Ari.

"They wanted you to think of the man you loved. So they could send something after him. It's a thing that looks like a snake, called a heart seeker."

"One moment," said Grimm.

A minute later Rosa came to the door.

Grimm nodded to her. "Princess Arianna, Rosa would like to arrange a safe trip back to your hotel. Isn't that right, Rosa?"

Rosa gave him one of her sour looks and walked out with Ari behind. With the princess disposed of, we could talk.

My bracelet hummed for a moment, and my hand tingled as Grimm assessed the wound. "You need stitches. Evangeline, if you don't mind?"

"I'll get the kit," said Evangeline.

We got a lot of practice. If I had to go to the emergency room every time I needed stitches I'd have an office there instead.

Evangeline came back, and began to thread her needle. "You want local?"

"Please."

Her eyes narrowed the slightest bit. Grimm always disapproved of painkillers. In this business it was too easy to reach the point where you never wanted to feel again. She took out a syringe and jabbed it into the nerve cluster. I winced as pain like a stun gun shot up my arm. The pain faded to a dull tingling, and she began to stitch.

"Tell me everything," Grimm said.

So I told him about the snake and the bite. I told him about the blood, and how it felt like it was cooking my brain. He listened the whole time, nodding to himself.

"Now dear," he said, "I need you to think clearly, and tell me exactly who you sent it after."

As if I hadn't had a bad enough day already. I waited for Evangeline to tie off my sutures and put my hand to my head. It was going to be quite a competition for which hurt worse. "Liam. I thought of Liam."

Evangeline watched me, her hand covering her mouth. I had a sickening moment where I imagined her telling Grimm about the phone, but she kept her mouth shut. Grimm closed his eyes and took a deep breath.

I waited for him to yell. To scream. To tell me how I'd once again managed to make another massive mistake, and ask aloud what I always figured he wondered: Why on earth he took me as an agent in the first place.

He nodded, like he had through the rest of my story. "You've had quite a day, Marissa. Go on back to your office and I'll call you when my SWAT team clears the MRI room."

I left the two of them there and pretended I didn't hear their muffled voices through the wall.

STAFF MEETING, NEXT day, and we were all in the room. Even the part-timers, though it was clear some of us were allowed to ask questions and others would have to keep their questions to themselves.

"The good news," said Grimm, "is the first son of a leading royal family is not cursed." He said the word *curse*, and a tickle slid down my spine, like when you bite tinfoil. "That's about the only good news. I've received six months' worth of wishes in three days, and they all ask for the same thing: safe transport to Fae, Avalon, or any one of the other realms. I've even had requests for passage to Inferno. All the wishers are magical, and all of them are scared. Alpha and Beta Teams, you have your positions. I need ears throughout Kingdom." Half the room stood up and left. Shopkeepers, maids, you name it. Grimm had ears everywhere.

"Gamma Team, I think you are more likely to hear useful information, but you must be discreet, even if it means delay." The Gammas were hags and hangmen. I couldn't stand them, but they could walk into the low streets of Kingdom the same way I entered Main Street, and no one gave them a second glance or a first knife to the belly.

That left me, Evangeline, Clara, and Jess. Clara and Jess used to work for Grimm. Clara was easily sixty, a good twenty years older than Jess. The road map of scars on her made me want to leave this business more every time I looked at her. Grimm had a pension plan, but I didn't know of anyone who had lived long enough to claim it.

"Clara, I need you in the Court of Queens. Someone near to the prince is targeting him, and I'd bet another royal over anyone else. Jess, you'll take the princess's family. If someone didn't want Arianna to find a husband, a curse would be an expensive but traditional method," said Grimm.

"I swear that girl is cursed," I said, and Jess gave me a look of disdain. She looked like a carbon copy of Evangeline, except that her face wasn't gashed. The two could have been mother and daughter, but were quite possibly half sisters. Odds were the same djinn continued to get lucky all over the city just by promising women wishes. If what women wished for was nine months of pregnancy and eighteen years of responsibility, he could definitely grant that.

"Amateur," she said. "People are plenty crazy without talking curses. I've seen mothers cut their daughters' throats for a pound of Glitter, and you want to go bringing curses into it. Stick to being the pretty face, it suits you better."

"Better than it suits you." I didn't appreciate Grimm bringing in other agents. I already had to compete with Evangeline for good assignments. Two more ways to divide the work meant I'd be working twice as long. With djinn blood like Evangeline, she could twist me into a pretzel before I could fight back, but I wasn't going to let her temper or attitude back me down.

She threw the briefing papers across the room. "I don't have to tolerate this, Grimm. You should get some real help." She paraded out of the room.

"She certainly hasn't gotten any more stable," said Clara. She looked at me. "Girl. Marissa, do you understand what you are suggesting? Do you have any idea how much Glitter it costs for a curse?" I didn't know what Clara's heritage or talent was, but in a lot of ways she seemed more confident than Jess. In about every way she seemed saner.

"I have blessings. Got them free after donating blood. I bet all you've ever gotten was a cookie and juice."

A look of recognition and fear ran through her eyes, and she glanced at Grimm for a moment. "Magic creates. Something he should already have taught you. Turning it to destroy something is difficult and dangerous. It's ten times more difficult, and a hundred times as dangerous. For what it costs for one curse you could hire an army to conquer a kingdom."

"Forget I said it." I kept my eyes on the table until Grimm let me leave. He and Clara sat in the room, laughing and talking about years gone by. I wanted to go back in and ask about the curse. I wanted to ask about Liam, and if he was safe. But not while Clara was there. I could image what she'd say about me working the wrong man on a setup.

Later, when we were alone, I asked Evangeline. "Someone's already spending that kind of Glitter on a curse for the prince. Why not Ari too?"

Evangeline shook her head and went back to filing her nails. "Because she isn't worth the effort. Cursing her would be like cursing you: a complete waste of Glitter."

Thirteen

EVANGELINE WENT BACK to the site of my mugging to get the pie box, while I was tasked with a more mundane problem: a lich. They're what happens when a warlock dies before his time. I believe it ought to be a requirement that every warlock attend weekly mortality counseling sessions, because I've never met one yet who thought it was time for him to go.

As usual for this kind of assignment, I brought backup, though more of the staple-slinging than the gunslinging sort. He was a by-the-hour, by-the-book sack of slime named Frank. We approached the brownstone and I felt it right away. It wasn't the subtle shift of my Agency bracelet. The place actually looked creepy. From the swing out front that kept rocking itself to the wind that played with my hair at the entrance to the courtyard and nowhere else.

"You ready?" I asked Frank.

He straightened his black-and-white suit. "Not entirely, but one never is. Remind me sometime and I'll tell you about the first one of these I ever did."

"Not while you are on the clock. Grimm's orders." Like most of the contractors, Frank worked hourly, which was nice, since Grimm didn't have to give him medical and dental. I knocked on the front door and it swung open slightly.

"I'm Marissa Locks, here on behalf of the Fairy Godfather. I'd like to talk this over," I said to the empty hallway. "Give you a chance to go peacefully, uh, wherever it is you need to go."

The building gasped as if it were waking up and taking a few breaths.

"Into the light. Tell it to go into the light." Frank gave me a thumbs-up for encouragement. The estate management firm we were handling this for didn't care where it went, so long as it stopped gobbling up anyone who stepped inside.

I glared at Frank until he looked away. Once he shut his mouth I turned my attention back to the task at hand. "All right. You had your chance, now we do it the hard way."

The door swung wide, inviting me in. I stepped away. Grimm and I had played "spot the horror movie goof" for the first eight months I worked for him, and one does not ever go through a door that opens on its own. For that matter, if your cat is down in the basement, you don't go looking for it either. The cat has four legs with which to climb out on its own.

"Sic 'em," I said.

Frank approached the door, stapler in hand. He pinned a dozen papers to the doorway and stepped back.

I signed the summons and stuck it to the door frame. "I'll see you in thirty days."

As we started to leave, every window in the building opened and slammed shut. The doorway flung itself wide and out of the darkness rushed a form of blackness wrapped in rage, clothed in bitterness. "What?" That one word took at least five syllables. That's long enough for the entire goblin constitution.

"Those papers constitute legal notice that I am beginning

the eviction process. I had them notarized, and since I don't think ghosts sleep, you've got plenty of time to review the terms and conditions. Should you decide to accept a peaceful transition, contact Fairy Godfather by ether-net." I finished the usual spiel and started to walk away. Beyond the threshold of its house, it couldn't do much more than yell at me.

It put a claw to the dried jawbone that formed its chin and thought for a moment. "Exorcism," it said, hissing as it did.

I'd had this argument before. "Eviction. Cheaper and faster. Meet Frank Cole. Frank's under retainer and specializes in property law. So, take your time, read up on your rights, and when I come back in thirty days, we'll work this one of two ways. Method number one," I drew a line in the air for emphasis, "you leave voluntarily. You go wherever it is liches go when they aren't haunting property that isn't legally theirs. I hire a hazmat team to come in and clean up the mess you left behind. Trust me, judging from the smell, it's a mess."

It reached out for me with skeletal fingers, cold seeping off of it.

"Method number two involves accidentally delivering a truckload of salt to the place, accidentally burning the whole damn thing down, and salting the entire lot all the way up to where those nice surveyors placed the pretty little flags."

The lich slowly withdrew its hands, fixing me with glowing eyes that were meant to induce nightmares. I waited, humming softly to myself, until an exasperated groan whistled through its jaws.

"I've gotten scarier things than you from carnival games. Move out." When I last looked back it was haunting the doorstep, probably trying to figure out what "rights of remainder" meant. Frank wasn't a priest, but he passed his bar.

Grimm didn't mind working with the odd hangman or executioner. You know, respectable professions. Lawyers, on the other hand, Grimm couldn't stand, so it always fell to me. Frank was fine in my book. He worked for greenbacks, and he knew his way around the property code. In my book that made him not only magical, but damn near a wizard.

BACK AT THE Agency, Evangeline had struck gold, if an empty pie box fished from a Dumpster could be considered gold. It was a sad comment on my life that I was excited to see it. Grimm already had it put into the Visions Room. The Visions Room was weird even by Agency standards. For those of us without the Sight, it worked like a little window into the spirit world. Prisms covered each wall, and I couldn't go in there without getting nauseous. Grimm checked for traces of what had been in the box.

"Curse." Evangeline mouthed the word so as not to bring down the wrath of Grimm.

"I can read lips in sixteen languages, you know," said Grimm.

I looked through the window. "Fifteen. Pig Latin is not a language."

"Tell that to the Three Little Pigs. If I can deliver Christmas Mass in it, it's a language."

I gave up. "So what is it? And don't bother saying a pie box."

Grimm gave me a look of contempt. "I'd say it's a pie box, but that's because you asked the wrong question. The right question, my dear, is 'what was in it?' Be precise."

"A curse," I said.

He shook his head. "A curse shell. So a curse can move about in daylight and even cross the midnight boundary without evaporating."

"You said there aren't any real curses anymore," said Evangeline, "and any time I thought I was working against a curse, all I had to do was remember people are clever, people are resourceful, and people are a thousand times nastier than curses."

"That's sound advice, my lady," said Grimm, "and you would do well to keep it in mind, but there is no point in pretending it is not what we believe. It is a curse. Even more, it is an old curse, of a type rarely used even when they were common."

"Wait a minute," I said, "the fae blessings, they're like a curse, right?"

Grimm nodded.

"So why don't they need a shell to follow me around? Why don't they evaporate at midnight?"

"Marissa, didn't I send you to college for four long years?" asked Grimm.

He knew the answer was yes, which meant he wasn't interested in the answer. They did need a shell to keep safe, they had to. Then it hit me. "They've already got one." Me.

"Clever girl," said Grimm.

I think I should have asked the Fae Mother about the fine print before I accepted.

"Enough pining about bad decisions, my dear," said Grimm. "I consider the question of what was aimed at the prince closed. The next order of business is to determine exactly what was aimed at the prince." If this was another of Grimm's "think it throughs," he'd lost me, or maybe I'd slept through that lecture.

"Why are we doing this?" I asked, "You don't usually do things out of the goodness of your heart." Thing was, I was certain there was goodness at times.

"I haven't trained either of you in spell craft, you know," said Grimm, turning away from the mirror. The bald spot on the back of his head reminded me of a bowling ball. "And that was not an accident on my part. I believe magic is most powerful when it supplements your natural strengths, not when it replaces them." He didn't bother adding that magic-and-Marissa was almost always a disaster. "This kind of curse, this method of delivering it, is beyond even the Black Queen. It bears the mark of another fairy."

I tangentially knew other fairies existed. I mean, Grimm wouldn't work much out of state, and even then, it was at rates designed to make people choose more mundane methods of solving their problems. I'd never talked with another fairy, or even talked to another fairy's agent. "Or the fae.

Another fairy wouldn't have mistaken me for the princess." Grimm didn't deal with fae often, or if he did, he didn't involve me. We had the occasional customer who confused fae with fairies, which was similar to confusing a birthday candle with a volcano. The fae had their courts and kings and queens, politics and intrigue. Fairies, on the other hand, created the fae for entertainment, if you believed what Grimm let slip.

Grimm crossed his arms and shook his head. "My dear, I am certain another fairy is involved. When we read the future, it's the intents we are looking at. I intended Ari to carry the bottle of wine to the prince, and so that is what would have shown clearly. Our last-minute change would have been almost impossible to foretell. Reading intents is something not even the fae would attempt."

This made sense. Grimm had tried once to explain how he influenced events, and the closest he could get to it was describing it like making a path in tall grass. Sure, someone might stray, but odds were strong they'd stick to the path. Grimm was good at leading people. I decided to take the opportunity to ask something that had been bothering me for a while. "Grimm, how's my debt looking?"

Definitely caught him off guard. He glanced around the room. "Evangeline, would you be so kind as to check on the princess?"

"Doing something else, somewhere else." She put down her nail file and walked out.

When she was gone, I shut the door.

"That kind of question doesn't come up out of nowhere," said Grimm, his voice stern.

"Answer the question, please."

"Look at your vial, Marissa. What do you see?"

I pulled it out of my shirt and felt it grow in my hand. It was barely half full. I closed my eyes, unable to stand to look at it.

"What did you expect, my dear? It's only been six years."

Anger poured through me, mixed with fear, and I snapped my eyes open and looked at him. "I expect I work my ass off. I work nights and weekends and every holiday known to man and magic. I walk into war zones and hostage situations with only a gun and a few spells, and most of the time I do a damn good job. I expected more."

"A lifetime of Glitter takes time to build up, but that's not what this is about."

"Evangeline has been here fourteen years in May. Clara and Jess, how long did they work for you full time?" I said, the frustration rising in me. "Did Clara actually pay you off, or did you demote her to part-time because she got too old? And Jess has so many brain injuries she ought to be collecting disability. I'm never getting out, Grimm. I'll be doing this when I'm sixty, and I'll still be alone."

He held up one hand as if to stop me. "Clara has done favors for me for fifteen years. She has a grandson who has a condition I'm happy to help with in return. Jess I only call in emergencies, which this is. And if you will keep my confidence, Evangeline spends Glitter as fast as she earns it, and has ever since the accident. If you want a different life, make different choices."

"I want to go see Liam."

"No."

"I sent a curse in his direction, I owe it to him to make sure he's all right," I said, trying not to let the desperation show through.

Grimm shook his head. "Most curses, particularly against high-value targets, are of a ransom nature. The most popular of the heart-seeker era was sleep. The prince rides in, kisses the maiden, and revives her. They live happily ever after because while the prince paid to have her cursed, he didn't pay to have her killed. Your accidental prince is most likely having the afternoon nap of his life."

"I want to be sure. You said you wanted to know exactly what was used against Mihail. I say Liam's the answer." I was on fire now, I knew I had him.

"He's more like the problem where you are concerned, my dear. I will send Evangeline to check on him tomorrow.

If he's sleeping I'll arrange a guard to make sure nothing improper happens to him."

"I want to go," I said, sounding more like a little girl than an adult.

Grimm leaned in as if getting a better look at me. "I think you underestimate your skills, Marissa. You are exceedingly good at what I ask you to do. For that reason, it is likely you are the last person he would want to see."

Fourteen

∾

I WAS IN Upper Kingdom, and it should have been fantastic, but my heart was in a speeding convertible breaking every traffic law available on its way to visit Liam. Liam Stone. He had a last name, and I got it from Evangeline before she left. I didn't usually collect last names; they got to be a liability. I sat in a bus moving ever closer to the heart of Kingdom, only a few blocks from the palace itself.

Evangeline was checking in on my accidental prince, and I was doing homework on Ari's almost one, trying to figure out how something as basic as a potion could have failed. The bus finally got to within a few blocks of my stop, and I walked without fear on the high streets of Kingdom. Here you were more likely to meet a king in his convertible or a queen returning from the spa than a dwarf or a witch. Everywhere I looked, I saw police. Some stood on street corners, some rode white horses through the crowds as they made way for yet another royal procession, completely fouling the bus schedules.

I walked up to the doorman and presented my Agency card. "Marissa Locks, here to see Queen Mihail. I have an appointment." The Second Royal Family was orthodox. When the prince took the throne, he'd never use a first name again. It probably made telling whose coffee mug was whose more difficult.

In the old days each royal family built a castle. These days they owned skyscrapers. Somewhere at the top of that building I hoped I'd find answers to our princess problem. The doorman looked at my card, glanced at my Agency bracelet, and waved me in. I understood the look of disdain that he gave me. I was a fairy's hired help, but at least I was human.

Truth was, Upper Kingdom was almost all humans. We pushed the dwarves and the elves and most all the other friendly creatures out to Middle Kingdom centuries ago. They could check our bags or deliver the mail, but actually live near the palace? No way. All the nasty things got to live in Lower Kingdom, kept in their own private slum.

Inside Mihail Tower, the lighting was clear and magical, giving the lobby soft shimmers that made the marble floor swim. The last time I saw an effect like that was when I mistakenly drank three Dixie cups of dwarvish liquor. That stuff tasted like cherry soda. Grimm said I proposed to the marble lion outside my apartment building and passed out in an ethanol coma. I never drank dwarvish liquor again.

I approached the elevator. No buttons, just a smooth, steel panel. As the minutes passed by, I waited and the elevator neither opened nor came. In frustration I slapped the steel panel. For my trouble I got a static shock that left my hand tingling. I heard the elevator coming from far above, a rattling hum that echoed through the metal. While I waited, a piano player tickled out a tune that echoed in the empty lobby. At last, the door opened and I stepped in. There was no elevator man, and no buttons.

It shot upward like a rocket. Gravity tried to pull my stomach out through my feet as I rose. The elevator doors slid open to reveal a suite entirely of windows, wide open. All around me was the city by day.

"Finally," said a woman. I recognized her immediately as

Queen Mihail. No flowing gowns or high crowns. She wore a clean-cut business suit and handed her tablet to an assistant as she strode across the marble to meet me. She wore flats, not heels. "I was wondering when the pawn would arrive."

I'd have been upset, but I'd gotten used to how royalty spoke and acted. The princes and princesses were a bunch of worthless brats, but I kept my tongue in check around their parents. As we moved across the building, a man followed. I had thought him an assistant, but he was too wide, too heavy. Bodyguard or personal assassin.

"Pawn, that's Shigeru. You needn't fear him."

Shigeru bowed to me, and I returned it, hoping I remembered the correct angle and length for an honorary bow.

"Don't be afraid, girl, he's not magical, he's Asian." I had two Korean girls in my class at community college, and I knew Asian magic—it was hard work and high expectations. The tattoo on his arm matched that of the ninja assassins Grimm occasionally hired for government work. That meant Shigeru wasn't dangerous. He was deadly.

"You are late," said Queen Mihail, taking a seat on a couch edge by a window. "Sit."

Now, I wasn't afraid of heights. It doesn't pay to be—too many ledges, ladders, and crevices—but sitting on the edge of the couch I could look down the building. The farther down I looked, the more dizzy I got. "I'm sorry I'm late. I couldn't figure out how to call the elevator." I actually thought I was fifteen minutes early. Grimm has this theory that me showing up early was actually a harbinger of the apocalypse. If he was right, every time I showed up late, I actually saved the world. You'd think he would thank me for it.

"My elevator isn't called. It's sent. I told it to pick up the head of the investigation and only the head of the investigation. I called Fairy Godfather five minutes ago, and you just showed up."

Something was wrong. I'd accidentally stepped into a mystery, and all I had to go on were Saturday morning cartoons with a talking dog and monsters in masks. Something had gone wrong in the time it had taken me to bus through Kingdom and get here, and I was going to be damned if I let her throw me off. I'd look like an idiot. I'd make Grimm look like an idiot.

"Show me where it happened," I said, taking a stab at it. She rose and I followed her up a sweeping staircase to another floor. She placed her hand on the door. It glowed for a moment, and opened. Huge, messy but recognizable: I stood in the middle of a bachelor pad. Mihail's apartment.

My bracelet tingled against my arm. That meant they had enough Glitter to put cancellation wards over the whole top floors. Grimm wasn't going to be watching over my shoulder. "I need to look around," I said. Then, drawing on many Saturday mornings' worth of TV, I added, "We need to search for clues." Only problem was, I was an agent, not a private investigator. In Kingdom, if you tried pulling the mask of a monster, it would probably pull the skin off your head.

"Shigeru will watch you. Don't try to take anything." She left us alone.

"You are not an investigator." He came over and stood behind me.

"No. I'm the messenger girl, errand girl, that sort of thing. I was supposed to be filling in a questionnaire about the prince's magical tolerances. We had a basic love potion fail on him."

"You assume the prince is capable of love. May I have your gun for safekeeping?" I hadn't put a hand on my purse or looked at it once, but he knew. "It would make me less, how to say? Tense."

It wasn't like shooting him was an option anyway, so I took it out, pulled the clip, and handed it to him.

"Thank you." He tucked it into a deep pocket in his loose black pants. "I assist the royal family in all positions, so I will answer your questions."

"Is there someplace we can sit? Trust me, I'm not going to take anything he's touched."

I think a smile almost made it out, but he stifled it. "You have met the prince."

"Yeah. We've talked more than I'd like." I was actually glad I had met Liam instead. Three dates with Mihail would have triggered my gag reflex. His apartment was actually decorated with paintings: paintings of himself.

"Look, when I get back, Grimm's gonna want to know what happened, and I don't want to look bad. I'm a messenger, but even a messenger wants to do good by their boss. What'd she call Fairy Godfather about?"

Shigeru leaned back and blinked, his eyes getting wider. "The prince, Mihail. He is missing. Kidnapped."

That did it. I took pride in knowing when to call for help, and when to handle things myself. "You get bracelet reception anywhere in here?"

"That corner. Wards are weakest there. You're above most of the normal interference, anyway."

I wandered to the corner, stepping over discarded laundry and avoiding anything that had so much as touched the prince. The moment I hit the corner my bracelet shook like it was going to tear my arm off. The wall was all glass and the view made me want to hurl, so I took out the compact and focused on the tiny mirror.

"Grimm?" When I saw him I knew things were bad.

"Marissa, where are you?"

"Mihail's apartment. Don't worry. I showed up and the queen figured I was here to look into it. I need an investigator and the cops. This isn't my area of expertise, Grimm."

"There's a secondary team on their way already and I've contacted the police, as they should have to begin with. Simply tell the queen you don't believe her son's case is getting enough attention, and you've dispatched a squad to handle it."

"I dispatched them?"

"Let her believe what she wants to."

I heard Evangeline's voice, distant and broken. "Let. Me. Talk to her."

"Not now," said Grimm, but I could feel her reaching through him.

I had this horrible feeling in my stomach and needed to lean against the window. "What's wrong?"

"We'll discuss it when you return," said Grimm.

I felt Evangeline reaching out again. "Tell her."

Grimm dropped his eyes. "There's been an accident at Liam's house."

"Show her," said Evangeline.

Grimm didn't usually connect us like that, and while his magic reached into our ears he almost never did anything with our other senses. "You need to trust your own eyes," he always said, but I felt my vision slipping away. I stood, too tall, and at the wrong angles. I was looking through Evangeline's eyes. It had been a house, or a barn, or a house with a workshop, I don't know. Everything left was charred chunks of wood and twisted bits of wrought iron.

Evangeline strode across the charred ground, each step so foreign I was sure she'd fall over. She reached down and shook the ashes from something. A silver snake—the curse shell. Its eyes were lifeless; it rattled and clinked as she picked it up. Grimm cut the link to Evangeline and I sagged against the window.

"He's not dead, I already checked," said Grimm. "I can't seem to find him."

"I gotta go." I snapped the compact closed. My gaze wandered out over the city and the world spun, slick with tears and fear and pain. Hands seized me and led me from the window, and I was unwilling to resist.

"Sit," said Shigeru, and I collapsed onto a couch by a king-sized bed. "Bad news." He sat on the edge of the bed.

I nodded. I struggled to find my voice, to focus on my job. "Team of investigators coming. Cops too. Some of them are friends, sort of."

"I will restrain myself. I do not believe you will take anything. When you are ready, the doors beside the elevator lead down." He put his hand on my shoulder as he spoke. "Bad news and good news are brothers. Where one is, the other is never far behind."

My eyes ached, my head pounded, and I blew my nose on a tissue and tossed it in the trash by the bed. That's when the dressing mirror caught my eye.

It was long and narrow and ugly, obviously a family relic from a time when fine copper mirrors couldn't be had. The thing was a silver mirror, the old kind, with a silver platter painted and polished until it held a dim reflection. The polish had long since worn off it and the silvering looked like sludge that had run down the mirror, leaving lumps. What bugged me was the feeling I got when I looked at it. It's the same feeling I got when Grimm watched during an assignment. For a moment, the desire to touch it seized me. The thought of Mihail's hand doing the same washed over me like cold water, and the moment was gone.

I met the queen on the way down, Shigeru close behind.

I looked her straight in the face, always the best way to lie. "I've decided this case deserves more attention. I've ordered a team of investigators, and contacted my most trusted detectives. I made it clear there was no higher priority."

A speaker chimed, and the doorman spoke. "My lady, a group begs admittance."

"I will send the elevator. Allow them in," the queen said. "Pawn, come with me."

Shigeru followed along behind us, padding softly on the carpet, so close he almost brushed me. She led me to a granite serving room separated by low marble walls.

"You'll take care of the investigation, won't you?"

Grimm had told me to let her believe what she wanted to, but the look in her eyes made me worried. "Yes, Your Highness. I'll be overseeing it personally."

She popped the cork from a wine bottle and poured rich red merlot into a glass. "It always falls to us when trouble comes. A man may make money, and earn Glitter, and make a thousand decisions. When trouble comes, it is a woman who deals with it."

"I do what I'm told." It was a somewhat truth.

"Then listen to what I'm telling you. My son has done something, or offended someone. I do not know what or who, but I will be the one to deal with him. When you find him, you will contact me. My gratitude will be impressive. I can give you rewards your Godfather cannot."

I shouldered my purse, eager to get back to the Agency. "I'll find him."

She raised a glass of wine to me. "I hope so. My generosity is legendary, and it will fall on everyone who aids you." She took a sip and considered me, as though she could scry the future in the wine. "Fail, and my wrath will be legendary as well."

Fifteen

ROSA MET ME at the door with a shotgun. Strictly speaking, not aimed at me, but you don't really have to aim a sawed-off shotgun. She swung it toward me. "You, get in there." She turned her attention to the crowd. "The rest of you will take a number and have a seat." Her paperwork skills might have been lousy, but her personal touch was something I aspired to.

I ran down the hall and slammed the door to Grimm's office. "Where is Liam?"

Grimm flickered into the desk mirror. "We're in the conference room, if you don't mind."

"I do. Where is he?" I sat down in one of the chairs and waited.

"Marissa, please?"

Evangeline came through the door and joined me, putting her feet up on Grimm's desk.

"Ladies, I don't like you two meeting in here. Too many toys, and some of you have shown a tendency to act first and think second."

Clara opened the door. I looked at her white hair and

wondered what she'd seen over the years, and where those scars had come from. I thought they were only on her face, but now I saw they ran down her arms as well, and most likely covered every inch of her body. She looked at me and Evangeline. "Nice to see things haven't changed around here." Clara limped over and took Grimm's mirror out of the chair.

"Clara, you are sixty-two. Act your age," said Grimm. "Put that back."

Clara sat it up against the wall and took his chair. "I heard you met Queen Mihail. I knew her when she was just Irina."

I had the beginnings of a migraine. "She threatened me. Said she'd reward me if I succeeded and punish me if I failed. Said Grimm couldn't protect me or reward me the way she could."

"That woman," said Grimm, "is invoking powers beyond her control."

Clara turned back to look at Grimm. "Wouldn't be the first time. She wants her boy back, right?"

I nodded.

She opened a drawer in Grimm's desk and began to pick through it. "Then we better get him. When Irina gets angry, she doesn't get violent. She hires someone else to get violent for her."

"She thinks I'm in charge of the investigation." I had everyone's attention now. "It was a misunderstanding. Grimm, you'd better have an idea of how we're going to find that prince, or I am going to suffer the consequences. I told her we'd find him."

"If Irina threatened you, she'll punish us all," said Clara, her eyes narrowing. "Do you have any idea what that woman is capable of?"

I stifled a keen desire to see if I could strangle her faster than Evangeline could intervene. "No. I was born less than a century ago, so I don't quite have your range of expertise."

"Then how are you going to find the prince?"

"I don't know. I'll think of something."

The look she gave me would make a kobold soil his pants. "Remind me exactly what it is you do around here? Oh, yes. You're pretty. You know, you're plain for a pretty girl. Does Grimm have to spice you up for dates?"

"*That is enough!*" said Grimm, shaking the desk with his anger.

I was done being cordial. "What is your problem with me?" She could talk about my looks all day. I had a mirror with me at all times, and no delusions. My mirror might talk, but it didn't lie.

She leaned forward on the desk. "You have no business being involved. You show up and don't have the sense to wait when Irina is obviously throwing off thunderclouds. You got mugged, for Kingdom's sake, and used to launch a curse, and you couldn't even aim it at the right person. You're carrying fae blessings around with you like they're a puppy."

She stood, and for a moment, I saw an image of what she must once have been like, and a sad prophecy of what I might become. She pointed her finger at me. "I have a family. They live in this city. That curse is old, and powerful enough to level twenty city blocks. You jet around with your curls and your smile and treat it like some sort of adventure. Now you bring down Irina's wrath on us?"

I looked at Evangeline, but she kept her eyes down. I glanced at the mirror. "Grimm, what do you want me to do?"

Clara spoke before he could. "Settle down and act like an adult. Let your friend and Jess worry about your crush, and let me try and put a lid back on Hurricane Irina before innocent people get hurt. Grimm, do you want her tripping around with a set of blessings while we try to fix this?"

"That what you think?" I asked Evangeline.

She at least had the decency to meet my eyes this time. "I think you need to be more careful, M. I promise you I'll find him and make sure he's safe."

Clara spun Grimm's chair to face the mirror. "Make a decision, Grimm. I won't work with her. She's too much of a liability."

"Clara, I need you to handle the Court of Queens," said Grimm. "You wouldn't be working with Marissa anyway."

I snapped my fingers for Grimm's attention. He hated that, but I did it because it worked. "It isn't my fault with Queen Mihail. I was in the wrong place at the wrong time."

Clara took a pack of cards out of Grimm's desk and began to shuffle them. "Wrong place? Or right place? You've got things attached to you that wouldn't hesitate to make a change in your favor." She began to deal cards to me. "Anything else like this happen? Strange coincidences? Improbable accidents? People mistaking you for other people, bad things happening to people you don't like?"

My jaw felt numb for a moment as I thought back. Ari getting sick. Me getting mugged. The elevator.

Clara tossed me a card. Ace of spades. "Grimm, slaughter a few bunnies and ask if magic was involved in any of those 'accidents' you've been telling me about. Or don't. You know the answer as well as I do."

Grimm disappeared and I waited as the minutes ticked by. I took the deck from the table and began to deal cards to myself. Aces, kings, and then queens. Always. I went through the cards and picked out the two of diamonds, then turned it back over. I focused on it while I reached across the table. At the last moment, something pushed my hand. What I came up with was a ten. The best card left in the deck.

"See?" Clara crossed her arms and looked at me like I was a schoolgirl.

Grimm reappeared in the mirror, and he looked worried. Almost afraid, though he's never afraid.

Clara looked up at him and grinned. "Could've saved you a few rabbits. What did you always say? 'Clara is right.' So nice to hear that again."

"Marissa is not responsible for the potion's failure," said Grimm.

I waited for him to speak. And waited. And I knew a defense wasn't coming. "I didn't do anything," I said.

Grimm ran his hands through his hair. "My dear, I've

used enough rabbits to keep Alice in Wonderland for the rest of her life. You have powerful forces acting on your behalf."

"Grimm, you know how blessings work," Clara said. "You want her involved when something like this is going down? This is a conjunction. You're several thousand years old. Act your age for once. Or if that's too much to ask, act mine."

I looked at Evangeline, and saw the word didn't mean anything to her either. I waited until Grimm glanced at me, and I asked, "Conjunction?"

"Something nasty," said Clara. "Every so often magic goes head-to-head with magic, and the rest of us try to survive. Imagine the world is a silver platter balanced on a ball. Now imagine they're playing soccer with that ball, and we try to keep the platter from tipping over and killing everyone. Now imagine you are tap dancing around on the platter with a couple of live bowling balls at the same time. Grimm, ditch her."

"Or you could send her back to the nursing home," I said, and smiled as a look of anger crossed Clara's face. "I've never let you down before. Say the word, and I'll go get her walker." The clock ticked the seconds away, and I began to get nervous. "Grimm?"

He closed his eyes for a moment, like he does when he's trying to read the auguries. "I'm sorry, Marissa. I've pushed you so hard, and asked so much of you, and you've always delivered. I asked you to deal with Queen Mihail, so this is my fault as much as anyone's."

"And?"

"I think it is time I reevaluated how I use your services."

I bolted upright in the chair, stiff as a board. "You've used my services for six years without complaining. Everything you ask, I do. I do it right, every time."

"Not every time," said Evangeline.

"Go get the Root of Lies, and we'll do this again. I told you what I saw, I did what he told me to, and now you want to sit there and tell me to be more careful?" She looked away.

"And you," I said, turning on Grimm. "You wanted me

to deal with the queen and I did. I have nothing outside of
this job. I do nothing but work for you, and I do it well. So
don't send me off somewhere like I'm the latest kid whose
parents pawned them off on you."

Evangeline refused to look at me. Grimm stayed silent
for a moment before answering. "Marissa, I know what your
life is like. That's why I'm doing this. I'm taking your company card and removing your access to the Agency. You
will not be allowed to work here until I agree you are ready."

I felt my purse shift and I knew he'd taken the card. "I
pay my debts," I said, rising to my feet. "I may not have
magic, and my mother might not have been a djinn's whore,
but I'm the best agent you've ever had. Admit it. You ask
me to kill an imp, I shoot it till it's dead. You ask me to
climb a beanstalk, I put on my climbing gloves and climb
for days. You ask me to break someone's heart and I do it
every time, even if it kills me."

"Marissa," Grimm said, "I think it is time for you to
leave."

Tears mixed with white-hot anger. "You can't kick me
out. I have to work. It's the only way."

He didn't answer.

"So how does this work? I leave? You just send me
away? I'm the first debt slave to get fired?" I swung out of
the chair.

"My dear, you are not fired. I'm changing your assignment to give you time," said Grimm. "Take Princess Arianna home."

My jaw was clenched so hard my teeth hurt as my insides
roiled. "What if I say no? What are you going to do to me?"

He looked out at me, his lip pursed. "You won't. We have
a bargain."

"You want to kick me out, at least do it right. Take
everything." I rummaged through my purse, dumped the
gun on his desk, and yanked the Agency bracelet off. Finally, I took the vial from my neck and threw it at the mirror, cracking it along the bottom. I walked away. I could lie
and tell you I held my head up, but I didn't.

Ari was sitting in the lobby, which looked a bit emptier than before. Grimm had obviously told her to wait for me.

I kicked her bags as I walked past. "Come on. I'm leaving."

We got in the car and I drove fast where the traffic let me. I was angry but not suicidal. At the gates of the Avenue, I slammed into the curb and threw the car into park.

"This is as far as I go. Take your bags and walk." I'd been crying the whole way there, and she'd at least had the good sense not to say anything about it.

Her mouth hung open, and fear crept into her eyes. "I don't understand."

"Fairy Godfather said for me to take you home, and I am. Get out. Walk."

She looked at me again, her face adrift with something between horror and disgust. "I can't go back."

"I've heard that a dozen times before, princess. Walk in, say 'I'm home,' and you're back."

She grabbed her bag from the back and stopped. "She'll kill me." Ari's lip began to quiver. Something in her tone said that wasn't a metaphor.

Ari sat on her bag, staring at the curb. "I ran away from home. I paid Fairy Godfather with every bit of Glitter Father gave me. Fairy Godfather said he would find me a prince. He said everything would work out."

"He says a lot of things." It didn't make sense. I'd spent enough time listening to people lie in this business that I could see it coming. Ari was telling the truth, and Grimm had to know. He'd never send her someplace that wasn't safe. I thought about Grimm's words. "That bastard." I'd never seen a birth certificate, but I'd put money on that being his first name. I knew this was something I'd regret. "Get in the car."

She tossed her bag into the back and slid into the shotgun seat. "Where are we going?"

"Home. Mine."

Sixteen

~∾~

I HATED GRIMM some days. It wasn't the debt-slave thing, because labor laws made that more like a job than a sentence. It's because he knew I didn't like Ari. I'd never been able to stand princesses, with their natural luck and expectations that the world revolved around their rose-scented navels. I waited at the apartment door while she carried her bags up.

She walked into my apartment and wrinkled her nose. "Do you ever open the windows?"

I walked to the living room and pulled at the window shade. "When I moved in I had this idea I would look out the window and watch the stars at night." The shade finally retracted, showing my fabulous view of a brick wall.

"You could bake a pie on the countertop in here." She forced the window up. It groaned the whole way.

I pointed to the side. "Your room is the one to the right of the front bathroom."

"Is that the guest room?"

"Don't know. Never had guests." It was true. While I

once did have a nasty infestation of gremlins, I'd never had anyone human visit. It was still a point of debate in my mind if Ari broke that record or not.

She went into the room to drop her bags, and I decided to check the fungal levels of the food in my fridge. We'll say I had enough mold in there to cure an epidemic of tuberculosis, and my milk had gone through puberty and turned into yogurt.

Ari waited for me to complete my scan of food that had more hair than Bigfoot. "Do you have a bed?"

"Yes. I have a nice memory foam one. You can sleep on the couch."

"There's nothing in the guest bedroom but a litter box." Ari didn't whine, but she was awfully good at complaining.

"I've never had guests. I always hoped my parents or my sister would visit, but it's never happened." At the thought of my family, my stomach turned. Babysitting a princess wouldn't get me any closer to free. The only thing I'd be at the end of the day was older.

I ordered takeout, and we ate in silence, her on the couch and me at the bar. At least, we tried to eat in silence. She yapped the whole time. I'd crushed the necks of poodles that were less annoying.

"Why didn't you paint the walls?"

I looked around, I think for the first time in six years. The walls were a pale green like the color of my counter. A loaf of bread sat there, camouflaged and waiting to attack the first person who attempted to make toast. "This is temporary."

"How long have you lived here?"

"Five and a half years." I was in no mood to play twenty questions. I didn't like the thought of having Ari in the apartment, but I didn't dare cross Grimm. "I get you're trying to be friendly, but I'm tired. So far today, I got threatened by a queen, yelled at by a senior citizen, demoted by my boss, and I walked out of my job. While I appreciate the whole family drama aspect you are wrangling, I'm going to bed." I left her on my couch and went to bed, dreaming about a day I'd give anything to do over.

WHEN I WOKE up, I did the best I could to boil my skin off. The shower raked me, leaving my skin bright red, but I wanted to scour the film of that day off me.

As I dried, I felt it: the bracelet on my wrist. My hand went to my throat, where the vial hung. I wrapped my towel around me and walked out into the bedroom. On my pillow sat a small gift box, mint green with a gold ribbon. I untied the ribbon and opened the box. Inside were my gun and a couple of extra clips. The card was written in calligraphy.

Stay safe—G.

"What's that?" Ari poked her head into my bedroom.

It was a good thing the gun wasn't loaded; I'd have had a princess with a higher than average number of holes in her. "I need a towel," she said, "and some toilet paper would be nice."

"A jerk left a gift on my pillow." I put the gun in my purse anyway. "Get dressed. We're going to the track." I'd spent the better part of six years running, whether I was sick or well, rain or shine. When I emerged in my tracksuit, I found Ari in the front bathroom, repeating her shopping list to the mirror. I peeked in the door, which I told myself wasn't snooping, since she'd done it to me earlier. "Grimm?"

Ari sighed. "I called the Fairy Godfather, but I guess he's too busy to show up. So I just told him what I needed and why."

"Who do you see in the mirror?"

Ari mistook it for some sort of test, scanning each section of her reflection. She squinted, her eyebrows furrowed. "Me. A little bit of you."

"If you have a problem, the only people you can count

on to help are the ones you see right now. We'll check the alleys around here, find you something to sleep on. Now get dressed."

So I went running, Ari in tow, and we ran for miles.

We stopped only because if I didn't, I'd need an aid car to drag her home. She gasped for air, hands on her knees. "Why are you so obsessed with running?"

"I figured you would understand wanting to run away from something."

"Yes, but when I run, I go somewhere." She pressed her hand to her side as she stood.

"Part of the business. I'm not bad in a fight, and Evangeline is downright deadly, but there are still a lot of uglies you would be better off running from than fighting. Ever watch a horror movie?"

Ari sat in the grass and rubbed her ankles.

"Those girls make it a quarter, maybe half a mile and they trip or start wheezing. When you're being chased by something with more heads than teeth, you want to be able to look over your shoulder and say 'I can do this all day.'"

So we ran some more. Good for the soul. I also went to the store, and I'm proud to say I bought food that was neither past its expiration date nor preserved with more chemicals than ingredients. When the elevator door opened to my apartment floor, I was still introducing Ari to reality. "You need to lower your standards. There was nothing wrong with the last two mattresses."

Ari almost dropped her bag of groceries as she spun to glare at me. "One had bedbugs, and the one before that had a dead crocodile in it."

"Alligator. You can tell by the shape of the nose—" I stopped, staring down the hall.

Packages and mail lay in heaps beside my apartment door. A gnarled old postman dumped another bag at my feet and glared at me. "You don't deserve this, killer. I hope they all contain anthrax."

"You know, after the trial I was told I'd never get a

package from Kingdom again." I let a smug grin spread across my face. I'd won after all. "And you're not even a gnome. What does it matter to you?"

"We're members of the same union." He looked at Ari and smiled, then scowled at me. "If we had any say in it you wouldn't get so much as a postcard, but we're not picking a fight with the Fairy Godfather."

Ari looked at the tags with me. "Who is A. Locks?"

I almost punched a hole in the wall. "You are. That bastard."

"This stuff came from Delaware. I thought he'd just, I don't know, conjure what I needed."

I helped her drag a brand-new mattress in through the door along with a dozen other boxes. "You don't know Grimm. Never spend magic on what you can buy. Cash is cheap."

She dumped a bag of mail out on the couch. "You've got like six jury summons here, and a letter from the district attorney."

"Never saw a point in showing up for jury duty. I already know I'm going to vote guilty."

Ari's mouth made a tiny *O*, and she put her hand to her heart. "What about justice?"

"It is justice. Whoever they are, they're guilty of making me show up for jury duty. Also, whatever that letter says, I had nothing to do with the murder. Get pulled over with one little dead body and it takes years to sort out."

I left her in her room attempting to insert nightstand dowel peg 12 into hole 234 and went to my laptop. There sat another package from Grimm, mint green, with a bow. A big one. A heavy one. I opened the box and slid out a book. A large, black book with thick skin binding, though what animal it came from I can't guess. *Spellcraft and Curses*, read the title. Under that it had the words *A Pop-Up Book*.

Ammunition for the most dangerous weapon you carry—G

I walked into the bathroom and grabbed the bracelet. "Grimm, send whatever you need to by post. Anything else is a waste of Glitter." I knew he heard me.

IT HAD BEEN a long time, at least six years, since my last vacation, and I spent the first month in a haze. At first I couldn't sleep through the night. I woke up every few minutes, sure I heard Grimm calling like usual. I'd make my way to the mirror like always. He never answered.

As the days of my forced vacation stretched to weeks I got used to being alone with my thoughts. Every day we ran at the track, Ari and I, and ate a salad lunch in the shade of the park.

I briefly took up hating Ari as a hobby. Briefly, because Ari didn't fit the norms for a princess. That and the fact that I didn't have anyone else to talk to made it hard to do a quality job of hating her. Sure, I might have trapped her in the building basement a few times, and I can tell you that a princess will definitely fit in a five-cubic-foot chest freezer, but you can only do that so often before it gets old. After that, she wasn't interested in visiting the mausoleum or the bomb shelter. I pride myself on doing things right, even if it's loathing someone I'm stuck with, so eventually I gave up.

We sat on a park bench as other runners went past. "So tell me: What's it like being a princess?"

Ari gave me a smile and laughed. First time I'd heard her do that in a while. "When I was a little girl it was nice. My dad would take me to High Kingdom on holidays and we'd bow before a greater king, or watch the ogres on parade. When I was older it was uglier. I saw the politics behind everything. I listened to Mom and Dad argue."

"Sounds normal from what I remember."

"I knew something was wrong when they stopped fighting. I knew it. A few days later, Mom told me she was sick."

We stood up to make a few more laps and call it done for the day.

"How come you never use your, uh, abilities?"

The look on her face was pure grief. "She never trained me. Mom always said it would be tomorrow, or next month, and then her tomorrows stopped coming. I can feel it, down inside, and sometimes I can see things. Like the things that follow you."

I stopped short, hand on my knees. "You can see them?"

"Sort of. They move around a lot like pixie lights, but faster." She ran off.

"Where are they now?" I asked as I caught up.

"It's almost noon. They're inside you, of course."

I didn't ask anything else, but my feet felt heavier with each step. As we walked along the sidewalk from the park, I got worried. For the last few years I'd been hunting things and hunted by things so often that I got used to the feeling. Today though, I knew something or someone was watching me, something considerably more substantial than a couple of blessings. I knew better than to ignore that feeling.

"Ari, how do your legs feel?"

"Tired. Tell me you aren't suggesting another round."

Her water bottle was nearly empty and she looked drenched. I didn't look much better. "Not suggesting it, but we might have a problem." I scanned the cars, the people, and I spotted him. A man crouched down behind a car, staring at us. I gave Ari a push and we ran for my building.

From the moment he leaped over the car, I knew he was a wolf. As he ran, he changed. His hair grew long. His stride changed from footsteps to bounds. I have no idea what the people on the sidewalk saw—probably convinced themselves it was a homeless man who hadn't shaved, or a rabid dog chasing two women. We hit the entrance to my apartment building, and dashed to the elevator.

I held the Door Close button as we passed floor after floor. "If he knows where I live he'll take the stairs and get there first, so be ready when the doors open."

The elevator dinged one floor from mine and as it opened I nearly put a bullet into an old man with a beard. He held his hands up. "I'll wait for the next one."

I heard the wolf growling as we approached, and fired before the doors opened, driving it back into the wall. I didn't have any silver bullets, so the worst I could do was hurt him. My neighbors were calling 911, but the smart ones would keep their heads inside their apartment. The wolf fell backwards, and I put a bullet into each leg.

"Give it back to them," he said, oblivious to the pain and the blood. "Give it back or they'll kill everyone." His eyes were streaked with red, and spittle ran from his mouth.

"Give what back? We already returned the child."

He shook his head and convulsed in pain as the wounds began to close. "We didn't take it. You must have. Give it back, please." He dragged himself away from me toward the stairwell.

"I don't know what you're talking about." I followed him, ready to raise his lead content if he so much as hesitated.

The wolf rose to his feet, blood dripping as the wounds sealed. The look he gave me wasn't rage or hunger. It was despair. "Then we are all dead."

Seventeen

IF I HAD a dime for every time I've heard "We're all going to die" or "I'll kill you," I could afford a better apartment. You can only listen to so many threats of destruction, doom, or death before you start tuning them all out. So I followed the wolf out of the building, then went home. The first year I worked for Grimm, I treated every threat as personal, every invasion as imminent, and every apocalypse as inevitable. One evening, Grimm presented me with a bound book and pen, and asked me to keep a record of every time I rang the emergency bell. A year after *that*, we sat down and reviewed. Tyrannosaurs remained extinct. Intelligent apes completely failed to take over anything but the government. Several boy bands did rise to fame, but the only thing that proved was that there was no accounting for bad taste. So when I got back to my apartment, I penned the wolf's words down right under the line that said "Bell-bottoms are the next fashion fad" and went on with life.

When I told Grimm to send me whatever else he wanted to by post, I expected a few more boxes. Judging from the mountain of packages piled against my door, either Grimm had shipped me everything in his private library or Ari had stayed up all night watching the Shopping Channel again. I hoped it was the Shopping Channel. One heft of the packages said most of them were books though.

Ari stood at the stove, cooking dinner, as I unwrapped. "What are all these?"

The girl could cook. Her dad had bought her chef's lessons at the Culinary Institute for her fourteenth birthday. I figured if she was going to sponge off me, a meal or two wasn't so much to ask. I tossed another book into the I-can't-read-Ancient-Sumerian pile. "Grimm's trying to keep me busy. It's like school all over again."

"I wanted to go to school, but she wouldn't hear of it." Ari stabbed a defenseless fried egg for emphasis. From what little she said about her stepmother, this was about normal.

"Community college is cheap, but don't tell that to Grimm. He still acts like sending me was the greatest act of charity ever."

"Dad would never dream of letting one of his children go to public college. It was Ivory Tower League or nothing. Better we nobility didn't go at all than mix with the common folk."

I poured a glass of wine for myself, and after a moment's thought, a smaller one for her. "That him talking or you?"

"Do I look noble?" She gestured to herself. "My sisters looked the part, and they all took their places in the courts and the balls and did what Moth—, what Gwendolyn wanted, so things were okay for them. But she and I kept fighting. Arguing, yelling, screaming and . . ." She bit her lip so hard I was afraid she'd cut herself.

"She hit you." I knew how words became fists, but I'd never thought that royalty did that sort of thing. The smell of burning eggs filled the apartment.

Ari kept her eyes fixed on the stove, and when she spoke it was through gritted teeth. "She has magic too."

I thought for a moment. In fact, the more I thought about it, the less those birthmarks on Ari's back reminded me of birthmarks, and the more they reminded me of the scars I'd seen on battle mages. I knew that sometimes moms and daughters didn't get along. I didn't think that they'd ever use magic like that on each other.

"When Dad brought me the Glitter, and he told me where to go, I went. I am never going back to live in that house. Ever. I will sleep on the street. I will live in a Dumpster and fight with the rats." Now sobs punctuated each of her words. "I will die before I go back."

She turned off the stove and opened the window to trade smoke for air. "I'm sorry. I'm not hungry right now."

Ari went to her room, and I pretended I didn't hear her crying. That night I opened books, and there were a lot of them, but the last book was the one that caught my eye. The cover was burned, as were the edges of the pages, but the spine still held the print. *An Account of Her Majesty Queen of Thorns, the Black Queen*. I opened the cover and a note fell out. I recognized Grimm's script, though given that he has no hands I can't say how he writes.

I keep my promises, but read this one last—G

Of course I thought about ignoring his warning. I certainly wanted answers I knew I'd find inside. The other part of me thought about a couple of blessings bound to me in a way that I couldn't shake off. So I picked up my copy of *Spellwork and Curses* and read more. When Ari came out to make breakfast, I was still reading.

She took out another carton of eggs. "Final exam tomorrow?"

"Reading about curses. Sort of a recurring theme with me."

"After breakfast let's get the run out of the way. I want to enjoy the sun afterward." She leaned out the window and looked up at the clear sky.

I had other plans. "Not today. We're going for a different kind of workout." The wolf had me worried. Not because I thought his threat would come true. Up until now I'd thought Ari and I were a couple of ants in a hill of millions, but the wolf had found us. Or found me. I wouldn't mind an attack every now and then if I were alone, but with Ari around, I could never truly relax. After breakfast, we drove down the interstate, out of town, to a dingy shop built into a hill.

Ari watched the road signs as we passed. "Where are we? I've never been this far south."

I opened the door and the sounds of gunfire rang out.

Ari flinched with each pop and roar.

I waved her on in. "It's a gun club, not a shootout." After I checked Ari into her class, I practiced my normal shots, then did a few rounds of movement shooting before checking on her. She stood, dwarfed by the instructor, with earmuffs tightly on. Beside her sat a tray of gleaming steel death, everything from a revolver to a shotgun. I remembered my first trip here. How the gun had leaped in my hand and the stench of spent powder.

He guided her as she leveled her gaze, sighted, and squeezed. When the gun went off she nearly hit the floor, but I didn't laugh. She pushed the old man away and sighted up again and squeezed, and this time the gun only leaped a bit. And again, and again, and again. I sat for hours as she worked her way through the weapons. Revolvers she hated, and she rejected the tiny palm gun right away. After a few hours the range owner motioned me over to the booth.

"What'd you like for her?" I asked.

"Something smaller, but she ain't budging. That girl's made of brass."

She came over and pulled out her earplugs. "I want number six."

"That doesn't fit in a purse. That doesn't weigh less than ten pounds. I'm not even certain you can buy ammo for that if you aren't military or police," I said.

"I'm not going to carry it. I'm going to keep it handy at home; if I shoot something, I want it to stay dead."

It was a pain in the ass to get a carry license, and I'm convinced the only reason I had one was that Grimm worked his magic on it. The real kind. It was time for a late lunch and a drive across town. When we pulled up at our new destination, Ari understood what I had in mind. She looked at the kanji written across the window. "Awesome."

That's what everyone said before the bruises.

We walked into the dojo, and I waited. When Mrs. Roselli came out, it was like talking to a penguin in a gi. She was two inches shorter than I, and weighed about a hundred pounds more, with olive Italian skin, gray hair, and bifocals. She looked fat, but six years of lessons had taught me her body was covered in layers of pure mean. You did not mess with Mrs. Roselli more than once. She taught the first self-defense course I'd ever attended, and my arms still hurt thinking about it.

"Mrs. R," I said.

She gave me a hug that nearly crushed my ribs. "Marissa, have you come back to learn to break the bones?"

"Evangeline's got that covered, but Ari here could use a little help. Living with me is turning out to be a little more dangerous than expected."

"You don't become a ninja overnight," she said.

I held out my credit card. "I was thinking something more basic. Right now, she'd lose a fistfight with a Girl Scout."

I paid the private lesson fee, and I watched. Watched Ari learn how to stomp the inside of the foot. How to grab someone by the ears and push her thumbs into their eyes. When the lesson was done I had one battered, bruised, and beaten princess. I almost felt bad for her. Mrs. Roselli hugged Ari and told her how great a student she was. When I took the class I got yelled at before, during, and after.

"Do you do this every week?" Ari took the complimentary ice pack that came with the class and pressed it to her hip.

"No. I passed that one a few years ago. Let's head home." I had this weird moment when I said home, and thought of her there.

That night I had an idea. While I was exhausted from my all-night study session, I wanted to make more progress. So after dinner, I dumped a book called *Spell Well* in Ari's lap.

"You wanted to learn magic," I said. "Help me get through this."

So we sat up until midnight and compared notes as I struggled through yet another chapter of curse material. Afterward, Ari disappeared into my recliner, spell book in hand.

When I finally slept that night, I dreamed of the Fae Mother. In my dream, Ari's dressing mirror lit up like the sun, blasting white light until she stepped out. I floated in my dream, watching her move through the apartment, looking at my books, and giving a disapproving nod to my sink full of dishes. She watched Ari, sleeping in the recliner, then moved on to my room. I thrashed, pinned by my nightmare, unable to raise a hand to defend myself. The Fae Mother leaned over my bed and whispered something.

I sat up in bed, dripping with sweat and shaking in fear. I clicked on the light and grabbed my gun from the pillow beside me, but my bedroom was empty.

In the living room, Ari snored softly, still clutching her spell book. When I was finally certain we were alone, I lay back down, unable to sleep. It wasn't my nightmare. It was her words, which at first I didn't think I heard. The longer I lay in the darkness, the more certain I was I knew what the Fae Mother had said: "Find it."

Eighteen

WE HEADED OUT early, not even waiting for breakfast. I drove and Ari sat in the front, the *Spell Well* book in her lap. She wore a light green pantsuit that Grimm had bought for her during her makeover, and had straightened that wild auburn hair into long, obedient locks. She looked less like an intern and more like an executive.

"You ready to hurl lightning?" I asked.

She gave me a frustrated glance. "I don't understand all the words, and I can't do what little I understand. 'Gather thyne energy.' Okay, that's no big deal, but 'send it out along a spindle drop,' that's barely English, let alone understandable."

I shrugged. "You're doing better than I would. I've got zero magic talent. I can't even draw a protection sigil. Thank Kingdom I can draw a gun."

"After yesterday, I feel like an honorary agent." She gave me a little grin, like a child who'd discovered a new toy.

Right about then, it occurred to me how stupid my plan was. One day of firearms training barely taught Ari how to avoid shooting herself. One class of self-defense probably made her more dangerous to herself than anyone attacking her. And now she had this idea that being an agent was good. It made me sick to my stomach.

"It's no honor. Anyway, Grimm's got a strict 'No Princesses' rule for his agents. Some sort of human resources violation. I don't think I'm even an agent anymore. I got demoted to handmaiden."

She shut the book and put it beside her. "How'd you start working for Fairy Godfather?"

I thought of all the different lies I'd used in the past. Recruited for my talent, chosen for a rare gift of prophecy— I'd come up with a lot of lines. "My sister was born sick. She needed a miracle to keep her breathing, and she needed it soon." I shifted lanes, gaining speed as I spoke. "Mom and Dad were getting desperate, and that's the key to finding Grimm. You have to need him badly if you are a normal person. Folks with Glitter can walk right in."

"I needed his help." Ari's statement seemed like a challenge, one I wasn't interested in taking.

"I remember some of it. Dad crying, and Mom being upset, and Grimm talking to me from a mirror. He said he could help Hope, and he would do it, but there would be a price." I swerved around a truck and punched the accelerator down, flying along so the wind hurt my eyes.

"So I said yes. I thought when I was done, I'd go home and my sister would be waiting for me. I thought they'd all be waiting for me, but the truth is, I won't ever be free. I earn Glitter for every job and I work every chance I get and I'll never be free." I jingled my Agency bracelet. "Basically a part of him. Keeps me on a leash. Lets me talk to him. Lets him talk to me."

"So throw it away and leave."

I couldn't help but laugh. I snapped the bracelet off and threw it out the window. The wind whipped it away.

Ari turned to see where it landed. "You ever visit your family?"

Her question touched a sore spot in my heart. I had a gap there the size of my memories, and I spent a lot of time not thinking about it, not mentioning it, and praying every time I woke up that that day I wouldn't be reminded of what I'd lost. I slammed on the brake, skidding over to the side of the road. There were so many things I didn't want to explain to her, and yet I needed someone to understand. I didn't talk about this with anyone. I wasn't even sure Evangeline knew about the memories. In fact, I hoped she didn't. She'd take it as another sign of weakness.

"When I came to work for him, I was sad. Couldn't work, couldn't learn. So Grimm made me a deal. I let him hide most of the memories of my family. If I ever pay him off, I'll take them back and I can go home."

"Home as in where?" She took off her sunglasses to look at me. For a moment I felt like her eyes saw right into my soul.

"With them." Where else could there possibly be?

Ari squinted at me like she used to before contacts. "How old are you?"

I knew how things were supposed to work. You got older. You moved out. You lived on your own, but the normal order of things never seemed to apply to my life. Everything had changed on that bitter December night.

I'd spent six years telling myself that this was "for now," or "only until." Even if I were free, I wouldn't be that sixteen-year-old girl. Mom and Dad would welcome me for visits, I was sure. The truth was, I was never going home. I'd left on my eighteenth birthday, too foolish to realize what it meant.

"Mom and Dad said this was until . . ." I couldn't bring myself to finish it. I held up my arm and showed her the bracelet, hanging where it always did.

Ari reached out to touch it, making sure it was really there. The look of pity on her face made me jerk my hand away. Agents didn't get pity until their funerals. We kept the silence the rest of the way.

THE WOLF TOWN was off the main highway, but I knew long before we arrived, something was wrong. The smoke-houses had no fire and the air stank of rotten meat that I hoped was pig. No guards at the branch road, no eyes on me as I pulled into town.

Ari wrinkled her nose. "What is that smell?"

"Meat." I hoped she wouldn't ask more.

I got out of the car and looked around. "Anyone here? I want to talk." My voice echoed back to me with the sound of crows.

"Come on," I said to Ari, and I headed over to the building where Billy had gone to negotiate with the wolves. The odor of death filled the air as I opened the door and a cloud of flies buzzed out.

Ari vomited at the stench of decay. I was used to it.

The wolves lay dead where they had stood. Some slumped at tables, some lay on the floor, and the bartender draped across the bar. The worst was the flesh. Whatever it was had torn the skin from their bodies, tossing it onto the ground a few feet away.

Outside, the air smelled sweet with only the aroma of rotten pork.

Ari gagged again. "What? What happened?"

"Something magic. Fae magic." The fae guard's ability to tear people apart was legendary. Most legends had a grain of truth behind them. This one apparently had a boulder.

The larder, where the children had been kept, stood closed. I opened the door, praying that Billy and Evangeline had been to town recently. Inside, tiny figures slumped against the back wall. Flies spared me the need to check on them. I kicked the larder door in frustration and anger, glad that Ari wasn't there to see me cry. She'd seen that enough already.

I was headed back to the car when it attacked: a half-wolf, tearing across the street toward Ari. She saw it and froze. I cursed her for blocking my shot, but it was already on her, teeth bared. It bit her once on the shoulder and rolled away, gagging and choking. I didn't give it a chance to get up.

I put two bullets into each leg and another into its stomach. With the third bullet the half-wolf collapsed into the dirt. I rolled it over with my foot and put my gun to its head. It changed slowly, becoming more human. Ari approached, her arm dripping red.

"Tell me what happened or I keep shooting. Then I re-load, and I shoot you some more."

"The fae came for it, but we didn't have it anymore. They took it. You took it," said the wolf, now almost a man.

"Exactly who took what?

He convulsed and shivered, pain and fear wracking him. "The servants of the mirror."

Nineteen

❧

I LEFT HIM in the dirt, choking on his own blood. Wolves could survive a lot, and if he did, I didn't care. I wasn't usually a killer, though he frustrated me. Wolves were smarter than goblins, but pronouns must have given them headaches. "It" was not a proper name, though I suspected "it" might be as close as the wolf could come to naming the thing.

I took Ari to get her celebration stitches and slipped the doc an extra twenty to claim pink was the only color suture thread they had left. I'm pretty sure she knew. Ari held her arms and rocked in the seat as we drove across town. "How do you deal with it?"

"Get used to it. Wolves are like that. I didn't use silver bullets, so it's not like it will kill him." I cut across lanes to take my exit.

"No, the pain. How am I going to sleep tonight? What if I turn into a werewolf?"

You can guess what color her wound wrapping was. Best twenty bucks I'd spent in a while. "This whole business is pain. When it goes well, there's less, and when it goes bad, there's more. There is always pain, it's just a question of who is hurting." I glanced down at my own wounds, still traced in pink scars. "And the whole wolf-to-werewolf thing is an urban legend. If it makes you feel any better, he's probably panicking about turning into a were-princess."

I pulled into the Agency parking lot and didn't even bat an eye at the security guard. I had to act like I belonged there, and Ari was with me. I wasn't surprised when my bracelet didn't open the service door, so we went through the lobby like the plebes.

I gave Rosa a smile and she gave me the stink-eye like always. "Hey Rosa, buzz me in. I need to talk to Grimm." If I had walked through the door with wolf blood splattered on me from head to toe and a severed arm in my mouth I wouldn't have gotten a worse reaction.

She hit the buzzer. Not the door buzzer. The emergency one we had installed after a wraith attempted to devour Rosa's soul. Poor wraith took one bite out of her and died.

"What in Kingdom are you doing here?" said Grimm from the lobby mirror. "And why is she not safely at home with you? And what happened to her?"

Before I could answer, Evangeline came bursting through the front door. The moment she saw me she stopped cold.

"Evangeline, I told you not to call her," said Grimm. "We had this discussion. Friend, yes. Call, no."

"She's not my friend. I didn't call," said Evangeline.

Then things became a lot clearer. Behind her came Jess, wearing a blue silk outfit that should not have looked that good on someone her age, and behind her, Liam.

I simultaneously felt sick and happy and dizzy. That's quite a few feelings to have at once, but I've had practice.

He saw me, and everything flipped over. First it was recognition, and then surprise, hurt, and anger. I tried to smile at him, but all I could remember was how I had left him. He looked bad, scraped and cut, like he hadn't slept in a year. He reeked of wood smoke.

"Get her out of here," said Grimm, "and take him to my office."

I watched Liam as he walked past and through that white staff door. "Grimm, we have to talk."

"We have to do no such thing, Marissa. You have zero appreciation for what it has taken to find him, and I can't risk you upsetting him right now."

"No, you and I have to talk, but I need to see him afterward. A wolf found me at my apartment."

"Did you teach him to heel or play dead?"

"The fae killed the wolves. Most of them, at least. Whole village is dead, more or less."

I knew the look he gave me. It was the "Don't you dare say another word here" look. I'd gotten it a lot. "Rosa, buzz her through." He turned that gaze back to me. "Watch yourself, my dear. You are on one misstep probation. I will toss you out of this office for a year at least. You go where I tell you to go, you be silent when I say to be silent."

Liam was inside, and so I did what Grimm said. "Ari, stop picking at the stitches and come on." We walked down the hall.

Evangeline blocked the way to Grimm's office. "Conference room, M. Please?"

Evangeline had always been there for me. She got me my first sutures, and bought me ice cream to celebrate the first time I broke my leg. When I couldn't sleep for a week after that shaman went on a rampage she came over, stayed up, and turned out the lights. She'd also always made it clear that she didn't understand why Grimm took me in the first place. It wasn't all that surprising that she got along better with another half-djinn than me. So I went to the conference room.

Grimm appeared in the conference room mirror. "Tell me everything, princess."

I was screwed.

So I listened as Ari started with breakfast, and how we ran every day, and about how I was always reading the books, and about how my front bathroom has only plain white towels. Eventually she ran out of boring things to talk about and explained about our wolf visitor. She moved on to my attempt to teach her to shoot, and I could see how this was going downhill the whole way. By the time she got to the wolf town part (after describing my driving as "almost as crazy as Evangeline's"), Grimm had his eyes set in that glower that said he was going to yell at me for a few hours. Since he didn't have a throat, it didn't get sore.

Ari explained about the bodies. The children. The wolf, and the fae. That part she handled well, since I sounded like a crack shot and a commando and scout all in one.

When she finished, Grimm stepped back and crossed his arms. "You are to tell no one about this. Marissa, we'll discuss later how taking your charge to the wolf town was keeping her safe."

"The wolf said the servants of the mirror took something. You send Evangeline or Jess out there to do bargaining?" Grimm had a habit of getting things done, and if that meant extortion or blackmail, well, sometimes it worked better than bullets.

"No, Marissa, and neither did I send Clara, since you are going to ask."

"Pity. I'd pay money to watch her beating off wolves with a walker. She's practically jerky already, so the wolves might pass on eating her." The moment I said it I wished I'd kept my mouth shut.

He glared at me and I knew I was about to be royally chewed out.

That's about when the shouting started. It was Liam, and I think Evangeline. Liam pushed his way through the door. His fists were clenched, his jaw was set, and even in the refrigerator cold Grimm insisted the office be kept at he was sweating. The longer I looked at him, the warmer I felt myself.

"I'm done with this," he said. "I'm going home, and you two ladies can go—" He stopped, looked around. Looked at Ari. Glared at me. "Where is he? I heard the son of a bitch in here."

"I'm right here," said Grimm.

Liam approached the mirror, his hand held out like he wanted to touch it. "Some sort of hologram?"

"Indeed, sir. Most people can't tell, but obviously you are too clever for me to fool. Now, if you don't mind, I would like to run a few tests."

"I do mind," said Liam. His face turned purple and sweat poured off him. "I've had a hell of a month, you know that? Every time I go to sleep I wake up somewhere different, in the middle of a fire. Then those two show up and offer to take me home. This is not home."

Grimm crossed his arms and nodded. "Sir, would you mind humoring me with a request? I promise it does not involve needles."

"Will it get me out of here? "

"It would certainly be a step in the right direction. I have a medical bracelet of sorts I would like you to wear. It allows me to monitor your affliction."

Evangeline stepped forward with it. The bracelets, as I understood it, were a piece of Grimm. Thing about it was they couldn't be forced on you. You had to choose them. Since Liam didn't have a contract it wouldn't be binding, but I was sure it would give Grimm a better understanding of what we were up against, and maybe a little control over it.

Liam clipped the bracelet into place. In the next few seconds, he seemed to deflate. His face cooled and he relaxed his shoulders. "Can you, can someone tell me what is going on? I want to go back to my house."

"It is gone," said Grimm. He was never one to take the bandage off slow. "As are the other places you've slept. The police are looking for a serial arsonist."

Liam put his hands on his head, and I saw steam rising where the sweat glistened on him. "I don't, I don't remember. I woke up and it was hot, and everything was burning. Even the metal. That doesn't even make sense."

"I can help you, Mr. Stone, and I will. I believe the bracelet will control your episodes for the time being. First we will find you housing."

"He can stay at my place," I said.

It just slipped out, and Liam skewered me with a glance. Grimm got there second, but his death stare didn't feel like much. "Marissa, your guest room is occupied. And of course, Mr. Stone, how would you feel about spending time with Marissa?"

Liam looked at me full-on, the first time he had done anything but glare at me since I first saw him, and it made me shiver and want to cry at the same time. "I'd rather be roasted on my own forge. I'd rather have my hand nailed to this table. Do you have any idea what you put me through? I had the best days of my life with you, and I felt like I could share with you, and you didn't look through me, you looked at me. Then you take me to that restaurant—why couldn't you do it in private?"

I was struck into silence. I knew this was coming, and yet every word hit me harder.

"You had to do it in public. Tell everyone how I made the mistakes. How I misread the signs, and you leave me there in a room full of people and they whisper." He kept clenching and opening his fists, like he was barely in control.

"You know what the worst part was? It wasn't the end. It was the beginning. That's the thing I keep going over. I went down to the pier to be alone, and I look up and there you are, and the sun hits you, and I keep thinking you're glowing." Liam looked down at the table and hung his head.

"I'm so sorry," I said.

He snapped his head up, his jaw set, his mouth square. "Don't you dare say that. I spent the better part of a week waking up and wishing you'd call me and do it all over again just so I could be with you. Now I'm having black-outs. I'm waking up miles from where I went to sleep and I think I'm setting fires."

"Mr. Stone," said Grimm, "I do not believe you are directly responsible for these fires, and as I've stated, I believe I can help with your problem. I'll arrange appropriate housing." Grimm's eyes flashed to me. "And a treatment protocol."

"Why?" said Liam, his voice suspicious.

"I feel for your predicament, Mr. Stone, and I know that Marissa would demand I help you anyway."

He could have left that last part out. Without warning, Liam seized the stapler at the end of the desk and hurled it at the mirror, shattering it from top to bottom. "I don't want your help if it has anything to do with her."

I spun my chair to the door. "I'll go. Stay and I'll go. I won't come back, I promise. I swear."

I hit the lobby door so hard it broke, rushed into the hall, and cursed the elevator that never seemed to come.

Ari stood behind me, silently waiting. We rode down to the parking lot without speaking. When the door opened she finally asked. "Who was that?"

"My most recent professional mistake."

"I've made a lot of mistakes. I don't look at any of them the way you look at him. What did you do?" She followed along behind me to the car.

I put the car into gear and swung out of the lot. "Let me tell you exactly how we get a prince and a princess together."

Twenty

~

ARI STARED AT me the whole way home as I explained. "And you do this all the time?"

"It works. At least it does when I get things right. I meet Mihail, break his heart, you show up at the right time and put it back together. You're holding his heart already at that point. Love is easy. Love is cheap."

Ari shook her head. "I don't buy that. Love is something special that happens when the world aligns just right."

I pulled into my building's garage and turned off the car. "Well, in that case, I've spent the last six years aligning people. Except this time I screwed up. I saw Liam, and I thought for sure I saw the magic on him."

Ari looked at me like I had a third eye. I knew a doctor in Kingdom who specialized in removing third eyes, but had never had the occasion to use him. She raised one eyebrow. "You saw the what?"

"Magic. Prince magic? Princess magic? I swear, you folks look like magical snow globes when the sun hits you right. I saw it on him. I thought I did. Grimm figures I was looking for a boyfriend."

Ari spent a moment waving her hands wildly around her head and looking at them.

"Settle down. Any more shaking and you'll have a seizure. You can't see it?" Admittedly, Ari was hardly a first-string princess, but she had enough magic about her to look like a disco ball at times. That was the seal bearer in her at work.

She shook her head. "How many boyfriends have you had?"

"Counting Liam, one."

"How many friends do you have?"

"Counting you, one." I looked at her and was relieved to see a smile. That feeling down inside me, like autumn sun, was new and different. Then I remembered: This was what it felt like to be happy.

That evening, as we ate dinner, I thought about what Grimm had said. I wasn't to talk to anyone about the fae. That meant he didn't want me scaring anyone, and that meant Grimm didn't know what was going on with them. The fae had killed the wolves and looked for something. Something the wolves thought we took.

"I was thinking," I said, "maybe I can help you. I'm not sure I understand magic. Grimm says if I were any less magically inclined I'd start cancelling spells out, but I got an A plus on my English lit projects. Might as well have gotten my degree in deciphering strange languages."

"You know as much as I do about using magic." Ari ran her fingers over the spine of her book as if doing so would extract knowledge, or give her a spell to wash the dishes. It didn't, so she put down the book and picked up a sponge.

When the dishes were done, we studied in earnest. It turned out I wasn't terrible at magic. I just lacked any ability with it. Of course, if magic tomes were written in plain English, things would have been easier.

Salaium bound in round, for instance: Why not say "Pour a circle of salt around the princess like she's a slug?" Not that I ever poured salt on slugs. Once Grimm showed me what slugs were actually here for, I loved those little slimy monopods. Every time I turned over a board and saw them crawling back and forth, part of me was happy knowing at least that day there wouldn't be a demon apocalypse.

I admit I considered trying to shrivel up Ari until she went away. The problem was I had grown used to having someone to talk to. So I poured the table salt in a circle around her, and I only sprinkled a little on her hand. Just to see what would happen. Getting the circle set up, of course, led to the more difficult part.

Ari drew in her energy for the thousandth time. I felt it when she did, and I've got to say if this is what the witches in legends were like, I bet they could tear things apart. The dishes in the cupboard clinked and shook as if we were having an earthquake.

Ari brought her hands together and whispered to herself, "Now focus."

A tiny light glowed, like a firefly, and that's about when the first lightbulb exploded.

"More focus," I said. I had a bag full of broken lightbulbs from the day's practice already.

She bit her lip and the firefly became a match, glowing soft orange. Pictures flew off the wall, flying across the room to bounce off the circle's edge. Ari cupped her hands like she was holding a baseball. "Now, take form."

She drew her hands out, and I held my breath. The book said this would simply conjure a foxfire. Given that we were only a few hours from sunset, a night-light creature wasn't going to do much. What appeared between Ari's hands crackled and hummed like an electric sun.

Every dish in my cabinet broke at once.

Every light in the apartment went out. Through the walls I heard angry yells and the sounds of feet shuffling. Apparently, Ari had not only broken the bulbs, she'd blown out the power to the whole building.

Ari's eyes snapped open and the foxfire blinked out like yet another bulb. "Crap."

"I'm out of bulbs, out of power, and we're eating on plastic tonight."

"It's not my fault." Ari's voice trembled with frustration.

I brought out a flashlight, because the single window in my apartment didn't let in nearly enough light. "It's not mine either."

"Actually, it kind of is."

I swung the flashlight to her. Sweat rolled down her head from the effort, and her hair clung to her face. She rubbed her palms together and glared at me.

"Go on," I said, taking a seat.

She stepped out of the circle. Regardless of what anyone tells you, princesses aren't slugs. "Those things with you go crazy every time I get started, and they start bouncing everywhere. Closer I get to doing a spell right, the angrier they get."

Great. My blessings didn't like it when my only friend did her stuff. That kind of ticked me off. Somewhere along the way I'd started thinking of her as my princess. Kind of like my cold sore. And nobody picked on my princess except me.

"I think they're eating the spell power and converting it into, well, I don't know. Destruction," said Ari.

I was completely frustrated. Then an idea came to me. I looked at my hillbilly bookcase (pine boards and cinderblocks) and found it: *Spellwork and Curses*. If there's one thing I'd learned about apartment maintenance, it was that it might be hours before we had electricity again. I once watched the building supervisor throw the same breaker over and over, in hopes that it might restore power. "Let's head to the park and see what we can do. We can at least study until sundown."

Ari looked over the book. "Curses? You said they were a blessing."

"It's kind of a gray area from what I gather."

We spent the rest of the day at the park and came back to an apartment building with power. I read late into the night, and in the morning I had a plan. The only problem was it required something I didn't have a way to buy: Permission.

I stood in my bathroom, using the sink mirror to call. "Grimm, I know you can hear me. I need to use the Visions Room. Please."

He slowly faded into view in the mirror, and if he ever slept I'd say he was worn out. "I'm sorry, my dear. I am a bit occupied at the moment."

"I've been doing my homework, and I've gotten to the point where I need to do lab work."

"Fine. You can come in after ten and use it for an hour."

"How is he doing?"

"He is deeply enchanted, my dear. Even worse, it is a type I can't identify, though I have a theory. I suspect, in fact, it is a salamander charm."

"He turns into a lizard?"

"Amphibian," said Ari, apparently tired of eavesdropping from the door.

"A salamander is a creature of fire. It fits the pattern, prince into frog and such. It matches the evidence as well, his home being burned down, but there are aspects of this curse that are baffling."

"Did he hurt you?" Ari asked Grimm.

"Young lady, I don't understand your question," said Grimm.

"He broke your mirror," said Ari. "Did it hurt?"

Grimm laughed a gentle, deep laugh. "Young lady, I have had so many broken mirrors in my time I have lost count. Only obsidian may break our portals in a way that hurts. Even that wouldn't kill me, it would just be quite painful."

"How is he?" I asked again, knowing Grimm would know what I meant.

"He is angry, and sad, and hurt. Everything I've ever asked you to make a prince."

"I'll be in tonight. Call if he's there late, and I'll make sure to wait."

Grimm didn't leave. He looked at the floor a moment, then back at me. "Marissa, I might have been overly harsh with you. I regret not taking the time to explain more. I'm not punishing you for a mistake, whether you believe that or not. I'm doing what is best for you. You've never taken more than a day or two off, and the pressure of this job is hard to handle even if you are a fairy."

"See you tonight, Grimm," I said. I couldn't decide if I should be happy that Grimm had almost apologized for dismissing me, or upset that he thought I couldn't handle it. "That was a private conversation," I said to Ari.

"Sorry." Ari had never shown a tendency to apologize for snooping before. "I'm worried about you."

I CANCELED THE morning run in favor of study time, though my blessings made it impossible to get any sort of spell work under way. We spent the day doing absolutely nothing, which was as much work for me as actually working. That evening, I drove us to the Agency, trying to time it right. Too early, and I'd run into Liam. Too late, and I'd waste precious time. I was relieved to find my bracelet worked, letting me in the back door.

I took Ari to the back corner of our office. "This is the Visions Room." It looked like a large closet until you noticed the four-foot-square window in the side. And the blacklights. And the prisms. "It should let me see the same thing you see."

"M!" said Evangeline, nearly scaring me to death. She came over and hugged me. Before I'd met Ari I'd always thought of her as my friend. Now I wasn't so sure. More like a sister who can't stand you, but knows that killing you would get her grounded.

"You can take the scarf off around her." I glanced at Ari, trying to give her warning.

Evangeline unwrapped herself.

Ari did well, focusing on her eyes and keeping her mouth shut.

"You get used to it after a while," said Evangeline. "Well, maybe you do. I don't think I ever will. Grimm said you'd be in tonight. Guess you aren't grounded as much anymore."

I hit the power-up button to start the lights. "Going to get a look at my blessings. Try to calm them down."

"I don't think you should talk to them," said Evangeline. "You want to see something nasty? Check this out." She punched up the Visions Room monitor and brought up a picture. It was Liam, and I could finally see the curse I had sent after him. It looked like a net of barbed wire, but the loops were curved like scales, and it was tattooed in spirit ink across his entire body. "Never seen anything like it. Jess says she hasn't either, and she's old."

I spent a moment admiring the man under the curse, wondering what his skin felt like without one of those flannel shirts he always wore. I shook away the thoughts and focused on my current problem. "I gotta get in and see if this works." I'd taken aspirin in anticipation of the migraine the Visions Room would give me. I opened the door and walked in. The ceiling was low, but this was one case where losing the genetic lottery worked in my favor. All I had to do was stand and wait for the lights to activate. When they did, the light was simultaneously brilliant white and deep purple. The prisms kicked in, splitting the normal light away and bending the magical energy down to the visible spectrum.

My eyes focused, and I blinked a couple of times to be sure. "You two seeing what I'm seeing?"

The speaker in the box buzzed and Evangeline spoke. "Kingdom help you, M. We can see them."

Ari had said they looked like pixie lights that dashed back and forth, but obviously she needed a pair of magic bifocals to go with the contacts. Across from me sat two creatures, like tiny children, except children don't have six-inch claws, or three toes and fingers, or a mouth full of razor-sharp teeth. They looked more like piranha than people. Their tiny bellies pooched out like they'd swallowed a poodle or two, and they hunched over so that their tiny fish faces hung forward. I smiled at them and they returned the grin with a mouth that could swallow a cat.

Evangeline buzzed in again. "M, you want out, pull the safety latch."

"They'd come with me." I was sort of wondering if I'd be

able to sleep at night knowing what followed me everywhere. "Listen up, you two. I know you can understand me. I also know you aren't bound to my will. I have two names. I'll give you each one, and I promise I'll speak it at least once every day." I'd done my bit, finishing up curses and spellwork. You didn't speak of a curse because it gave it power. It fed it.

I pointed to one. "You. You are Beatus." As I said the word it shimmered, becoming brighter, and it quivered like the name had stroked it. I looked at the other. "You are Consecro." If the thing had rolled over on its back it couldn't have been more pleased. "You are my blessings, and from now on you go with me by my permission." That was all I needed to do. Simple, and hopefully effective. See, the key to naming something was that it had to accept the name, and know you called it that.

Beautus and Consecro. Latin for blessing and curse. I'd chosen the names with care, because everything they did for me seemed to cut both directions. I couldn't remove them, but I had learned about harakathin. Naming them gave them power, but it gave me power over them, as well. Giving them permission to come with me was more symbolic. What mattered was intent, and I was intent on being in control of my own life. I opened the door to the Visions Room and watched as they faded away. "Let's go, Ari. We've got studying to do."

Evangeline shook her head and leaned against the Visions Room wall. "M, this is not a good idea, and you are so good at bad ideas. Giving those things names? Giving them permission to come with you? Grimm's gonna blow a gasket."

"I can hear you two," said Grimm, showing up on the mirror facing the monitor. "Feeding a curse is a terrible idea. Feeding a blessing is only mildly bad. They are connected to you, my dear, and will react violently to separation."

I looked at Grimm. "Speaking of violence, what's going on with the fae?"

"They are preparing for war, my dear. A war between the realms."

"The fae and the goblins? The fae and Avalon?" I had a bad feeling about the way he said it.

"You know better than that, my dear. Their foray into the wolf village was only the beginning. I don't know why, since you are going to ask, but the authorities are attempting to negotiate, and the police and the military are doing what they can to prepare." There wasn't going to be such a thing as preparing for that. I saw what happened to the wolves.

"Then there's the matter of the prince. I wouldn't expect you to be able to tell," said Grimm, "but there were traces of fae magic everywhere in his apartment."

"Tit for tat?" I asked. "Someone snags a fae child, so they grab the prince?"

"My dear, it certainly appears so. Though why they'd want Mihail I can't say. There are half a dozen better targets in Kingdom."

"I'd kidnap a kobold before I took Mihail." The more Grimm explained, the less I understood, but I didn't like the idea of keeping Ari out any later than absolutely necessary. There were things that came out to play after midnight that even I did my best to avoid. "See you round, Grimm. Evangeline, keep an eye on Liam for me."

"Of course. He's staying at my place." She didn't bother looking up.

"What?" I said, looking at her with horror.

"Calm down, M. Not like that. Your friend gets a lot of attention from the wrong crowd these days, and it's a full-time job for me and Jess to keep him from winding up in the wrong place at the wrong time." She walked over and gave me a hug. "Don't worry, I'll keep him safe for you."

"Is he any better?"

"Nah, if anything the curse is working its way deeper into him. And where you are concerned, he's not any better. He still can't stand you."

Twenty-One

❧

I STOOD IN my living room. "Blessing, curse, come here. I need you two to stay calm while Ari does practice, okay?" I couldn't see them, but that didn't stop me from talking to them. I had a cat for a while. It disappeared one day while I was gone and hadn't shown up since. I still worried every time I moved the bed that I was finally going to find it. Having a couple of blessings was like having a cat, only I didn't have to feed them. In that regard, they were my kind of pet.

Ari touched up the circle and stepped inside. "All right. Let's do this."

"I bought an entire case of lightbulbs. Just in case."

She ignored me and I felt that chill as the magic ran through the apartment, gathering about her. Now she held a globe of light in her hand without breaking a sweat.

"Consecro, Beatus, good job," I said, hoping to keep them from a rampage. The vase on my table quivered a little but otherwise things were quiet.

Ari took a deep breath. "Be." A fountain of light erupted in the apartment, blasting out like a wave from Ari, painting everything it touched with a rainbow of colors. It rushed back into her, collapsing and taking all the light in the apartment with it.

A pale purple glow lit in the darkness. A globe of light that hovered before her. The globe floated forth like a tiny lightning storm, stopping at the edge of the circle. I walked around it, marveling. It resembled a thundercloud, shimmering with micro-lightning. "That's amazing, and beautiful. Hey, you okay?"

Ari looked like she was about to faint from the effort of stepping out of the circle. She stumbled, and I helped her to the recliner. "So tired. Feel like I stayed up all night. And I hurt." One little glow bug and she was wiped out.

"What do I do with the foxfire?" It floated against the edge of the circle like a miniature cloud, lights playing across the surface as it tried to reach her.

She coughed, and her voice came out in a whisper. "Let it go."

I stepped on the edge of the circle, and it floated out. The lights flickered and a bolt of static electricity shot out at me. My hand convulsed like I had grabbed an electric fence. "Stop it." It shocked me again.

"I can't," Ari whispered, the best she could do.

That was obvious. Lying on the recliner took every bit of strength she had. The table flipped over, the pictures went flying, and the foxfire shrieked. It bled light from wounds that something raked across it. As the fire drained outward like blood, it illuminated the invisible claws and teeth of my blessings. They floated in the air, devouring it like honey-glazed ham, their teeth lit up like tiny electric swords.

Ari slept the better part of two days, and when she did get up, she looked like she had the flu.

"No running." She shuffled to the fridge.

"Not today." I sat with a book in my lap. "How you feel?"

"Tired, but not dead. Need to move."

"I think we should put a hold on magic until we can figure out what it is doing to you, but if you are up for a trip, I'm thinking about going into Kingdom."

"What do you want there?"

I held up my book. "Near modern history of the fae. Volume sixteen, but it ends over a thousand years ago. I'm hoping there's a bookstore with the last volume. Also I need a spirit prism. Tired of not being able to see where my pets are."

"They're on the mantel like usual." Ari glanced at the fireplace. "I can see them better today. They don't look like lights. More like hot dogs with legs and arms."

"The fae didn't always keep to themselves, you know that? At one point they nearly took over the entire earth realm. Several times, in fact."

Ari took a drink from her coffee. "Have they actually seen this place? Why would they go to war for it? What I saw through that portal made Earth look like a dump."

"I think Earth's like a middle ground. Goblins, fae, even the fairies with their mirrors. They're all connected here, so I think if you want to get to someplace else, you have to go through Earth." I closed the book and put it aside. When she was ready, we headed into Kingdom, and since it was a nice day, we took the bus.

Kingdom on a Wednesday was about as close as it ever came to normal. Whole place ran on a seven-day cycle, becoming more and more magical as the weekend approached. Noon on Wednesday was the peak of normal, which meant it looked a lot like any street in the city: weird.

Ari looked a lot better now; the air and the movement were doing her good. "Any idea where we are going?"

"There's a bookstore up at 116th and Cross." I pointed it out on the map of Kingdom Grimm had given me the first time I came here.

We walked along the high streets of Kingdom, under the watchful eyes of a number of cops, all the way to the bookstore. As I passed the Isyle Witch's shop a shiver ran down my spine. I left Ari at a singing flower stand while I went inside the bookstore and found my book. It was tiny, less than three hundred pages long, but the cost left me nearly choking. Three weeks' worth of work in a tiny golden pile.

"Get the book?" asked Ari as I joined her outside.

"I got it, cost me three weeks' worth of Glitter, but I got it. Let's find an artifact shop and get out of here before I spend every ounce of Glitter I've got. I need to find a spirit prism and we can go have lunch." I hefted my book, bound in brown paper and tied up in ball twine for safekeeping.

"This way," said Ari.

Walking down the streets of Kingdom toward the exit was a lot easier. All the magic in the place pushed me out toward the normal world, and if I wandered, I knew I'd find myself at the gates every time. Ari, on the other hand, would inevitably wind up at the castle. She cut over a couple of streets, and I followed, resisting the temptation to open my book and read.

Ari stopped. "Mother—I mean Gwendolyn went here for all her spells."

Dread washed over me, making my skin prickle. "Anywhere else. I'll pay double to buy it anywhere else." We stood outside the Isyle Witch's shop.

"No, you won't." She walked right in. The stench of toads wafted out of the door as she opened it, and the bell rang as it closed.

I held my nose and went inside, wishing I'd have asked where we were going first. Inside, my eyes struggled to adjust to the dim light. "Ari. Ari, where are you?"

"I'm right here," she said, standing at the counter.

The witch saw me and grinned, showing rotten teeth. "Handmaiden. You honor me with your presence."

Ari gave me a look that said I'd have trouble explaining this later, then she turned back to the witch, and when she spoke, it was a command. "Get me a spirit prism."

"For what? Your eyes are like my own. You see." The witch leered at her in a way.

If my skin was crawling before, it was ready to run at this point, and drag me with it out of the shop.

Ari looked right back into those yellow eyes without a hint of fear. "None of your business."

The witch snarled at her. "Witchling, you should watch your tongue in the presence of your elders. I could teach you much if you'd learn respect."

"The prism," said Ari. "I'm not a witch, I am a princess, and the seal bearer of the third Family."

The witch laughed. "Where do you think witches come from? You have fresh wounds from wild magic on your soul. It won't be long now." She wandered into the back of the shop.

Ari glanced at me. "What does she mean by *handmaiden*?" She sounded a lot less sure of herself now.

"Not now, please. I told you I'd go anywhere but here."

The witch emerged from the backroom with a black cloth bag I knew contained a prism. "Pay and be done."

I did, trying not to care about what it cost me. That tiny pile represented an entire month helping a little old man spin used dental floss into gold. By the time I'd finished that assignment, my smile shone bright white.

She weighed the Glitter. "Are you pleased with my work, handmaiden?"

"It didn't affect the man, so I think not." I walked over to the counter to stand beside Ari.

The witch's hair flared up in clumps like gray tentacles, and the safety bonds on her wrists glowed bright red. In Low Kingdom she would've already thrown a spell or two at me. "I swear by the low streets, by my own casket twice buried, that the potion was good. If it did not work, then some other power opposes you. And my gift to you, did you use it to win his heart?"

"She said it didn't work," said Ari. "Are you deaf as well as blind?"

"Not your man, little witchling. Hers. You should use it soon. You have little time left." As I took the prism, she seized my hand. The restraints on her smoked, burning her, and the heat seared my skin. She held on with an iron grip as she peered at my hand. "See, she has marked you as her own. Remember me with favor when she comes, handmaiden."

"Let her go," said Ari, and I felt the magic rushing in around her with her anger.

The witch let go, and I yanked my hand away. She looked at Ari with those yellow eyes and spat. "She will drink your soul."

On the street I sat at the curb and caught my breath. "I'll explain, I promise. I just need time."

That's about when the sky split open. At least that's what it looked like, white line shining so bright it made my eyes hurt. From the tear in the sky riders came forth, riding down the beam of light like a path to the street blocks away. The colors and sounds told me immediately they were fae. That and the fact that they were riding on a beam of light, a trick I didn't see many other races attempt. They touched ground several blocks away, but when the lead rider spoke, it was like he was screaming in my ear.

"Heed our warning: return the Seal or bear the price of war," he said. "You have until the equinox." A drop of blood dripped from my nose as his words cut through me. Around me people fell to their knees as his voice tore into them. Ari didn't seem to be hurt, though she looked straight at him. The gold and maroon of his uniform shone brighter than the sun, and the sound of his horse's hoofs echoed throughout Kingdom. He turned to each of the four directions and repeated the warning.

A mounted policeman rode toward the fae, his horse mad with fear, and the fae warrior raised his hand.

I owe Ari my life. I couldn't move a muscle but she dragged me backwards, into an alcove. A blast of blinding white light rushed through the street, sweeping back and forth like a searchlight. It cut off, and the street was silent, dead silent. The hoof falls grew louder and louder. The fae rode down the street, looking to see if anyone else dared challenge them. They stopped to look straight at us, and I knew that with a single spell I'd be obliterated.

Ari stood before me, her fists clenched, and returned

the fae commander's gaze. For a long moment they traded stares without a word. A portal tore open in the sky. He gave the command, and their horses began to climb on the beam of light that shone from it until they disappeared. In the streets of Kingdom lay dozens of bodies, their skin torn from their bones. Old, young, women, and children, it didn't matter. They were all dead.

Twenty-Two

I DON'T REMEMBER how we got home. That trip was exactly the reason I didn't like shopping. I went out looking for a book and a prism, and I almost got destroyed by the advance scouting force for a warrior race. That's why I avoided the mall most days. Not that I'd ever seen an army of magical warriors kill everyone on a street before, but once was more than enough.

I heard Grimm in the mirror as I unlocked the door.

"Marissa, princess," he called from the bathroom.

"We're okay," I said, knowing he could hear fine.

I walked into the bathroom, where Grimm waited. "I found out you two were in Kingdom this morning, and I was greatly worried, my dear."

Ari held up the bag with my prism. "Doing a little shopping."

"Marissa, did you see the fae?"

"Saw them. Heard them. Almost got cooked by them. My ears are still ringing. Grimm, I've been reading as fast as I can. What's a Seal? I'm sure the answer's in a book I should've read by now."

"It is, my dear, but I believe you've earned a little direct education. A seal is a barrier for a realm. In this case, the fae Seal, for the Realm of Fae," said Grimm.

"So every realm has one?" I knew there were seven realms, seven royal families.

"Earth is not sealed, my dear, but all the other realms are. Without their seal, one could cross into Fae anywhere, instead of the agreed-on and prepared portals. One could strike at the heart of a realm and walk away without ever passing a guard."

I held up my book package. "I'm only up to about a thousand years ago, but the fae had a lot of enemies back then."

"And now," said Grimm. "They believe someone in the city has rendered them vulnerable, and will do anything to coerce us to return it."

Ari tapped on the mirror to get Grimm's attention. "Who has the Seal?"

Grimm detested being treated like an aquarium fish, and frowned. "Young lady, if I knew that, I would have already alerted the authorities. Honestly, it isn't anywhere as best I can tell. This isn't like Liam's curse. I knew he was alive, I just wasn't looking for the right form. The Seal isn't present at all. Anywhere."

"Someone destroyed it?" asked Ari.

"Killed, young lady. You kill a seal. If they had killed it, we would know for certain. The effect would be unmistakable, and leave a crater the size of an office building. I want you both to stay out of Kingdom and stay away from the Agency. I can't keep everyone safe, but I will do what I can." Grimm exhaled, and I wondered for the first time ever what the limits to his power were, beyond his stingy nature.

"Grimm, you mind if I skip around in my reading a bit?" I asked.

He looked at me in surprise. "I was certain you would have read the history of the Black Queen first. Of course. Consider it a reward for diligent effort."

"Is it the whole story?"

Grimm began to fade. "No, my dear, but it contains what you want to know." He left us alone.

It wasn't easy to fall back into a vacation rhythm when I knew a war was fast approaching, but I did. It's not that I didn't care, it's that there was so little I could do. Grimm wouldn't let me come into the Agency, and frankly, I was beginning to feel like I was normal again.

I sat in the chair each night, reading the history of the Black Queen, which was primarily concerned with who she killed and how (the answers are: a lot of people and in grotesque ways). She wasn't all that creative either. Thorns through the eyes, thorns through the ears, thorns through the—okay, in some ways she was creative, but it was all the wrong ways. Late one evening, I finally found what I was looking for.

"Ari," I said, and she came out with her hair in a towel. "About what the witch said—"

"You don't have to explain. It doesn't matter." Her tone was cold, and her eyes looked past me, lost in thought.

I read aloud. "'She called them, and they came, those who bore her mark, and they knelt before her to receive her blessings. Her handmaidens swept the land like a plague, the shadows that went before and after her.'" I closed the book, tired on so many levels. "The witch said 'She' marked me. Can you see it?"

Ari came over and took my hand. "I still don't see magic that well, but I don't see anything. You know what I've been reading about? Witches. She told me the truth. We're the same. Witches were all seal bearers once. Then they started using wild magic." Her eyes were open wide, her face looked nearly panicked.

"I thought witches gave birth to witchlings." I'd actually never given any thought to the matter, but now I understood Ari's concern.

"Evil witches can't have normal children. Their sons are satyrs and the daughters gorgons. Witches were seal bearers like me."

I thought about my blessings, and how almost everything they'd done caused me more trouble. "It's just a name. We decide what we are."

She almost smiled at me, but looked away. When she spoke I could barely hear her. "I'm not sure anymore."

The doorbell rang, and it was not time for the daily mail. I grabbed my gun and approached the door. "Beatus, Consecro, I might need you." I had no idea what the little guys would do in a pinch, but from what I read, some curses were capable of pulling your intestines out through your nose.

I hated peepholes. They required you to put your eye right up to the door and when (not if) something poked a claw through the door, your head was right there. So I had a camera installed a few years ago.

The man standing outside wore a fine gray suit and showed no signs of rabies or fangs or the normal problems you see in the city.

Ari looked at him with me. "Assassin?"

"Doesn't look respectable enough for that. Probably a lawyer. Either way, go hide." I put away the gun and opened my door.

The man reached into his coat and took out a scroll. "I'm looking for Arianna Thromson. I have a message for her."

"What is it?" asked Ari, breaking our agreed-on rule that she hide in the bathroom until I gave her the all clear. She took the scroll. Those Kingdom types still wouldn't use phones or text messages. Ari read the first few lines and her eyes went wide. A tiny sob escaped her, and she dropped the scroll, backing away.

I stepped into the doorway between them. "She's not going back, and that is not negotiable."

The messenger caught my tone and raised his hands. "I'm not taking her. It's her invitation to the funeral ball."

I slammed the door on him, knowing he was waiting for a tip, and read the scroll. The first bit was your usual proclamation stuff. I skipped over it to the silver writing that identified the actual message.

*We celebrate the passing of King Torsten Thromson,
and his rich life, this Friday, the twenty-second, at
eight in the evening—her Majesty the Queen.*

Ari lay on the couch and curled into a ball, tears streaming from her eyes. She began to sob and rock as pain finally found a voice. Her tears ran like a river for hours.

I wasn't used to having anyone around to comfort me. Agents became best friends with pain, and sorrow rented out every spare room in our lives. So I sat beside her, and held her hand, and listened to the silence. Her sadness found a counterpart in me, and without Grimm or Evangeline watching, I finally felt free to let it out. When she finally fell asleep, I covered her with a blanket and settled into the recliner.

In the morning, she woke me up to talk, looking at me with eyes ringed red. Her pale skin made the purple bags under her eyes look worse. I sat up and gave her a hug that only caused her to gush more, as though I'd squeezed the tears from her.

"I have to go, M." She looked at me, pleading and watching my face as though she thought I might say no.

"Let me get dressed, I'll take you anywhere." I rolled out of bed and winced, a headache born of shared tears.

"I have to go to the funeral ball. I have to say good-bye. My stepmother will be there."

I understood. Ari's stepmother wouldn't lay a hand or spell on her under my protection. If her stepmother wanted to try going a few rounds with me, I'd welcome the opportunity. My only real concern was my bad history with celebrations. They almost always ended in disaster, which I attributed to bad luck, and Grimm attributed to me not being able to keep my mouth shut. "We'll go together. I'll take care of everything."

We sat together in silence, because grief didn't come with words. I thought about my own family and wondered. Would they have called me if someone died? They hadn't called for anything else, but part of me felt certain that Mom or Dad would have called if something awful had happened.

Later I went to my bedroom to make a call. "Grimm, did you know?"

"I heard, Marissa. Please convey my sorrow to her." He didn't bother coming into view, which meant he was doing a thousand other things at once.

"I'm taking her to the funeral ball on Friday in Kingdom." I wasn't asking if it was okay.

"Of course. Would you like Evangeline to come along? Your track record at parties leaves something to be desired."

I thought about the second, and last, time Grimm threw a birthday party for me. I got to find out what a radiation decontamination procedure felt like. The best gifts may be experiences, but that one was definitely not the best present ever. "That would be great. When do I get to come back to work?"

Grimm snapped into view, his face pale and hair disheveled. "Princess Arianna is my responsibility now, and therefore yours. Take care of her, and I promise I will have you back to work as soon as possible." He sounded more tired than ever.

"You find the Seal?"

"We are looking everywhere." Grimm's chin was set, and the look on his face was nearly a scowl. If I didn't know better, I'd have said the most powerful magic wielder in the city was powerless.

Twenty-Three

❦

EVANGELINE SHOWED UP early on Friday, knocked on my door, and marched right past me to squeeze Ari until I thought she would choke her. She stood a foot taller than Ari, but they managed it. Evangeline put her hands on Ari's shoulders like she was a child. "I brought a dress for you." Evangeline nodded toward me. "And I'll keep an eye on her to make sure she doesn't ruin things."

Ari's voice was hoarse. "Thank you."

We dressed, and I understood why Evangeline had brought a new dress for Ari. Almost all of her outfits looked fit for a rave rather than a funeral, but not this one. It was magnificent. Forget sweeping trains and all that; they aren't comfortable or easy to move in. This was sheer and black with a liquid shine. It looked like someone wove a fabric of tears. Looking at the dress made me sad. On the shoulder it had a golden emblem sewn in thread I think was real gold: her family crest. I preferred black slacks and shirt.

On the way there Evangeline actually drove somewhat somberly, proof in my mind she was set on being nice. When we pulled up outside the ballroom, my nerves about got the best of me. See, I might have mentioned balls didn't usually work out well with me. The first one ended with police in riot gear. The second one ended with a fire, and the last one, with the hazmat squad having to wash down everyone.

Evangeline let us off at the front steps and waited for the valet while we went on in. She didn't have an invitation, but then again, she never did. Men had trouble saying no to her when she had her veil on, and they had trouble saying anything when she had it off.

"Lady Arianna," said the doorman. "I'm delighted to see you." She gave him a hug, which was completely against ball protocol.

"The Princess Arianna Thromson, and guest," called the announcer, and a low buzz swept across the ballroom. Kingdom balls were like high school lunchrooms, except alcohol and cleavage were mandatory. They ran on gossip as much as Glitter, and I'm certain Ari was the subject of many tales. Just another reason for me to dislike them.

"Arianna," said a woman, and I felt a storm rolling in. She was dressed in black, of course, and her hair was red like Ari's, but that's where the similarities ended. She was as tall as Evangeline, and her eyes were dark brown, almost black. Her makeup was perfect.

"Gwendolyn." Ari made no attempt to hide her contempt.

"I will always be Mother to you."

I gave Ari a squeeze. It wouldn't do to have a throwdown on the stairs. She relaxed a little. "I've come to see Dad." She shook my hand off and disappeared into the crowd.

"Have we met?" asked the queen, and as she did, I had this feeling. Her voice seemed familiar, her face was alien and repulsive, but I couldn't quite place her.

I gave her my best smile. "Of course we have. You didn't think I'd forget, did you?" It wasn't the answer she was expecting, for sure, and I took the opportunity to go after Ari.

Funeral balls were one of the creepier parts of Kingdom.

They're a holdover from the old days, when people would gather together and bury the dead, but having a coffin at one end of the ballroom inevitably killed the desire to dance near it. Ari stood alone, waiting her turn, and I joined her.

She latched onto my arm like a drowning woman grabbing a rope. "I can't do this." Her makeup was sealed with Glitter, but magic didn't work well against grief. She was starting to streak from the tears.

I took her hand and we approached the coffin. As was traditional, a bin of polished rocks sat beside the coffin, and I took a handful. At one time kings had been buried with diamonds and rubies, but that had two effects: It encouraged grave robbing and it drove up ghoul dental bills. These days they used pretty rocks.

He was older, starting to turn gray. Maybe in his fifties, but he had a regal air about him even in death, and I thought I could see a hint of Ari's chin. I left a handful of stones and let her stand by the coffin. She took his hand and leaned in to whisper to him.

"I don't think we had a chance to complete our conversation," said the queen, who had come up behind me.

I made no attempt to hide the threat in my voice. "Leave her alone. If you put a hand on her, you'll find out what color the emergency room walls are this week."

She sneered, staring down at me like a few inches of height made a difference. "I know who you are. You're the little tart he sends around to do his dirty work."

Evangeline sauntered up, her every step drawing the attention of each man she passed. "I'm the big bitch he sends around. You look like you bruise easily, Your Highness."

Ari turned away from the coffin, her face set with determination. "What do you want, Gwendolyn?"

"You will call me Mother. I want you to come home. It's time to begin your training, under my care."

"I am not coming back." Ari crossed her arms and stepped back.

"This discussion is not over," said the queen, and she reached out to grab Ari's hand. Several things happened at once. Evangeline swung at the queen's hand, a simple downward smack with her palm. Evangeline was fast. The queen was faster, pulling her hand back before Evangeline could touch her, and backhanding me.

The blow wasn't hard. It caught me off guard and off balance. I fell backwards, my hand caught the rope and pulled the entire vase of stones over on me. I'm telling you, at balls it's like I'm cursed. The good news was no one was staring at Ari or Evangeline. They all stared at me as I clambered to my feet and walked away. Warm blood trickled down my lip where the queen had struck me.

"Let's go," said Evangeline, grabbing Ari by the arm.

Ari shook loose. "I need to see them take him out." At midnight the reapers would come and the coffin would be taken to the cemetery.

Evangeline leaned down to whisper in my ear. "You've got blood on your face. I think the bathrooms are up the stairs."

"You got Ari?" I asked, as Ari wandered aimlessly in the crowd.

"Got her. The queen caught me by surprise. Won't happen again." I'd seen that look on Evangeline's face before. It would take a miracle to keep this party from ending in blood, and Grimm was a bit busy.

I looked around and found the queen, surrounded by a flock of bodyguards. Evangeline would tear through them like tissue paper if they bothered Ari. I headed off for the bathrooms.

The ballroom was standard for Kingdom. The entrance on one side led down a grand set of stairs to the dancing floor. On the far side of the oval room, another set of stairs led up to a refreshment table, private feasting halls, and most importantly, bathrooms.

At the top of the stairs stood a table of food, mostly ignored in favor of champagne, but I was hungry. I debated cutting a slice of cheese from the wheel. I loved Gouda, but it reminded me a little too much of the cheese in the Agency fridge. That's when I felt that familiar feeling, someone looking at me, and I looked over my shoulder. The huge mirror on the corner wall showed the dancers whirling in dresses, but the mirror itself was what caught my eye. Grimm didn't even try to call much in Kingdom, but that's exactly what it felt like.

In the bathroom I washed the blood off my lip. There, I sensed it again. "Grimm?" I asked, but he didn't answer. Then again, it was the lady's restroom, and we'd had a few intense discussions on appropriate places to talk.

Outside, I snagged a glass of wine from a host and watched the dancers below. Ari and Evangeline stood off to the side. The feeling of being watched surged over me again. I turned to the mirror and walked closer, as if by staring into it I could see through. My own face looked back. A nose too small, eyes too large, and a chin that showed no particular heritage. I reached out a hand to touch my reflection.

"That would leave fingerprints," said a voice.

"Show yourself," I said.

The mirror swirled, turning milky. In the center something strove with my mind to form, but I rejected the image it sent and countered with another. She came into view, an older woman. Sixty-five or so, with gray hair pulled back in a bun.

"Well met, Marissa."

"Who are you?" I asked, though I was sure I knew the answer.

"Your Fairy Godmother, of course. We should talk, but not here. Trouble follows you everywhere you go. I'd hate for you to spoil your friend's mourning. She'll take care of that all on her own."

"Where? And don't say the basement. I don't do basements."

She clucked her tongue at me in a disapproving way. "I was thinking over here." She flashed into a metal bannister. "This way," she said, farther down the hall.

I walked to the far end and opened a pair of wide doors. This was a feast room, large enough for a hundred guests or more to have their fill before a party. I peered into the shadows with the same suspicion I gave the mirror. "I don't do pitch-black rooms either."

"The lights are by the door," she said, and I turned them on. She stood in a massive mirror above the fireplace, a sweeping white gown over her gaunt frame.

I reminded myself I chose what she looked like, and she shifted to half-snake, half-grandma.

"That's impolite," she said, forcing herself back into gown form.

"What is your name?"

"Odette. You may call me Fairy Godmother."

I sat at the serving table where I could look at her without turning my head. "So talk."

"So rude. I'm not your enemy yet, darling, though that may change. I simply wanted to meet the girl I hear so much about. Marissa saved this, or Marissa found that—I've heard your name more times than you have, and never seen your face."

If there's one thing I couldn't stand, it was people who complimented me. Especially ones I'd never met before, who claimed to know a lot about me. This one had to have an agenda. "What do you want?"

"Why, to help you, darling." She smiled warmly and her voice sounded like Grandma's, after school.

I wasn't buying. I'd had a lot of people try to help me. Help me off a building, help me under the water until I stopped breathing, or help me find out up close and personal what my intestines looked like. Help tended to be deadly. "What do you know about the fae?"

"I know you carry their blessings. Why didn't he intercede for you? Or help you remove them?" Her eyes flickered with each question.

"What do you know about the Seal?"

"Ah, directly to the point. Good girl. I'm actually here because of it. Did you know what the word on the low streets of Kingdom is? They say the Seal was stolen by a servant of the mirror. You wouldn't know anything about that, would you?"

"I didn't take it." It occurred to me at that moment that "servants of the mirror" was no longer a unique term in this town.

"Obviously not, darling. The seal is a living creature, and pure magic. For one like you, with so little affinity, touching it would be torturous. Your friend, the princess. She's a seal bearer. She could touch it and it wouldn't so much as shock her. In fact, the experience would be empowering. Of course, she has plenty of magic. Tell me something, why is it after all these years he hasn't gifted you with magic?"

"Stop trying to get me to doubt Grimm."

She shook her head. "I don't need to do that, darling. You are already doing it yourself. How close are you to being free? You know, I don't keep people. Three tasks for me and their debt is paid. Why, even if I made it three years you would already be free of me twice."

I kept my face calm. "I'm almost there."

She gave me that wan grin and shook her head slowly. "I've had so much more experience lying than you, child. You are maybe halfway. Probably less. At some point you'll be injured, or maybe you'll make an honest mistake, and he'll sideline you." She flashed to a silver pitcher directly in front of me.

"Listen to me, child, while I tell you the truth: You will begin to spend your Glitter, and wait for him to allow you to work, and that day will never come. Do you know anyone who has paid their debt to him? Have you ever seen it happen?"

I didn't. I hadn't.

"You are evil," I said, but I wasn't sure anymore. I was asking those questions. All on my own, before she ever showed up.

She wasn't angry. She smiled that look that said she knew so much more than I did. "I give you my word, darling. I have never given someone something their heart did not desire. I grant wishes and give, it is my way."

"I'm done being vaguely threatened, and I'm done

listening to you talk about Grimm. I pay my debts, and I do what he tells me to. You can go now. If your agents lay a hand on Ari, they'll be leaving teeth under their pillows for you for a month."

I don't know which upset her more: the dismissal like she was a servant girl or the deal with the teeth. There are only two magical creatures that deal in teeth, pixies and efreets. Pixies take the tooth under the pillow. Efreets bring pliars.

Her eyes flashed the same way Grimm's did, and the silverware on the table rattled. "Don't think I can't harm you, girl. My wishes are weapons, and I can destroy you with your heart's own desires. Indeed, it is the only way. Or perhaps I grant the wish of those you love. Does the blacksmith wish to forget you? You mother, does she ever wish she had more time to herself? Without a young child she'd have all the time in the world."

I shook with sudden anger, and my hands clenched over something in my pocket. I slipped my hand in and found a few stones from the vase, and I started to laugh.

"How would you like to work for me? I pay your debt. You work for me. You could be free before the end of the year."

I did want it. Anger welled up in me like a fever. Anger at myself for wanting to accept her offer, rage at her for knowing how much I did. I shoved the anger down inside me with that same cold wall of emotion I'd practiced so much.

"I'm not going to skip out on Grimm. All the magic I need comes in ammo boxes, and I'd rather plunge an ogre's toilet every day than work for you." I stood, taking the rocks from my pocket. They were solid black, polished. I picked up a pitcher and threw it across the room. She retreated to the mirror.

"Child, do not raise your hand to me." Her face became stern, her mouth pulled back in a grimace, and her eyes narrowed.

"You threaten my friends or my family, and I will find a way to kill you, if it takes me a lifetime." I threw the stones.

They struck the mirror and it shattered, splitting like a spiderweb. The mirror bled, blood gushing from the cracks like I had sliced an artery.

She screamed in rage, a word that spun past me like the wind, and rooted me to the spot. I strained against the spell but it pinned me in place. The table shook and silverware went flying. The lights exploded in a rain of sparks. My blessings, it seemed, didn't like her any better than I did.

Then something appeared in the air. It popped into existence. A bottle, and a brush, and the brush began to paint the mirror. As it did the blood turned black and disappeared, and the mirror was flawless. The stench clawed at my nose, the smell of fleshing silver. As the brush wiped the last drop of blood clean, she formed again in the mirror.

"I return your blow threefold, foolish girl." Her skin was pulled back so tight she looked like a talking skull, and her flowing white dress now looked like woven bones.

"Get it over with," I said, steeling myself.

Instead the spell released me, and when I looked up she stood there, her normal self.

"Not yet, darling. A blow struck in haste is a blow wasted. When the time is right, I will give you my gifts." She faded out. "Only when you have received the third may you ask, and I will grant your request. Only then will I kill you."

The giant clock in the ballroom rang over and over, and as I counted it, I realized it was midnight. I had lost hours to the fairy's voice. I ran out the door to the ballroom, and heard the shouting before I could see them.

"You will come home," said the queen. Most of the guests were huddling near the entrance, but Ari stood before the coffin, between it and the queen.

"I don't think you understood my friend," said Evangeline, and I knew her tone. It was the harbinger of pain and violence coming.

I ran down the stairs. "Leave her alone."

The queen turned to face me. "Hold your tongue, fairy whore. You turn cheap tricks and pass them off as magic, but you would make more Glitter on your back."

She looked to Ari. "You choose them over me? Then I decide. Until you return to my house and accept my training, you are not my daughter, and you're not of this family. I cast you out of this house and Kingdom."

Ari let out a sharp cry as if she had been punched in the stomach, and Evangeline grabbed Ari's wrist. The doors to the ballroom slammed open and the reapers entered, sending guests rushing to the walls. They marched through the ballroom toward the coffin, and the queen stepped aside as they passed, their robes trailing. They seized the coffin and marched out, and the head reaper waited. Evangeline seemed to be wrestling with Ari, trying to put something on, but my view was blocked as the head reaper approached me.

He didn't speak. He looked at me with his empty skull, and I felt his gaze on me, like when Grimm is watching. He bowed before me and followed the others out. Evangeline pulled Ari out the front door, and I followed, running up the stairs and out the door.

Evangeline ran to the valet booth, dragging Ari with her. "We've got to get out of here. She's fading."

The valet wandered off at his normal pace. I realized what was wrong. The queen couldn't change who or what Ari was. Sadly, she'd be a princess and seal bearer for the rest of her life. The magic of Kingdom did follow strict rules though: Stripped of her family title, Ari wasn't just thrown out of the family. She was being removed from the place. As I watched, she faded from view, disappearing completely.

"Where is she?"

Evangeline looked around, checking the street signs. "You don't want to know. That part of the city isn't somewhere you go in daylight, let alone midnight."

"I'm going after her. We'll meet you at the gates. Grimm, if you can hear, let me go." I pulled my Agency bracelet off and threw it at my feet. The world wrenched sideways, and the shimmering lights of Kingdom disappeared. Abandoned cars sat against the curb, missing tires and burned.

That's when I heard someone scream: someone who

wasn't Ari. I took off in that direction because any scream is a bad scream. I rounded the corner, and there in the middle of a gang of men was Ari. One of them was rolling on the ground, clutching at his crotch while the others laughed. I cursed this tiny dress purse with no room for my gun.

I whistled as I approached. "I've had a bad night, boys. I think it's about to get better." A couple split off to meet me. They weren't expecting what happened next. There wasn't any reason to.

I raked the first one in the eyes and followed it with a knee to the groin, grabbed the second and bent his arm until I got a nice clean snap, and let him scream for a moment to give the others something to think about. Ari swung a broken bottle and hit one of them in the head. He fell like a bag of sand and the others decided they were done.

I walked up to her and gave her assailant a kick. "Sorry I missed the fireworks." She had been crying, but it was anger as much as fear or sorrow. I heard the thugs in the alley. They were coming back, and this time they were bringing friends. "Take off your shoes," I said, and she did. We ran. I think they followed for a few blocks, but we ran all the way, all the way down and across, and we didn't stop until we hit the gates, where Evangeline was waiting.

As we spun through the city, Ari drooped over and dozed. Evangeline clicked on the light to check on her. "Some night, M. We're going to have trouble with the queen, you know."

"Yeah, but she's not who worries me."

"Something worse than an angry royal?"

"You have no idea."

Twenty-Four

~

I GOT TO the Agency bright and early the next day. The waiting room was empty—Rosa had put a closed sign on the door and hung signs that read "Caution, Biohazard," "Now Entering Tuberculosis Infection Zone," and "Jehovah's Witness Meeting Today!" at various places in the halls. Even the most desperate wishers wouldn't risk catching Jehovulosis.

I entered the conference room, which normally only held this many people on poker night. Jess and Clara, Evangeline, Ari, and myself.

Grimm waited while Jess and Clara took turns giving Ari hugs, and then cleared his throat. "We are no closer to finding the Seal, despite your exemplary efforts. The fae, on the other hand, grow restless. The fae realm lies exposed, and they believe someone in this world holds their Seal."

"Plus," I said, "there's a fairy godmother in town." In the silence that followed I watched Grimm digest this.

"Marissa, I would ask if you were certain, but I know the answer." Grimm crossed his arms and looked at me over his glasses.

"That's crazy," said Clara. "You gonna let her move in on you?"

"No, I am not." Grimm kept his voice calm and low, with an unmistakable threat in his tone. "At the moment, there are certain problems. Foremost, that I have no idea where she might actually be."

"Do the bunny thing, and then mug her in an alley," I said. "It worked on me."

Grimm shook his head. "You need to read more. I can't enter another fairy's domain any more than she could mine. The traditional way is to break her original mirror. As I stated, we don't know where it is."

"Then rumble with her directly." Clara sat forward at the table like she was giving orders to him. "Even if you can't approach her, you could make it bad enough that she'd move on. These tweens you hire nowadays might not understand, but I've seen what you can do."

Grimm closed his eyes. "You have seen what I can do against normal creatures. Weaklings, like the fae, or the demons. Fairies cannot directly interact, our powers repel. We cannot approach each other."

"Her mirror is at the hotel. She spoke to Marissa there," said Ari.

Jess gave her a look of contempt. I'd gotten that look a thousand times from Evangeline, and learned to ignore it as best I could. Ari, on the other hand, started a Mexican standoff that could only end badly for her.

"No, young lady, her mirror, her original mirror is unlikely to be at the hotel," said Grimm. "It would be somewhere safe."

Ari looked at him. "Where is yours?"

Evangeline and I exchanged uncomfortable glances. Grimm would sooner give out his bank account numbers, vault codes, and turn over every bit of Glitter he owned.

"Someplace safe," said Grimm, and Clara smiled.

"Her name is Odette. That ring a bell?" I asked Grimm.

His eyes grew slightly wider, but he kept his face impassive.

I glanced around the room. "She suggested one of us took the Seal. She offered me wishes, Grimm."

An uncomfortable silence passed over the table. I kept waiting for Clara to say something stupid like, "You better not have taken them" or "Do you have any idea what you've done," but she kept looking to Grimm. Grimm fidgeted for a moment. "May I have a word with Marissa alone?" In the stunned silence, no one moved. "That is not a request."

One by one, they filed out. The jealous glare on Evangeline's face, the accusing look Clara gave me, and the expression of worry on Ari's face only added to my nerves.

I held up my hands. "I didn't take them. She said they are weapons, and she'd hit me three times."

"Why on earth would she do that?" Grimm's look told me how much trouble I was in. I'd seen that look when people brought frog princes in after a month, when the spell was permanent, or asked if they could visit a baby a year after the imp took them.

"Because she threatened my family." I swallowed, my mouth dry. "Also I hit her with a few pieces of obsidian. The mirror bled."

Grimm scrunched up his face like I'd slapped him. "You struck a fairy with obsidian."

"She fixed the mirror with fleshing silver and the blood just disappeared." From the way he looked at me, I knew that this was a thousand times worse than the blessings. Maybe more.

"She will never forgive you." His magic reached out and surrounded me. I felt it pouring through the bracelet like hot water, enveloping me. "While you are under my protection, she cannot so much as scratch you. I worry for you, my dear. There are ways to wound that do not leave a mark."

"You know, I think it's too coincidental that a fae child goes missing, the Seal gets stolen, and then a new fairy godmother shows up in town. Remember the magic show you took me to?" He once sent me to a theater where I watched it over and over until I could spot the cues and the hand movements that gave everything away.

"I do. If this is what we are meant to see, what do we not see?"

His question reminded me of something else eating at me. "I need to use the Visions Room."

Grimm rolled his eyes. "Keep playing with those things and you'll go blind."

"This isn't about my blessings. A witch said something to me. Something I need to check out. If Ari's spirit sight is as bad as her normal vision, I wouldn't trust her to tell me how many arms I'm holding up, let alone details."

Grimm's gaze went to my hand, and I wondered if he was telling me the truth about not being able to see the mark. I'd found an engraving of it in the book, but part of me needed to know if it was really there.

"My dear, the Visions Room is undergoing maintenance. I'll have the contractors work overtime to get it functional again. Someone has been putting tiny stress fractures on the prisms."

"Grimm, if I had the handmaiden's mark, you'd tell me, right?"

He flashed over to the cream decanter. Grimm leaned in toward me and spoke softly. "Spirit sight is not one of my formidable powers, my dear, but if it were, and if I could see it, and if you did have the handmaiden's mark, I still would not tell you. The mark appeared on dozens of girls during her reign. It was a curse of its own kind. These girls were thrown out of their homes, driven away, sometimes killed for something they could neither see nor control. Most never heard her call."

At that moment, the world exploded into gunfire and crashing, and I heard screams from the back room. Grimm was gone from the mirror. By the time I made it out the door and down the hall, the Agency was silent. A hole the size of a refrigerator was smashed through the back of the office. Jess lay twitching in a pool of blood, feebly trying to move her hands.

Ari came out from under the table. "It took him. A troll."

Liam was gone. I glanced out the smashed window, and my stomach churned. Panic flooded my brain, threatening to drown me.

"Run," said Grimm, in my ear, "straight for the window, and when you get there, jump." Grimm had never recommended suicide before, so I figured he had a plan. I sprinted down the hallway at full speed to the gaping hole and did a perfect swan dive. I fell toward the ground, and as I did, I passed the troll. It was climbing its way down the building, Liam still in hand. The pavement was coming for my head, and fast.

I saw a glint of gold as the magic took shape, right before I hit the concrete. It felt like pillows, rolling into pillows. I came to my feet wondering why we didn't use this more often. The troll dropped the last story down and landed on the trunk of a car.

Twelve feet tall, wide as a truck, with muscles like chewing gum, the troll looked at me and growled like an elephant and a lion mixed together. His sallow, yellow skin had mottled spots, and each hand had three fingers, long enough they wrapped clean around Liam's rib cage.

"Stop," I said, putting a bullet in one of its feet. "Or I'll shoot." I squeezed off a few more shots at the troll's knees. It dropped Liam in a heap and came for me, but I had practiced this a dozen times. I rolled to the side as it stomped at me. I put another bullet into its knee and one in its butt. It roared with rage and kicked backwards at me. I almost made it out of the way. The foot hit me like a hammer. I heard a couple of ribs break and went flying into a windshield. Liability did not cover troll damage.

That's when Liam picked up the bumper from the car he'd been dropped on and swung it, hitting the troll right upside its runty little head.

Troll skulls were mostly bone. It turned to grab him, giving him a squeeze for good measure until he turned blue. It lumbered off, dragging him along. I shook the glass out of my hair and ran. Straight across the tops of the cars I ran, ruining six different paint jobs. At the corner I jumped onto its back.

The troll grabbed me with a free hand, bringing me around to bite with a pair of jaws like a snapping turtle. Troll eyelids were heavy bone as well, but I put one bullet into each nostril, and let that bone hold the bullet in as it bounced around. The troll fell forward and dropped us.

The troll got up exactly once, at which point Evangeline came roaring around the corner at full speed, driving her yellow convertible straight into its chest. That was the sixth convertible she'd destroyed that year. Ari came running from the building to help me up, and as she slid her arm around me, I cried out. Broken ribs hurt.

Liam kicked the troll a few times in the head, managing only to stub his toe. I think he was trying to feel like he had contributed something to its death. He limped over to me, a look of wonder in his eyes. "You jumped out a building? And attacked that thing?" He reached out to wipe a speck of blood from my hair. "Are you crazy?"

Ari put her hands on her hips and looked at him with those blue eyes of hers. "No, you idiot. She's in love."

Twenty-Five

~~~

THE NEXT FEW minutes were some of the most awkward in my life. Liam kept looking at the troll, as if he expected it to evaporate. He'd look back at me, and I wanted to evaporate. I'm honestly not sure which of us had the bigger impact on him. If you go to the bookstore and look up books on "How to tell the man you accidentally cursed after dumping him because you thought he was someone else that you still have feelings for him," you won't find any. I speak from experience.

Once Ari decided there wasn't going to be a chance of me running into his arms, she ushered me inside to have my ribs x-rayed. I got nine celebration stitches on the back of my head, and by coincidence, pink was the only suture color available. There isn't much you can do for broken ribs except wait, and so we went home. There I called Grimm, to thank him for the magic.

Grimm chuckled and gave me a smile. "Marissa, your heart went out the window first, I only thought it right you follow it. Anyway, I don't do that nearly often enough. It felt good to stretch my muscles, as it were."

"Magic is a supplement for your mind. That's what you taught me." I'd heard that statement so often my first year, I dreamed about him saying it. "How's Liam doing?"

"My dear, do you remember when you met your first harpy?" The smile fled his face and now he looked serious.

I certainly did. I stayed locked in my room for about a week, and Evangeline had to pull me out by my heel. I detest pigeons to this day. "I remember."

"It's about a hundred times worse for him. No convenient stories about accidents or terrorists or hallucinations. Though I must say, I think you had a greater impact on him than the troll."

"Thanks." I didn't mean it.

He held up his hands. "In a good way. Give him time. It occurs to me, he might be more important than I had considered. Still, you aren't doing anything for a few weeks. You need to heal."

"We don't have time. The solstice is coming, and no offense, but I don't think even you can stop the sun." If there was an emergency, we'd deal with it now. Wounds were patient and would still be with us when more pressing concerns were dealt with.

He shook his head. "We don't have time to rush into things. I have two wounded agents and a puzzle that will take all my attention to understand. You'll feel much better with rest, my dear."

He called me his agent. That meant I'd be back to work, eventually. "Grimm, why don't you have any male agents? You let men drive, guard, and haul."

Grimm's face broke into a wide grin. "If you need something broken or burned or bashed, a man will do just fine. I have nothing against them, and they do those tasks well. If you need a problem handled, you need a woman. Now rest. Heal for a few days. You've taught me something important, Marissa. I'm done driving my employees to the breaking point." He faded away, off to commit a rabbit genocide, I'm sure, trying to figure things out.

* * *

I SLEPT FOR over a day. When I finally did wake up, I decided to finish a pet project. In one of Grimm's books I'd found plans for a spirit cypher, a fancy term for a box that let me see spirits. Think of it like one of those old-time daguerreotypes, except the prism went inside instead of film.

Ari and I built the box, painted it flat black, and I snapped my spirit prism into it. I turned off the lights and held it up. "Blessing, curse, come here." Grimm's Visions Room had thousands of these, ones that bend out normal light as well. The things I saw in there had texture and color. What my project showed me looked like a badly drawn cartoon, but it worked. I recognized them. Two feet tall, mostly face, and a set of teeth that would cost me a fortune in orthodontic bills.

"Hey. I missed seeing you." They seemed to jump up and down, but it got blurry when they moved fast. "Those rocks at the ball, pretty handy. That your work?"

One of them jumped up and down, which either meant "yes" or "I need to use the litter box."

"I have a question for you two. I know you can't talk, but I bet you see magic better than Ari. Can you see this?" I held up my hand.

One of them approached. My hand looked gray and almost shapeless through the spirit cypher. My blessing opened its mouth and a tongue like an octopus tentacle slithered out. I shivered as it sniffed my hand, and licked a spot on my wrist. The hairs on my arm stood up as it did so.

"Is it the mark?"

They both jumped up and down.

"Thank you. Stay close."

GRIMM GAVE US three days before he announced we'd had enough time to recuperate. I already knew what I wanted to do.

"Grimm, I need the pie box," I said, as we sat in the conference room. Liam hunched over in the corner, looking like a man lost in a city where everyone spoke a different language.

"We've already analyzed the curse," said Grimm. As he said *curse*, Liam winced.

"Yeah, but I've been thinking, and I'm wondering more about the box it came in. Where did they get it? I'm guessing my mugger was royalty, and you know as well as I do they wouldn't waltz into a grocery store and pick up a pie. I also doubt they'd trust anyone else to handle something like that."

Liam sat up. "You called it a curse. Not a disease."

"Sir, if the term disease makes it sound more palatable, I would be willing to use it instead."

"What is it?" His hands trembled ever so slightly as he waited for the answer.

"It's a curse," I said, and I saw the hope go out of him. "A living spell that attaches to you and changes you." Since the troll attack, he no longer glared in my direction, but he didn't smile at me either. Every time I left the apartment, I thought of driving over to see him, and every time I picked up the phone, it was him I wanted to call.

"Hold on a minute," said Evangeline, "I think it's time we cleared up a few things. You," she looked at Liam. "Sorry to tell you there are bad things in the world. Even more sorry to tell you you're carrying around one of the worst. You," she said to me. "Get over him. He's never going to trust you again. You," she said to Grimm, "should have been all over the fact that someone sent a troll after him."

"Evangeline, are you finished?" asked Grimm. "I've given thought to the fact that they were willing to attack here in order to retrieve him, and the only reasonable conclusion is they mean to reclaim the curse."

Liam put his elbows on the table and his head in his hands. "I'll give it to them voluntarily if I can have my life back."

"They'll carve it out of you," said Grimm. "Strictly speaking, they push your flesh through a soul sieve. What comes out one end is sausage to feed the ghouls and what comes out the other is the curse."

"I'm no longer interested in volunteering," said Liam.

Evangeline slammed her hands on the table, her face turning red with frustration. "I don't think any of you are hearing a word I'm saying. They sent a troll. Big, ugly, and horribly slow. If M hadn't done a swan dive on it, we could have eaten lunch, driven down to the next block, and still gotten there before it."

A grin spread across my face as I understood. "Trolls move too slowly. It couldn't possibly have been meant to get away with him."

"How do you know it wasn't going to eat me?" Liam looked at me, and for a moment I saw a glimpse of the man I'd met on the pier. I felt like I'd swallowed the butterfly garden at the zoo.

"Because it could have done that in the office," I said. "Instead it climbed down with you carefully. And it wouldn't do it on its own. Trolls have to be told to eat or they'll practically starve to death. It was taking you someplace close. Or to someone close."

"All right then," said Grimm. "Marissa, you may investigate the bakery if you so desire, though I suspect your box may have come from any one of a dozen grocery stores. Evangeline, you may take the others and begin a sweep of the area. You will search for evidence of a portal; that's the most likely method for removing Mr. Stone."

Liam put his feet up on the table. "What do I do?"

"You, sir, may watch cable television on my personal HDTV," said Grimm, "and I will order you pizza, and the beer of your choice."

Liam stood up. For a moment I thought he would pull his own hair out as he clenched and unclenched his fists. When he looked up, steel resolve replaced the despair I'd seen before. "No. I didn't ask for this. I don't work for you, and I'm tired of being poked and prodded and watched like some sort of freak. I'm going to find out what happened to me and who did it. I'm going to get rid of this thing. Then I'm going back to my life, my workshop, and making little wrought-iron butterflies to sell to the tourists."

"Search is out of the question," said Evangeline. "I give it a fifty-fifty chance the portal's still active. You step on it, and you're wherever they meant to take you in the first place."

"Fine," said Liam. "Marissa, you'll take me with you to this bakery. On the way I want to know everything you know about this curse. Consider it a date."

"There you go, M. First agent in history to get a fourth date," said Evangeline.

I knew from Liam's tone it was anything but. "Okay." I looked around, wondering where my constant companions were. "Come on, blessings. You and I are going down to check out a bakery, and I'm going to need you to help keep me from blowing my diet."

"Marissa, were you hit in the head again? The MRI room is available if so." Grimm peered at me as if I'd started a conversation with a poodle that didn't involve bullets.

"No. I've been working on a relationship with my little friends. If they have to come with me everywhere, it's going to be by my permission."

"What did I tell you about feeding those things?" asked Grimm. He shook his head in frustration.

"Since when did I do as I'm told?" I asked, and grabbed my keys off the table. Inside, I knew the answer: always.

Ari grabbed my hand as we walked toward the car. "You want me to drive? You two could sit in the back."

She was hopeless, in my opinion. "Do you know how to drive?"

The look she gave me was answer enough, like I'd caught her watching the Shopping Channel with my credit card again.

I patted her on the back. "Thanks, but I choose life. I'll ask Evangeline to teach you. She taught me."

Ari looked a little queasy at the thought.

Grimm gave me the address from the pie box, and as

we drove I could tell Liam was staring at me, waiting. So I gave him the spiel about curses, and did my best to answer his questions.

He slumped back in the passenger seat until I thought he'd dozed off. When he spoke, I almost swerved. "Enough about curses. Tell me what it is you do."

"I told you already. I work for Grimm. For Fairy Godfather."

"Granting wishes?"

"Solving problems, more often. Most of the time what people wish for isn't what they need. They need their baby back from an imp, or they need a pair of deadly slippers retrieved, or they need a troll to stop punching holes in the taxicabs that drive over the bridge. People need things, and I get them done." I'd rather have crawled into a witch's oven willingly than had that conversation right there and then.

"What about me?" He still wouldn't look at me, staring pointedly out the window.

"I made a mistake. Two, actually. I was supposed to be working a prince." I knew there was no going back now. First I picked the wrong man and dumped him, and then I sent a curse his direction. Lots of women cursed their boyfriends after breaking up with them. Not every ex-boyfriend wound up transforming into a flaming lizard.

"You make it sound so romantic." His tone had grown cold as the January wind.

"Something went wrong with Grimm's auguries, and I met you instead."

"You mistook me for the guy you were supposed to be putting the moves on." When he said it like that it sounded dirty.

"Yes."

"So what was mistake number two?"

I didn't answer until we turned into the bakery parking lot. "I'd done that assignment so many times. I was lonely, and I was sad, and when I met you, it just happened—"

"So many times? How many times have you done that before?" His voice was hoarse, and I felt his anger smoldering.

"At least twelve. I forget sometimes. It's easier," I said, knowing exactly how he would take it.

He spoke in a voice cold and dull. "Do you do the same thing with all of us?" His hands gripped the leather seat rest until it nearly bent.

"Yes. Meet at the pier or someplace public. Have an accidental meal I arrange. Walk. Dance."

"Kiss," he said, and I could feel the hurt I had sliced so professionally into him.

"Yes. Then we break up, and you are ready for the princess to come into your life and put it back together. Ready to love someone. Someone else." My sense of professional pride gave way to raw shame. I'd always regarded setups as a game, but never considered that it was one I always lost.

I put the car in park, and he practically leaped out, so eager to be farther from me. "Well, you did it right. I couldn't be more ready for someone else if I tried."

Twenty-Six

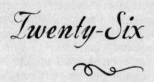

THE BAKERY LOOKED wrong from the beginning. Everyone thinks of bakeries as little shops where a fat man pulls bread in and out of ovens. Modern bakeries looked like factories, factories that should have been full of workers. As we walked through the empty lot, I knew something was wrong. At eleven o'clock in the morning there should be people everywhere. I didn't see a single fat man.

Ari checked her map. "Fairy Godfather ever get the address wrong?"

"Fifth Street Bakery" read the sign on the office door. I gave it a pull and found it locked. "Not that I've seen, but there's a first time for everything."

"Shoot the lock," said Ari. She'd obviously watched too many television shows.

"Or we could look around. Most deliveries happen at night, and at the big places, they leave supply doors unlocked so you don't have to let the truck driver in." I walked around the side of the building, with Liam and Ari trailing. Experience paid off. At the back of the building I found three delivery bays, one standing wide open. From the doorway, a sour stench billowed.

"Do all the places you go smell like this?" asked Ari. Wherever she grew up, hideous stenches didn't make too many guest appearances.

"No, most of them smell worse." Inside, the machinery still hummed as though at any moment it would start up. The huge ceiling lights flickered. I sniffed and decided I'd smelled much, much worse. I once took care of an ogre with irritable bowel syndrome after he raided a Thai buffet.

Liam pointed to a vat. "Rotten bread dough." From the oven line, I smelled the char-burned smell of wasted loaves. I heard something moving, a shuffling sound that became the patter of running feet.

Liam heard it too, and even Ari stopped her humming and backed slowly toward us.

From behind a row of ovens, a man in white leaped. Flour covered him from head to toe like a ghost, but blood ran from his mouth, and as he came, he screamed.

I swore at myself for not having my gun out. The man leaped over a stack of pallets, his arms flailing toward me, his eyes wide and empty.

Liam caught him with a gut punch. Liam was taller than me, thicker, and he had a blacksmith's arms. He about punched through the man, smashing his fist deep into the man's stomach like so much dough.

Ari stared at the man, and started squinting, even though I knew she had her contacts in. She took off at a run straight for him, shouting, "Get back! Don't touch him."

Liam ignored her and stepped on the man's chest, pinning him. Ari pushed on Liam, like a flea trying to move a bulldozer. She put her hands on the side of Liam's face, forcing him to look at her. "Can't you feel it?"

I dragged a fifty-pound bag of flour across the man, and as I stepped over him he tried to bite me.

"Get back," said Ari, pulling at my arm. She had a tone I'd never heard from her before. She leaned closer, looking at his face. Blood caked his mouth and ran from his eyes. "You," she said to me, "keep an eye out for others. Beefy, you go get another bag of flour. And don't let him touch you."

I pulled my gun, scanning rows of assembly lines. "Want to explain what I'm looking for?"

Ari put her hand on the man's forehead. "Others. He's probably killed them all by now, but if there are others, it would be bad." She knelt on the man's wrist so he couldn't scratch her.

I watched the empty floor, stealing occasional glances at her. "You said no touching."

"You're not a princess, and Liam's not a prince. It won't affect me the same way. It's magic. Some sort of poison." Her voice had this weird echo to it as she spoke, and the magic that drifted off of her looked like a snowstorm.

Liam lumped a couple more bags on the man's legs and arms. "Is everyone around here crazy?"

I could live with his anger at me, maybe. I didn't feel like letting him direct it at Ari. "She's not crazy. She's a princess and the seal bearer for her house. She's also my friend."

"How long were you hired to be her friend for? What the hell is she doing?"

Ari knelt over the man. I recognized the feeling of static electricity that swept across me. A wind whipped through the bakery, sending tiny tornadoes of flour spinning, but Ari wasn't paying any attention. With an ease that made me nervous, she gathered her power.

She held her hand over his head and closed her eyes. A green mist seeped from his nose and mouth, forming a cloud above him. The mist solidified, taking the form of her family crest for a moment, and then the wind rushed in and tore it away. Ari fell over, crumpling to the ground.

The man opened his eyes. "Where am I?"

I ignored him, rolling Ari over. She was breathing, thank goodness.

"What did you do?" I asked, brushing her hair out of her eyes.

She tried to sit up. "He was poisoned. I took it out."

When she made the foxfire, it took her days to feel better. Either she was getting better at magic or curing poison wasn't as hard, because she didn't look like death this time. Sweat rolled down her face and her hair clung to her face. If I'd known that magic was that much of a workout, I'd have said forget the laps, and made her sling spells.

"Where am I?" the man asked again.

"You're in a bakery," said Liam, "and that stuff on your mouth and face is blood."

The man's hands went to his face. His fingers ended in bloody stubs where he'd torn the fingernails out. His crusted lips quivered as he spoke. "Accident. There was an accident."

"What happened?" I asked, leaning over him.

"Too many hours straight, I told them. Too dangerous, but they insisted. She said a war was coming."

Ari failed to get up for the fourth time. "I need to rest."

Liam walked over and hoisted her like a two-penny nail. He carried her over to the office. Plenty of nice chairs in there, for sure.

I held up my phone. It showed a picture of the heart seeker, coiled up lifeless on Grimm's desk. "I'm looking for something."

His eyes went wide. "I didn't know you worked for her. Please don't hurt me. Just take them and go. They are in the kitchen." With his free hand, he pointed to a small kitchen where they tested dough before large-scale production.

Inside, the stench of rotten food and something wet and dark filled the air. Where the light cut in from the doorway, a hand lay, smeared in blood. I felt for the light and clicked it on. I caught my breath. Bodies lay scattered across the floor, but I'd seen a lot of bodies, and that didn't bother me anymore. On the center island stood a baker's rack, and on every level were rows and rows of apples.

Now, you might be tempted to think I had an allergy to apples, or I considered myself more of a citrus girl, but those apples were only related to fruit in the same way a hand grenade was related to a pineapple. They oozed magic. It took every ounce of will I had to avoid touching one.

Apples went out of style as weaponry about four hundred years ago, at least. See, until the invention of the explosive shell, you had to convince your enemy to actually take a bite. It only took one or two times of seeing a prince turned to applesauce that people started eating oranges instead.

The invention of the explosive candy shell was supposed to be the next big thing, but by that time there were easier ways to kill people. Only witches and hags still considered apples a decent form of self-defense, because of who they most often used them against: each other.

Poison apples worked best against those with magic in them. The explosions made hamburger out of a normal person. If you had a protection spell, the goo the apple scattered ate away at the spell, and then snacked on the person. The more magic, the better it worked, unless you were a princess, of course. For them, the worst thing that happened if they ate a poisoned apple was they got to take a nap. Those girls got all the breaks.

I took a few steps farther in, checking the other bodies. The smell nearly overwhelmed me.

Liam came to the door and stood looking at the carnage. He'd obviously never seen death firsthand. He recoiled, forcing his eyes closed, with an awful grimace. People only did that the first five or six times they saw a massacre. "What the hell happened in here?"

"You might want to stay back." I opened my compact and called Grimm. "You probably want to see this."

His eyes appeared in the compact and I moved it around so he could get a full view. Grimm spoke with authority, his voice deeper, his tone grave. "Marissa, get out of there. I will call the hazmat team immediately. Don't let anyone into the building."

I closed the compact, and that's when the feeling hit. The feeling of being watched, like I had at the ball. "Where are you?" I shouted to the empty room. The whole place was stainless steel, where it wasn't spattered with blood. "I know you're watching." I felt a hand on my wrist and nearly broke Liam's nose.

"Come on. You heard your boss."

A particular body caught my eye, one that lay across a serving platter. A body sheared in half like a giant razor blade had cut it off at the waist. The platter was an old one; black tarnish marked it as true silver. The edge I could see was dull gray, the same color I had seen in the feast room in Kingdom. Fleshing silver. I reached out, pulled the body over, and recoiled. The body was Clara, her eyes dark pools of blood. The other half of her body had to still be wherever the mirror once led.

"Come on," said Liam, giving my arm a pull.

Before I could move she spoke.

"Most have the sense to fear me, darling," said the Fairy Godmother, her voice coming from Clara's ruined face. "Or flee if they live under my shadow."

A mist blanketed the world, the way it had when the Fae Mother spoke to me. I felt Liam pull on my arm, or some-one's arm, and he was yelling, I think.

"Once you strike me, and thrice I return it. Your desires are delicious. What shall I give you, that you may under-stand the error of your ways?"

I fought to let go of the mirror but it stuck to my finger-tips like frozen steel. "I don't want anything from you."

"No, but you do want something. Your family. For your first wish I give you the truth of your family."

Something like a train hit me, and I landed in snow. Maybe not snow, the memory of it, cold and cutting and bitter. "Stop interfering," said Fairy Godmother, though not to me. "On second thought, there's always room for one more." Someone joined me in the memory. I knew with a sinking heart it was Liam, meshed in her spell.

"You've forgotten so much, darling, about your parents' wish. I give it back to you and more. The important part isn't the what. It's the why."

I would have told her off, but I could neither speak nor

move. The memories started to come back. This was my
house. I remembered so much about it, baking cookies and
playing in the tree and a thousand days of summer. A smile
came to my heart as I realized I knew where home was. I
remembered everything.

Mom and Dad stood outside in the wind and the cold,
and they were fighting. Mom's raven black hair held down
in her hood. She grabbed Dad's hand. "There isn't time.
We must call him now." As she said it, I knew what night
this was, and a sickness swept over me.

"There's got to be another way," said Dad. I remembered him holding me, the way he smelled of shaving
cream, aftershave, and how rough his chin was. His eyes
were as blue as hers.

"They are lovely," said Godmother. "So unlike you.
Where did you get those plain brown eyes?"

My mother turned her back, facing the storm so it
lashed her. "It's the only way, Roland. He'll take good care
of her, and when she's free, she can return to you."

"To us." I saw the hurt on my dad's face, along with determination. His hands were balled into fists, his entire body
tense.

Mom dropped his hand. "She wasn't yours to begin
with, and she's not mine. I've raised her for you, but it isn't
the same. Not the way Hope is."

Dad shuffled his feet, kicking at the snow. "Make the
call."

Godmother ripped the world from me and formed it
again, oozing into place like molten wax. I was sixteen,
with too much makeup and my hair looked like it was at
war with my head. I sat at our kitchen table, Mom and Dad
behind me. On the table stood my makeup mirror, and in
the convex side I looked like a clown.

Grimm looked out from the mirror, and the look on my
younger face was one of awe as he spoke. "This isn't how
things normally work. Roland, I didn't expect to hear from
you again."

"You know why we called you," said Mom.

"I do," said Grimm. "Young lady, do you understand?"

I didn't. I couldn't, but my teen-self looked to Dad and nodded.

"You would work for me only until their debt is paid," said Grimm.

I knew now how long that could be. Teen me was all too eager to please. "I'm getting a job at the Burger Hut this summer to practice."

Grimm laughed. "I'm sure you will do wonderfully, Marissa. So do we have an agreement?"

I looked at Dad and he nodded. Mom wouldn't look at me, but I knew what she wanted. What I wanted more than anything was to please her.

"You will fix Hope?" I watched Grimm with all my teenage skills of lie detection.

"I give you my word, young lady."

Young me paused and looked up to Mom. Even at sixteen I had the good sense to think before I acted. "How long will this take?"

"It doesn't matter," said Mom. "You'll be an adult soon. You're getting a head start, Marissa."

Young me glanced back to Grimm, and I saw a tiny smile flicker across Mom's face. "I'll do it."

"Then it is done," said Grimm.

Mom hugged Dad and started crying.

Young me felt something at her wrist and held it up. A tiny gold chain hung from it. "That's amazing," she said.

Grimm began to fade away. "I give these to all my employees. I am never far away now. Call me if you need anything."

"How many years," said Fairy Godmother, whispering, "have you traded your freedom for their happiness?" If I had a mouth to scream, lungs to sob, or eyes to cry, I would have. A cry of despair rose within me, but without an outlet, it could not drown out her whisper. "Twice more, child, and then you may ask for your death."

The floor stank of blood and sour and death, and yet the feeling and smell was so rich it was actually good. I blinked and had eyes.

Liam loomed over me, looking like a giant. "Here," he said, picking me up like a bag of flour, "We're getting out of the building like the mirror man said." He cupped his hands and yelled. "Princess, move it."

With his help, I limped to the door.

Ari came walking out of the offices with a box of papers. Her jaw was set and her free hand clenched in a fist. "I told you to call me Ari."

I was lost in memories I'd dreamed of having back, dreams that I knew would be nightmares from now on. I remembered it all. The fighting, the crying. The endless meetings with doctors that had culminated that night. The night my parents had traded me to Grimm.

Ari came running to me. "M, are you all right?"

I couldn't answer. I could barely walk. Only Liam's incessant pull on my hand kept me moving long enough to make it out of the building. The hazmat team came pouring in, followed by the bomb squad, and the police.

"I'll drive us back to the Agency," said Ari.

I tossed the keys toward her. At least it would be entertaining to see her try.

Liam caught them, holding them out of her reach. "I want to live."

When we got back to the Agency, I stayed in the car, in the dark parking garage. I still heard Fairy Godmother's voice in my head, and the images wouldn't go away. I knew now why I'd made a deal with Grimm to hide my memories.

"I'm sorry," said Grimm from the rearview mirror, "Liam has explained what she did."

"He knew it was a spell?"

"He knew it was something. It's not the sort of thing he would forget. Nor will you now. If I attempt to modify your memories again, it might kill you."

I sat up and my head spun, or the world spun around me. "You said she couldn't hurt me."

"Marissa, I said she couldn't so much as scratch you. I never said she couldn't hurt you. That would have been a lie."

I grasped for reasons, anything that would make what I saw, what I knew, untrue. "Would she tell me the truth?"

Grimm didn't answer immediately. He rubbed his forehead with one hand. "If it hurt you worse than a lie? Absolutely. You will understand in time what a parent would do to save their child. For now I would like you to come and speak with Ari. She's proven herself resourceful, and you should see this. There will be plenty of time for tears later."

There's always plenty of time for tears.

I went through the front door of the Agency and plowed through a crowd of people who didn't get the meaning of the term *no appointments*. In the conference room, Ari stood at the head of the table, the box of papers beside her.

She looked at me and the fierce expression on her face softened. "M, I'm sorry to bother you. I thought you would want to know. In the office I started going through their files, trying to figure out how long it had been shut down. No bread baked there for over a month."

She passed around an order form. "On the other hand, they've gotten sixteen shipments like this."

Liam looked at it a moment. "Someone's got an aversion to doctors."

I snagged the paper from him. Apples. Thousands of apples. I looked to Grimm. "They doing what I think they're doing?"

"Yes. Someone is preparing for a war."

"Run down the owner of the bakery, and you'll find out who," I said.

Ari gave me that smile of hers. She pulled out another paper. "I can help there."

"'Health inspection schedule for part C,'" I read.

Ari shook her head. She tapped the company letterhead, and Evangeline let out a low whistle. "Is that what I think it is?" she asked, though I was certain she was right.

Ari traced the letterhead with a finger. "My family crest."

Twenty-Seven

LIAM TOOK THE report. "That's the symbol that appeared in the smoke when you did your hocus pocus on the man."

"She's her family's seal bearer," I said. "All her magic has that mark, or it will." Everyone stared at Ari. At least for once it wasn't me.

Grimm cleared his throat. "Did I hear that wrong? Or did Mr. Stone say the princess was using magic?" He kept his tone soft and calm, but I've heard him speak like that before.

"So what did you find?" I asked Evangeline, hoping for a quick topic change.

Ari had this worried look on her face. "I've been learning it myself from the books you sent." I needed to work with that girl on when to keep her mouth shut. Come to think of it, I needed help with that myself. Perhaps we could take a class together.

"We found nothing," said Evangeline. "We searched three blocks in every direction, and there's nothing. I don't know where the troll was headed, but it wasn't going to a portal. Maybe they were going to pick it up with a dump truck or something."

"You are not to use magic," said Grimm. The building trembled slightly, and a corner of his mirror split. "Magic can be deadly, young lady, particularly wild magic."

Ari shook her head, but her voice stuttered as she spoke. "I'm not using wild magic."

Grimm's face was bright red, and splits appeared in the mirror from the edges as he screamed, "*Of course you are!* Those books were meant for Marissa. They were training lessons for an entire generation of witches. Seal magic is impossible to learn on your own. Training takes years and it must be learned from one who already knows how to control it.

"You have taken the first step down the path of the witch, princess. Think long and hard about how far down that road you wish to go." He turned that gaze on me, like a school principal and cop in one. "What on earth possessed you to share those with her?"

Desperate to divert him, I brought up what I'd wanted to tell him, meant to tell him the moment we got a bit of privacy. "Clara," I said. "Clara was at the bakery. She's dead." It stopped him in mid-rant, and I heard a tiny squeak I knew had to be Jess. "What was she doing there?"

Grimm looked shocked. He wavered in the glass, his image becoming fuzzy, and then sharp again. "She was visiting with Queen Mihail when last we spoke," said Grimm.

Jess and Evangeline stood up together. "We're going to go see her," said Evangeline.

"I've got a few enhanced interrogation techniques that will have her telling me anything and everything," said Jess.

"You will not," said Grimm. "I share your desire for blood, but I require proof. Since it is trouble you desire, I would like you to accompany the Kingdom Police to see Queen Thromson. It is her company who was manufacturing these weapons, and she knows full well what they were meant for."

Liam raised his hand like he was in school. "I actually don't know what they were meant for."

"Mr. Stone, they are weapons nearly perfect for killing

the fae," said Grimm. "Someone wants a war. Marissa, you will go and revisit Queen Mihail. Ask her what Clara was looking into. I will not rest until her killer is in the ground."

Not justice, I noted, revenge. Given how Jess looked at the moment, wherever she went off, there'd be more bodies than the city morgue could hold.

"Princess, no more magic. We will discuss this matter more when time is not of the essence."

Ari wiped her eyes. "Yes, sir."

"Grimm, can you tell me if Queen Thromson was the one who mugged me? The curse came in her pie box from her factory. Also, I need something to keep Ari in Kingdom," I said.

The dais at the head of the table glowed as Grimm invoked his power, and a tiny gold band dropped onto the table. A ring.

"I will research Queen's Thromson's whereabouts. The ring will last until midnight," said Grimm.

Typical. I flipped it to Ari and we headed out.

"I'm coming with you," said Liam as we rode down to the garage. "I'd like to meet the man who was supposed to get my curse."

I thought of Mihail. "Trust me, you don't." I wondered if he would ever trust me.

I knew I should head into Kingdom immediately, but I sat behind the wheel, drumming my hands. An idea kept flitting in the corner of my mind. The more I looked, the more it retreated to the periphery.

"Are we going to actually, I don't know, go somewhere?" asked Ari.

I put the car in gear and drove out in a way that would make Evangeline proud. We hit the interstate and I pushed the pedal down to the floor.

"Where exactly are we going?" asked Liam as the yellow stripes flew by in a blur.

"Back. Back to where this started." The more I thought about it, the more certain I was.

"How do you know where it began?" asked Ari. She'd

called shotgun and forced Liam to fold himself into a pretzel to sit in the backseat.

"Simple." I caught my exit. "It's where my life went crazy."

"You jumped out of a window after a troll," said Liam. "Crazy you've got."

"Troll's nothing," said Ari. "Tell him what you told me about the shaman. Or the orphans. For that matter tell him about the beanstalk."

I let the miles roll away in silence, working up the courage to speak. "I jumped out after you." We pulled off at a gas station and bought four bags of supplies. I believed in being prepared.

Ari had waited in the car, reading a magazine. When we hit the road again, she wouldn't leave well enough alone. "From what Grimm tells me, your life has only gotten better this year."

I shook my head, confused. "What do you mean, 'from what he tells you'? What did he tell you?" Grimm knew most of my secrets. He probably knew them all, but was too much of a gentleman to mention it.

"We talk from time to time, but like I said, I don't think you had it too good to start."

I smacked my hands on the wheel. "I was Grimm's most trusted agent. I had my own office. I was almost halfway done paying off my debt, and even the freaking gremlins stayed out of my way when I went into Kingdom."

Ari turned the page of her magazine. "You had an empty apartment. You had a phone in your apartment that never rang. You had four forms of life in your fridge that could probably survive on Mars. I think what I found in my closet was a cat."

"You found Mr. Sniffers? How is he?" I was both elated and terrified by this.

"Flat." Ari put down the magazine to look at me, which bugged me since I had to keep my eyes on the road. "What kind of life did you think you had?"

I glanced in the rearview mirror at Liam, wondering

why Ari chose now to bring this up. Then I realized I didn't have any dignity left where he was concerned. "I didn't worry about now. I kept thinking about when I'd be done, princess." I didn't need to say that dream was gone. I might one day talk to my parents, but things would never be the same now that I knew.

Ari watched out the window as the dairy lands rolled past, and my stomach felt heavy with guilt. I knew how she hated to be reminded of her title. I risked taking my eyes off the road long enough to look her in the eye. "I'm sorry. I always thought there'd be something for me beyond this."

Ari reached over and took my hand and squeezed it until I was sure my bones would crack. "Then make something. You never told me what your name was. Your real name."

I thought about it a moment. Marissa Lambert didn't fit me anymore. I didn't even want their name. Not now that I knew the truth. Even thinking about it made me sick. I wasn't going to cry in front of Liam. "Locks. My name is Marissa Locks."

Ari narrowed her eyes and frowned. "That's the name he gave you."

"No, it's the name I'm taking for myself. It'll save me a fortune in monogramming and a trip to the DMV. It's my name now. Grimm can call his new girls something else." I cut the wheel and slid onto the dirt roads.

"Here?" asked Ari, recognizing the smokehouses, and I nodded.

"Where is 'here'?" asked Liam.

"Wolf town," I said. "Stay in the car."

We got out. Wolf town still stank of rotten meat and death, but I knew we weren't alone from the moment my shoes hit the gravel. A few of the smokehouses were going, trails of ash winding from their chimneys into the sky.

"Careful," I told Ari, "I don't want to piss them off if I can help it." The car door opened behind me and I heard Liam step out. "I said to stay in the car."

He walked up behind me so close I could smell the wood

smoke on him, that scent he always had. "I've been twisted into a yoga position for the last hour. If I don't stretch, I'm going to die of a blood clot."

"Wolves," I yelled, my own voice echoing back, "I'm not here for trouble. I want to find out what happened." In the shadows I heard footsteps and paws on gravel. My arm ached with the memory of my bargaining trip.

"Look out," said Ari, and I saw a wolf come running out from between the buildings on all fours, at full speed, straight for Liam. Why it was the thugs always went for the man I didn't know, but I was ready this time. I shot it in the stomach. I aimed for the chest but wolves run fast.

Liam looked more than a little queasy at the spray of blood. "When you said wolf town, I didn't think you meant wolves."

"Keep an eye on that one." I waited, listening to the sound of cows in the distance.

Liam waved to me. "Hey, um, you might want to—Oh, crap." His eyes grew wide and his jaw went slack. The wolf continued to morph, growing longer, skinnier, and uglier. Liam took another nervous step away and backed into me. "Werewolf?"

"Just wolf." I went over to have a talk. "I said I'm here to look."

The wolf pushed the bullet out of the wound, and it dropped into the gravel. "You're back to kill us. Back to finish what you started."

I shook my head. "If I wanted to kill you, I'd have packed silver or maybe the flamethrower. I need to look around. You wolves leave me and my friends alone, we'll take the unguided tour and leave, okay? If you'd waited, I would have offered you a trade."

I walked back to the car and returned with my plastic bags.

"What is this?" asked the wolf.

"Every piece of beef jerky in the store, lunch meat, and two cans of bacon bits. We didn't have time to go to the pig farm."

He sniffed it and looked at the label. "There's a month's worth of sodium in one of these. You are trying to kill us."

"Take it or leave it. We want to look."

The wolf rose and snarled at me. "How about I carve something better out of you?"

I stood my ground. I needed to figure things out, and I was certain this was the place. "You don't want to do that." I looked at Liam. "He's cursed. Take the wrong bite and you might wind up with it too. I drink so much caffeine my blood should be a controlled substance, and I eat so much junk food I'm considered an additive by the FDA."

The wolf looked at Ari. "She looks tasty."

"Princess."

He spat on the ground in disgust and opened a can of bacon bits. Once he'd consumed the can, the wolf grinned at me with almost human teeth, baring them in a smile that looked all too hungry. "Next time bring pigs."

I went back and shut the trunk. Ari came up behind me and grabbed my shoulder. "Why didn't he want to eat me?" She almost sounded upset.

I patted her on the back. "I've heard princesses taste like gym socks boiled in iodine. Didn't you ever wonder why the dragon never eats the princess?"

She sniffed her hand and tentatively touched her tongue to the back of it. I went back to the wolf. "How did the fae child wind up here?" I took the safety off the gun for emphasis.

"A gift. Payment." He backed away, none too eager to get another bullet.

"For what?"

"Figure it out yourself, Red."

I wish I'd picked something else to wear on my first visit. I turned away from the wolf. "Come on." Liam followed me. I went to the bar first, trying to figure out what it was that had bothered me so much last time.

"So what are we looking for?" asked Liam as we walked across the street.

I opened the door and a plague's worth of flies flew out.

The inside smelled like someone had combined a morgue and a Crock-Pot. "I don't know."

He left what little food he'd eaten in a puddle at the door. I walked through the bar as my eyes adjusted to the dim lights. Each step sent tornados of flies up behind me. At the back, I swiped a glass and the nearest bottle.

Liam came along, trying to dodge flies. I held out a glass. "Drink?"

He mumbled something through his sleeve as I wiped a fly from my glass. I'm fairly sure it was something along the lines of "How can you drink in here?"

"You get used to it. Not my first massacre cleanup."

He took the drink and managed to down most of it.

I looked over the bar at the dead bartender. "They were just sitting here. Drinking their beer, watching the game. The fae came in and killed them all." I took a closer look at the bodies closest to me. Like those by the door, their skin lay in crumpled heaps near the wall.

Liam still looked sick, so I grabbed a bowl of peanuts from the end of the bar. "Take a handful of peanuts. It'll help calm your stomach and keep the smell out of your nose."

He looked at the bowl in the dim light, and sniffed it.

"I ate at Froni's with you. This place couldn't possibly be any dirtier. Have a peanut."

He took one out and chewed it, then choked, spit it out, and wretched over the bar. "Not a peanut. I think it was an earlobe." After a moment, he regained control of his stomach. "What does this?" He managed to speak and cover his mouth at the same time, as he gestured to the bodies.

"Fae magic. Big white beam of death. Solid concrete would stop it, but most buildings around here are cinderblock or wood. They cast it from the door and killed everyone."

Liam slipped off his stool and headed to the door. Leaving, I guessed, for air with fewer legs and wings. He stopped at the door and turned around. As he walked from side to side I watched his gaze, and in an instant I understood.

I walked to the door and looked. When last I came here it was too ugly, too bad for me to tell, but now I saw the same thing he did. There was no way someone had stood at the door and done this—the wolves at the bar and the wolves at the back were killed from the same direction. We hit the door and ran out into the air, which smelled so sweet.

I looked around. "Where's Ari?" I'd left her by the car, but now the square stood empty. I ran through the wolf town, listening for footsteps in the shadows, hearing a door shut somewhere. "Ari!" I yelled, and Liam came after me. "If you hurt her, I'll finish what the fae started." No one answered. Above the wind, I heard her soft sobbing.

I followed it back, back closer to the square, to the wolf larder. The door stood open and in the shadows Ari knelt, tears streaming down her face. "You can't tell, can you? You don't know what happened here."

"What was it?" I went over and stood by her.

"Death. It didn't kill them the normal way. It tore them out of their bodies. Smeared their souls across the ground."

I took her shoulders and turned her away. "You didn't say anything about this last time."

"I've used a lot more magic. I see better now."

"What were you doing here in the first place?" asked Liam, and I told him. About the wolves. About the pigs. About the kids. "You come down every week to negotiate with wolves. To trade for children?" He'd had a lot to take in in the last few weeks.

"Every week. They've always found new ones."

He looked inside the larder and winced, growing pale. "What if you skip a week?"

I shook my head. "They'll make fresh bacon bits. They had a fae child."

"I can tell. It's like a footprint in the magic. He was here a few days at least." Ari put her hand out toward the door, like she could reach out and help them.

"The wolves ate one of these fae?" asked Liam.

"No," I said. "If they had, the fae would have already killed every living thing in the state. They took a fae child.

The question is how they got to him in the first place." I walked out of the larder and back into the square, gauging a line from the bar. Grimm made me take geometry twice, the second time on my own dime. I hated him for it then and loved him for it now.

The blast that killed the wolves in the bar and the children in the larder had come from the same point, and I walked back along the buildings, peeking in through windows to confirm my theory.

Ari followed me with Liam behind her. "Marissa saved him." I ignored her story. I'd either come out sounding like a commando or a clown, I was sure.

At the far end of wolf town stood a barn. The white paint curled on the doors and the roof sagged inward, but the blast line led straight up to it. I pulled on the door and it didn't budge. Liam braced his foot against the door. "Let me help." He strained until it slid back.

Ari held out a hand, reaching for something I could not see. "It was here." She focused on nothing, her eyes looking beyond the dirt in the barn. "The seal was here."

"How do you know?" I asked, but I knew that tone. She wouldn't have said anything if she wasn't sure.

"I can feel it. They took it through here."

I walked into the barn, looking at the smooth dirt, and a pattern in it caught my eye. I took an LED flashlight from my purse and shone it on the floor. It was only part dirt. A block of marble, black with gold veins stuck out in the center, and carved on it I saw runes—runes I recognized.

I opened my compact. "Grimm."

His eyes appeared and widened in surprise. "I thought you were headed into Kingdom." I wasn't sure if it was annoyance or amusement in his voice.

"I keep hearing I need to make better decisions. So I did. You know those books you sent me?" I didn't wait for him to answer as I turned the compact to show him the engravings. "The seal came through here. That's some sort of gate, but not one I've seen you use."

"That is not a realm gate," said Grimm, his voice dull

as he worked to control his emotions. "Turn around and look behind you."

I did and shuffled along in the dirt until my toe ran across something. Liam and Ari helped me rake away the dirt. This circle I recognized. It looked like the standard gates I'd hop on to go to Avalon or anywhere else.

I ran my finger over the engravings. "Isn't this missing the directional runes?" I did read those books, and while I couldn't activate a gate at all, I understood the basic concepts.

"Indeed," said Grimm, "one could bypass the realm seal and appear almost anywhere." That someone would have to be completely crazy. Without directional runes, a gate flickered between a thousand points. The odds of winding up half in one and half in another were better than I liked. Traveling through a realm gate with no directional runes might save baggage fees, but it was a sure way to wind up in several pieces.

"So what is this?" asked Liam, walking on the black marble.

"It is a demesne altar," said Grimm. "With it one could go directly into a fairy's demesne. Perhaps even to their home."

"You know, you've never even had me over for dinner," I said.

"My dear, a fairy's home is like the fae realm, only a thousand times stronger. You'd be insane before we had cocktails."

I looked from gate to gate. "So someone takes the Seal out through here, and through that thing. I'm pretty sure they didn't take it to you, so I'd bet on Godmother. Grimm, we're getting out of here and heading into Kingdom."

"Be careful, Marissa. It took me over a month and three dozen pigs to make up for your choice of uniform last time. I'd like you on your way."

Standing here I once more felt the wolf's teeth tearing into me and I shivered. "Don't worry. I'm not considering renting a place. The whole town makes my arm hurt."

"Why?" asked Liam.

I didn't feel like recounting my bad decision making to him. "Our world doesn't look like this to the fae. The boy could barely move. The wolves were coming, and I didn't have time to get him and me into the van. So one of them wound up taking a nice chunk out of my arm."

Liam walked over, and I pulled back my sleeve to show the jagged scars that ran along my arm. "You fought with one of those things over a kid you don't even know?" He looked at me with surprise as we walked to the entrance of the barn. "How did you keep them away from the kid?"

"I was wearing a red jumpsuit with a hood. Created a diplomatic incident, from what I gather. And yes, I picked a fight with them. It's my job."

A guttural growl came from outside the barn, and I saw a tiny pack of wolves had gathered. "Little Red Riding Hood came back," said one of them. "Not even a huntsman could save you this time."

"Help," I said, and Ari and Liam helped me slide the barn door shut. A wolf thrust his hand in as it closed, and we smashed it with the door. Outside, the shouts became growls and howls.

"We can kill them," said Liam. "Wolves may be big, but they aren't that big." Something slammed into the barn door, cracking a plank.

"These might be the extra-large variety," Ari said.

I looked up at the old hayloft. At the top was a hay door, and the wolves wouldn't be at that end. Another blow nearly punched through the wall in one spot.

I pointed to the ladder. "You two, up into the loft and out the hay door. You'll have to jump and run." I took the car keys from my pocket and tossed them past a disappointed Ari.

Liam caught them backhand. "What are you going to do?"

"Keep them occupied. Get to the car, get back to the Agency."

Liam crossed his arms, and Ari put her hands on her hips.

Behind me, an enraged wolf nearly ripped the door off the rails.

"You," I said to Ari. "You are my responsibility. And you," I said to Liam, "are my fault. Get back to the car, get out of here."

The wolf tore a plank loose and stuck his head in. "No peeking," I said, and rewarded him with a bullet.

Ari gathered in magic. "I'm not leaving you."

Liam nodded, and rolled up his flannel sleeves. "I think I'm done running."

I had an idea. I hit my bracelet, since I didn't have time for the compact. "Grimm, can that altar take us to your demesne?"

"Traffic jam?" asked Grimm.

"Wolves. They want to lodge a complaint about my hood, in my spleen." I emptied one clip on anything that moved or tried to reach through the broken planks, and slammed my spare into the gun.

The marble began to glow. "Hold on, this will take a moment to get ready." The runes were etched with gold and they began to pulse, slowly, then faster. With a roar, the alpha wolf tore loose another plank and pushed through the door.

I shot him twice, and he landed on his knees, laughing. He stood up and began to walk toward me as I sent bullet after bullet into him. I dodged one swipe from his claw, but he wasn't putting a lot of effort into it. I realized why. Other wolves were climbing in behind him, squeezing through the ruined door.

Ari yelled, not a scream, but something like anger and fear in one. A bolt of lightning leaped from her to set the fur of two of them on fire. The first wolf leaped backwards.

Liam walked toward the wolf. Whatever he was cursed with, the bracelet was barely holding it in check, because I heard the curse speaking in a voice like gravel. "Bad doggie. How about playing with me?" In his hands he held a hay fork, long curved tines rusted from years of disuse.

"Grimm," I said, "We need to be going now."

Like the dais in his office, the altar shone like a spotlight, a shaft of golden light illuminating the barn. "Almost ready, my dear."

The alpha wolf swung at Liam, and he ducked. Liam hit the wolf with the handle end of the fork, first in the head, then in the stomach. Liam raised the pitchfork with both hands and gave a guttural shout. He slammed it down, ramming the tines through the wolf's leg, clean into the dirt. The wolf howled in pain and backhanded him. As Liam rolled up, I saw blood leaking from three slices on his head.

"Come," said Grimm. I grabbed Ari and pulled her toward the altar, which now shone a rainbow into the darkness of the barn. With a howl, the alpha wolf ripped the tines from his leg, tearing loose a tendon.

We ran, Liam and Ari and I, straight for the altar. As the light engulfed me I looked over my shoulder. The alpha wolf came for us, loping on four legs. He gathered himself and flew through the air, fangs bared. Then we were nowhere.

Twenty-Eight

~∾~

ONLY A MOMENT of blinding light separated me from the wolf. I landed at a run, stumbled onto the carpet, and smashed my thigh against a table. Ari slammed into me, giving me another bruise, and I could only hold my breath as Liam repeated it. We landed in the back room of the Agency. Filing boxes, plaster statues, and lava lamps from the sixties covered the floor. "This is your demesne?"

"Of course it is." said Grimm. "Where else would I need to exercise my power? Mr. Stone, those wounds on your head require stitches. Princess, you may clean up in our wardrobe department, and Marissa, I'd like to see you in my office."

Grimm waited in his office for me. As I limped in, he looked over me with concern.

I figured a preemptive strike might get me out of trouble for disobeying him. "Where'd the wolves go?"

He gave a small laugh. "Empowering the portal takes time and effort. Changing where it goes is trivial."

"So where exactly did they wind up?"

"Have you ever seen the inside of an active volcano?

They have." Grimm gave me a wide grin. Maximum effect for minimum magic was his modus operandi.

That's when the building started to shake. At first, it felt like a minor earthquake. The building began to sway ever so slightly.

Grimm shouted, "Marissa, into the Visions Room, immediately." I ran as fast as I could, through the halls, and locked myself inside. The crystals began to shiver and hum.

"Grimm? What's going on?" Inside the room, everything glowed an eerie purple.

I heard his voice from outside. "My dear, I told you your blessings would object to being separated from you. The portal took you, but not them."

The crystals rattled like wind chimes, then one split, and another. A fountain of white light shot through the wall, two orbs of that rocketed toward me. They blew through me, leaving my hair standing on end, and circled me so quickly it looked like I stood in a tornado of white.

"Beatus, Consecro, calm down." As I spoke their names, the white glow intensified. Another set of crystals shattered, but they slowed down, becoming visible as distinct orbs of white. At last they hovered in the air, out of my reach. I couldn't tell if the expression on their sharklike faces was fear or anger. "It's all right. I'm not trying to get away."

I opened the door to the Visions Room and stepped out. Most of the fluorescent lights were broken, and the agency looked like a typhoon had blown through.

"I just had the Visions Room repaired," said Grimm. "That is why I prefer that you drive. Though you seem to have trouble navigating."

"I was supposed to go to Kingdom." There was no point in avoiding it.

Grimm gave me that wry smile of his. "My dear, I trust you. Though the matter of Clara's death is not one I'll wait to resolve."

"The Seal came through wolf town. I think the fae child followed it, or maybe he was near where it was and they grabbed him too. That Fairy Godmother must have it, Grimm. What would a fairy want with the Seal?"

He nodded in agreement as I mentioned her. "Seals generate more magic when safely in place. Killing one would be of almost no value by comparison. Help me find out who killed Clara, and I will take care of this Godmother, no matter the cost."

"I can take her."

Grimm had almost no sense of humor on a normal day, and it was clear from the way his eyes went narrow he thought I'd actually try to take her on.

"I'm kidding," I said, "I'll leave the scary fairy to you." I could have broken Grimm's mirror a thousand times and not earned his wrath. Maybe his annoyance, but not his wrath. If I'd ever seen Grimm like this before, I'd probably have thought more about my words at the funeral ball.

"Fairy Godmother talked to me through Clara's body. I'm sure she had to do with her death."

He didn't respond. He closed his eyes and exhaled.

I pulled up my pant leg to get a glimpse of my latest bruise. "I have a theory about how they meant to get Liam out. Ask Evangeline if you found anything painted with silver. Fleshing silver. Would've been close. The troll was meant to deliver him to it."

Grimm disappeared, so I headed down to Wardrobe and cleaned up. I kept three sets of black pantsuits at the office, just in case. In case of the normal things, like getting bitten by a wolf or clawed by an imp. Using a fairy portal to escape a pack of wolves out for vengeance was unusual even by my standards.

I was dressing when I heard the explosion—sounded like someone had set off a bomb outside. I headed for the front office, glad that I'd at least had time to put on my sports bra. People in the lobby milled nervously, trying to figure out if they should run or stay put, and if the shirtless woman with a gun was more or less threatening than whatever waited outside.

I ignored their stares and walked down to the hole the

troll had smashed in our hallway. Outside, smoke billowed from an alleyway across the street, and sirens wailed. The explosion had blown out every window for a block.

"M, I think Grimm did it," said Evangeline as she came up to survey the carnage. "I told him there was a Dumpster with a huge blob of silver on it, and he started glowing. The mirror in my office melted."

Ari and Liam peeked out of the door and came walking down to join us. Ari pushed past me to get a better look. "What was that?" We watched as the fire trucks gathered and began to spray foam.

"Only Grimm knows," I said.

Liam jogged down the hall and came back a moment later, having retrieved Grimm's mirror from his office. He carried it with ease and leaned it against the corner so that Grimm could see.

"Thank you, Mr. Stone." Grimm's voice sounded like he was almost laughing. "I think that will send an appropriate message."

I stepped out of the way so that Grimm could see better. "What exactly did you do?"

Grimm started laughing. "I sent a message to the new fairy in town. It's tragic. A satellite misfired and fell to earth. Quite fortunate that it missed everyone and obliterated a Dumpster. A miracle, really."

"You crashed a satellite to destroy a Dumpster?" asked Liam.

"I didn't have an asteroid handy. I sent a message to the party responsible for your close encounter of the troll kind, Mr. Stone. That sort of mirror is intimately linked to the fairy who empowers it, and I'm sure right now she has a nasty burn or two. I wouldn't have risked anyone else coming into contact with her anyway."

I watched the firefighters spray foam on the fire. "I'm not sure that's an appropriate response."

"That's exactly what the dinosaurs said. Kindly return my mirror, when you are done appreciating my handiwork." Grimm faded from view.

I realized Liam had been staring at me the whole time. I'd never understood why it was that men saw me in a bikini and didn't look twice, but if they saw me in a bra, it was scandalous. If I'd known I was going to be modeling for Liam, I'd have chosen the push-up bra.

He caught me looking at him and turned away. His face wasn't angry anymore, but I knew I'd killed my only chance at a relationship. Or had I? I left him there in the hallway and went back to get my shirt. By the time I was done getting dressed, Grimm's mirror was back in his office. I had business there, so I went to finish our discussion.

"Grimm, did you send the cops after Queen Thromson?"

"According to her law firm, she only created enough apples to defend her family." Grimm's tone said he felt the same way about that claim that I did.

"Bull. You show them the records Ari found?"

"Marissa, I believe the bulk of those apples were actually delivered to Kingdom forces. My ears tell me Kingdom believes they can win a war against the fae if need be. That means someone has given them the means to do so. The authorities are not inclined to quibble over a few illegal weapons when a threat like the fae wait in the wings."

"So she makes a bunch of weapons for them, keeps a few for herself?"

Grimm nodded. "It appears so."

"So the question is, how did she know the fae were coming? What about the curse?" I stood up and walked to the armory wall.

"I'm certain she's responsible, but I can't prove it." The frustration in Grimm's voice was palpable. "Someone blurred her position with a spell such that I can't tell where she was or was not. Even if she did perform the curse, since it only affected a commoner, we'd have no legal recourse against her."

So Ari's stepmother would get away with trying to curse another royal simply because she hadn't succeeded. "You still have my potion?"

"Second column, third down. May I ask why you would want it?"

I slid out the box and it opened for me without a sound. In the black velvet lining sat the love potion the Isyle Witch had given me. "I need it." I ran my fingers over it. A tingle shot through my hand, and I curled my fingers around it.

"Marissa, I do not think that is wise."

"I can fix things. You say magic is a supplement for your mind. It's no different than you using a potion on Mihail." I started to slip the potion into my pocket and my hand went numb.

Grimm spoke from the chrome shelving before me. "My dear, I do not think you understand what you are suggesting. These are completely different situations."

I felt his power radiating out along my arm, holding it still. "Let go of me. You said it was mine. I'm taking it." I struggled to move my hand, but it hung limp at my side.

"Please, Marissa. Put it away. Allow me to explain."

"I said I'm taking it, Grimm. If you want a potion, pay for it yourself. I know you've got the Glitter." A cold pulse of energy rushed from the vial, and my eyes locked onto the door to his office. I was done. This discussion was done.

"It's not about the magic," said Grimm, his eyes narrow, his face red. "You don't understand what you might do, and I won't allow you to harm yourself like that. Put the potion away, Marissa."

I felt my hands move of their own accord and watched them put it back in the box. I fought with all my might, but all I could do was induce a tiny tremble. My hands slid the box back into place and he released me.

He had never done that before. Ever. "You . . ."

"I'm sorry, my dear. You gave me no other choice." He wouldn't meet my eyes.

"You made me." My voice shook as I said it, and my face felt hot. I was dizzy and nauseous, and my throat felt like I swallowed the desert.

"Marissa, I don't enjoy—"

"Don't. Just don't." I summoned every bit of willpower I had and the cold emotional wall I had used so many times on so many princes. I walled it away, the fear, the feeling of being violated. "I'm going into Kingdom." My voice was cool and calm, a facade I prayed I could keep up until I was out of his office. "I'm going to go see if Clara left anything behind, Godfather."

He didn't say anything.

I went straight to my car, and found Liam and Ari waiting in the garage. Pink sutures stuck out of Liam's head like tiny ribbons. I left the Agency, wondering how I'd ever bring myself to come back.

I spent the next hour fuming in the car as it crawled toward Kingdom. There's a traffic jam in Kingdom every single day, caused by the bleed over from the Avenue underneath, and we sat in traffic going nowhere when he spoke. I kept my hands on the wheel to keep them from shaking.

"Did that really happen?" Liam asked.

"Trolls? Wolves? Portals? Yeah." Every inch of me wanted to scream at him to leave me alone, and at the same time I wanted to wrap my arms around him and close my eyes and forget about being Grimm's marionette. I couldn't do either.

"No. What the Godmother showed me. Your parents put you up to that deal."

I shoved away the fear and the pain, putting on my mask of fearlessness. From behind the wall of cold it was easy to answer now. Easy to see what my life had been, and what I had done. "Yeah, it's real. All of it." We sat in silence and inched a half a car length forward.

"What is it like working for him?"

I held up the bracelet. "Most days it's like a job. Some days a good job, but it's never a choice."

"So can he make you do something?"

I tried the next lane over in hopes it would move faster. It didn't. "He could. His requests aren't requests at all. So you do what you have to do, and you tell yourself it's what you want to do, because in the end it's the thing you are going to do." I glanced in the rearview mirror and saw Ari staring at me. She knew about not having choices.

Liam spoke so softly I could barely hear him. "You said you made two mistakes with me. What was the second one?"

I wanted to tell him. To swing the wheel over and jump across the seat and hold on to him. I thought of what happened in Grimm's office. What if Grimm didn't want a relationship cutting into my work time? What I wanted wasn't a factor in my life. "It doesn't matter." It didn't, I told myself. It didn't.

We pulled up at the entrance to the queen's tower, and I left the car out front. The doorman saw me coming and tried to explain, but I pushed past him and banged on the blank steel elevator panel. The doorman whispered into his phone, and I felt the elevator activate.

It came down and opened, and inside stood Shigeru. "The royal family is not present."

"We're here as part of another investigation. I'm looking into a murder."

Shigeru's face stayed as emotionless as mine. "I can give you access to Prince Mihail's floor, but I am not permitted in the living quarters when the royal family is not present. I am confined to my quarters while I await their return."

"You search us when we come down. I promise we won't take anything. Where are the king and queen?" I put my money on out of town, maybe out of the realm.

"They petition the High King to make war against the fae and recover their son." Shigeru whispered in Japanese into the elevator. I remembered the queen's comment about it being alive. Probably a command.

"So if we can find him and bring the prince back, they'll back down?"

He laughed, a sharp, static, almost cough. "You have not spent enough time with Queen Mihail. She will seek war regardless."

We crowded into the elevator and rode up. When it opened, we walked out onto the black marble flooring. Ari whistled.

"What a setup." Liam squeaked a boot on marble tiles.

"I'm glad you like it," said a voice I knew all too well. From behind the elevator came Prince Mihail, a gun in his hand. He was missing his shirt, his pants were unbuttoned, and on one arm hung a woman who was more silicon than flesh. You can buy magical breast enhancements, to be sure, but silicon is cheaper.

"Is this her?" asked the bimbo, and I saw a gleam of dryad green in her hair.

Mihail walked over to me, keeping the gun carefully pointed at my chest. "No. She's a girl who keeps getting in the way. This is her." He pointed the gun toward Ari, and she turned red.

"Her?" asked the dryad. "You were going to marry her? She's fat and flat. I have handmaidens who would make better princesses."

"Yes, I was going to marry her," said Mihail, "and once I was done wiping myself with her, I was going to throw her out that window."

"Do it now," said the dryad.

I felt Ari gathering her power, and this time she was furious. She threw a blast of light from her hand, and the dryad screamed as it burned across her.

"Run," said Mihail, shoving her.

She did, right across the room, toward the dressing mirror. She stepped into it and disappeared. Liam's breathing became ragged, and his face turned the color of blood. Wisps of smoke curled out of his clothes.

"You, you're the one who stole my curse," said Mihail.

"What?" I said.

"I was supposed to receive it. Had a nice nullification potion on board so I didn't burn down my favorite restaurant. The problem with transformation curses is you can't take them. They have to be sent, and that one required 'A fair maiden, with love's first bloom in sight.'"

Ari rolled her eyes. "What idiot came up with that idea?"

Mihail looked offended. "That's the curse's purpose. To

separate two lovers. All you had to do was think of the right person. Me, and the curse comes to me. Instead you think of this lout and give it to him."

"You cursed me?" said Liam, looking at me.

Ari spat at Mihail. "You would have made a great salamander."

He laughed a deep, natural laugh that told me we were in trouble. He looked at Liam. "Turn around or I shoot them both. Then lie down on your face."

Liam did, and Prince Mihail knelt on his back. He gestured with the gun. "You two, over there."

"What did you do with Clara?" I asked.

Mihail gave me a vapid grin, trying his princely charms. Didn't work. "You know, I never did like her sitting around. She wasn't afraid of Mother, and she asked so many inconvenient questions. She had the gall to look around in my things. So I sent her away."

"Where?"

"Through the mirror, of course. There's someone on the other side who would love to meet you. To know all your little secrets. I don't need any more taste testers for apples, but I'm sure my friend could find something entertaining to do with you."

"Playing with fairies is bad for your life expectancy. Your mother would not approve."

The prince glowed at the mention of his mother. "I'd bring you along but really, I hate traveling with companions. Too much like flying coach for my tastes." He looked around at his many, many portraits. "I've always enjoyed matching decor. When the solstice comes, this whole city will be ashes, just like you." He pulled the bracelet from Liam's arm and ran for the mirror.

Twenty-Nine

~

I DIDN'T WATCH him leave. I was focused on Liam, who groaned and convulsed. Without Grimm's bracelet to restrain the curse, he was changing. His clothes caught fire and burned right off of him, leaving his skin untouched. Liam began to change, and I understood. The fires. The waking up miles from where he went to sleep, the strength. His arms grew longer and his skin turned reddish green and hardened into scales.

"Get away," he said, flailing at me as his fingers shortened and widened into claws. The rest of his words became hisses and gurgles. Grimm had told me once that when a prince got changed into a frog, his nervous system was the last thing to change. They felt the entire process. Most required counseling afterward.

Ari pulled me by the hair until I followed her. I looked back once more, and I knew why Grimm hadn't been able to find Liam. The curse wasn't turning him into a salamander.

He was a dragon.

Ari pulled me toward the kitchenette. "Come on."

Liam's voice was gone, replaced with the guttural hiss

of an ancient lizard. As he stood up, I got a good look, and it was bad. He was only half dragon, like a man and a komodo mashed together. He walked on two legs and bounded on four. His head was long and his face ended in a mouth full of teeth. With each step, his claws chipped the marble, and his skin was now covered in bright red scales with a tint of shiny green. Liam raised his head, inhaled, and set the couch on fire with a stream of flame.

As I ran through the kitchen, I hit a chair. Liam's serpentine head whipped around to follow me. With a roar, he ran on all fours across the apartment. I picked up a plate and threw it at him, simultaneously whispering an apology. It smashed into his head, and he ignored it.

As the dragon came through the kitchen, plates and cups flew from the cabinet, smashing on his scales. My blessings objected to me getting roasted, which might have been the first time we agreed on anything. Liam shook bits of glass off of his nose and turned to come for me. He turned too quickly on the kitchen tile, and his hind legs slipped out from under him.

Ari dragged me into the bathroom. "In here."

We slammed the door and threw the lock. I leaned up against it. The dragon shuffled along outside, sniffing at the dense oak door. We were in the prince's private bathroom. Black marble and white marble, like everything else. The man had a singular sense of style.

I checked the door to make sure it was locked. Dragons weren't known for using doors, but somewhere in that thing was Liam. If any of his intelligence remained, a doorknob wouldn't slow him down.

Outside, the sounds of crashing and smashing told me the Dragon-Liam was saving his fire for something more edible. As the hours passed, I cracked the door to check from time to time. Every time, he lay a dozen feet away, smoking drool dripping from his mouth. "I can't believe he's in there. Grimm's going to flip." Thinking of him, I tried the bracelet once more, but we were on the opposite side of where Shigeru said we'd get service.

"Why didn't you tell Liam how you felt in the car?"

I clipped and unclipped my bracelet, twisting it in my fingers as I passed the time. "It doesn't matter what I want, or what I think, or what I feel. I'm trapped in a bathroom, trapped in a job, and trapped in this life." I watched as the bracelet snaked itself around my wrist, and clicked into place. "I was going to use a potion on him."

"A love potion?"

I nodded.

She scowled at me. "Didn't you read the spell books? A love potion works best when there isn't any feeling between two people. If you gave it to him, he'd feel love for you all right, mixed with anything else he already felt."

Her words were like cold water on me, as I worked it through. "He'd hate me and love me."

"I don't think he hates you. You don't see how he looks at you. But if you used a potion it wouldn't ever be real love."

"Grimm made me put it back. It was like watching a puppet show from inside the puppet."

Ari reached over and gave my hand a squeeze. From outside, I heard something definitely crystal and probably ugly break. Ari looked at the door. "How long does this dragon episode go on?"

"One of Grimm's spellbooks said transformation curses lasted about six hours or until the victim went to sleep." I glanced at my watch, wondering if dragons took catnaps, or just ate cats as snacks.

"Why doesn't it push down the door? Or burn it down?"

Now, I might not have made it all the way through "D" in the *Beast Lexicon*, but I'd peeked at a few of the more interesting subjects. "Why would he? The dragon part of him has everything it could ever want. A princess, locked in a room in a tower, with no chance of a prince showing up to give it a lance-ectomy. Trust me, he'll stay there for the rest of our lives." I propped up a set of bath mats, curled up in the bathtub, and dozed.

I woke to a humming sound. In the dim light of the bathroom, Ari's ring had begun to glow, emitting a green and yellow light. I shook her awake. "It's eleven thirty. Your ring goes off at midnight." Outside, a clatter of dishes let me know my scaly admirer still roamed the floors.

Ari peered under the door. "Is there an office building here? I could walk down the stairs there."

"I think there is, but the top is about thirty stories below us. Grimm, we could use some help." I put my hand on the bracelet and thought of him as hard as I could. He didn't answer.

I unlocked the door slowly and listened. There was no sound in the apartment, but as I cracked open the door, I saw him. Dragon-Liam had swept the furniture out away from the bathroom and lay on the marble, facing the door. He wrapped a long tail around his body, lashing back and forth like a cat. Wisps of smoke drifted from his jaws, and with each breath he rumbled in a way that shook the floor.

Ari's ring began to pulse faster. "I've got to get out of here."

"Spell him. Like you did the bimbo."

Her face turned pink, and she shook her head. "I can't do it on command, and I don't think I could hurt a dragon either."

I looked out again, and saw him sitting with one eye fixed on the door. "I'll go to the left and lead him around. Get ready."

She ignored me, looking in the mirror. Her mouth moved as she worked something through. "I've got an idea. I've read a lot of history books in the last month. There's a story that shows up again and again. The princess uses her charms to calm a monster and lull it to sleep."

"A dragon?"

"Not that I've read, but the principle is the same. I'm a princess, so it has to listen to me."

A memory came to me and I nodded. "Like the hellhound?"

"Exactly."

Dragon-Liam still waited, flipping his tail back and forth

lazily as I watched from the bathroom. "I don't like this plan. It has too much chance for charbroiled princess."

"I don't like the idea of pancaked princess either. Hold the door in case I need to get away." With that, she stepped out.

Dragon-Liam heard the door latch and raised his head, fixing her with a glowing red eye and turning from side to side to try and get a better look. Ari hummed as she stepped forward, a soft lullaby. As the tune filled the quiet, he closed those wicked jaws. She took one step, and another, and began to sing softly, something country western.

Dragon-Liam's head shot up, and he squinted at her, first with one eye and then the other. A low growl came from him that echoed in the apartment, followed by a tiny squeak of fear from Ari. His lips curled back, revealing long fangs and a forked tongue.

"Ari," I yelled, as he filled his lungs. She ran through the door, and I slammed it. Flames burst on the frame and her sleeve was on fire. She flailed in the bathroom while I beat at her with a towel. "Put it out!"

So I shoved her into the shower and turned it on. Once she was completely drenched, Ari looked like a half-drowned kitten. Well, one that had taken a nap on a barbeque. "I don't understand. I'm a princess, it's supposed to work."

We sat in the dark as midnight ticked closer and the ring made a continuous warning hum. I leaned against the door, listening to the sound of claws on marble. "Everybody makes mistakes. I thought he was a prince, remember? I even told Grimm I could see the prince shine on him, and I believed it enough to fool the Root of Lies."

She gasped, staring at me like I'd admitted eating the last pint of ice cream. "You have to try it."

I glanced at my phone. Twenty minutes and Ari would be taking the express elevator down. "Why not?" I asked, getting up. "When I go out there, I want you to run to the elevator. Don't stop, don't look back. Keep going. If I let you get killed, Grimm will resurrect me and kill me twice." I opened the door and stepped out to face the dragon.

It raised its head at me, and every nursery rhyme I could think of went out the window, so I just talked.

"I'm sorry this happened," I said, taking a step toward it.

"This is my fault. Don't punish Ari for it." She would be out the door, and hopefully headed for the elevator.

"I'm the one who thought you were a prince, not her."

The dragon turned its head to look at me with the other eye.

"I'm the one who sent the curse for you."

It growled and the eyes flickered with flames hot enough to melt marble.

"It wasn't supposed to happen. They told me to think of the person I loved." I was so close I could touch it now, or it could tear my head off with a single snap of its jaws.

"I lied to you in the car. My first mistake was thinking you were a prince, and I'm sorry. I'm so sorry. My second one I'm not sorry for, and if you need to kill me for it, I understand. I let myself imagine you could be mine. That I would be allowed to love you. That you might love me." I put my hands on its jaws, running my fingers over the rough scales.

It took a deep breath in, and I heard the fires rumble inside it.

"My second mistake was falling in love with you. I won't ever be sorry for that." I waited for a flame that would burn without end. Instead, I felt a heavy weight on my shoulder.

Dragon-Liam's head rested against me, and from its mouth came the scent of wood fire and smoke. As I tried to hold him, he slipped forward, and curled up in a ball around me, a gentle curl of smoke coming from his nostrils. He began to snore.

Ari stood in the bathroom doorway, a look of awe on her face. "That was amazing."

I disentangled myself from Liam and dragged her to the elevator. Six minutes. "You were supposed to go. And why could I charm him if you couldn't?" I whispered to avoid waking Liam.

"He's not my prince."

Her words stung me. "I'm not like you. I'm not a princess."

Ari grinned so wide it looked like her face would split open. "To him you are." She signaled the elevator, which apparently could be called from the inside.

"We can't wake Liam. I'm not sure how long it will take the curse to wear off, and there's no way I'm going to risk leaving you on the street at night."

Ari reached into her pocket and pulled out a stamped metal business card. "The Agency," it read, and below it, our address. "Grimm gave it to me in case you left me somewhere." She hopped out of her shoes and ran across the floor in socks. She tucked the card into Liam's curled claws.

"He'll be safe here, but first I need to do something." I tiptoed across the room to where the dressing mirror sat and laid it facedown. Now no one could come through to threaten Liam, and if anyone tried to get past Shigeru it would be a mistake they wouldn't live to regret.

As my hand touched the mirror, I heard her voice.

"You are foolish beyond measure, girl. Few risk my wrath a second time," said Fairy Godmother.

"I'm not afraid of you." My heart was so full of joy it was true.

"Twice now I return your blow, darling. I give you your deepest desire."

"Leave her alone," said Ari, running toward me.

I felt a tremble as my blessings raced through the room.

"My second wish to you is given," said Fairy Godmother. "Once more and done."

Ari grabbed my shoulder. "Are you okay? You glowed for a moment. It was weird, and bad."

"I don't feel so good." The bracelet on my wrist fell limp and crumbled into the Glitter that made it. Our eyes met for a moment as I realized what it meant. Ari lashed out at my hand, but her hand passed through mine like I was made of smoke.

I fell.

I told Ari we were thirty stories above the normal buildings. More like fifty. I'd never considered leaving Kingdom at the top of a skyscraper. After a moment it felt like I was flying instead of falling, except the earth came rushing toward me to give me a big, terminal hug. *So this is how it ends*, I thought, and Godmother whispered, "Not yet." The world twisted, and I crashed into what I think was a dresser, smashing it to pieces.

In the darkness someone screamed. A girl. I stood up and recognized a bedroom. A man came charging into the bedroom, throwing me to the side. "Get away from her." He pushed her behind him.

"I'm sorry," I said. "I'm sorry."

He looked at me a moment and turned on the bedroom light. "Marissa?"

I was in my old bedroom. I was home.

Dad came walking toward me, looking at me like I was a ghost. He threw his arms around me. "Finally."

Mom came through the door in a robe. "Marissa, what are you doing here?"

That was not what I expected for our six-year reunion. "I'm home, Mom. I think I'm free." I glanced down, and sure enough, there was nothing on my wrist. I was finally free. My eyes started to fill with tears, but this time it was joy.

Right about then, the lights trembled and the doors shook. The girl, Hope, my sister, cried out and clung to Dad as the earthquake grew worse. A lightbulb shattered, and then another. I recognized this. Fairy Godmother transported me all the way to my home, but my blessings had been left behind. They were coming. They were ticked.

I stumbled out of the bedroom and into the kitchen, where the plates went flying out of the cupboard and the faucet sprayed like a fountain.

Dad followed me. "Honey, what's happening?"

"It's the fae blessings. They're coming to me."

Mom's face went ashen white. "You led a harakathin to our house? You'll kill her."

Part of me felt confused, trying to figure out how Mom knew about blessings. The other part of me knew if I didn't get them calmed down they might destroy the whole house. "I can calm them. They get upset when they are separated from me, or around spell power."

"Magic," my mother whispered. Her eyes grew round, her mouth opened.

"They eat it. Beatus, Consecro, calm down." If anything, the trembling grew stronger as I spoke their names. It sounded like a train was hurtling toward the house.

"You named it?" screamed my mother.

"Both of them. It lets me control them better," I said as the stove caught fire.

My dad shoved me toward the door. "Get out. Get out before you kill her. What did she do to you? Hurt us, but don't kill her."

"I don't understand." It didn't make any sense. Mom and Dad didn't know of magic. If they had, Dad would have made a lot more money.

Mom shoved me past the threshold right as the windows exploded into a rain of glass. As I passed it, I felt a burning sensation. My blessings were home.

"You came to kill her," said Mom. "You knew what would do it."

"I have no idea what you are talking about, Mom. I got transported by accident, sort of." All my dreams of this day, they'd never included words like this, looks like this.

Mom fixed me with that look I could never avoid. The one I got when I spilled grape soda on her new carpet. The one I got when Dad caught me with a can of beer, sputtering and choking it down. "Hope. The one we returned you to Fairy Godfather to save. You've come to destroy her heart."

The words made no sense to me. I tried to work it through and failed. "Grimm said he'd fix it. He'd heal her."

"He gave her a new one. A mechanical one," said Dad. "A magic one." Hope stood at the doorway. She had Mom's black hair, and eyes as blue as Dad's. Dad ran back to scoop her up, and took her inside.

Mom walked toward me, her face covered in that look of disapproval I had come to take as love. "Don't you have a life of your own now? Go back to it."

"I've waited for this day for six years. I missed you so badly I had to have the memories taken. I wanted to come home every day and every hour. What did I ever do to you?"

Mom looked back at the doorway. When she saw it was empty, she walked over and stroked my hair, pushing it back out of my eyes. "It isn't what you did, Marissa. It's who you represent. As long as Roland held on to you, he held on to her. I couldn't compete with a ghost. And then we had our own daughter, born of our own blood."

Through the broken windows, I heard Hope sobbing. I was sure I could keep my blessings in check. Maybe. "You wanted me to make a deal, I made a deal, Mom."

"For your sister," she said.

"For you. I knew you wanted me to. That's the only reason I agreed." Tiny bolts of anger gave my words force.

"Of course I wanted it. Until you've held a child of your own, don't judge me. I traded your freedom for her life. A trade I would make again any day."

I shivered as her hand brushed my shoulder, torn between the urge to hug her and the need to scream at her. "I know what you told Dad that night. I loved you, Mom. Why didn't you love me?" My voice came out like a squeak. I felt like I was a tiny girl, begging her to pick me up.

She bent down to look in my eyes. "You act as if I didn't try. You were a wild girl, always given to mischief and destruction. Name one of your birthdays that didn't end in a trip to the emergency room or with a visit from the fire department. Name one party you've attended that didn't end in a fight or an accident. I tried, Marissa."

My hands shook and the porch light exploded in a shower of sparks as my blessings drank in my anger. She glanced to the broken light and shook her head. "You have no control over those blessings. For the sake of your sister, go back to your life. I've made my choices, and I'll bear the consequences."

Anger flared over my sadness and my hands stopped shaking. "You made mine too. You said I could come home when I was free."

She let go of me. "Could you live with yourself if those things harmed your sister? I doubt I could stop you if you decided to go back inside, but the girl I raised was never a killer. Perhaps you truly have changed."

I stood in the silence, in the darkness, considering the choices I was finally free to make. I never thought the first choice I'd make on my own would be to give up the thing I'd dreamed about most. "I love you, Mom. Tell Dad and Hope I said I love them too." I turned and walked into the night, and grief went with me.

Thirty

〰

IT TOOK ME two days to get back into the city, hitchhiking. The first person to pick me up was a truck driver with a load of cantaloupe. He spoke only Spanish, and the only Spanish phrases I'd ever heard were from Rosa. Judging from his reaction, Rosa said mean things. My second ride was an elderly couple who explained that Jesus loved me. Jesus had actually kicked me out of his truck for repeating a phrase Rosa had always said meant "Thank you very much." My last ride was a trio of stoners. I'd eaten casseroles less baked. They didn't understand that "No" meant "Keep your hands on your side of the car," "I'm not lifting up my shirt," and "If you try that once more I'm breaking one of your fingers."

When I finally got back to the city, I smelled like the high-altitude seating at a rock concert. I dropped them off at the emergency room to get their fingers splinted, and took a cab to the Agency.

I almost didn't see it in time: the building was cordoned off. I had the cab driver stop a block away and let me out. I merged with the flow of people, walked past on the other side, trying to look only when others did.

The signs said biohazard, the guards posted said magic. I'd been around enough that I could recognize the difference. Rent-A-Cops wear bad polyester uniforms that never quite fit them. Whatever these things were, they wore Rent-A-Cop skins the same way. When they moved, their skin sagged and something evil peered out from their eyes at the people passing by.

I headed for home, because there was a decent chance Ari would be there instead. I had no way to know if Liam had already followed the card back or not. When I walked into my apartment, I saw the answering machine flashing.

I ran to it, figured which button actually played messages, and waited. When I heard Ari's voice my heart leaped in my throat.

"Marissa, I found Liam at the gates of Kingdom and brought him back with me to the Agency. Grimm says you—" In the background I heard screaming, Rosa shouting something I no longer believed meant "Merry Christmas" in Spanish, and the roar of a shotgun. The message ended. Whatever happened at the Agency, Ari and Liam had been there. I reflexively put my hand to my wrist. And found nothing. My mirrors were glass and silver now, and I couldn't call Grimm with a word.

I remembered the words of the Fae Mother. She'd tried to tell me. To warn me. I had my freedom. And that was all I had. I'd dreamed a lot about being free, but never dreamed it would cost me what it did. I'd been up for over twenty-four hours, and as tears blurred my eyes it grew harder and harder to keep them open. I collapsed on the couch and passed out.

When I got up, I had a headache as determined as I was. I looked again at my bare wrist. I finally had the freedom to do wherever I wanted. To my surprise, I wanted to do what I'd done for the last six years. I unlocked my gun safe and took out my spare nine millimeter.

I was going to rent a car, head downtown, and run over

the first couple of guards. The others, I'd shoot. I didn't know if Ari or Liam were still in the Agency, but I'd kill anything that got between me and that office. I was still in the shower when I heard the knock. A special knock, one I'd taught Ari when I first brought her home, as a way to signal me when a freezer I'd locked her in was low on air. I'd used the same code with Evangeline when I came to work myself.

I ran to the door, dripping the whole way, wearing only a towel. I threw open the door and someone tackled me, rolling me onto my stomach and pinning my arm behind me.

"I'm going to kill you, you bitch," screamed Evangeline. In any other building, maybe the neighbors would have called the cops, but you can bet mine had learned ignorance really was bliss.

I felt something pop in my shoulder, and pain flared down my arm. "You're breaking my arm."

If anything, she leaned down harder. "I never thought you had it in you, you know. That plain little face with just enough brains to be deadly. He told me what happened. You two had one little spat, and you went and did this?" She reached for something, and I heard the soft beeps of a cell phone.

"She's here. Of course I have her." She leaned over and said softly, "M, I want you to know something. If you lie to us, she's not going to kill you." She gave my hand a squeeze until something cracked. "That's my job."

After a few minutes I heard someone else come in, and Evangeline yanked me to my feet.

"Sit," said Jess, "so we can talk."

"Listen—"

She hit me backhand across the mouth like one swats a fly. "I tell you when to answer. Where is he?" She wiped my blood off her hand on the tablecloth.

"Liam was at the Agency."

Wrong answer. Jess grabbed me by my hair and twisted my head. "Grimm. Where is Grimm?"

"I don't know, call him." It was harder to breathe with my head at this angle. When she finally let go I slumped back over.

Evangeline dangled her broken Agency bracelet in front of me. "We've been trying for the last two days. Where was his original mirror?"

"Something's happened to Grimm?" I asked, and I think that's about when they realized something else was wrong. Jess let go of my hair and looked at me.

"Fine. Grimm had us getting the truth out of people about the Seal. I hear you like this thing." She reached into her purse and pulled out the Root of Lies. "You know what this is."

All I could think of was how desperate Grimm must have been to let them take the Root of Lies out of his office. It was something best locked away, buried and hidden.

She reached out with it, running the claw down the side of my face. It shifted and moved, but the nails didn't dig into my cheek. I jerked away as it moved, tickling the skin at my throat, caressing me under the chin.

Jess shuddered, and looked queasy. "That's wrong." She forced my hand up to it. The tangled mass of thorns at the end separated, leaving only finger bones that ended in thorn points. It flexed underneath my hand, tracing a pattern on my palm, and wrapped around me with a grip like steel.

Jess took me by the hair again. "Did you have a fight with Grimm?"

There was no point in denying it. The root would literally tear it out of me if I did. "Yes."

"Did you betray him?" asked Evangeline.

"No," I said, ignoring the thing squirming in my hand.

"Did you sell Princess Arianna or Liam Stone to that fairy bitch?" asked Jess.

"No."

Jess leaned in to look at me, like she could do a better job than the Root. "Do you know where Grimm's original mirror is?"

"No."

Evangeline and Jess stood up and walked to the door, leaving me.

"Hey, hang on. If you're going to the Agency, I'm going too." Part of me wanted to check on the delivery staff. I liked Bill and the other cargo handlers. Rosa, on the other hand, might be gone. There was always a silver lining. I knew that Evangeline and Jess shouldn't be allowed out in the city like this.

Evangeline looked at me with that look of scorn mixed with pity. "There isn't an Agency anymore. We were lucky to be out working when it happened. Last thing Grimm said was that someone dumped a bag full of Glitter off with your name on it. The courier said they'd purchased your contract."

I stood up and walked toward her. "Think about it. Am I worth that much Glitter to anyone?"

For a moment she was my big sister and teacher again. She shook her head. "No. You aren't."

I'd seen Grimm talk Evangeline down out of rages in the past. "It's the Fairy Godmother. She must have done this." I'd been able to reason with Evangeline in the past, but I'd always had Grimm to back me up.

Evangeline looked down. Ever since her accident she only showed anger, if she showed any emotion at all. "You didn't have to listen to him break. Have to feel it. We're going to find this Fairy Godmother's mirror. We're going to tear through any and everything that gets in our way, and return the favor."

"Where are Ari and Liam? They were at the Agency." I knew now I couldn't persuade Evangeline to let me come along, and I wasn't crazy enough to argue with Jess.

Jess came over, her motions fluid like the rise and fall of water. She exuded an air of deadly confidence without Grimm to keep her in check. "Building's empty. The guards keep wishers away. They could be anywhere."

I shook the Root loose from my hand. "I'm going with you. We can clear out the guards and start figuring out where they went from there." I struggled to my feet, unwilling to be pushed around any longer. Even though I knew I didn't stand a chance in a fistfight with her. "I can help you. Let me help."

Evangeline shoved me backwards so hard I fell into my table. "When are you going to understand? There are bigger problems than your boy toy and someone's leftover princess. The fae are coming."

Jess shouldered past her and put one hand on my shoulder in a subtle threat. "Come noon tomorrow there's going to be a full-on war in Kingdom, and without Grimm, you can't even set foot in it."

I held up the Root. "At least take this thing. You can use it to find out where Fairy Godmother's mirror is."

Jess shook her head. "We're done asking questions, and it likes you." They walked out of my apartment like it was a social call. I'd spent six years in that apartment. It never felt so empty. I never felt so alone.

I DROVE A rental car down to the gates of Kingdom. Without Grimm's magic I couldn't even see them. I turned the corner more times than I could count. No matter how many times I closed my eyes, or walked, or wished, nothing happened. The shops still sold gloves instead of gauntlets, and the flowers in the flower cart were cut instead of dancing and singing. Being inches from the streets I wanted to be on didn't change who I was.

After hours at the gates and dozens of failed attempts, I finally gave up. I walked a few blocks to the pier and ordered a bottle of wine. I listened to the wind and the chimes until nightfall. I looked in my purse, where I had crammed the Root of Lies. That was the real reason I had driven here. I meant to throw it in the water, but honestly, the river was polluted enough already. In less than twenty-four hours, this place would be a war zone of fae killing everyone and Kingdom forces killing the fae. And I couldn't do a damn thing about it.

So I walked to the carousel and got on board. I found the horse I'd ridden with Liam, and ran my hand down the carved mane. With all the cash in my purse, I paid the operator to keep it running while the world spun away. Memories and wine kept me floating all evening. It was the dead of night when the operator finally shut it down. The pier was empty now, silent and dark. The trash of the day skittered in the sea wind as I walked back up to look at the avenue one last time.

I didn't even have a way to reach Fairy Godmother. She'd promised me one more wish, and I figured there couldn't be anything worse than what she'd already given me. Then I thought of my nightly reading. That *Near History of the Fae* book described a dozen different ways people used to treaty with the fae. Most of them were bloody, which fit my mood perfectly, but required equipment and victims. For the oldest and least reliable method, I had everything required.

I knelt in the dark by a puddle and ran my fingers along my eyes. As much as I'd cried in the last month I should have been dehydrated, but I was still plenty drippy. I moved so the moon hung reflected in a puddle, and flicked my tears onto it. The pool rippled and became solid like a mirror.

I felt the presence. "I'm ready for my third wish. Bring it on."

"Marissa, is that you?" said Grimm.

Thirty-One

~

"YES!" I SHOUTED, not caring who noticed.

"I'm sorry I cannot see you. My current situation has left me weakened. My mirror has been broken."

"Grimm, I need your help."

He was silent for so long I was sure I had lost him. "I don't understand what you need my services for. You have enough Glitter in that vial for two happily ever afters."

My hand went to my throat, and I felt the vial. I tried to process what he said. I hadn't even thought about it. I held it up and looked, and sure enough, it shone full. "I thought it was to pay you."

"Marissa, I've always taken my payment up front, split equally between your debt to me, and your own account. The vial was for your own benefit, when our working relationship ended. I hoped when you left this life, you'd buy a better one."

"I didn't make a deal with Fairy Godmother. She said freedom was her second blow to me."

Grimm was quiet again, but when he spoke, I heard pride in his voice. "I want you to go, Marissa. I cannot give you your family or your memory, or any of the things I would have wanted to, but you have to leave. You cannot help here."

"Ari and Liam got taken, and Evangeline and Jess are going ballistic without you. Where was your mirror?"

The puddle rippled as he spoke. "Even I don't know. It was safer that way."

"How'd they find you?"

"Clara handled my safekeeping, my dear. I thought the knowledge died with her, but apparently not. I want you to know I am sorry for how we parted. Now leave. You are no longer bound to me."

I wiped the tears from my eyes. "I pay my debts, Grimm. This is my life. I can't go home. I don't think I ever could, but from now on at least I'll do things my way."

The wind kicked up, sending waves through the puddle. My tears could only buy me so much time before the spell broke down. I turned the vial over in my hands. It was a ton of Glitter. Enough to buy me that ever after I always said I wanted, or maybe just enough to go after what mattered to me now.

"See you soon, Grimm."

What I did next was crazy and desperate, and that's the only reason it worked. I took off the vial and tossed it into the gutter. I couldn't afford one single speck of hope on me for it to work. I walked to the corner of the Avenue and closed my eyes. I thought about my family. About my mother. My sister. Ari, and the way Liam had looked at me when I'd told him what I did. I wrapped my sorrow and pain like a cloak about me, and I walked forward. I made it fifteen, maybe twenty paces. I tripped on the curb and went flying into the street.

Rough cobblestones gouged into my hands, and when I opened my eyes I knelt in the filth and the sewage of the Low Kingdom. Only the occasional street lamp flickered while a pixie burned to death. I glanced back at the gates. These were made to keep victims in, not out. Thorns and razor-sharp glass jutted from them.

A drunken man towered over me like an ogre. "You'll not be getting out that way, lass."

He reached for me, and I tripped him, throwing him into the gutter. In my worst Scottish brogue I answered, "You'll not be getting me that way, lad." I checked my running shoes and ran. In the low streets of Kingdom, a chase is like a fox hunt, and soon I had everything from kitsune to a few wolves stalking me. They were used to following city girls who stumbled down the wrong street, not agents with a thousand miles under their soles. Plus, I wasn't running for the sake for running. For the first time in my life, I was running toward something instead of away from it.

I rounded corners, splashed through waste piles, and, generally speaking, ran like hell until I found it. Low Kingdom almost exactly mirrored High Kingdom, and the Isyle Witch's shop lay exactly where I expected. No bond statements on her door, and the cages and jars lined the outside window, but I walked in without fear. Inside, a true cauldron bubbled as she stirred it.

She looked at me with those yellow, diseased eyes and nearly dropped her ladle. "Handmaiden, it is not yet time."

I reached up to my neck, where I knew the vial would be. Like my old Agency bracelet, it was mine and couldn't be lost or stolen, but now that I was past the gates, nothing would kick me out of Low Kingdom. High Kingdom, on the other hand, remained a problem. "I need to be able to go to High Kingdom."

She cackled with glee. "One both blessed and cursed could walk the streets."

The thought made me pause. A person torn between blessings and curses could walk the streets of Kingdom. My blessings gave me enough grief trying to help. In a way, I already had a curse. "What does it cost?" I plopped my vial on the magic scale, and it didn't even move.

"Harakathin are expensive."

Another idea came to me. One that made me frightened and hopeful at the same time. "What if I already had one you could use? One you could change." The scale swung up, hanging far lower. "Do it." I watched years of Glitter drain away in seconds. Years of blood, bruises, and broken bones. Years of living someone else's life.

The witch swung her hand up in the air and seized something, and I felt it scream as she plunged it into the cauldron. As it boiled, the steam formed a mist that filled the shop. She lifted it up out of the cauldron, and in the mist I could see how it had been twisted. The teeth no longer fit in its mouth, it had two tails, and when it moved it shook, with fear, rage, or both.

The witch held out a claw toward me, beckoning. "It must be claimed."

I reached for the curse and it swiped at me, baring its teeth. "I claim it. It is mine." I felt it burn inside me, connecting to a part of me I couldn't see.

The witch bowed her head. "I am honored to be of service, handmaiden. You have needs?"

"Fleshing silver." I handed her the vial.

"You dare paint a way to your battle? I see why you are her chosen." She disappeared into the shop and came out with a flask, made of rusted metal. Only a tiny trace of glitter remained in my vial.

I took the lid off and the smell curled its way into my nose, the cloying sweet stench of brined cat. "One last thing. I don't have spirit sight. Can you show me the mark?"

She held out her hand, with bony knuckles and long nails. "The price is blood."

I took her hand without flinching.

She muttered, and I felt the power gathering around her like it did when Ari cast a spell. My hand burned, like it was on fire. Welts rose on my hand, traced in excruciating agony, and the blood ran along them. At last, she let go, and I saw the mark. It began at my wrist and followed up along the back of my hand, a rose with a ring of thorns encircling it. "Thank you," I said.

"It is not safe on the street. Not all fear our queen yet. Leave by the upper entrance."

I looked back, and the doorway had changed. Through

it I saw High Kingdom. I walked out, finally able to walk that street by my own will and power. Kingdom soldiers in white lined the streets, and the few people standing outside looked nervous. I turned my back on High Kingdom, and headed down toward Dwarf Town.

I wandered the streets for hours, lost, looking for one tiny house in a warren of tiny houses. They all looked the same, and without Evangeline to guide me, I would be wasting hours, maybe days I didn't have.

I took one more wrong turn, and found myself back on Main Street. Shops stretched back toward the gates, and ahead lay the palace. Off on the right stood the Kingdom Post Office. I bit my tongue, and headed inside, waving to the door gnome, who tried to trip me as I passed. I stood in line, watching the clock tick ever closer to six o'clock. I knew that at six sharp, they'd lock the doors and let out the asps. Exactly where they got buckets of asps, I neither knew nor wanted to.

At five fifty-seven the crowd began to thin as folks with better survival instincts decided to come back another day. At five fifty-eight, a stampede of people exiting the building nearly crushed the door gnome. Only an old woman stood in line before me.

She pushed a handful of pennies across the counter. "I'll take one hundred and seventy-eight stamps, please."

The counter gnome picked up a penny and nibbled at it. "These are zinc. Not worth as much as the copper ones, and we don't accept either."

The old lady pulled out her dentures and placed them on the counter. "Ou an ave ees ooo," she said.

"No glitter, no stamps," said the counter gnome. He looked up at the clock. My watch said I had just enough time to not make it out.

I pulled the vial from my neck and set it down. "I'll pay. Give her the stamps."

He glared at me and handed them over, one at a time. In the background, the door clicked. The clock above the grand hall began to chime. From the corners of the room snakes slithered, emerging from holes near the base of the wall.

The old woman threw back her hood and stood up straight. "No ordinary woman am I. You look upon the great enchantress Elinda. For your kindness, I will reward you."

I hopped over a snake and stood on one of the chairs in the lobby. "I need to find a place in Middle Kingdom."

She waved a staff that appeared in her hand in a puff of smoke and began to chant. I felt magic rushing in around me, gathering for her spell. She shrieked and fell over to the side. Asps hung like fringe from her ankles.

"Seriously? You can find anywhere in Kingdom, but you can't even summon a pair of asp-proof boots?" I scooted the chair closer and closer to the counter, where the counter gnome grinned at me.

"No substitutions, exchanges, or refunds," he said, pushing a pile of stamps at me.

I considered trying to shove them down his throat, but the security systems here made Grimm's look like a "Keep out" sign. If I were lucky, I'd lose a hand to a laser beam. If I were unlucky, it would be a mutation spell, and I'd gain a hand or six. "I came to say I'm sorry. I'm sorry I ran over Bernie."

Snakes covered the floor of the lobby, so deep they writhed upon each other, crawling back and forth. The counter gnome rang a bell.

I waited for security to come over and push me from my perch into a pile of poisonous snakes. Instead, gnomes began to gather behind the safety glass. Five, fifteen, and then a hundred of them at least. Tiny gnome faces watched me from across the counter as they crowded in.

"Go on," said the counter gnome.

I'd done a lot of things I was sorry for. I'd also done a lot of things I should have been sorry for, but wasn't really. Fortunately I'd also told a lot of lies while working for Grimm. "I'm sorry I ran over Bernie. It was my fault; I should have been looking more carefully. In fact, I'm sorry for every gnome I've ever hit."

Their eyes went wide.

Too late I closed my mouth and fixed my gaze on the counter.

The counter gnome walked to the edge of the counter, his tiny hands balled into fists. "How many of us have you run over?"

I chewed on my lip for a moment. "How many do you know about?"

"Just Bernie."

I finally let out the breath I'd been holding in; a long, steady sigh. "In that case, he's the only one. And I'm really sorry."

One of the gnomes grimaced at me.

"I mean, I shouldn't have been driving at all. It was dark, and I had no business driving when I couldn't see what, I mean who, might be hiding in a pothole. I am sorry for every mean thing I ever said about gnomes. I'm sorry for the time I used a priority mailbox to send regular mail. I'm sorry I kept a little plastic basket you delivered the mail in. I promise I will never spindle, punch, or fold again."

"What do you want?"

"I made a pickup here a while back. Signed for it to do last-mile delivery myself. I need the address it was going to. You said you kept a copy for your trophy wall. I need the address."

"Not good enough," said the counter gnome, and his audience applauded.

"I'll throw in a pile of stamps. Also, I'll sign anything else. You can all have a signature to put on your wall."

"Anything?" asked the counter gnome.

"Anything. You name it, I'll sign it. I need that address."

He pushed a button, and the glass over the counter slid upward. I leaped over it, happy to be away from the snakes, and followed him back to his office.

He pointed to the chair. "Sit."

The chair was about six inches square. Heck, the gnome's desk was the size of a clipboard. If it weren't for government regulations I wouldn't fit in the room at all. Another gnome came in with a box of pens, and I began to sign, thankful that the arm Evangeline hurt wasn't the one I wrote with.

Hours had passed and my hand had cramped into a claw before we were finally done signing things. Every scrap of paper in the place had my scrawl, along with most of the office furniture. I'd signed the counter gnome's desk seven different times itself. He looked in a mirror to admire my signature on his rear before pulling up his pants, and then walked over to the wall. Behind a glass picture frame I saw a shipping receipt with my name and an address scrawled in Dwarfish. He handed it to me. "Here. Just promise not to drive so fast."

I took it gingerly with my bad hand; my good fingers hurt too bad from holding the pen. "What exactly was Bernie doing in the pothole?"

A grin spread across the gnome's face and his eyes lost focus as he daydreamed. "Trying to set a world record for most time spent in a pothole without getting run over. He almost made it too."

BACK IN DWARF Town I wandered the streets, watching for a match to the puzzling symbols. At last I found it, on a tiny side street near the bottom of Middle Kingdom. The streets of Dwarf Town were empty. The dwarves knew that most of Kingdom was about to become one gigantic no parking zone. I found the house at which we had made our delivery. The symbols matched perfectly.

See, while I'd always known that fleshing silver could clear up acne and get bloodstains out of cotton, at the ball, I saw Fairy Godmother use it on her mirror. Evangeline and I had dropped off fleshing silver here.

Since most dwarvish clothing was so filthy it could basically run around on its own, I didn't think he was using it for cleaning. And acne? Dwarves had such bad acne that if you wanted a cream cheese bagel, all you needed was a plain bagel and a dwarf who would let you squeeze his cheeks. That left only magic mirror repairs.

I knocked on the door and got no answer. A strange symbol was written on the door, but the color of the paint, bright red, identified it as a warning. I tried the door and it opened.

"Can you not read?" said a voice behind me.

I turned and saw a dwarf guard, a heavy hammer in his hand. "The Red Death lies within. Enter if you will, but if you try to leave, I'll have your head."

I pushed the door open and crawled through. Inside, someone had painted the walls brown and black. After a moment, I realized it wasn't paint. Something had splattered every ounce of blood in a dwarf over the walls. Dwarf blood spread poorly and didn't cover well. I picked my way through the house and finally up a staircase. The top floor contained only a tiny bed, but what caught my eye was a door. It should have opened a hole in the roof. The house was only two stories high, with a tiny conical roof. This odd door hung on one hinge, splintered. I stepped through it, into a room that could not possibly exist in the same house.

The room was completely empty, with warped wood floors. Out of a porthole window, I saw an ocean of blue-green water. A massive picture frame filled one wall, and the floor was covered in mirror shards. I picked up a tiny fragment and felt his familiar presence. This was Grimm's original mirror, and it lay in a thousand pieces.

I knelt in the shards and began trying to piece them together. It must have been hours before I found the first two. I slid them into place, matching their curves. My fingertips were bloody from a dozen tiny cuts, and splinters of glass stuck from my fingers like I was a cactus.

I painted a strip of silver along the crack, and it solidified. The shard still showed the room, but I also saw, or thought I saw, a ghostly outline. I found another shard, and another, and sealed them into place. I found the next one. That's when I realized I could see him, looking out at me with those quiet eyes like always. I slid another piece into place, and as it sealed, he spoke.

His voice had a weird echo in it, like a long-distance call. "If you don't mind, my dear, I will offer a hand."

"Be my guest." The sea of glass quivered, shook, and slid. One piece flicked through the air to snap into place, and another, and another.

"Silver," said Grimm, and I painted them. Now the shards moved like mice, scampering to the right places. As I painted them in, the glass flew faster and faster. At last the flask of silver rose out of my hand.

"Marissa, hold out your hands."

I did, and the splinters flew from them like darts.

The fleshing silver rose out of the vial, assuming the shape of a spider web, sealing the last tiny specks.

When Grimm spoke now his voice echoed in the room like he was yelling. "Ah. That feels better."

I would have hugged him if it were possible. "Good to have you back."

"I owe you my existence, my dear. I don't mean to sound ungrateful, but may I ask how exactly it is you can be here without my geis?" I'd never seen Grimm look like this. His grin was so wide it had to hurt, and at the same time I thought I saw a hint of anger in his eyes, or determination.

"I paid a witch most of my Glitter to curse me."

He nodded his head. "Of course you did."

"I need your help. I have to find Ari and Liam, and I have a score to settle with a prince."

Grimm nodded. "You have it. We'll discuss the matter of your payment when we are done."

"I know. I'll do whatever it takes." I knew that was coming. Nothing is free in life, not even death.

He opened his mouth in surprise and wrinkled his nose. "Marissa, I meant my payment to you. But first we have business to deal with."

I looked out the door into the dwarf house. "We can't go out the way we came in. There's a guard who thinks the house is infected with the Red Death."

"My dear, this is why I insist you keep up-to-date on your plague immunizations. Red Death, Black Plague, you needn't fear any of them. Where, may I ask, did you find fleshing silver?"

"My favorite witch." I held up my hand to show him. "I have the mark."

He followed the pattern on my hand where the blood had dried to scabs. "Of course you do."

"Why? Why would she mark me? I don't have magic, I don't have scales or breathe fire, I don't have Glitter. She could have a thousand people, why me?"

Grimm crossed his arms. "The Black Queen is dead, Marissa. I saw her body burn myself, and you have felt her bones with your own hands. I don't know how she reaches from beyond the grave to do this, but I understand her choice." He paused, searching for the right words. "Do you know what a handmaiden does?"

"Apply hand lotion? Trim cuticles? File nails?"

He leaned in, and it felt like I was back in training, being taught by him for hours. "Maybe now, maybe here. In her day and age, you would be called my handmaiden."

I shivered, remembering how the Root reacted to me in my apartment. "I will never be her agent."

"Of course you won't. Now let us make ready. I'd like to take you to the Agency."

"Things didn't work out so well last time I used a portal." I glanced around nervously. My blessings had a penchant for breaking glass when they felt threatened.

Grimm waved his hand. "You're allowed two pieces of luggage, my dear. I'll bring your pets as well."

I nodded. The floor under my feet caught fire as green flames burned portal runes into the floor. The world folded in on itself when the portal activated, then grew outward again. We were in Grimm's office. "We're going to arm you." The doors on all the safe boxes clicked open.

I headed for the wall. "Spells. I want the big boys. No more playing with elemental magic."

"I think not, Marissa. Magic has never obeyed you. Open the third drawer in, twenty-seventh up." It was a long black case, engraved with writing I'd never seen. Inside were seven perfect silver spheres. "Pick one up."

I tried, but my wrist looked like a swollen sausage and every time I lifted my arm higher than my waist, streaks of fire ran down my side. "Don't think I can aim anymore."

He glanced around the empty room as if checking it for watchers. "Just this once, Marissa, I'll make an exception." I felt my wrist pop, and nearly threw up in my mouth as my shoulder wrenched itself right. With teeth gritted, I held on as my muscles and tendons stretched back to the right places. "I wouldn't get too used to that, my dear."

I let out the air I'd held in on a groan. "Don't worry. I won't ask, I promise." Now, however, my hands worked perfectly well to pick up one of the silver orbs. I took one in my fingers. It felt like putty on my fingertips. As I held it, it changed, becoming longer, harder. It transformed into a perfect bullet.

"Each of those took fifty years and the blood of a seventh son to make. There's nothing I know of they won't kill and let me be absolutely clear on this: I do not want you to be concerned about the cost. Use them to kill anything that gets in your way."

I knew Grimm ran orphanages and drug recovery houses, but I'd never heard or seen the paperwork for a blood bank. "How'd you get them to volunteer their blood?"

He looked off into the distance. "Volunteer may not be exactly the right term. One does not capture the essence of death with a vial full of blood."

I loaded the rest of the rounds into a magazine, and slapped the magazine into my gun. "One last problem, Grimm: I can't bother with a cell phone. Need my old bracelet back."

"No." Grimm looked at me over his glasses, his jaw set.

"No?"

"Those bracelets are for employees." The dais next to his desk glowed, and on it formed a perfect silver circle. "That is one for a partner."

His words took a moment to make sense, but over the months with Ari I'd remembered what happiness felt like. This was it. Freedom meant being able to go and being free to stay, and that simple choice made all the difference in the world.

"Give me a moment," I said, and I ran down the hall to the Visions Room. Inside, I waited for it to start, and as the light drained away I looked at my blessings and my curse. The damage was worse than I thought. How the thing had survived I couldn't say.

"Blessing?" It came forward, glowing. "I'm going to need your help." I reached out to the curse, and he nipped at me again. "Curse, I want you to come too. You may be a curse, but you are my curse. I claimed you."

Grimm appeared on the mirror outside. "Marissa, there isn't much time."

"Is there ever?"

"You'll need to get there quickly, and the Agency cars are missing."

It was about time I got the princess treatment. "You summoned me a pumpkin?"

Grimm rolled his eyes. "I called you a cab."

Thirty-Two

~

ON THE WAY over, I brought up a few tiny details I thought Grimm might have overlooked. "Let's start with where exactly we're going." Impromptu worked fine for me. In fact, it was something I did better than planned. The problem with impromptu in a cab was you could run up quite the fare. Also, when there was a fae army heading straight into downtown, it was not the right time to go for a sightseeing tour.

Grimm spoke from the rearview mirror. "Ari is at the castle. Liam is a bit more difficult to locate, since he isn't wearing his bracelet anymore. Speaking of which, do you like the new one? It should work in Kingdom as well."

"Fantastic, though I might want one in gold. If you want to find Liam, try looking for a dragon."

"How obvious, in hindsight." His eyes lost focus for a moment. "Half dragon, Marissa. I thought I trained you better. Also at the castle."

"Prince Mihail is working with Fairy Godmother. He knew about the curse. Said he wanted it. Ever heard of someone wanting a curse?"

Grimm waited in silence until I got his point. "A half dragon is something you would have to see to appreciate," he said.

"Seen him, touched him, got the scale marks to prove it."

Grimm shook his head. "If a man learned to control that sort of power, he would be worshipped and feared."

The cab pulled to a stop and I blinked. "Grimm, we at the right place?"

"I'm certain of it." We were parked outside the castle. The old castle. "Listen to me, Marissa: Within the castle there may yet be paths to her domain. Promise me you will not enter any mirrors."

"Fine." I reached for the door and it locked.

"Listen! You have read about the Black Queen and how her lies became truth as she spoke them. Within our domains it is so for the fairy. It is not just material we may bend."

"Kinky. Now let me out."

"My dear, this is no joking matter. In her realm, her choices would become yours, her thoughts yours. If you followed her, the person who returned would be only what she made them."

The door unlocked.

"Ok. Mirrors bad." I exited the cab, paid my fare, and set off to save my boyfriend, my best friend, and possibly the city. In that order.

The first clue someone had taken up residence at the old castle was the troll. Seeing a troll in Kingdom wasn't unusual, but this one wasn't looking to lie on a street corner and collect coins for marrow. It lumbered out to meet me. I pulled my gun from my purse and gave Grimm's super bullets a try, putting one right through its belly button.

In the movies, you always see people shooting to the head. Head shots may get more attention, but I'll take a solid body shot any day, because you are ten times as likely to pull it off. The troll rippled like water, and the flesh melted from it, leaving a smoking skeleton where it had once stood. Nice.

"Grimm, any idea where I'll find Ari or Liam?"

The new bracelet worked perfectly, and he snapped into view on the door knocker. "Ari is your priority. Without her power Liam becomes just an interesting prisoner."

"Why is that?"

"They'll want to recover the curse, not just kill Mr. Stone. A soul sieve takes immense energy to separate a curse from a person's body and soul. Torturing a seal bearer would supply that power."

I'd looked up a soul sieve after Grimm mentioned it the first time. The drawings resembled a food processor the size of a room, thousands of enchanted blades that would slice a body to pieces. Once the magical deflectors engaged, the soul would leak out one end as a slimy green liquid, the curse out the other, to be captured.

I pulled on the door, and it ground open. At one time, there was an entire team of liveried house servants to open those doors.

The castle was big. The new castle was about seven times the size, because it housed most of the actual government for Kingdom, but the old one was plenty large. Too large to go exploring in all the nooks and crannies. Fortunately I had a good idea where to find Ari. See, Fairy Godmother was sort of a stickler for tradition. Apples, snake curses. Myself, I'd keep the prisoner on the ground floor, in a blind hallway with murder holes in it. Ari would be in the tower, for sure.

I opened door after door, and finally called for help after finding my sixth empty conference/ball room. "Grimm, I could use help. Directions? Maps?"

"My dear, I would love to assist, but I have to point out there's another fairy at work here. Her magic is countering my own to the point where simply communicating is difficult. Once she is aware of your presence, even that may be impossible."

"Nice knowing you, Grimm." I reached the main chamber of the castle, and I saw what stood between me and Ari. Grimm would have hired mercenaries, a whole freaking boat of them, if he were going to guard a castle.

Godmother hired wolves. I'm guessing every wolf that wasn't in the wolf town was in the castle, plus they must have been having a wolf family reunion with folks from out of town. They lounged in the central chamber, dozing or scratching, in wolf, human, and every form in between.

The other thing to note was that wolves made lousy guards. Mercenaries would have patrolled the grounds, set up perimeters, that sort of thing. All the wolves did was sit around and gnaw at their fleas.

"Marissa," whispered Grimm in my ear, "don't attack them. I've sent help."

That's about when I heard the howling. From a hallway across the chamber, came a pack of wolves at full speed. Their mouths were frothy, and their fur matted with blood. They weren't hunting. They were running. Behind them, two women walked out, calmly, slowly into a cloud of wolves. Jess and Evangeline.

Evangeline was dressed like always, loose black pants and a sleeveless purple top. Jess wore something that looked like she had wrapped herself in the night. It was a long, sleek suit that clung to her curves like it was painted on. The fabric glittered as she moved, but otherwise it was like light simply disappeared into her.

The wolves circled and growled, and Jess pulled something from a sheath on her thigh. A knife. A simple double-bladed knife. The blade shone in the light and I knew it was silver. If the wolves in the chamber had any sense at all they would have run. One wolf attacked and the pack converged.

Jess and Evangeline moved like a sea of fury. Evangeline broke bones and bent limbs like taffy. Behind her Jess carved wolves the way one carves a turkey. I knew I wouldn't eat dark meat again for a while.

A heap of dead wolves lay at odd angles along the floor. The alpha wolf stopped and howled, called back his pack, halting the attack. The wolves ran from the hall on two legs and four, leaving the wounded behind.

In the silence I felt safe to leave the shadows of the hallway. "Hey."

Evangeline spun toward me, and I nearly caught a knife with my throat. "M, I thought I told you to stay someplace safe."

"I'm done taking orders. Ari and Liam are here somewhere. Any guesses where?"

Evangeline thought about it a moment. "There's a blind hall at the back of the west wing according to my map. They've probably put guards along the walls. They'll shoot anything that moves in the hallway."

I grabbed her arm. "The Princess Arianna."

Evangeline shook her head. "Tower's up the main stairs across the hall." Evangeline took a tiny map out and pointed.

"The half-dragon will be in the dungeon," said Jess. "Only place with enough stone to keep him. Also, as I recall, it's down the hall from the soul sieve. I'll head down there to find him, you two go get the princess." She jogged off down a hall into total darkness without fear.

I felt something coming. The ground shook and the chandeliers swayed. With each step, the wine sloshed from bowls where the wolves had filled their bellies. The formal arches at the end of the main chamber buckled and the doors caved in. I knew now why the wolves ran. The thing that walked in was like a wolf, only larger and heavier. It had white fur covering it and one eye slit so the lid never closed. It stepped forward, crushing the wounded wolves underfoot without so much as glancing down.

It growled, and I recognized words in the voice. "Red Riding Hood," and "Fenris."

I wished I'd worn something else on that first visit to the wolves. Anything else. I could've worn a bikini and caused less commotion. Come to think of it, I'd never caused a commotion in a bikini, but a red sweatsuit was now on my "does not look good on Marissa" list.

"M, get out of here," said Evangeline. She was smiling, a true smile, one that made the cuts on her face hang wide open, and her eyes were wild, wide like she'd found a treasure.

"I don't feel like fighting fair," I said, pointing my gun at it.

Evangeline stepped in front of me. "This one is mine. The Fae Mother said he was coming." She pulled off the veil and threw it on the floor.

Fenris began to shake and roar with laughter. He held up one paw, splaying the claws wide. Claws that ended in a green tinge that looked like rotting death. I knew in that moment exactly what Evangeline had gotten into a fight with.

I put my hand on her shoulder and pushed her aside. "I said I'm done taking orders, and all I need is a clear shot."

Fenris leaped at me, a blur of flying fur. Something hit me from the side. I flew through the air and crashed into a bench. Evangeline had thrown me a good eight feet. She had always fought barehanded, but now she held knives in her hands, wicked, curved knives, with blades that twisted.

Fenris swung at her, and she dodged. This time she sliced him, carving meat from bone all the way up to the shoulder.

He fell to the side, howling. As I watched, the skin knit itself back together as though it had never been torn. "Run," I yelled, but they were already at it, claw and blade, in a dance so close it was impossible to separate them.

I needed a clear shot, and there was as much Evangeline as wolf in my way. They moved back and forth across the floor, and Fenris shifted like putty as he did. Sometimes on four feet, sometimes almost a hulking man, always a blur of death. Evangeline had blood running from her face, and her purple top shone with what I hoped was wolf blood. He went for her throat.

Like a tornado of blades, she rolled under him and came up on the other side. They stood a few feet from each other, and Evangeline tossed something to the floor. A wolf ear, and it didn't grow back. I edged around her, trying to get a clean shot, but she sidestepped, keeping herself between me and it. The wolf swiped at her, almost a feint, and came away missing two fingers. They didn't grow back either.

"You have no idea how long I've waited to do this," said Evangeline.

Fenris howled with rage, but in the middle of his howl, she attacked, driving him backwards. With every step, she moved him, with every slice, she whittled flesh from him. Wolf skin lay like ribbons on the floor. She slipped. Maybe she was too tired. Or too hurt, or maybe she was just human, but one inch made all the difference. Fenris whipped a claw around, catching her by her single braid. He brought his other claw in, raking across her abdomen. Blood gushed out but she didn't even bother trying to hold it in, she swung the knives around, stabbing him through one eye, and then the other.

Fenris dropped her in a wet mess, raising claws to eyes. Already, the eyes took shape again, filling in the sockets.

My first bullet caught him in the stomach, and as the magic rippled out he screamed, a wolf howl of agony. The second one followed so close it almost took the same hole. The third one I put right through his eye.

He fell backwards, flesh dripping like sizzling fat, as Grimm's corrosive magic warred with his healing powers. The flesh turned black and dripped away faster than it could regrow. I didn't wait to see him dissolve. I was kneeling on the floor, watching Evangeline die. She was my teacher. My mentor. Some days almost a friend, and I couldn't do anything for her. In the movies, you always get to say good-bye. You get to tell someone what they meant to you, and maybe hear they cared for you, but she was gone. Her eyes lay open, but empty.

"You killed Fenris. The wolves will not be amused. They'll make bacon from your breasts for that," said a voice I knew. A voice I hated.

"Mihail, it's past your bedtime. Your mommy wants you to come home." I closed Evangeline's eyes.

He stood on the steps that led out of the chamber and up to the main tower.

I advanced on him, not caring why he didn't have the good sense to run. "She says I'll suffer if I fail to keep you safe. I could do with a little suffering right now." I wasn't about to waste one of my magic bullets on him. I was going to kill the bastard myself. I'm not usually a killer, but I have my limits.

He held up an apple, crisp and red with a candy shell. "I think not." It glistened under his fingers. So perfect. So magical. "I think I'm going to toss this your way. I might get a little mess on me, but that's a risk I'm willing to take. Then I'm going to go upstairs and enjoy a little 'there's not going to be a wedding night' sex with the princess."

Something crashed into his head, and he fell forward. I winced as the apple bounced down the stairs. Tiny cracks split open on its surface as it rolled up to me, and it bubbled on the broken edges.

"My name is Ari. It's not a hard name to remember." Ari stepped out of the shadow of the stairs. She had a cut on one side of that cute little face and a black eye. Her scalp showed where several patches of her hair had been torn out, but she was alive, and she ran down the stairs to me.

"Marissa! It's here. I can feel it."

"The fae Seal? Grimm said it wasn't anywhere. He was thinking maybe on a different plane."

"It's here, I'm certain of it. It's near my cell." She looked down, and saw Evangeline. The color drained from her face and she took my hand. "I'm sorry, M. I'm sorry."

"I'm going to kill someone for her, that's a promise. Starting with the prince." My hands shook, and my eyes blurred with tears that were neither fear nor sorrow. That's when the spell hit. A standard binding spell, nothing fancy. I wasn't watching and I wasn't ready. It hit me so hard it knocked me off my feet.

Ari managed to stay on her feet. In fact, the spell hardly did anything to her besides ruffle her hair. One of these days I have got to be a princess. She looked up to the stairs, where Queen Thromson stood in a completely impractical gown. Sweeping and shiny, and leaving absolutely nothing hidden. She might as well have been wearing plastic wrap.

"Gwendolyn," said Ari.

"Arianna, I told you to call me Mother."

"And I said to call me Ari. You are not my mother. Let

us go. There is still time to get the Seal back to the fae before they destroy the city. How could you do this?"

Ari's stepmother—I mean, Gwendolyn—walked slowly down the stairs and knelt by Mihail.

"Why would I give it back? It took me so long to take it from them. Daughter, war brings opportunities. The Kingdom authorities will suffer heavy losses. There are bound to be casualties in the Court of Queens. And who better to lead as High Queen than your mother? The fae believe they come unopposed, and they will die by the thousands."

"So will most of the people in the city."

"There are people who matter, daughter, and people who don't. Get used to it. You matter. Your friend there does not. Who should I spare? You or her?"

Mihail rose to his feet, looking more than a little bleary. "Neither. Kill them both." He walked over to the queen and kissed her, softly at first, and then with passion. "How do you like that, little princess? Your mother is ten times the temptress you are, and luscious in ways I would love to show you."

Ari giggled. "I'm so happy for you. The prince I can't stand and the stepmother I hate. I hope you two have a long life together. I do." I felt the power rushing into her, and the spell around us lessened. The queen felt her magic too, and a look of rage passed over her face.

"Magic? You have taken the path of the witch? I'll kill you myself before I let a child of my house do that."

"I am a seal bearer, Gwenny, and not part of your house any longer."

The binding spell on me weakened. I could move, though it still pressed in like being smothered under a mattress.

"You have used your power before touching a seal, Arianna. You are a witch, tainted with wild magic. And as such, I will strike you down." The queen raised her hand. When Ari did magic there was this feeling like water drifting over your skin. When the queen did it I felt like I stood in a whirlpool. Ice grew at the queen's fingertips, absolute elemental cold.

I stood, but I couldn't quite aim, and running wasn't an option under twenty tons of spell.

She flicked her hand at us, and an orb of pure cold floated lazily our way, freezing the stone underneath. Ari hadn't moved, not one inch. In the midst of the queen's magic I hadn't noticed that she'd built a spell of her own, a round disk that grew darker and darker at the edges. She spun a shield. The winter orb struck her shield, and for a moment everything stopped. The orb exploded, unleashing a blizzard.

I'm convinced Ari's shield saved us. I had ice on my skin and the floor was covered in snow, but a cone of protection extended back from where she stood. I could finally move. I couldn't sling a spell to save my soul, but I could toss an apple. The broken apple at my feet lay coated in ice. I grabbed it and did my best baseball impression, hurling it straight at the queen. It was a thing of beauty, right up until she caught it.

She held the apple an inch from her hand by pure willpower. The apple's protective shell shattered and magic oozed out onto its skin. The queen tossed it aside without regard, and as it passed, it touched Mihail. Brushed his hand, really, but a sliver of candy fell from the apple, and I saw for a moment the spell contained inside. A spell designed to twist and destroy magic. Magic like princes have.

He screamed as it crawled up him, leaching out of the apple shell like an ooze and devouring him. As it did, he stumbled backwards. How he ran, how he moved at all, I can't say, but his wailing trailed off up the staircase.

"Burn," said the queen, and I realized too late she had gathered another spell. Not ice. Fire. The hellfire wreathed her hand like a thing alive, and I knew Ari was too weak to block it.

"I don't think so," said a voice from the dungeon tunnel, and Liam came running out. His wrists had cuts from the manacles, and the marks on his face were probably all bruises. "Don't you dare touch her."

The queen glanced at him and flicked her wrist, letting the flame go. It leaped out at him, wrapping his form, so hot I had steam burns from the ice melting. The hellfire raged and leaped across the furniture, burning the dirt and wolf bodies. In the inferno, something moved.

Liam came out of it wrapped in fire, clothed in it, covered in it. He shook his hands, wringing the flames from them like water.

He glared at her, his mouth pulled back in a thin smile. "That tickles." In his voice I heard the curse speak. "I've got a little fire of my own." Smoke began to billow from his mouth as the fire welled up inside him.

I pulled the trigger.

I'll never know how she got the first spell off in time, catching the bullet. Anything else, I think she'd have stopped cold, but this was no apple tossed by an angry woman. I shot her with a magic bullet, designed to kill magic things, and it didn't stop, it slowed down. As it did, the bullet changed, becoming something like a tiny death reaper.

The queen screamed and with a surge of power threw the bullet into the stone. So I gave her another one, right between her eyes, and again she caught it. With each spell, she changed. White streaks rippled through her hair like water, and as she forced the bullet to the side, wrinkles dripped like rain down her face.

"I've still got one more." I carefully put the sight on her chest.

She ran, and I wasn't about to waste my last bullet on a bad shot. Liam grabbed me and nearly crushed me in a hug. The fire raced along him but felt cool to the touch.

He leaned over and whispered in my ear. "I have these dreams. I used to think they were dreams. Dreams of fire and rage and destruction." He let me go for a moment but kept his head close to mine. "I would wake up and tell myself it wasn't real. It couldn't be. Then you showed up and it's trolls and wolves and people with guns, and I needed it to be a dream."

Outside the hall, I heard the screams of wolves and the sound of armored feet approaching. Help was on the way. I considered how the rest of this year had gone, and I knew it was more trouble.

"I can hear inside it. I remember. Did you mean what you said there?" I couldn't speak, I could barely nod, and then he swept me up into those arms so I could smell the smoke on him. "Then I don't want it to be a dream anymore."

"Ahem," said a voice, and I looked back. The hellfire had gone out, and Liam was very naked. I also didn't appreciate where Jess was looking, and I'm pleased to say Ari had found a convenient speck of dirt on the ground to study. About then the wolves came back, and they brought company. Big company in suits of armor.

"This day just doesn't quit," said Jess. "I'll deal with the wolves, you three go find the queen." The armored creatures marched forward, clattering swords and shields. I felt in my purse for another clip and shivered as the Root of Lies caressed my fingers. I'd have to ask Liam to burn the thing later.

Liam walked toward the wolves like he was going out to greet friends. "You know, up until now my curse and I haven't agreed on much. When it comes to you, we're on the same page." He glanced at me, and his eyes shone as if they were on fire.

I think for a moment the alpha wolf considered running. Did I mention that wolves were stupid? It leaped at me and Liam caught it like a bug, slamming it into the ground. A growl came from deep in his chest, and he swung it overhead by the arm, slamming it into the ground again. He wrenched over like he was vomiting, and fire belched out, blanketing the wolf.

Liam looked up at me, a tiny drool drop of fire hanging from his lip. "Get out of here. I've got serious mood swings." I had trouble understanding because his teeth were changing.

I ran for the tower, and realized that Ari limped along behind me. "Ari, stay here. I'm going after the queen."

"Not without me. I've got a score to settle with her." She wiped blood off her cheek and ran after me.

I helped her up the staircase, looking back to see my boyfriend one last time. He was mostly dragon now, and even though he had scales and horns and was ripping the entrails out of a wolf, he made my heart thrill. "Grimm," I said, and there was no answer. "Grimm, are you there?"

When he spoke, his voice broke up. "She knows you are there, Marissa. Hard enough to keep in contact at all."

"The Seal is here. Ari can feel it."

His voice came through louder this time. "My dear, that's not possible. The fae would have simply taken it."

"Grimm, she's hiding it. Even you can't sense it here. How would the fae?"

He paused for a moment, long enough that I thought perhaps we'd lost our connection. "A locus. She's joined her demesne to the castle, creating a locus of power. It's like a black hole for magic, it would conceal even a fairy. If you can get the Seal far enough away, the fae will be able to sense it and they'll come for it. They won't be able to put it back in place, but they'll stop the fighting. They have already begun their attack."

"Fine. One Seal, coming right up."

"Get going. I'm going to tell the fae you have the Seal and are bringing it to them. Don't make a liar of me."

Thirty-Three

~⚬~

IT SHOULD BE a law that if you put in a tower, you have to put in an elevator. At one point, the castle had a large lock of golden hair, but the cost of detangler spray and a bout of lice spelled the end for it. Any way you look at it, a staircase that long was a violation of common sense. How you'd get a princess in a wheelchair to the top, I had no idea.

It didn't help that Ari was worn out from her spell battle. After the first three-dozen landings, we came to one where a door lay open. Two goblins sprawled on the floor, their heads split open.

Ari gestured. "That's where they were keeping me."

I looked inside. Standard princess prison cell. Rose-scented stationary was a dead giveaway. "Wait. You killed two goblins?"

She blushed. "I meant to knock them out."

"Use the flat part of the axe next time."

She held up her hand, as if reaching for something. "The Seal's near here."

We followed the stairs on up, and I threw open the last

door. We stood at the railing, on top of the old castle tower. To the east, I saw the lights of magic like fireworks at ground level, blinding sweeps of white light, as the fae swept their death magic to and fro, and red explosions as apples rained down on them. Ari pulled my hand, hauling me back inside.

She had her eyes closed. "When Moth—when Gwendolyn hit me, it nearly knocked me out. I realized I can see magic without using my eyes." I had a brief shiver as I thought of the Isyle Witch and her eyes without pupils.

She reached into the stone. "Here." It rippled under her fingers. Something clicked, and a hidden door swung open to a room that would have hung in the air beyond the tower. Inside it, a lightning storm raged a thousand times over. As I looked at it, I realized it was only one ball of lightning. It was the Seal. The walls and floors were mirrors.

Ari looked at it with her eyes closed. "How are we going to get that to the fae?"

"We aren't. You are."

She snapped her eyes open and glared at me. "I can't use my magic. You saw what happened last time."

I had. I also saw what happened to the queen, and I didn't want that for Ari. "I don't think it's something you do. It's something you are. You are the seal bearer for your family."

"That's not what that means. I have the family seal on me, and that's what gives me magic."

I grabbed her by the shoulders and looked her in the eye. "Think about it. The royal families weren't given magic to use against each other. They were given it so that they could seal the realms. When the Fae Mother spoke to you, she said you had to become what you are. You are a seal bearer."

Ari shook her head. "That's not what she said. She said I would become a witch." She started toward the door. "I'll try."

"Wait," I said. "Grimm said it would be in Fairy Godmother's demesne. It's kind of like a gateway to where she actually lives, and I'd bet anything magic entering there will raise all kinds of trouble. Stay here at the door, I'll bring the Seal to you, and you can carry it out to the fae."

She reached inside the hidden room and touched the floor. It rippled under her fingers, and as she pulled them back a drop of glass fell to the mirror. After a moment, it became solid again. I pushed on it, and felt only glass.

I thought for a moment about Grimm's warning, but as long as Ari stayed out of the room, I wouldn't be going through the mirror. So I stepped out of the stairway and into the hidden room. The mirrored floor held my weight, thank goodness, and I walked up to the Seal. It looked like the foxfire Ari had summoned, only bigger, angrier.

I reached out toward it, and flashes of light played across its surface. Grimm had said the Seal was alive, so I figured maybe it could be reasoned with. "I need you to come with me. My friend there is a seal bearer, and she'll take you home." The room shook in a way that felt far too familiar.

"Hurry! Your blessings are hungry for it," Ari yelled.

I remembered what had happened to Ari's foxfire and grabbed the Seal. It burned like I'd grabbed a power line, sending pain rippling through my hands and down my body, but I forced myself to take a step. I could move it.

"Child," said Fairy Godmother, "you are foolish beyond compare."

I took another step, and my arms jerked back and forth as the Seal resisted me.

"Come on," Ari said. "One of your blessings is fighting with the other one."

I hoped my blessing was fighting to keep my curse away, but it was equally possible they were fighting over who got the first bite. That's when I realized I could see Fairy Godmother in the mirrors. All of them. She was no longer the beautiful gray-haired Queen; she was the emaciated woman in a gown of woven bones.

"Once you strike at me, and thrice I return it. Few receive my third gift."

I managed a couple more steps. Just a little farther to

the door. The mirrors went blank, and then lit up. It was like looking out a window on a hurricane. They no longer reflected the Seal. Instead, black clouds boiled in them, and an eerie green light filled the room. "Come," said Fairy Godmother. I felt the floor change. The next step, my foot sank into the glass an inch, and I pushed the Seal toward Ari. The next step I sank up to my knee. When I raised my foot, glass pulled like taffy along with it.

Ari leaned in and snagged the Seal. It clung to her like a child, zipping in circles around her and sending bolts of lightning off. In the reflection of the mirror, I saw my hara-kathin drawn to it over and over, but each time they approached, a glow surrounded Ari and pushed them away. The glow drifted off from Ari like a cloud, but as the Seal orbited her, the glow drew inside her until her skin shone like she was on fire.

"Take it to the fae," I said.

Ari held on to the door frame and leaned out, hanging over the floor. "Give me your hand."

I sank to my waist in the mirror, and swung my purse like a rope toward Ari. It hit something invisible in the air and bounced to the side. In the mirror, I saw my curse hovering there, his eyes glowing. A claw wrapped around my waist and pulled me under.

I fell through the mirror and beyond.

I LANDED ON grass and clamped my hands over my ears. If the voice of the fae had sounded like thunder, the sounds of birds twittering rushed through my brain like the squeal from a microphone, and the bright glimpse of green seared into my brain. The intensity of this world washed over me like a wave, tearing at my mind. Even the softness of the grass brought pleasure to the point of agony. Then Fairy Godmother spoke.

"Hush," she said, and the world grew quieter. I opened my eyes, and I lay on a vast field of green as far as I could see. My purse had fallen through the mirror, and my driver's license and everything else lay scattered in the grass. "You must not go mad yet, darling, or you will not appreciate your third wish."

I looked for Prince Mihail. "Where are they?"

She floated backwards a few steps. "The queen and her pawn? This was not their checkmate."

"I've won. Ari will take the Seal back to the fae and end the war. They will know what you did. You took the Seal. You hid Mihail. You took the child."

"And then what, darling? What will the fae do against one of us, the old ones? They are only our dreams, born when our minds wandered. Not unlike yourself."

"Why? Why start a war?"

"The fae kill the Kingdom, the Kingdom kill the fae, and the people of your miserable slice of world belong to me. Such an irony, in that dull, dreary world, the people grow magic."

"You started a war for magic?"

She tipped her head. "What else would be worth it? Humans are unremarkable. They grow and die in the blink of an eye, and when they wield magic, they are feeble and clumsy. Still, I assure you—if you took every bit of magic and killed every dream in that city, tomorrow something amazing would happen. Do you know what it is?"

My bracelet glowed white as Grimm tried to reach me. "Enlighten me."

"They'd get up and go about their miserable little lives, and before they could even make it out the door they'd have a tiny hope. Maybe today they wouldn't get yelled at. Or today they'd win the lottery, or today they might find love. That pitiful race creates magic it can't even use. But I can."

I spotted something lying in the grass and smiled. "It is beautiful here."

She returned the smile. "I am glad you like it, darling. You will never leave." She swept her hand, and the sun swung toward the horizon. "I like it best at sunset."

Rising to my feet, I took a few steps away. "How far does it go?"

"Beyond forever."

While she spoke, I picked up the gun and hid it in my palm, and picked a glorious pink flower. "I have something for you." I turned to her and held out the flower.

She bent to smell it, and I pulled the trigger. The gun roared, a muffled, mechanical noise foreign to this world, sending out that last magic bullet in a burst of smoke. The bullet exploded into a cloud of butterflies.

I knew she had toyed with me, but she wasn't frowning. She was smiling. "So clever. So cunning and courageous. No wonder he took you as his agent. No wonder she marked you as her own. So stupid."

My hands felt like lead, and my arms hung limp.

"You don't like that gun," she said.

Fear gripped me as I realized I didn't. I hated it, in fact.

"You want to throw it far away."

My arms shook as I clenched my hands down on the grip.

"You need to throw it."

This was a thousand times worse than Grimm compelling me. That felt like someone else moving my arms and hands. This was different. She spoke of need, and I felt it. I threw the gun with all my strength, flinging it away. I swung at her with my fist.

"Back," she said, and I was flung through the air, landing in the pile of debris, where my purse overturned. Something streaked through the air, whistling like an incoming missile. Two Harakathin, one golden white and one sparkling purple. They flew at her, biting and tearing and scratching.

I rolled to my feet in the grass and a gleam caught my eye. In my purse had been the Root of Lies. In my world, it was an ebony claw like tree roots, but here it was dull bronze. I touched it. It ran like liquid in my fingers, becoming a curved dagger. A weapon. I picked up the Root and held it against my arm. While I held it, her power over me seemed weaker.

Fairy Godmother crossed her arms before her. "Away." My harakathin were flung out of sight, but I knew they'd be back. I stood and walked toward her. "Yes. Come to me, darling." She reached out to embrace me. I flipped the dagger over and sliced up and back, attempting to cut her throat. On the upstroke I missed her artery by a centimeter and the downstroke cut her cheek clean through her lip so her teeth showed.

"*Down!*" she screamed.

The world crushed me to my knees. It felt like the sky lay across my back. She bled, and the drops turned to Glitter as they fell. "Never has one dared to strike at me in my home. Never has my blood been shed. You will wish for death, and never find it granted."

The Root of Lies lay a few feet from me, the blade writhing as it drank the fairy blood. I saw two comets come shrieking through the sky, blessings and curse returned, but they bounced off of her like she was stone.

"I will devour your curse children later, but first I must complete my promise to you. I owe you your third wish."

I laughed at her.

"You don't think I can hurt you more," she said, and she waved her hand. The sky became a mirror, and I looked out at the main hall of the castle. Ari walked like a sleepwalker, carrying the Seal before her, right through the middle of the hall. Wolves lay shredded or burned, and only the armored knights remained. Liam tore the head from an armored knight as it approached Ari, and sent a burst of flame at the others.

"I can be her." She shifted, her face running like wax until Ari stood before me. She spoke in Ari's voice. "I can be your friend, darling. Or I can be him." Now Liam stood on the grass plane. "I will sweep you off your feet. You are mine now. You agree to it."

As she spoke the words I felt something snap into place between us. A feeling I recognized from the night I was sixteen. I forced my image of her, demanding she appear as the gray queen, and she did.

Blessings, I said in my mind. Their faces snapped to me, watching with eager round eyes. They could hear my thoughts, something I probably should have realized. *Please, take the Root of Lies and stab her with it.* Beatus immediately flew to it and seized it, but before he could turn around, he was tackled by Consecro.

"Your playthings amuse me," said Godmother. "As does your request to them." She could hear my thoughts, which definitely was not good.

She held out her hand along mine, and beckoned to them. "We will play a game. Let them decide."

The harakathin rolled in the grass, biting and squealing and screaming until Consecro used the dagger like a club, bashing Beatus. He limped over, the dagger in his hands like a broadsword.

Please, I thought, *please let it be her. You are mine.* He kept his little snout down, and he refused to look at me as he approached. He raised the dagger, a gleeful smile on his face. And he brought it down, driving it through my palm.

Pain shot through me and up my arm like I had never known. As my blood touched it, the dagger changed back, becoming the claw root again. It clasped my fingers like an old friend, letting my blood dribble onto it.

"I have seen your desires," said Godmother, "and I fulfill them. I grant you your third wish. You will never be alone again." I felt her presence descend on me like rain, pattering into my heart and mind, pushing on me, and all the while the claw writhed in my hand. As it did, an idea took form. I pushed it away, refusing to let it take focus.

I shaped my mind, calling on all the need in my heart, to see her as I needed her to be, and she changed. "Yes," she said, "yes." Her gray hair became black and her pale skin tan and the smell of the rain became the scent I knew from a hundred nights of reading with her or doing homework. It was the smell when she hugged me when I was sick, and when I opened my eyes, Fairy Godmother was gone. I stood with my Mom.

I gripped the Root of Lies in my hand as she hovered over me, overpowering me. Becoming me.

"Ask," she said, feeling the question that came to me every time I saw Mom.

I waited, waited until I could feel her taking over my thoughts. I finally asked the question I knew I always had.

"Mom, do you love me?"

She breathed out a scent of warmth and kindness I'd never known. I knew the truth.

"Of course I do."

There was one heartbeat of peace, one moment of silence, and I felt the Root tear in to me. Touching the Seal felt like electric death, and I thought I'd felt the worst I could. All the pain of six years, all the broken bones and stitches, it was nothing. The Root of Lies shot up through my skin, tearing through my arm and into her. She screamed and fought, but it held her as tightly as I did, and the thorns cut into her lungs, choking her screams into whistles. Still it grew, curling around her and through her. Thorns sliced into my scalp where our heads touched.

She writhed and twisted as the thorns consumed her. Glitter ran from her like blood as the thorns burst through her skin and thickened, blackened. The thorn branches holding me to Fairy Godmother crackled and broke. I collapsed forward, and lay in the grass, alone with pain and blood.

Something bumped into my chest, and I realized Beatus and Consecro stood before me. I willed them to come, and they did. First Beatus, then Consecro, they snuggled up next to me. In this world, I could feel them. I put my good hand on Consecro's head and held him close. The sun set for the final time on this world, and without Godmother I could never leave. I curled up with my harakathin and waited for the end.

I FELT HIM coming before I saw him, a rumbling like an earthquake, a light shining like the first sunrise on earth. His light swept over me, shining like a spotlight, so bright it blinded me. In the light, I saw Fairy Godmother was gone. The Root of Lies had grown through her, tearing her apart, replacing every piece of her with thorns. Where she had stood, a thorn tree loomed, bent into the shape of a woman. She was dead, and the Root was destroyed. A ball of blazing light settled before me, brilliant like the rainbow, brighter than the sun.

"Marissa, my dear, what did I tell you about mirrors?"

When I looked at Grimm, there was this odd moment. See, I'd never seen him from the waist down, so I didn't have an image of what he looked like. He looked like a butler. He looked at his legs. "I had hoped you would give me a more striking figure."

"It suits you." I began to shiver violently, though I no longer felt the cold. Thorns stuck out through my skin in places, and my hand was a pile of ruined flesh where the Root had grown through it.

Grimm reached down and took my good hand. "This is my home now, and in it, you are what I make you."

I winced and looked away, waiting for the wrenching healing to begin.

"Marissa, here I am not limited in my abilities." Grimm spoke softly, patiently.

I opened my eyes in time to see a burst of light wash across me. Warmth like fire raced along me, tracing my wounds, numbing the pain. The thorns dissolved like butter and the cuts healed. My skin grew tan and smooth. I wished Grimm would heal like that more often. Only the scars remained on my hand, tracing out in white the handmaiden's mark. "You can't do anything about this?"

"I'm afraid not. Your scars are not something I can take from you." A table appeared behind him. "You said once I've never had you over for dinner." Food grew on the table from a vine, with goblets and platters. "It never occurred to me to, shall we say, turn down the volume on my realm. Would you like to have dinner?"

Though I no longer ached, I was tired beyond all knowledge. "I want to go home. Rain check?"

"Out through the mirror is a more difficult task," said Grimm, "but one I can handle. We'll go through fae to retrieve Ari, and that means you must sleep. I would not have you ruined for your home by the journey." A portal sliced itself out of the air, and through it came the colors and sounds of fae, pale against the colors here. "Do you trust me?"

A bed appeared, a luxurious four-poster bed with deep satin sheets and silk pillows. As I touched them, all the weariness of six years came on me. I barely managed to climb in before my head became too heavy to keep off the pillow. Grimm leaned over and tucked me in.

"Sleep, my dear, and dream." Sleep wrapped around me like a warm blanket, and took me home.

I dreamed we traveled down a tunnel made of diamond, but the diamond moved in waves like the ocean, and mighty voices thundered around me as I passed. The Fae Mother came to me, gliding on the wind.

I trembled when she reached out to me.

"Peace. You do not need to fear my touch here. The Princess has restored our Seal. We have ceased our war. But yours is only beginning."

I remembered her words so long ago when she blessed me. The Black Queen would come. I would drink of a river of pain.

"You must tell her. She must become what she is, if there is to be hope."

"Who, Ari?" I asked, and she nodded. Behind me, I realized Ari traveled with us, her eyes shut tight. My bed had changed into a box that looked disturbingly like a coffin.

The Fae Mother brushed my cheek. "You will bring the end of the world, and carry its hope." She drifted away, carried by the wind. We sailed on a river of rainbow, until darkness wrapped me and I truly slept, until I heard his voice.

"Go on, kiss her," said Grimm. "It is traditional."

I opened my eyes, and I saw Liam's face. He smiled at me in that way I had waited so long for, and I flung my arms up around him. I was free. He was mine.

Thirty-Four

~∾~

I STOPPED BY the Agency on my way out of town, and of course Liam went with me. Jess asked for one more look at Liam's curse. I watched him through the normal monitor, almost as pleased to see him shirtless as he was to see me.

Jess had him turn around enough times that I figured she was no longer looking at the curse. "That's one hell of an entanglement." She shook her head.

"I've seen worse," said Grimm. "It's been a couple of millennia since then, but with two of you working on it, I'm certain you could earn enough Glitter for a cure. I doubt it would take more than a couple of decades."

I let out an offended gasp. "What happened to the 'No Men' rule?"

"I'll make an exception in this case."

"No thanks. I'm looking forward to getting back to doing art." Liam put his flannel shirt back on, buttoning each row with care.

"I could use the services of a half-dragon," said Grimm, and he morphed into his temptress form, a lush woman with purple locks of hair. "And you'll love the way we sign our contracts."

I hooked my arm into Liam's and pulled him toward the door. "Vienna, Grimm. We're taking some time."

"I'm well aware of that. Leaving me to handle cleanup from the largest war in sixty years. I'll be overseeing reconstruction of Kingdom for the next six months, so don't think you'll get out of it." I shook my head. "Running DNA tests on the remains of half of Kingdom's army isn't my idea of relaxation."

Grimm shifted back to his usual self. "Well, I've got offers for work in the old country. In case you get bored."

I tossed Ari the keys to my apartment. "You'll keep an eye on it while I'm gone?"

She looked at the key ring. "No car key?"

"I want you alive when I come back."

Jess came over and put her hand on Ari's shoulder. "I taught Evangeline how to drive. I can teach anyone."

Ari turned a little green. "I don't have anywhere else to go. Mother's banned me from Kingdom, I don't have a job. I was supposed to marry for happiness."

Grimm cleared his throat. "In light of past events, I've been considering an opportunity for new agents. I offer medical, dental, and employee education plans. You'll need the medical and dental more than the salary."

"Sorcery?" said Ari, a note of hope in her voice. She practically beamed with excitement.

Grimm crossed his arms and gave her a stern look. "College, young lady. A smart agent is an effective agent. Though were you to excel in your normal studies, we might negotiate access to other training resources."

I shook my head. "I thought you had a 'No princesses' rule."

"Rules are made to be broken," said Grimm.

Ari sat back in the chair, her eyes closed.

"Of course, young lady, there's the matter of how we sign our contracts."

"Not gonna happen." Ari threw a pen at the mirror for emphasis.

We walked out without looking back. Ari would be fine. We rode down in the elevator and caught a cab for the airport. I snuggled up to Liam and put my head on his chest. He put an arm around me and squeezed me so tight my ribs hurt. "Is this the ever after I keep hearing about?"

I thought about the prophecies I'd heard from the Fae Mother. I ran my fingers over the scars on my hand and made a decision. I couldn't get back what I once had. I didn't know what might come. But I could enjoy the now. "I don't know, but at least I've got the happy."

TURN THE PAGE FOR A SNEAK PEEK AT THE NEXT
GRIMM AGENCY NOVEL

Armageddon Rules

COMING SOON FROM ACE BOOKS!

IN MY DEFENSE, I didn't mean to start the Apocalypse. It wasn't just my personal aversion to oblivion; I had a clear financial motive: The end of the world is bad for business.

Speaking of business, that Monday began the same way almost every Monday had for the last three weeks, with a plague. Last week it was frogs.

I rolled into the office at about nine forty-five, and, as usual, the Agency was pure chaos. Rosa—our receptionist—was opening a fresh container of Taser darts and we'd only been open for forty-five minutes.

"Miss Locks, you gotta help." A man in an orange jumpsuit with "Corrections Department" stamped in block letters down the side grabbed my shoulder as I walked past, spinning me around. "I gotta get me a wish."

Strike one: Escaping from a garbage pickup crew. Strike two: Putting grubby fingers on my brand-new tweed top. Strike three: Calling me "Miss" instead of "Ms." Locks. Far as I was concerned, Miss Locks left the building the day I turned eighteen and hadn't been seen around here since.

"I'll make a few calls." To the police, if possible. To the morgue, if necessary.

He nodded gratefully and sat down on a bench.

I slipped through the "Staff Only" door, made it to the kitchen, and had almost poured a cup of coffee before the screaming started. One should never face disaster without caffeine. So I got my coffee and headed back out to the lobby, strolling through the door to see exactly what we'd been struck with.

Rats ran everywhere. They scrabbled on the walls, gnawed on the furniture, and covered the floor like a shag carpet from 1973. In the middle of the lobby stood a teen-age girl, six feet tall, rail thin, with platinum blond hair. Her clothes hung in tatters from bony white arms, and red blotches surrounded each of her many, many piercings. Her extravagant collection of tattoos spoke of poor impulse control and even worse decision-making skills. She looked up at me with baleful eyes. "Please. I need help."

I glanced around the room. The couple nearest the door held a cage with a toad, the kobold soccer team waited for Grimm to refuse to help them, and the guy on the end still hadn't figured out this wasn't a payday loan joint. I opened the staff door and waved to her. "Come on."

Rosa glowered at me, mumbling curses in Spanish. She hated when I picked clients, and if she had her way, we'd take them one at a time, from number one to number six hundred in exactly that order. Even if fifty-three was a starving fungal giant and sixty-two was a samurai with a serious shitake addiction. To her credit, Rosa kept her mouth shut. One does not argue with the boss.

We headed down the hall to a conference room, me, the girl, and enough rats to supply a hot-dog factory running three shifts, seven days a week. I took a seat on one side of the table, she took a seat on the other, and the rats took seats *everywhere*. Flicking one off my knee, I began the interview. "So what exactly do you want me to do for you?"

Tears smudged the sludge of makeup she wore, and she waved her arms around. "Duh. Isn't it obvious?"

Absolutely. Obvious that she needed help. Figuring out which kind first, that was the hard part. I walked over and ran my fingers through her tangled, crispy hair, took a good look at all sixteen rings in her ear, and the tasteful depiction on her shoulder of what was either Bob Dylan as "The Man in the Long Black Coat," or a velociraptor playing acoustic guitar. "We can help. First, let's take out those piercings. I'll get you some alcohol and a prescription for some antibiotics. Your hair is crunchy from whatever you used to bleach it, and the tattoos are going to take years to remove."

A rat jumped into my coffee and poked its head out. The girl stared as I fished it out by the tail, set it on the table, and handed it a sugar cube.

"What about the rats?"

I took another sip of coffee, which tasted Parisian, with a hint of rat. "What about them?"

"The only thing I need is for you to get rid of the rats." She shivered.

I pushed a box of tissues across to her. "What's your name?"

She scratched out a tissue and wiped her eyes. The tissue caught in her makeup and left shreds clinging to her cheeks. "Elizabeth. I like Beth."

I brushed the rats off the table between us and leaned forward, my mind already made up. "Well, Beth, I have good news and bad news. Good news is I can help with the hair, the piercings, and I've got a lady in my wardrobe department who can teach you how to use less than a pound of cosmetics a day. The bad news, I'm not going to do a thing about the rats."

She stared at me as her brain tried to process what I said. I leaned across and patted her hand. "You look hungry." Truth was, she looked like one of those commercials for starving kids.

"I can't eat. Every time I try to eat the rats take it from me."

I should've asked about her credit. I should've asked Rosa if her application was complete, but one look at her said I'd found my charity case for the week. "I'm going to order a pizza or two. I'll have one of my employees bring a barrel of garbage up from the Dumpster to distract your companions. I need you to sit tight for a bit, okay?"

She nodded and put her head down on the table. Walking out the door, on the way to my office, I made a mental note to have the table cleaned, or burned, or both.

I HAD A big office, almost the biggest in the Agency, which was only right, since for most things, most days, I was in charge. I was a partner; the junior partner, but definitely not a silent one.

I pulled a towel off the full-length mirror in the corner and made a call. "Grimm, how's it going?"

Grimm snapped into view in the mirror, looking more like an English butler than a sentient manifestation of magic. Grimm was the Fairy Godfather, founder of the Agency, once my boss, and sometimes my friend. He could grant wishes if he wanted to, but most people didn't need wishes. They needed solutions to their problems.

Just so we're clear, I had no magic. I wasn't a princess, witch, half-blood, or anything like that. The only magic I could work was performed with bullets, bacon, or boobs. Anything that couldn't be handled with the big three, I called in Grimm. I didn't call often.

He smiled, making the wrinkles in his face crease together. "Marissa, my dear, it is only Monday. Do you require my assistance already?" His voice always reminded me of some nature documentary narrator.

I shook my head. "Nah. Nothing we can't handle yet. Got a new piper though. She can't be more than seventeen."

Grimm slid his glasses forward to look at me over the thick, black edges. "What, may I ask, is she piping?"

I shrugged. "The usual for newbies." New pipers, particularly girls, always started with brainless, easy-to-influence creatures like rats or teenage boys. "If we can get her trained, this year's poodling will go a lot easier."

He raised one eyebrow and pursed his lips. "And if you can't, my dear?"

"She can supply Kingdom with organic, free-range rats. Can you tell me where Ari is?"

Arianna, my right-hand woman, my best friend, my Girl Friday, or at least Girl Thursday. At her name, Grimm's lips turned down. "I already checked. She slept through her alarm, missed her bus to the Agency, and failed her civics test. On top of her Department of Licensing disaster, she's planning to call in sick."

Ari had spent the last two years in college. Grimm and I had running bets on what she planned on majoring in. Grimm always said, "Do what you are best at." From what I could tell, Ari was going to major in failing the driver's license test. "She failed this weekend? Couldn't you intervene?"

"Marissa, I *did* intervene. She mistook the accelerator for the volume control and drove three blocks through the market at full speed. Again. It took every bit of magic I could pull off to make certain no one got more than a little run over."

"I'll go fetch her." Ari could've walked into the Agency by that time, so it had nothing to do with the bus. Except another possibility occurred to me. "Did she fail one of your magic tests too?"

Grimm's expression said it all. He wouldn't meet my eyes, his face turned down. "Not exactly. She failed my pretest."

Grimm had spent the last few years training Ari in magic. He traded passing tests in college for new lessons on how not to kill herself with magic. I remained unconvinced it was a fair trade. Grimm said he was taking his time because he didn't want her exposed to evil. If that were true, he wouldn't have made her take calculus.

I picked up my purse and took my jacket. "I'll be back soon. The piper's in 2A, I suggest nobody opens the door. The kobolds need to be turned down, Rosa will send away Payday George, and there's a frog prince waiting in the lobby."

Grimm sighed and faded out of view. I wonder at times what he ever did without me.

ARI LIVED IN a brownstone about twenty minutes from the Agency. Technically she lived alone. I knocked, and she answered without bothering to check the peephole. Her yellow sundress with matching hat made her pale complexion look a lot better, and she kept her red hair pulled back so that it didn't fall into her face.

I pulled my nine millimeter from my purse and pointed it at her. "What have I told you about answering the door without looking first?"

Ari ignored me and shuffled back inside. "I can see through the door, M, and Yeller would take care of anyone who bothered me." At the sound of his name, a dog the size of a Shetland pony padded forward. Only Ari would keep a hellhound as a pet. He looked like Cujo crossed with an alligator and a zombie. None of those crosses improved his disposition.

He stared at me, the gun in my hand, and began to growl, long and low. I put the gun away, since I'd grown somewhat attached to my hands. "Hey, Yeller. I have a poodle for you in the trunk of my car." Yeller bared his teeth at me.

Ari left the door open and walked down the hall. "Come on in, M. I'm making tea."

I *hated* Ari's apartment. She lived there because it was the only thing she could afford. She could afford it because it was haunted, and I don't mean "things that go bump in the night" haunted. I mean "things that devour your spirit."

Inside, the apartment still looked as if the previous owner lived there (which he didn't) and like he was still around (he was). Ari brought out a teakettle and poured three cups, then sat back on a couch, the cover of which looked like woven hair. She clinked her spoon against the cup, like ringing a dinner bell. "Larry, I'm having tea with Marissa. Are you going to join us?"

The basement door blew open, and a ghastly form made of shadows flowed out.

I nodded to it. "Larry."

It looked at me with those dull red orbs that passed for eyes, a look that said it would rather be devouring my spirit than sipping tea. "Marissa."

That one word took five syllables. I didn't have the patience to talk with liches. I was *supposed* to have evicted this one a few years ago. Evictions were cheaper than exorcisms and worked about as often, but the day I went to court to close it, I made a nasty discovery.

I still remember standing there in my business suit with my property attorney at my side, while we waited for the lich to fail to make an appearance. They never showed—being bound to the place of one's death limited mobility options. Right as the judge was getting ready to approve it, the courtroom door swung open.

In lurched a postman, his mailbag still hanging from his side. He moved in awkward, jerky movements like a teenager at his first dance. The postman staggered to the bench and handed a scrawled paper to the judge. A few minutes later, when I *should* have been filing the new deed, I was sitting outside asking our lawyer how we got beat by a possessed postman.

I spent the better part of the next year fighting him. Well, technically him. Whether it was the grandma in her walker, or the hipster on his single-speed bike, they all developed an unholy knowledge of property law when possessed by Larry the Lich. I think the low point was getting hit with attorney's fees by an eight-year-old boy.

At that point we actually did research and discovered that before death, Larry the Lich had been Larry Gulberson, attorney-at-law. That was before he took up a more respectable profession, committing unspeakable acts of evil.

So we negotiated a new contract. Technically, Grimm and Larry did, and Ari sublet the top three floors from an undead spirit of wrath. He wasn't a terrible landlord for someone bound to this plane only by the sheer weight of his hatred and malice. Ari claimed he wasn't that bad, once you got past the glowing eyes, spectral form, and tendency to devour the meter man. She always did find the positive things.

Ari went with me when we needed to hunt uglies. She helped me out when I needed to tame something nasty. Even if she was part princess and part sorceress, I trusted her. It'd always been somewhat of a toss-up as to which I detested more, princesses or sorceresses. In Ari's case, I made an exception.

I stood at the coffee table. "You're late. Work started hours ago."

"I didn't feel like coming in today. Summer semester tests are next week and I need to study more." Ari made a terrible liar, her cheeks bright red, her hand over her mouth.

"I need your help with a new piper. She's a mess. Got so many piercings she looks like a tackle box, and more tattoos than the Detroit Lions cheerleading squad. I could use a hand." I took my tea and sat down beside her. As I did, I winced where the fabric of my pants rubbed fresh burns.

Ari looked at me and nodded. "Liam singed you again?"

"Yeah." My boyfriend, Liam, burned with more than desire.

Ari stood up. "I'll get you some ice. Where'd he get you this time?"

I gave her the look.

She stopped for a moment, then opened her mouth. "Oh. You want burn cream?"

"No. Remind me to ask Grimm for help when we get back to the Agency. Now, come on, we've got work to do. I'm sorry about the driving test. I'm sorry about the magic test, and I'm sorry about the civics exam. I've got a lobby full of potential clients and I'm missing my right-hand woman."

Ari stared at me for a moment. "We don't get the results of the civics test until tonight."

"Well, in that case I have a feeling you'll be doing the makeup exam. Now go get dressed for business and we'll try doing something you're good at." She left me with the lich, and as she walked out the mood in the room changed.

I knew Grimm negotiated safety for folks who stayed out of the basement. As the lights flickered and black smoke began to ooze out from the lich like tendrils, I kept my cool. "Larry, you hear about her driver's test?"

The tendrils paused for a moment and stopped snaking toward me. Larry nodded.

"When it comes to driver's tests, that girl is cursed."

The lich shook its head, managing to keep it attached. Not bad for someone who'd been dead a few years.

"Sorry," I said. "I don't mean actually cursed. She just has really bad luck."

Again the lich shook his head. Then he drifted over toward one of the towering bookcases and began to point one by one to black-bound tomes, as if counting. It stretched out a skeletal hand toward one and beckoned to me with the other.

If it were anyone other than Grimm who laid out the contract, I'd have worried. We rented a truck to move the paper version of the contract after Grimm drew it up. I took the book out and looked at it, trying to make sense of the triangle-based hieroglyphics.

"I don't read anything but English." I went to put the book back, but it held out a hand, stopping me. One claw touched the book and a vaporlike mist seeped out. Through the mist, the letters crawled like maggots, rearranging themselves into words I could read. Also, I wasn't hungry anymore. *Celestial Law, Volume Three Hundred*, read the title.

I opened the book, and a wind began to whip through the room, blowing Ari's mail into the air and flipping the pages until at last it died down. Again the lich did the maggot words thing. I read the chapter title. "The Exchange Principle."

I struggled through the first paragraph, then followed a bone finger to a single sentence. "For everything given, something must be taken. For every blessing, a curse."

At the words *blessing* and *curse* I shivered for reasons of my own. Blessings, curses, no real difference. I've had a curse do great things for me and a blessing do awful things. I had one of each. "This isn't about me. I was talking about Ari."

It shook his head again and pointed up the stairs. Then my mind got to thinking. Princesses were ridiculously lucky. They had innate magic that made things work out for them. Vicious creatures like hellhounds loved them, evil creatures like wraiths tolerated them, and hungry creatures like wolves would rather eat gym-sock soup than a single bite of princess. But maybe, I thought, all this came at a cost. If the only cost was not being able to drive, that was quite a bargain.

"Larry, are you trying to devour Marissa again?" Ari stood on the stairs dressed in a standard black business suit with white shirt. She looked almost professional, but still cute.

The lich shook his skull and held up his hands.

"He was explaining something to me. On his best behavior, I promise." I exchanged a glance with the lich and returned the book to its place. Then I took Ari and got the hell out of the haunted house she called home.

J. C. Nelson is a software developer and ex-beekeeper residing in the Pacific Northwest with family and a few chickens. Visit the author online at authorjcnelson.com.

From #1 *New York Times* Bestselling Author

PATRICIA BRIGGS

||||||||||||||||||||||||||||||||||||||||||||||||||||||||||||||||||||||||||

FROST BURNED

||||||||||||||||||||||||||||||||||||||||||||||||||||||||||||||||||||||||||

A Mercy Thompson Novel

Mercy Thompson's life has undergone a seismic change. Becoming the mate of Adam Hauptman—the charismatic Alpha of the local werewolf pack—has made her a stepmother to his daughter, Jesse, a relationship that brings moments of blissful normalcy to Mercy's life. But on the edges of humanity, what passes for a minor mishap on an ordinary day can turn into so much more . . .

After a car accident in bumper-to-bumper traffic, Mercy and Jesse can't reach Adam—or anyone else in the pack, for that matter. They've all been abducted.

Through their mating bond, all Mercy knows is that Adam is angry and in pain. Outmatched and on her own, Mercy may be forced to seek assistance from any ally she can get, no matter how unlikely.

"Patricia Briggs writes one of the best heroines in the urban fantasy genre today in Mercy Thompson."

—*Fiction Vixen Book Reviews*

patriciabriggs.com
facebook.com/AceRocBooks
penguin.com